A Flower Amidst the Flames

The Flower and Flames Saga: Book 1

Brett Shaffer

Double Infinity Press

A Flower Amidst the Flames

Copyright © 2023 by Brett Shaffer

ISBN-13 Paperback: 979-8-9886145-0-0

ISBN-13 Hardcover: 979-8-9886145-1-7

Book Cover by Angie Alaya

Map illustration by Megan B

Printed in U.S.A.

To mom and dad, for always encouraging my stories

Keyica
Quoxia
Seya Mountains
Pits of Baraxat
Majeria
Desert of Polokaz
The Shadow Groves
Pietrovran
Sehrlic Forest
River Thex
Ikradal
Twisted Rivers
Sea of Kifalia

ONE

With a shuddering breath, Belyx felt the cold steel graze her slick skin. She staggered back, hand trembling with adrenaline as she readied herself for another strike. The target was swift, but she had honed her skills for every potential misstep. Failure was not an option. With gritted teeth, Belyx advanced once more. Her blade crept closer to its mark. One final move, and—

"Sloppy as usual," Madame Jewella declared, her face twisted into a frown.

Belyx gritted her teeth and set down her now bloodied sewing needle. She put her bleeding finger to her lips, trying to hide the pain. It wasn't the pain that bothered her, but the thought of the scowl she would receive from her unruly burgundy curls coming free like a cascade of wildebeests storming down a mountain. She knew she should have tied them tighter for her lessons.

"I almost had it this time. The hole slipped away from me," Belyx said, hoping to explain away her mistake.

Madame Jewella lifted the freshly sewn gown and her frown deepened. "I can't even compile a list to describe the atrocities. This piece will go in the 'no' pile. Why is it that your grandmother and mother were both naturals at this art, yet you possess the hands of a drunken mine worker?"

Madame Jewella didn't really want an answer. But she couldn't help wondering, did mine workers actually have unstable hands?

"It doesn't come as easy to me, I guess," Belyx said, trying to keep the frustration out of her voice.

Madame Jewella ruffled her rather humongous gown while checking her perfectly primed silver hair. As if that would hide the multitude of wrinkles sprouting from her face. Did being an instructor have an age limit? "A princess never lets a setback define her day. Honestly, you look like you walked into the night. Did you even sleep?"

"Of course, Madame," Belyx lied, keeping her voice even.

"A princess never lets one know she didn't get a night's rest. Very uncivilized," Madame Jewella said, reciting one of her many famous proverbs.

Belyx tried not to roll her eyes. "Yes, ma'am."

"The chosen dresses will be shown tonight," Madame said as Belyx followed her, continuing her rampage of insults ranging from how pathetic Belyx was to her favorite, "I'm going to tell your father." As if he would do anything, anyway.

The design room was at the top of the stairs. Belyx smiled at the etching of a rose on the door, standing for Velena Rose Designs. She ran her finger along the imprint, daydreaming about the three generations of hard work and passion they put in.

"I don't see what you are beaming about. We are behind the selection schedule your grandmother gave me. Now let's attempt to salvage something," Madame Jewella said as she walked past dress after dress, most of which Belyx had worked on. The maidens may have assisted her, but Madame Jewella didn't need to know.

The collection had about twenty dresses. The wealthy customers of Aikradal expected to have a line every year, and they needed to keep up with the current styles, which Belyx had meant to study, but she was busy with other, more important things.

Madame held up a voluminous gown crafted from bright pink tulle that stretched all the way down the bodice. The twists in the sleeves bore tiny crystals as if it came from the night sky. Underneath the peach colored material was a white acetate that circled across the bottom in a wavy hem. It was Belyx's favorite.

"So last season." Madame discarded it on the ground like a piece of trash.

Belyx fought back the heat in her face and continued smiling, almost reciting one of Madame's proverbs. *A princess never has time to frown.* Bile crawled up her throat. *A princess should not murder her teacher.*

"What about this one?" Belyx held up a silk gown to Madame. The dress trickled accents of yellow and brown, spiraling down the bodice until it flowed to a back drape. It reminded her of the Sea of Kifalia and how it reflected the natural lights. Madame's glower slightly lifted. That was something.

"Fine, but I want a few edits before it goes out. Major. Ones."

"Yes, Madame."

They spent the next hour rifling through the rest of the designs. A ball would be hosted later that night to display them. Boutique merchants from all over were coming to bid on their favorites. The palace needed that income right now.

Madame had finally chosen the last one, and they moved on. "I hope this year bodes better. Our number of sold dresses is dropping every showing."

Well, then hire someone else.

Not that Belyx hated designing clothes; it was not her passion, like writing poetry, dancing, avoiding princess lessons, and, of course, being a member of the Order. The previous month, she passed her skills test and enjoyed the freedom of exploring the kingdom. Not stuck with Madame Unpleasant.

Madame opened her detailed scroll as she passed a couple of maids clad in purple hoods.

Their presence in protecting the castle was a needed comfort, but she wished they would save her.

"Next, we have to find Captain Thomas and help him appoint the guards. Your father is busy, so he asked you to be in charge of the selection process. Please make sure they are qualified." She arched a brow to imply Belyx would fail. As if her kingdom had the funds to be picky with who they selected. Since the uprising of the gangs, guard numbers have been dwindling faster than Madame's hair line.

"No problem," Belyx replied, following Madame out of the palace. Outside, they were greeted by the Captain of the Guard, Thomas Beckert. He wore newly shined armor with a cross sword insignia inlaid on the shoulders, and his long blonde hair was tied in a clean top knot. Belyx couldn't help but blush at the sight of him. He was only ten years her senior and the youngest captain ever. Her father admired his courage and determination. Why couldn't he trust her more, too?

"Pleasure, Captain. Who do we have today?" Madame asked, intruding on Belyx's thoughts. Thomas pointed to the recruits, a motley crew of skinny and massive young men who looked like they hadn't slept in days.

They stared at Belyx as if she were the last jewel on earth. She couldn't help but wonder why they couldn't do more to help the homeless youth who were forced to join the guard for a free meal and housing.

"Recruits!" Thomas's voice startled them, surprised by his youthful authority. "Start at the beginning of the line and come forward. It will serve you well to obey our princess and impress her." He circled his thumb over his glinting blade, a nervous tell.

He leaned into Belyx. "I can only select two, so hit them with your best shot." Her shoulders swilled. Why did her father want her doing this? What skills did she possess for choosing the right guard? They all appeared adequate. Maybe she would pick two at random. "First one! Up!" Thomas commanded.

A tall, skinny one approached and bowed. His unkempt, curly hair rolled from his head. "Sir Beljo, your highness. I was top of my class at the academy and led an assault on the recent bandit raid. I hope to be considered." The wavering in his voice prevailed his inexperience.

If he had an arduous time sounding confident to a dainty princess like Belyx, how could he lead a fight?

She eyed this man up and down, surprised by how thin he was, but she had seen small people cause damage before. Thomas coughed, interrupting her thoughts. "Any questions you wish to ask, Princess?"

"Yes. Of course." Madame's ice-cold stare pierced behind her as she stumbled. Trying to take pieces from her strategy lessons, she asked, "How would you handle a traitor?" This was a difficult subject and temptation from the gangs ran deep.

The man, or boy, more like it, wiped the sweat from his damp neck and cleared his throat before answering. "I would always be loyal and report it to my Captain." He looked at Thomas but made eye contact with Belyx again. "No bribe would ever claim me. I swear by The God."

It sounded way too rehearsed and, based on his appearance, he would have a price.

The next one sauntered up. He was of average height, but the thing that stood out to her was his voluminous locks of red hair. Her own curls paled in comparison. Being jealous of a boy's hair was a new feeling. "Greetings princess and Captain. My name is Camryn Fried and I wish to be a guard." His voice radiated youthful exuberance. He may have been attractive if Belyx had time for such frivolities.

Belyx cleared her throat. "What motivates you to be a guard?"

Without a hesitation, as if rehearsed, he answered. "I'm tired of the people bad-mouthing the palace. I understand you are trying your best and I want to do my part to help."

Why was he so hard to read? "What are the people saying?" It was an answer she knew, but it was helpful to have an inside opinion.

"The gangs. Your majesty. They are stealing people's loyalty through violence and intimidation. They have given up on the lower ring and are joining based on false promises, but I believe there is hope. The protests against the crown will not stand." Hearing it from the people was worse. The lower ring's businesses were also being uprooted by the gangs. The kingdom would fall if the council didn't act fast. *And then all of us with it.*

He spoke like a leader, reminding her of a younger Thomas. *I wonder if he feels the same way?*

"How can we be assured of your loyalty to all the temptations?"

"I will never join them. The Berserkers killed my brother. I want to make sure no one loses any more family to them. I want to train and fight hard."

Belyx resisted the urge to beam. "That is all, Camryn."

He blushed and Thomas sent him back and called up the next recruits one at a time, who all had their own success stories and reasons they should be a guard. They even answered moral questions the same. Where was the uniqueness of these recruits?

A woman joining would be something new, but Aikradal forbade such things. It must have slipped her mind. The Order provided a place for women. Which was why it needed to stay a secret.

Thomas hit his sword on the ground. "Alright, recruits. Please exit and return tomorrow. As you know, due to funding, we can only accept a few of you. We will announce the ones who made the cut this month. Take care." The men bowed to them and left.

Thomas turned to Belyx. "Not bad. You had a couple of them sweating for sure. Usually your father just—never mind."

Belyx was glad he didn't finish. Grief had affected her father, even thirteen years later.

"Well, she could have asked more pressing questions, but I suppose not bad." Of course, Madame had to give her two coins.

She ignored her chide. "I would say the top two choices are Briton and Camryn. They seemed more energetic about it." Passion was a potent weapon. At least, she hoped.

Thomas nodded, as if he sort of agreed, but was afraid to make Belyx upset. As if he was more critical than Madame or her father. "It shall be put forth."

Belyx crossed her arms. "Well, fine. Are we done then?" *Please say yes!*

But her teacher cooed. "Oh, no you don't. You have more preparations for the dress showing tonight. The ballroom looks like there was a grand battle and our side lost."

Belyx wanted to fall over. "Yes, I almost forgot."

"A princess never forgets a task, no matter how small."

Of course they didn't.

She prayed no one would get hurt in the next couple of hours.

Madame Jewella adjusted the centerpieces for the scattered tables as Belyx hastily arranged them in a bid to take a quick nap. "Your taste astounds me," Madame Jewella commented. "But I will have a word with your father about your lack of attention. A princess—"

"I know," Belyx interrupted. "It won't happen again. I'm super excited about the show." She was as excited as a child getting a healthy snack instead of sweets. Madame Jewella licked her lips, as if to say, "you can't fool me," and continued fixing Belyx's mistakes.

The decorated ballroom exploded with sprinkles of silver festoons layered along the walls and mezzanines. Blood-red rose petals trailed across the floor, and the sun trickled onto the walkway where the dresses would be presented. Presentation was everything to sell them.

As Belyx started to lose hope in the event, Cook came from the kitchen, carrying a steaming pile of pastries that none of the guests would eat.

Well, only in secret.

"Princess, what do you think of my creation? I combined donuts with cream and wanted to test how it went," Cook said, beaming with pride. She was a force of a woman around the same age as Belyx's grandmother. She had been helping the palace a long time ago, when her grandmother reigned as queen.

After her mother's passing, Cook had returned to work for the Order, and she and Belyx had formed a memorable bond, as well as a mutual dislike for Madame Jewella. Cook sensed that Belyx needed to be saved. Her nostrils took in the gentle aroma of vanilla and sugar. The heat emanated against her skin. Madame Jewella would have a fit if Belyx put one in her mouth.

"They look delicious, Cook. I can't wait to try one," Belyx said.

Madame Jewella made a disgusted sound, but Cook merely smiled and rubbed the sweat off her deep brown skin, retying her wispy gray curls back into her bun. She worked too hard, and they didn't deserve her.

"The pleasure is mine. How is the collection?" Cook asked.

Before Belyx could answer, Madame Jewella interrupted. "Belyx has a lot of work to do. Carry on with your preparations, Rajabi," she said, using Cook's formal name.

Cook granted her a smile, and with her hurried hand movements, signed to Belyx, "tiring old bitch." She was thankful they had their own silent form of communication and stifled a laugh.

After Cook left, Madame Jewella scoffed. "We may need to talk to the healer about her sporadic hand gestures. I, for one, do not want something in my soup that shouldn't be there. Your father should find a replacement."

Belyx dipped her head and prepped more things. Madame Jewella would never understand the power Cook held. She could roast anything, and anyone who messed with the people she cared for.

"I say that dress is gorgeous!" Belyx rolled her eyes. When Lady Lim Grenald said anything was gorgeous, it wasn't.

"Just something from last year's collection," Belyx replied, glancing nervously around the ballroom. More people showed up than she expected. With the acerbic attitudes against the crown, fewer guests should have shown. Except a majority of the patrons were of the wealthy upper circle, who had little to no gang activity. It was the lower end of the kingdom who suffered, as usual.

Everyone was dressed in the finest silks and materials from all over. The cost alone could feed an entire kingdom, but there they all were, indulging in the fancy wine and silently judging one another.

The three ladies circled around her in the ballroom. The Great Hall was decorated to extravagance as the luscious floral pieces accented the checkered marble floors. Strings of illustrious material were woven from the ceiling with care and extended across the pristine walls, portraying paintings of historical battles. The spaced apart food tables had an array of decadent dishes prepared by Cook herself. Although if she tried any, the women would look at her as if she grew a second head.

In the center of the room, a wooden stage was brought in every year for the fashion showings. The skyline provided the right amount of moonlight and it was circular, giving the models plenty of room to walk. Showing all the angles made sure the buyers were making a smart investment.

In her worry about the production, she missed Lady Maria's question. "Apologies. What?"

Lady Maria Nebaska, best friend to Lim even though they always seemed in constant battle, said, with no effort to hide her impudence, "How will the collection be tonight?" She adjusted her spectacles and gave the other woman the *Princess Belyx is incompetent look*.

Stilling her thumping heart, Belyx went to reply when Lim butted in, as usual. "Last year's designs were just gorgeous! I still have mine!" She took a gentle sip of her wine and raised her eyebrows as if she declared something groundbreaking.

Belyx tried to finally answer when her aunt, sweet as ever, answered for her, also as usual. "She is doing great. I snuck a peek yesterday, and it is jaw dropping. You can find out later." She winked at Belyx as if she saved her. Lady Hannah Velena was the King's sister and despite their relatedness, they had zero in common.

"How come y'all always get to see it?" Lim wiped off crumbs from her gown. Her fake accent radiated. She said it was her heritage, but accents with that kind of drawl didn't exist, but everyone went with it. Who to question an advisor's wife? Not that Belyx would want to talk to him, either. "I just hope there is red in the collection. I never see any reds. It's a refined lady's color."

Maria shot Lim an annoyed look, for she always chose a red dress of some shape or form. She claimed it was the shade of danger and she wanted the world to know how treacherous she was. Especially when she decided not to "try" on her hair sometimes. *Dangerous indeed.*

Lim returned an arrow of her own, a toothy smile. "Anyway. Can we discuss the theme for the ball next year? It is all anyone is talking about." Lim brushed back her long blonde locks as if making them aware she lightened it to match the sun. The gray still protruded right through.

"Now, that is a good idea. What do you think it should be, princess?" Maria asked, fidgeting with her glasses again and her obvious new hair style. The brown was cut into a bob and curled at the tips. It complemented her tawny hue.

Although Belyx was drifting out of attention, she responded with the perfect answer. "I would say In the Garden, since the warm season is ending at this time. I say florals and illustrious bouquets." Based on their glares, it was the wrong response.

"Gorgeous!" Lim replied, not aware of her grimace beforehand.

They assumed Belyx was a clueless girl.

Everyone did.

"I, for one, love florals," Aunt Hannah replied. "It is my brother's favorite thing." A strand of silver hair fell out of her braid and she worked to put it back, receiving a stink eye from Lim.

These moments would be treasured...

"Maybe we can talk about it later." A clever deflection from Lim. She snapped her fingers in the air and turned her head at Belyx like she was marked for death. "What about you, princess? I know you are recently of age." She did a little dance, and Belyx wanted to crawl in a hole. "Whoever are you selecting to be your prince? This kingdom needs one someday." She gulped her drink, overlooking the glares. She waved her glass. "What? Oh, the king will live a long life, but one can't be too careful."

Belyx had suspicions her conniving husband fed her these ideas. She made a note to be apathetic to him at the next council meeting. Well, more than usual.

"I haven't decided yet. Too busy." This was true as Belyx had one proper suitor before. The children of nobles and guards were the only men available.

Maria fluttered her hand. "You are never too busy for boys. I certainly wasn't."

"We know," her aunt added with a side eye, but Maria ignored her.

Belyx hated this the most, and it was the same question that came all the time. *Who are you going to marry? When will you have children? It's your duty, etc.* It wasn't that Belyx didn't want to date, it was she found no men pleasing to her. They often tried way too hard, like one boy made her climb up a tall mountain trail to propose! Like she met him thirty minutes ago. Spoiled food lasted longer. Also, they probably wouldn't approve of her nightly activities. How her mother kept it a secret from her father was a mystery to her. "Well, the kingdom is struggling. I have to make sure everything is secure. I wouldn't want to marry a traitor who slits my throat in the night."

Although they would never make it past the door.

Lim blew out a puff of air. "Good God. Manners, princess."

"Apologies." Belyx didn't mean it.

"Ball goers!" the Master of Trade and Exports announced, saving Belyx from this conversation. For a short man, his voice boomed. He also loved to brandish his medals when he served as the guard ages ago, but he did his job well, as long as he didn't say anything weird. "The fashion show will begin soon! Please direct your attention to the stage." He shifted to the wealthy shop merchants, trying to curry favor. "Prepare your investments. This year will be a doozy!"

Belyx slapped her forehead for that remark. *Doozy? Yep, it turned weird.* They were doomed.

The designers were people she knew too well. They were dressed in the same high class silk no one could afford and acted like their opinion was the only one in the kingdom. Belyx waved to them and they shot her a look most people around here gave Belyx; a scowl. She had to please them though, as they possessed the power to cripple her palace... and they used it to their advantage.

A pit formed in Belyx's stomach. The show was about to begin. Belyx smoothed her ivory gown and took the stage. Everyone stared at her in awe as she stood, wiping the sweat from her palms. She cleared her throat, dreading the speech, but of course, a princess needed to woo a crowd. "Thank you for coming. This collection was inspired by layers and design."

Wow, what an inadequate description. Even Belyx forgot her own inspiration. "Enjoy these looks and we hope to see them in your stands." Flashing a well rehearsed smile, one she had practiced in the mirror numerous times, she returned to the crowd.

The first dress came out with a fury. Madame always said to "hook the fish from the beginning or they won't care." This was sure to work. The gown was encapsulated in glimmering silver swirling into a mystifying bottom. The tulle sleeves were woven in an asymmetrical line, accentuating the jeweled bodice. The way it flowed down the stage was like an ocean and as it turned, a crossed sword design was etched in the back of the shimmering silk. Belyx craned her neck at the shop keepers, but they wore the usual; a frown. *The next one will impress them.*

It did not. However, the sixth dress, which bore a handcrafted stone like bodice made from black leather, rose a few eyebrows. The off shoulder cape breezed behind the model like she was flying. She gave it a twirl at the end to show off the effortless movement. Women needed to move too, she had told the trainees who sewed it and sent them a silent thank you.

The presentation continued with head nods, lips pursing, scowls, head shakes, and minor clapping. The final design strode out, and the room was speechless. Belyx had never attempted velvet before, as it didn't cooperate with her sewing apparatus, but this one was gorgeous. The rich crimson floor-length gown glided across the stage, and across her waist was a belt encrusted with rubies sparkling in the moonlight. The sleeves were a bit unique, as they were slit down the middle, but gave an effect of freedom and modernness.

The bidding concluded and five out of the fifteen gowns were bought...It was the same as last year. At least she avoided a scolding from hell...for now.

Taking a wine flute, she downed it before a familiar face approached her.

"I think everyone is too picky," her grandmother, Dara, appeared beside her, sipping her wine, grimacing. "It gets cheaper every year." Her grandmother knew what she was talking about as her dress radiated beauty with the sapphire silk falling around her chest in a bow like fashion. She always said blue was the color of the youthful. Her face was painted to transcendence with blushes and coals, making her age twenty years backward. Her grandmother's hair was never messed up either, as her gray locks were wrapped delicately into a diamond encrusted clip. Appearances were everything to her grandmother, and pleasing such a person was always a daunting task. Suddenly, her own appearance shrunk.

Belyx circled her high-heeled foot awkwardly. "So, may I take that Goldfinger shipment assignment tonight? I spoke to the other Thorns, and they said it was fine." Her grandmother launched a glare at her.

"We discussed this. I only prefer you going out three times a week. Your sleep is becoming distressed. You look like you shared a cell with a donkey."

Belyx touched her face and sighed. Not enough makeup in the world would hide her fatigued appearance. "Fine. I just want to help."

Dara waited for the loud, drunk people to pass. It had reached that point already. "You only passed the trials a couple of months ago. I have plenty of members who need the practice. You have a responsibility on both fronts, Order and kingdom. Just relax tonight. Enjoy the party. Meet a boy."

"Grandmother!" More of this crap.

"I know, I know, but still, I'm serious. I overheard Madame telling your father your performance was lackluster. It needs to improve, Belyx. Your mother balanced it. Why can't you?"

Why didn't her grandmother understand doing assignments in the kingdom was all she was skilled at? These ridiculous parties weren't her and would solve nothing. Stopping the gangs would do something.

Belyx bid her grandmother goodbye and spent the rest of the night talking with other people while trying to be cordial and escape.

After everyone was dismissed, she retreated to her room and did exactly what her grandmother had told her to do.

For a few hours anyway.

After a failed attempt at sleep, Belyx opened her balcony doors in her chamber and took in the warm season breeze. The Sea of Kifalia's faint waves rustled despite being a couple miles away. It was peaceful and serene. The memories of her mom flooded again, but this time more elaborate. All the time she missed and would never have.

Her grandmother's comparisons tonight struck her. Her father would never utter a word about her mother as if she was a forgotten folktale. Her grandmother, the opposite, always brought her up like an over shared one.

Belyx didn't know which she preferred.

The portrait of her mom sat nicely on her wall. Her hazel eyes captured the effervescent light with her reddish brown hair, like Belyx's, tied into a neat pony. She was a woman who knew how to get things done, unlike Belyx. She kept back her tears and strutted into her closet, opening a secret alcove behind her illustrious gowns.

A tinge of excitement greeted her as she removed the outfit from its place. The leather top and bottoms were pristine, made from the finest of materials. Nothing overcame the durability and movement it provided.

The twelve knives sang to Belyx even louder as she slipped them into the desired sheaths across her person. After applying her dark wig and red contacts, she grabbed her poison pouch, the most important of her tools.

Belyx should be exhausted, but her kingdom was in danger. Anything going wrong haunted her. She would protect Aikradal, no matter the costs.

Two

Aikradal paled during the day than at night.

In the daytime, it was too formal. The times when Belyx would get to venture there, the citizens would smile and show unity despite the obvious fears of their crumbling kingdom. Everyone would spend money on useless items in the markets and try to fill the voids in their lives.

At night, Aikradal was filled with silent energy. Bustling crowds, beggars, and those looking for a good time roamed the dank streets, making it a dangerous venture. If the wrong person wandered out, it could be their last. The building's roof made the perfect place to watch as Belyx adjusted her sights. Although twenty feet up scared most people, she preferred the high areas. No wonder birds located their prey with ease.

Taking out her poisons and venoms, she counted them with care. The likelihood of their use was probable. A numbness crawled over Belyx's fingers. Her grandmother had warned her about going out again, but her thoughts wouldn't calm. Tonight was an exception. Before she left, she had convinced the other Thorns that her grandmother assigned her to this mission instead. The lie would creep back to her, but Belyx found it easier to ask for forgiveness than permission.

And what would her grandmother do? Belyx was the best Thorn in the Order with her determination. As well as dabbling in other ways to kill. Most of the others used poison, but Belyx favored venom freshly harvested from her snakes. The moonlight made them gleam, stored in their own vials. Each with their own uses. A grin spread across her face as she sifted through them. The viper's was for interrogation, king cobra's for hallucinations, krait's for paralysis, and black mamba's for emergencies. There was no cure for that one and she double checked the plug was on tight after dipping her hidden blade in it. The metal sheathed back with ease, and she continued observing the streets.

Belyx read in a report from Dara that the Goldfingers were buying weapons from other kingdoms and then selling them in the illegal markets. This crippled the Aikradal merchants and affected the taxes to the palace.

The Goldfingers were a prominent gang full of wealth and power, traipsing around in their fancy suits and new pistols, which the Aikradal guards hadn't even gained yet. Luckily, their strength was overshadowed by their horrible aim. Belyx preferred blades anyway.

The tug of exhaustion beckoned Belyx. Madame was right about her lack of sleep, but her mind was too distracted by such concerns. The kingdom was in danger of collapse and she would preserve it. The legal markets were closed at night, but the forbidden ones were not. Many kinds of goods were sold, ranging from fancy cookware to people. Although her mother ended slavery in the kingdom years ago, too often than not, it would sneak back into Aikradal. Any kind of slavery made Belyx sick and she would free them. Too often than not, the recruits for the Order came from these very places.

The landscape was vast, but she kept her eye out for the Goldfingers. They brandished their wealth like they owned the place. It wasn't an act of strength, but a display of deceit and Belyx would stamp it out.

Her eyes widened. Down at the edge of the markets, a horde of them were unloading a generic wagon filled with illegal items such as staves, blades, tobacco, other drugs, and even cattle used for farming. The cows chewed on their cud, unaware of the inflation they were about to cause.

The Goldfingers must have received these from another kingdom where they would use slave labor to cut costs and sell them for double the profits.

Belyx leapt from her perch, the crisp air tickling her ears. Rolling to break her fall, she advanced with the shadows as she was taught. Rumors of assassins lurking around the kingdom filled everyone's fears, but no one alive was able to prove it, like the Order intended.

She adjusted her mask as she hastened through the back way, passing a couple of customers browsing illegal howling monkeys. Saving them was not an option right now. *One thing at a time, Belyx.* Her grandmother instructed her to never do two things at once, for it was half effort on both and two times the failure.

Belyx rubbed her mother's rose pin on her shoulder for luck, something she always did before a kill; a way of remembering her during these tasks. Belyx's grandmother's paranoia almost kept her from being a Thorn, wanting to make her a Stem instead. Protecting the palace would bore Belyx to the grave. Although important, she craved other thrills.

The Goldfinger smugglers wore the usual garb, cotton and silk pants, bow ties and suspenders. The leader fancied himself on appearances. She guessed one needed to look proper to do illegal deeds. What a shame it would be to spill blood on such expensive clothing?

She counted five men, but more would come. If Belyx was to succeed at this, she would need to be fast. Counting her venoms one last time, she debated which ones to employ. The cobra toxin would cause them to act irrationally and give her time to strike and steal the carriage, leaving it at the mines where no one would think twice. Taking a breath, she crouched low, trying to mimic the wind.

Belyx approached the nearest member, smoking a putrid cigar. The stench made her eyes water. The man winced as she stuck him with a venom coated needle.

Nothing but a little bug bite... for now.

"Oi! Somethin' bit me!"

"Shut your trap and get back to work," the other goon responded.

Their teamwork showed no bounds.

The infected one began to wobble. Cobra hit the bloodstream directly, and the effects of this bane took a couple of minutes to kick in. Other drugs in his system must have sped it up. Tobacco was a commonly used drug and increased the blood flow to the brain; just what she needed. The Goldfinger started screaming and flailing his arms around.

The other Goldfingers rushed to his aid, leaving the merchandise carriage unguarded. Belyx was on her heels as she crept to the supplies and rounded the front when a sense of movement caught her eye. A cane came right to her side. Instinctively, she ducked and kicked his shin. The driver of the wagon grunted as he hit the floor, unmoving.

"What was that?" The other group members heard over the poisoned one's moans.

Belyx jumped in the carriage's driver's seat and whipped the horses. Giving a loud whinny, they charged away. The galloping sounds muffled the curses from the Goldfingers. Freedom was on the horizon.

She veered around the corner when a pistol shot thundered, and one horse went down.

The pistols were accurate sometimes.

Belyx had no time to grieve the horse as the carriage toppled over. The reins released from her grip, but it was no use as her body flung into the air. All her fall training was useless as she barreled into a pottery stand, shards of ceramic piercing into her arm. The pain seared as her ankle clicked, sending a fiery agony of hell up her spine.

The Goldfingers approached in haste with their pistols drawn. Belyx leapt up and limped away, gritting her teeth through the soreness as she pulled bloodied pieces of pottery out of her body, cursing at her clumsiness. The second she reached a safe alleyway, she dove under an abandoned garbage chute, ignoring the rotting stench of decaying food.

Four verses one wasn't bad odds for her. She had faced worse, but her throbbing ankle would be the biggest obstacle. Taking a focused breath, she concentrated on the henchmen and popped her blade out. Once she hit one, they would swarm her, but it was that or be discovered with no advantage.

"Find the bastard and we will gut him," the bigger one said. Everyone always assumed it was a man, hence why the Order would remain a secret.

The Goldfingers turned over scrap after scrap and they would locate her soon if she didn't act now. One put his leg in by the garbage chute and Belyx struck her prey.

With a screech, he went down.

The others rushed to their accomplice, as she expected, and Belyx pulled herself from under the chute and slit the fallen one's throat. The other three surrounded her, pistols drawn.

Grasping a knife in her ankle sheath, she launched it for the nearest one. The blade flew and landed in his chest before he fell on the dirt. Belyx dodged as the one on the left fired and the pellet shattered the brick behind her.

The gunman ventured too close as Belyx kicked him in the inner thigh, disarmed his pistol, and struck him in the temple with it.

Another gunshot. Belyx maneuvered as the bullet whizzed by her ear. *That was close.* Another blade soared from her grasp, but the biggest Goldfinger moved out of the way and smacked Belyx in the face. Hitting the ground, she stared down the barrel of his gun. The throbbing in her head intensified as she plotted a way out of this.

"You're no bastard," he said with an agape mouth. "You are a woman! A girl!" He pulled the hammer of the pistol back.

One shot would spread her insides on the brick.

Except he made a crucial error.

In a flash, he started convulsing and dropped the firearm. He fell to the ground and released his last meal. Belyx sparked up and kicked the gun away, leaning over the dying man.

The Goldfinger cursed as she lifted her hood. "This one is for the Order of the Rose." Crimson spit came from his mouth, unable to express his stupidity.

"You should be careful when you strike a lady. You never know what she holds in her other hand." Belyx held up her knife, coated with black mamba venom, a dangerous concoction that caused total organ failure.

The Goldfinger's face sank and turned a purple shade until he lay motionless.

Enemy screams closed in. More of them were coming and they would be hungry for revenge.

Belyx stumbled to the open street and the weapons in the wagon were already pillaged by God knows who. The first plan failed, but the Goldfingers would make no profit tonight. She kept to the shadows and limped back to the palace.

The climb up to her balcony with a bruised ankle proved to be quite difficult. After what felt like centuries of climbing, Belyx grunted as she hauled herself over the ledge. Her breaths escaped her body like fire. She wanted nothing more than to crawl into bed and sleep her troubles away until morning lifted its cruel head.

Belyx slipped through the terrace entrance and sighed, knowing she was in for it now.

Perching on her chair in the dim firelight, sat her Grandmother; dressed fancy like she was going out, despite it being the middle of the night.

Dara stared at her, twirling her necklace of The God that used to belong to Belyx's mother, rubbing her fingers along the two eight symbols overlapping one another, surrounded by a circle. The God represented infinite life and their people among it. The design reminded Belyx of the sand coins they would find at the beach as a child.

Her grandmother's aqua eyes didn't even flutter as Belyx responded, "I know, I know. I'm sorry. I needed some fresh air. It won't happen again." *It would.*

Better forgiveness than permission! Her ankle throbbed as she stepped, but she didn't bother hiding it. Her grandmother already knew as usual.

Her grandmother smoothed her silk gown, which sparkled sapphire crystals in the candle flame.

"Fresh air leads to damaged ankles now?" she asked with a slight grin.

"Would you believe I fell down the stairs?"

Her Grandmother arched a brow, calling her bluffs.

"It was no big deal. I couldn't help it. I needed to stop the Goldfingers."

Dara waited, never wearing a mad appearance, but it was almost worse when she was stoic, like a spider waiting for a poor fly to land. She finally replied, "Belyx, we are worried about you."

This was unexpected. "I'm fine."

"Historically, when one says they are fine, they are not." Dara's mouth curved upward, and she studied Belyx closer. This always led to an extra-long lecture and Belyx only longed to wash Goldfinger blood off her.

"You know the rules for assignments. Why would you disobey? I didn't let you become a Thorn easily. You swore a code and you can't keep assuming I will play favorites because we are family." Dara stared deeper into her eyes now.

The Goldfinger's guns were a ball compared to this interrogation. Belyx twitched a brow as Dara cleared her throat, shifting her tone. "Did you succeed? Any witnesses."

"No." *Maybe.* Would she check?

"That sounded convincing." Her grandmother chuckled. "The Order has been around for a long time, dear. I would hate for it to end, and that is why we have these regulations."

As if Belyx had never heard them before. *Like every week.* "I know, Grandmother. I have been distracted lately and I need some rest for the council meeting tomorrow."

Dara sauntered through her room, gazing at the decor in the room and rubbing the material of the curtains. "I always hated this color combination.

Silver and lilac scream like it tries too hard." Belyx stayed silent as her rambling usually had an end. "I only want you to be safe, Belyx. Living a double life is challenging work. We Velena women have done it for generations. You must focus your mind and think positive. That is the only way to get through this."

"Gee, I will just try." Belyx began taking off her assassin garb, and Dara put her hands on her shoulders.

"I know you miss her, but it's been thirteen years. Move on. Think about the good she did and channel it."

It would be simpler if her mother had sucked at everything. Instead, she left a bar Belyx could never climb over.

As Belyx continued to remove her clothing, her ankle stung again. Dara bent over to examine it. "Not broken, but could use some attention. I would see Amenthya about it. She should be up doing who knows what with her weird concoctions."

Belyx went to protest, but the pain in her leg grew. "I think you're right, but can't Freyja wrap it for now?" The last thing she wanted was to head back outside to the healer.

Dara went back and opened her bedroom door. "Freyja, she needs help." She winked. "You are lucky to have such a ready handmaiden."

Lucky didn't even describe it.

Freyja came in, her long braids swinging behind her, carrying in her herbs and gauze. "I would pay to see the other guy," she said as she bowed to Dara and then embraced Belyx, who flinched from her wounds.

Dara patted Freyja on the back. "Take care of her. Our princess had quite the night." She turned to Belyx. "Remember what I told you. Don't let this happen again, please. And also, see the actual healer tomorrow." With that, Dara bid them goodnight and left.

Freyja wasted no time in applying various gels to Belyx's cuts. She was thankful for her friend's gentle touch, despite her being able to break someone's neck in three places. "Thanks for waking up for me."

Her handmaiden kept working, the candles reflecting on her dark skin. "Oh, Belyx. I wish you would be more careful. You make my job harder sometimes."

"But I'm fun, right?" A sudden tinge of guilt sank deep into her gut.

Freyja was not just her handmaiden, but her protector. She used to be one of her mother's right after becoming an agent, but it lasted only a few short months. Regardless of her youth, she had never gotten over the guilt, but her instinct for danger and a kind heart made her a perfect Petal. One of her many duties was to make sure the Order members inside the palace were trained on how to protect it from any outside dangers. Freyja had a unique eye for that sort of thing, and she possessed strong leadership skills along with it.

However, her hardest responsibility was keeping Belyx safe. Despite the thirteen year age difference, Freyja was more like an older sister than anything else, and also a best friend. With the lack of girls at Belyx's youth around the palace, it was nice to have someone to relate to.

Like most members in the Order, Freyja was rescued as a young girl and recruited, but seldom talked about her time in Majeria as a slave, and Belyx understood the need to avoid the topic.

It was impressive how far she had come. Belyx only wished she had half the determination and resolve she possessed.

Belyx hoped to be promoted to Petal one day and be in charge of something. *Then I would have a say.* Although she was far too young and had many things to learn before then. Her grandmother always said to "never rush growing up, for the wrinkled apple never returns."

"Sometimes, you are fun, but not well into the moonlight." Freyja was almost finished with the wrapping.

"Sorry. I haven't been well lately. This turmoil and chaos is getting to me. I am only eighteen years old, for God's sake." Another flair of guilt, and she knew what was coming.

"You could have been sold into slavery at a younger age."

There it was.

Freyja tightened the bandage, and her ankle pinched, but relief climbed throughout her body. Which wouldn't last, however.

"I know," Belyx replied curtly.

Freyja picked up the rest of her things. The moonlight by the window bounced off her eyes, the reds swirling with the browns made her expressions pop. Another incredible detail about her, but now, it showed annoyance.

"It's okay. I am only messing with you, but in all honesty, please be careful. Her Majesty Dara is worried right now, and that is saying something because she never worries, at least to me. Aikradal must be in more danger than ever."

"That is the anxiety. I wish Grandmother would admit things are bad to me as well."

Freyja shrugged. "She only wants you to be protected. Remember, she lost a daughter then."

"She is right, though. I have to focus more."

They stayed silent for a while when Freyja embraced Belyx. Her couple inches of height advantage made for the best hug, and Belyx would cherish these moments. The possibility was strong that they may end one day.

"Your Highness, is there anything else?"

Belyx snorted. "You don't have to use titles when it is just us, you know."

"I know, and I don't care. You better sleep. You need to get up in about three hours." A hint of humor left her voice. Lucky for her, although she had to wake up too.

"Perfect." After she bid her handmaiden/protector/friend goodnight, she blew out her candles, drifting into a peaceful slumber.

An hour later, a nightmare shook her awake and then she stared at the wall. Any hope of sleep was out the window. Sitting up, she went to clean her knives.

They needed it.

THREE

"This is bullshit."

The curse slipped out loud, but the council's new plan was ridiculous and Belyx would never agree to it in a million years.

"Belyx, language," the king said. As usual, his eyes were sunken from lack of sleep, but that didn't inhibit the disappointed look he gave her. His wife's death was still affecting him to this day. Thirteen years was an excessive amount of time to be lost in grief, but that was how impactful the former queen was.

Belyx crossed her arms, forgetting the advisors, Counselor Kirk Sallo and Counselor Jaques Lorn, as well as the Master of Coin, Jon Gyra, Master of Trade, Roman Cruss, and the Captain of the Guard, were witnessing her childlike behavior. She took a calculated breath like her grandmother trained her to do and smoothed the front of her dress. Princesses didn't curse at people. Clearing her throat, she tried for a do-over. "What I meant to say is, we don't need Majeria's help with the gang uprising. We can handle everything ourselves."

Lord Kirk snorted. Like his wife, Lady Lim, he had trouble expressing his opinions clearly, only with passive aggressive jabs. The way he always flounced about in proper form made Belyx's blood steam. He always kept his pointy nose far up her father's ass, the king looked like he had a conjoined twin.

"You have a reply, Lord Kirk?" The acid in her tone was hard to hide. Why did he always, always protest her ideas like she was a five-year-old telling a make believe story?

He sipped from his fancy bubbly beverage Belyx probably couldn't pronounce. "You are aware of the limited resources we have in Aikradal."

"I concur with the statement," Master of Coin, Jon, added. His hands shook in his lap and Belyx pondered at how someone with as profound of a shake counted such delicate coins. *Maybe we have more money than we think?* No one knew his age, but he had served the last two kings, and that said something. His silver strings of hair barely stayed on his head and his skin was covered in dark moles. He made Madame Jewella look young.

"Thanks for the update," Belyx replied and received another glare from her father, but Captain Thomas snorted and she stifled a blush. At least he understood this was a waste of air. He was almost too perfect, like a happy retriever. No wonder Freyja had a crush on him.

Kirk pursed his lips, showing off his pathetic white whiskers below his nose. Could snakes grow facial hair? "The gangs are getting too much to handle. We have the Goldfingers smuggling illegal shipments across our markets. We have the Berserkers traipsing around, hurting people and causing a ruckus. The Cabarets continue with their mysterious doings, and don't get me started on the Whispers."

Lord Jaques scoffed, finally speaking up. He usually tried to stay out of things, hence why he was Belyx's favorite. "The weakest of the bunch, I'd say."

Kirk's vein popped out of his head like it did when he needed a fancy word to sound intelligent. "Do not underestimate the Whispers. They have more control than you know. The way they know everything is suspicious."

"Sounds like someone here is telling them secrets. Any ideas, Lord?" Belyx inserted. He always had such an obsession with the Whispers, Belyx would believe he was one if they accepted men into the group. Daggers from the entire table bore into her and she waved it off as a playful chide.

"At least the fae are no longer a problem," Master of Trade, Roman, added. "We have been keeping an eye on the kingdom and the rest of the continent, but none seemed to have slipped from us."

Her father's face stilled and Belyx's throat closed. The fae, the once peaceful group of creatures, turned evil when they murdered the former queen...her mother. How her father managed to eradicate them was a mystery, but he did it, and the world was free from those murderers. This was the only good news of this wretched meeting.

Shaking his enormous head, Kirk kept painfully going. "Anyway, we have four powerful collectives trying to usurp the throne right now, and we need support. Majeria is closest to us with loads of resources. My vote is for them."

Master Roman interjected, "Those pious fools would never help us in the first place. They try to swindle the trades every day!" and now Belyx nursed a small headache. At least he agreed with her.

"Majeria has a suitable fighting force who could destabilize these usurpers," Kirk replied, clenching his chair.

"The people's opinions of the crown are dropping," Master Jon said. "It is only a matter of time before they lose faith in us and join them. Have you seen the lower circles?"

Belyx had. Too many people lived in squalor thanks to the gangs taking control of the lower-level jobs and production. This created a lack of funds for the palace and led to fewer guards, crummy trade routes, and crime rates rising with no one to stop it. Even the Order couldn't contain such a mess. This last year was the worst.

The men continued fighting, and Belyx waited for an opening. Help from Majeria would be a horrible idea. The rumors behind their smuggling and slave trade were too risky to trust. Of course, they denied it, but Belyx had seen the streets herself. It was there.

"The rest of the kingdoms won't do shit!" Roman said curtly. "They won't even come near us because of these conglomerates, like a sort of sickness. Our whole trade is in the hole." His slicked back dark comb over shook as he went on his usual tirade.

With the pause in talking, Belyx lunged for her opening, like in a duel. "May I speak now?" That was meant to sound less vicious, but she had no sleep the previous night and cared little about their feelings. Everyone became quiet, focusing on her. This would not happen, and Belyx would use her tricks to prevent it. "Thank you. Majeria is going to want things in return. They always do." This was a stretch, as Majeria had never assisted them before, but their huffy princess had always been rude to Belyx. Since they met as children and despite Belyx being a secret assassin, Princess Viviene always ended up on top. The idea of groveling to her perfectly pedicured feet threw a hundred-pound weight in Belyx's stomach.

Her father cleared his throat. "What do you think, Lord Jaques?" Typical of her father to ignore her and ask someone else. Jaques had sense though.

Lord Jaques rubbed his chin of snowflake-like facial hair, and panned his head around the room. Unlike Kirk, Jaques didn't kiss ass and told it like it was. "Majeria is a volatile territory, your grace. Remember the rumors?"

Shockingly, Kirk interjected, "Oh please, that was years ago before—" He stopped and for good reason.

Her father turned a shade of crimson and Belyx smiled into her hands. Kirk making mistakes made her day. At least the ones her father would catch.

Belyx fired Lord Snobby a glare and continued her soon-to-be victory lap. "The gangs can be dealt with. They all have a weakness."

Kirk arched a brow. "Oh, tell us how you know so much about them. Studying hard from the safety of your chamber and sewing room?"

If only he knew. Could she slip him poison? *Too obvious.*

"The reports, obviously. I listen, too." Captain Thomas stifled another chuckle, and the king shot him fire. Belyx continued. "I say we start a campaign and pay the communities to report on them. Offer them things they want. The soldiers can't fix this problem alone, but our citizens can help."

"We have no money, naïve child." Kirk was treading in dangerous territory now. His drink was dangerously close to her hand. Master Jon's dark complexion shifted to a scowl as if Kirk offended his whole family by taking his words. At least he hated him, too.

"It is not always about the money. It is about power as well," Belyx said through gritted teeth. "Aikradal was built on this ideal, hence why our major export is weapons. The people are seeing us in a weak state. We need to take it back and change the narrative." Belyx paused and flipped her hair back. She didn't always say the right thing, but when she did, it ruled.

The king ignored her and looked at the rest of the council. Why was Belyx even invited to these? "I honestly don't know."

"Are you suggesting endangering the people of Aikradal by involving them in the activity of the gangs? The only ones responsible for their safety should be the guards. What kind of ruler endangers her people?" Kirk would soon regret his choices.

"Can you lay off her, please?" Captain Thomas stepped in, circling his thumb on his scabbard. Finally, someone who heard her.

Kirk rolled his eyes and turned to the king. "Aid from Majeria is the only way, your Majesty. We are spread thin. If this persists longer, we will be in a true civil war, where the citizens from the lower ring will have to pick a group or die."

Lord Jaques sat back in his chair and cursed. "At this point, let the damn gangs kill each other. We stay out of it." His eyebrows furrowed as if reevaluating his notion. "I am only being extreme, your majesty." Sometimes Jaques had wild ideas. At least Belyx would have less collateral damage on her.

King Terach shook his head. The wear and tear of ruling Aikradal was a stain on his soul. "I'm sorry, Princess Belyx and Jaques. Your plans are too risky. I have to follow Kirk on this one, but let's vote as a council."

"Terms of the vote, please," Kirk added, side-eyeing Belyx.

The king sat up and rubbed his drying hands. "If Majeria is to indeed assist us, we would have to throw a ball to honor them. Then I vote to offer control of our weapon production. They seem to have a knack for trade and turning a profit from it." He turned his eye at Master Roman. "With your help, of course." *All those weapons under Majeria's control.*

Belyx felt like she was in quick sand with no way out, forced to watch as she suffocated. The king looked at her. "The ball will fall under the princess." *Great.* "Those in favor of the ball, request for aid, and offering total autonomy of our weapons to Majeria?"

The vote concluded and Belyx lost five to two.

Belyx stormed out of the room.

It was everyone against her...as usual. Thomas even caved. The only one on her side was Master Roman, and the thought alone made her lose her lunch.

Her father's mental well-being thrust his own council on edge. Belyx made a note to talk to him later, except she and her father spoke less frequent anymore. The death of her mother and the uprising of the gangs painted the kingdom a harsh shade.

"That bad, huh?" Her handmaiden popped out from the tall pillars and offered Belyx chocolates. She always knew what she needed.

"They just don't listen to me." She chewed into the dark chocolates and her mood lifted...but not enough.

"A room full of men and no one listened to you?" Freyja caught a laugh and Belyx's ribs threatened to strangle her lungs

"And now I have to plan a ball and deal with perfect, judgmental Princess Vivienne." The name on her tongue even charred.

"I hate her too, but this conflict is getting scary, Belyx. I had to kill three guards today who were bribed by the Goldfingers, as well as stop one of those creepy Whisper clones from infiltrating here to spy. My tasks are becoming more difficult each day. There aren't enough Stems in the castle to thwart these threats."

"With no credit, of course." Secret assassins rarely received such praise. Belyx could tell the stress was getting to her. Freyja was a master with the coals, but nothing hid her sunken frame and half-closed eyes. When had she slept last?

Giving her a break was superfluous, and Belyx had her own challenges. As was said in council, things are becoming worse and none of those stupid men were aware without the Order, they would have been taken out long ago.

"Never." Freyja gave a close lipped smile and took the empty tray. "When is your next meeting?"

Belyx stuck out her tongue. "In about twenty minutes. I have to speak to Amenthya first. My ankle is searing, and it is making me irritable."

"What a surprise. You irritable?"

She nudged her friend. "Just kill some intruders for me, will you?"

Freyja winked. "Only for you. Afterward, I'll send Inka and Onka to your room to deliver lunch because I know you will be too stressed to eat, and no brilliant princess will drop unconscious on my watch."

Belyx beamed. "How do you always know what to say?"

"It's the trauma." It was always her answer.

"I'm serious."

"Years of practice then." She flicked her braids back and turned away.

Belyx made sure no one was around before embracing her. Princesses couldn't hug their handmaidens, but assassins could hug their protectors.

"Freyja did an impeccable job with this wrap," Amenthya said. Belyx tried not to wince as she removed the bandage. The air hugged her moist ankle. "Off late, I see." Amenthya lifted the wound up to the light and squinted to get a better look. Amenthya was always particular about her tasks. She was another rescue case by the Order, although her story was quite an odd one. One she didn't discuss.

Her grandmother rescued her south of Petrovkan, near the Twisted Rivers. She was a healer there too, in charge of keeping the Petrovkan slaves fit enough to work. From what her grandmother said, they took her from her family due to a massive debt. Like Freyja, she lived under the chain for a long time.

"What gave it away?" Belyx said with sarcasm. It was not the first, nor would it be the last time she came for a salve. Although, she usually wasn't this careless.

Amenthya let out a fake chuckle, the kind a healer gave an obnoxious patient, and opened a canister of a pea-colored substance. The mint aroma barely masked the rancid odor. As if detecting Belyx's disgust, Amenthya said, "Oh, stop. You could at least hide your grimace. The God themself blessed this brew. This is the best in the land."

A recipe she would never share. Even her grandmother didn't know. Dara wanted to hire more healers to apprentice under her, but Amenthya refused to teach her ways to anyone else. She wasn't too old, but it was still a risk to lose such an asset to the Order and the palace. In the last year, she had saved hundreds of people, Belyx included. The thought of losing her made Belyx's limbs numb.

The cream chilled her ankle and then seared it like beef on a spit. The throbbing instantly seceded. "I may need a bucket of that." Belyx poked fun, but Amenthya stayed quiet as she wrapped it up again. Belyx never quite figured out what she was thinking, but she didn't pry.

Wiping the excess viscous cream off her silk robe, she stood. "If that will be all, princess, I must see to my garden." She bowed and left Belyx, her white hair whipping behind her like a haunting specter. It was ironic how she used herbs for healing, while Belyx used them for harming.

As Belyx collected her things and stepped on her foot, the pain had subsided like magic. Belyx imagined what a healer's life would be like, actually bringing lives back instead of taking them.

Hearing day was by far Belyx's least favorite day.

It only proved to her the crime in Aikradal was getting worse by each passing moment. Hearing Day occurred once and month and they would start by dragging the arrested citizens in.

After listening to their pleas, they received judgment from her father and the council. Belyx hated being responsible for other people's fates, especially for petty things like theft. Stealing was wrong and affected everyone, but those poor people had no choice sometimes.

After the tenth one, Belyx couldn't stomach the turmoil her people were going through. The first was a man who took a loaf of bread to feed his family. Her father gave his ruling, and he had to pay a fine. (As if he could pay for it. He couldn't even afford bread). The council also gave him labor detail around the kingdom, cleaning and working on odd jobs for the guards. It was one way to have free labor, she guessed.

Another accused was a girl about fourteen years old. She escaped from an abusive home and her father reported her missing. Her own father doing such horrible things to her was unimaginable. Why bless the world with a child and turn around and harm them? These kinds of atrocities made Belyx's head spin.

"I see your predicament," her father said in a soft but forceful tone. The teenage girl trembled in her chains, surrounded by guards as if she would kill them. "But he is your father and you must respect his rules, even if they are un-reasonable. I sentence you to community service and I expect you to apologize to your father. You only get one."

Belyx looked away as the girl stared at her, as if the only other powerless woman in the room had any say. *Trust me, I've tried.* She barely had the energy to fight the burning in her cheeks as the sobbing prisoner was escorted out.

Lord Kirk blew out a breath like he carried an army up a hill. "They get younger every year, my liege."

"Indeed," the king replied, drinking from his goblet. His throat bobbed as the liquid slithered down. "This kingdom is losing its morals."

"I just wish the father was punished, too." Belyx regretted the words the moment she uttered them.

Kirk scoffed, and her father glared at her. "Mind your place. She disobeyed her own blood and obliterated his property."

"He was abusing her."

Her father stilled. "If you are to run this court one day, you must look at facts. People lie."

Belyx folded her arms. Of course people lied. She knew better than anyone, but the way the girl spoke of the abuse couldn't have been anything but true. People who harmed someone below them should be held accountable for their actions.

Her father drummed his fingers, as if deciding a punishment for Belyx's compassion. "Princess Belyx, you will sentence the next one. Don't disappoint me."

Belyx's whole tongue went numb as she tried to moisten it. As much as she hated watching these, doing the sentencing was worse. Usually they were easy, but the second they brought this next one in, her skin prickled.

The immense doors opened, and it was like the light had been sapped from the room. The pictures of past rulers appeared to have turned away as well. The guards hauled the towering man in. Across his body were snake tattoos slithering around his frame and his head bore a single obsidian top knot with a few strands coming loose. He kept his eyes down as they chained him in the center, as if embarrassed.

Lord Jaques leaned forward and whispered to the king, "Maybe you should do this one, liege?"

He shook his head and Belyx's throat grew sour. "Princess, proceed." A pit formed in her stomach she couldn't shake.

She took the man's paperwork from the guard and read it aloud, trying not to stumble. "Clad Gójsk is accused of..." Belyx gulped. "Rape and murder of five different victims. Three girls and two boys." *Girls and boys. Literal children.*

What kind of monster stomached such a thing? The regret not to stay in bed burrowed into her.

She tilted the scroll down and almost dropped it. He was looking up at her, his vibrant blue eyes pierced right into her soul as if he were peeling it away bit by bit. His tongue hung out like a hungry dog and behind his dry mouth sat a set of sharpened teeth. The criminal's aura made her crave a bath. Belyx curbed a shiver, wishing she was her assassin persona, Doneque, with her hidden blades and poisons. Here, she was just Princess Belyx. "Does the accused wish to rebut?" The answer was obvious.

He expelled his saliva on the ground like an animal. "Oh, I think I do." Snickering to himself like a demon, he spat again. "I wish I had a taste of you, princess." Her Father squeezed his knuckles, but didn't step in. "Crime will reign free. No one has control anymore after the death of the queen." The mention of her mother fired bullets down her spine. "Now, we have this oaf and bitch in charge." He licked his lips, showing more knife-like teeth. "Pathetic."

Belyx opened her mouth, but no words came. She had faced dangerous gang members and fought multiple assailants at one time, but he had a spell on her. Trying to check her shaking, she kept her bones from falling apart. Dots swirled in her vision. His stare was etched into her brain forever.

After what felt like years of torture, her father stood. "We find you guilty of a moral crime against The God and you will be sent to The Pits of Baraxat for judgment."

Everyone gasped.

The Pits were for the most intense of criminals. It had been months since they sentenced anyone there. The giant hole at the northern tip of the continent was where no one wanted to go. The kingdoms of Keyica would send their most notorious criminals to face judgment from the God Themself. Death was the favorable option.

The criminal made a guttural growl. "Your God will spare me. I do Their bidding!" He hissed like a dying animal.

Her father continued, unfazed. The years of experience aided him. The man shook in his chains and the guards held him back. Belyx found relief in his restraints. "You will be sent to the kingdom of Majeria on the morrow and they will escort you to The Pits. This is an official decree from King Terach in honor of The God and Their people." He struck his sword down and the guards dragged him away as he spat and screeched, the noises echoing after he was gone.

Belyx sat, hands still shaking. She avoided her father's eye contact. "That is enough for today." He glared at Belyx, and the rest of the council departed.

Captain Thomas put a hand on her shoulder. "You did great. Facing people like him can be a lot. I don't even know if I could."

Hiding tears, Belyx sank her head down. "How can I expect to rule if I can't even sentence a common criminal?" Every week, the criminals coming in grew and grew. The gangs made them hate the royals, and she couldn't do anything about it. Sure, she had the power to kill whoever she needed, but that wasn't enough. The propaganda against the palace was like an infected wound, threatening to fester until it died.

"He was anything but common, princess." Thomas stared out into the room. The sun had returned, and the light flared from the windows, making his blonde locks shimmer. "They told me I could never be captain because of my youth."

Belyx sneered. "But you are remarkable. My father wouldn't trust someone he wasn't sure of. Like me."

Captain Thomas ignored her self-deprecation, which she was thankful for. "It's harder than you think. The guards don't respect me and I have to work twice as hard to prove my worth every day. Half of them don't listen to me either, like I am a child playing pretend with a wooden sword. I wish they would see I am strong and can lead."

"You lead. You do it every day."

Captain chuckled. "Here I was, trying to comfort *you*." A close-lipped smile formed on his lips. "Well, *I* am proud of you."

Belyx sensed a sudden softness in the captain she couldn't place. "We are entering into a difficult time right now and I do not know how to solve it. My mother would get us out of this."

Thomas stared up again, his voice cracking. "She was an amazing woman. My trouble with reading was making me fail the academy. All the other kids and instructors said I wasn't trying hard enough and being a lazy boy." Belyx recalled students like him in the academy. They usually were sent to do grunt work. "The words just wouldn't come to me. I practiced every day, and it did nothing. I would get called on to read aloud and humiliated. One day, they were going to expel me and—"

"My mother swooped in." Of course she did. She always saved those in need.

Thomas smiled. "Right. Then she gave me a chance to join the ranks of the guards. I will always remember what she told me that day. 'Thomas, you are you because of what you can do, not what you can't do.' Those words have stuck with me ever since."

Belyx faintly recalled Thomas joining the guard fourteen years ago when she was nothing but a young girl. Her mother did everything thing right, and Belyx only dreamed of being as perfect. One day she would, but she had to keep fighting.

Belyx stood, the thoughts of her mother crept on her like stalking prey. "Thank you for the help, Captain."

"Anytime, princess." He bowed, and she left, forcing back her remaining tears, and trudged to her room.

Four

Inka and Onka came in at just the right time. Belyx was absorbed into her poems and needed a distraction. "Close the door." The steaming plate of seasoned pasta and beets made her stomach churn as she shut her notebook, trying to recall when she had eaten last.

"Cook said this would cheer you up," Onka said as she set the tray down. Her sister began to prepare it as usual, but Belyx waved her away, only to have her continue holding the food.

Right.

"It's ok for today, Inka. You work hard enough." Inka continued her routine and Belyx gave up. Everything had to be finished with her.

"I work as hard as I like," Inka added.

Onka elbowed her. "Don't disrespect the princess. We have talked about this," she said as if she was her mother, but Belyx didn't mind. Inka did what Inka did. How she became a Petal rank was a mystery to her, however. She had a brain different from everyone else, even her twin. Her parents exploited it by building favor with drug trades until a deal went wrong and Inka killed one of the dealers. After, her parents punished her by kicking them out on the cold Petrovkan streets. Did she feel guilty? It was hard to say, but Belyx believed deep down, she did. Her grandmother always made sure anyone with exceptionalities belonged here. Inka's analytical nature also helped her be a seasoned Leaf before her promotion. She gathered more information in a day than the average agent in a week.

Upon looking at them, the twins were difficult to tell apart. The maids both sported the same lavender servant's garb and wore their hair into short blonde bobs. It was when they started speaking that gave them away.

Belyx inhaled her pasta and vegetables. Onka, the ever caring one, asked in her quick staccato form, "Is it good? I can grab you something else if you need? Water? Seasoning? It would only take a second."

In between mouthfuls, Belyx eyed her as if to say, "it's fine."

"Sorry, Princess," Onka bowed again. Her nervous energy even made Belyx crave a breath.

Belyx wiped her mouth with a cotton napkin. "No, this is perfect. Thank you. You are free to leave. Next time I will make it down for dinnertime."

Inka bowed and left without a goodbye.

Onka rolled her eyes and sat down. Freyja's information spread like old ladies at a game of cards. "You think you can have a bad day and I wouldn't know? Please."

Belyx speared a lettuce leaf and plopped it into her mouth. Food always helped. "It's nothing. Besides me not getting a voice in council and I was volunteered to throw a ball for people I would rather not speak to or see."

Onka faked a gasp. "Planning a party. How bad..." Her humor never came across as she intended, but Belyx forgave her.

"Knock it off. You may outrank me in the Order, but I can still have my maid beheaded." Onka's lip quivered, missing Belyx's joking tone.

Belyx smiled and stared at her empty plate, wondering if she would catch a stomachache for eating with such haste. "I don't think we need Majeria's help and everyone is against me. *No surprise there.* I wish people trusted me to handle it."

"I see your point, but the council also doesn't know you are a badass assassin, and they don't think you can do much." Despite the eight-year age difference, she related to Belyx.

"I also mean as a princess. They won't listen to my plans."

"Well, you are young." Now Onka was annoying her. "I would wait until they fail. Then they will listen to you."

Belyx's heart sank as she uttered her next words. "By then, it will be too late. I can do it now."

"The gangs are out of control. They won't spare any of us if they breach. You heard Freyja, they are getting closer and closer."

The fork clanked as Belyx slammed it down. "I can handle the gangs. I've been training for this."

Onka scrunched her face. The one thing she did when things were about to turn honest. "Belyx. You were almost killed taking down a Goldfinger shipment, and they aren't even the toughest bunch. The Berserkers could rip anyone in two like they were meat."

"I know. I fought them before." A slight lie, but Onka didn't need to know she had help fighting them. Shockingly, they caused the least amount of crimes.

Onka bought none of it. Why did Belyx think she could fool a Petal? Especially one who was in charge of the Leaves, the group responsible for collecting information around the kingdom. Onka and Inka knew of everything happening more than a Whisper. Intel was the best weapon, but she enjoyed the smaller details of the kill assignments. Spying was still important, but the fight had to be messy.

As if sensing Belyx lulling in thought, Onka brushed the dust from her robe, collected from posing as a maid. "Damn these chores. You think dirt would just go away."

"I wish you didn't have to do all those chores." Belyx's double life was an extravagant princess. At least she didn't have to clean washrooms and take out putrid garbage.

Onka waved her hand. "It is no problem, but I hope men take these jobs soon. I could use a break."

"Wouldn't that be something?" Belyx couldn't even imagine. If men did these tasks, things would change in a heartbeat because The God forbid, they would be uncomfortable.

Onka twirled her string on her outfit and sighed. "It was better with her. She was strong."

Belyx looked away. Even though she was right, the thought of her mother stung. As if catching her words too late, Onka sank down. "Apologies. I didn't mean to overstep."

Belyx put a hand on Onka's shoulder. "You're fine. You don't have to worry about me. Actually, please talk about her. I know what she did for you and Inka."

Onka and her sister were rescued from Aikradal soldiers during a slave trade bust from Petrovkan. They were sent to train as maids when her grandmother discovered their exceptional observation skills and recruited them.

Onka blinked twice like she was surprised Belyx didn't launch her over the balcony. Although that would prove difficult. What Onka lacked in height, she made up for in raw skill. Spies needed to fight, too. "She made the Order stronger. Majesty Dara is great, but Queen Abigail was perfect in every way. It was a shame what happened."

Belyx stared out her window. Thirteen years it had been and the thought still sent her spiraling. Onka was right, her mother was entrancing. Even her death continued to haunt the kingdom. The monsters who murdered her deserved everything they received, but Belyx stifled those thoughts, drawing in careful, slow breaths.

After more tears and embraces from Onka, Belyx pulled away and wiped her face. "I think I am going to train a little before the evening ends."

Today was the day off from Madame and this meant assassin training with her grandmother. It was the perfect remedy to get over her mother. At least for now.

Onka laughed. "Well, not looking like that. Let me pick you out an outfit and do your hair. I know I'm not Freyja, but I can try."

Belyx nodded, and Onka ruffled through the closet as she followed. Despite the challenges she faced, her mother's blood was inside of her, and nothing would bring her down.

After Onka helped Belyx look her absolute best, Belyx snuck over to the giant rose garden on the far side of the palace grounds. The guard towers on the outside wall missed it and made a perfect spot for the Order's secret hideout.

The gardens led to a circular path where a stature of Dara's mother stood, Queen Margerie, who started the Order. The statue didn't portray her wielding a sword or anything violent, but resting, reading a story to her daughter. Queen Margerie gave Belyx's grandmother the garden when she was young, and Dara kept it blooming ever since. In the last fifty years, it expanded across the whole upper corner of the grounds.

In it lay bushes of multiple colors of roses. No one knew how they changed hues, but her grandmother always treated them like they were children and nursed them to grow. The bees retreated as the sunlight sank away and Belyx crossed over the grass, where rose bush plots were cut into intricate triangles. She held one to her nose, and the aroma soothed her. Rose scents were her favorite. The cold season was deplorable, but they would survive as they did every time. It would destroy her grandmother to have these bushes wilt.

Belyx went to another set of statues of children playing and checked to make sure no one was looking. With one click, she pressed the switch on the little girl and the floor creeped open, revealing a tunnel of stairs. She headed down and hit another latch to close the door behind her.

The dark hallway was lit by a sea of candle lights splitting off in multiple directions. Belyx took in the sights as she did every time she entered.

The various pathways led to rooms pertinent to the Order such as the recruit sleeping quarters, the weapons room, the conference room, the training hall, and Belyx's favorite; the poison garden and snake enclosure.

The room hailed to her like an old friend. She passed the usual poisons lining the plots the agents used. The flower that caught her eye was a vibrant red one, the belladonna. The sharp reds encapsulated the beauty, but also hinted at a warning. Belyx related to this, which was how she gained the assassin name, Doneque.

Past the other door was what she needed to check on. The room was under lock and key, so no inexperienced hands touched her babies. After a click of the latch, she pulled out her bag of collected street mice, trying to ignore their terrified shrieks.

"Dinner time," she called, throwing one into the opening of a giant glass container. A tiny snake slithered from its pond and devoured the creature with grace. "Good girl, Mira." Her blue-black sea snake stared at her with wide eyes, as if to ask for more. "You're tiny. You don't need anymore," she replied as she stroked the creature's scaly skin. Mira had teeth that were too small to puncture humans. The others, she had to be more careful.

"You're next, Kali. Stop the groveling." Snakes had the biggest attitudes. Her cobra, graced in a rare whitish pink color, tilted her head at Belyx, but went to town on the mouse.

A thud hit another tank. The snakes ate once a week and yet they acted starving. "Jay." The blue viper stared back at her. "What did we say about the banging?" Jay turned her head without a care. She knew who was in charge...her.

After Belyx fed her, she shifted to the last one and sighed. "Sleeping again, Gwyar?" The pitch colored black mamba slowly lifted her head. As Belyx's oldest snake, she was her most deadly. She found her stranded in the palace garden as a baby. Snakes were killed throughout the kingdom for their evil undertones, and Belyx couldn't stand to witness her die.

The mouse ran inside and Gwyar eyed it like she would handle it later. "Take care. I won't need any more venom for a while." She thanked The God for their venom's effectiveness.

Belyx sighed at an empty cage. Her egg was not boding well. She saved it by the river outside the Sehrlic forest. Months had passed, and there was still no sign of it hatching, but Belyx held onto the sliver of hope. Where did it come from? What snake lied within it?

The other members didn't understand her pets. They were useful creatures who did much for them. She bid the reptiles goodnight and headed out.

In the training circle were the Seedlings were practicing techniques while Dara meditated. Her grandmother was superstitious and claimed if she didn't pray every day, something bad would happen. Belyx feared it was inevitable anyway, but she would never utter such blasphemy aloud.

The students stopped their drills and waved at Belyx. They ranged from ages twelve to eighteen. Those older few would take part in The Budding soon. The freshness of her own Budding was still in her mind.

The recruits had multiple bruises on them from practice and from their pasts. Her stomach recoiled at what they had endured, but they appeared better here, and it was a start. Dara was a skilled leader, unlike Belyx.

Her grandmother opened one eye at Belyx and smiled. "You made it. Take a seat next to your gran."

Belyx plopped down and was silent for a few more beats. The only sound in the hideout was the students and occasional Thorn practicing. Focusing on her own thoughts was always a battle. "So, what is new with the Order, grandmother?" The thoughts won.

Dara inhaled a controlled breath of air. "You never could just be still. The God says to relax in their teachings." As if anyone around here relaxed.

"Well, nothing gets done then. I want to get this frustration out." Belyx fiddled with the soft mat underneath them.

Her grandmother laughed. "Oh, Belyx. When will you understand this is not what the Order of the Rose is for?"

Cue history lesson. Every chance she had, her grandmother lectured about the Order.. It's the morning, here's some history. I just ate dinner, here is a lecture. It's a thing she did.

Despite Belyx's audible scoffs. Her Grandmother continued. "My mother formed this Order to protect the kingdom." *I know.* "Men were doing nothing about the violence and disorder around the kingdom. They could have cared less about the trafficking, the drugs, and the harm against each other, especially against the women."

"Aikradal did pride itself on strength," Belyx said sarcastically.

"Exactly. She figured out a way to make it happen. Use the women. Who better to go unnoticed? I loved your grandfather, but he barely batted an eye at me. I envy my mother for her courage sometimes."

Belyx never met her great-grandmother Majorie, but the stories were incredible. A submissive queen, giving the credit for the crime rate dropping to her husband and never looking twice. Humbleness was a skill Belyx craved.

Queen Margerie had an organized ranking system. She would recruit girls and train them as Seedlings, testing their skills from disguise to fighting, and then when they were old enough, they would take The Budding and be placed into three prestigious groups. the Leaves, who were the spies. the Stems, who protected the castle. And the Thorns, like Belyx, who did the assassinating. It was one coordinated team under the pictorial of a rose. Her great-grandmother was truly a genius.

Petals were more complicated as they had to work with the main ranks to be chosen. Dara, Freyja, Inka, Onka, and Cook were Petals, responsible for the other ranks. A spot Belyx coveted, but she had a way to go. *One day,* Belyx thought.

Her grandmother eyed Belyx. "But the crime cycle is back. Our kingdom is in danger, and your father is doing nothing to stop it. It is up to us."

Belyx felt her heart beat faster. This was the motivation to help her proceed. "What do we need to do first? Kill the leaders? Threaten them? Expose their weaknesses?" Finally, she had the green light to cause damage and would gut the gangs like they were nothing. She shuddered thinking of it.

Dara continued walking to the center of the room to an ornately etched desk and pulled out a parchment scroll. "I appreciate the enthusiasm, but we can't just kill them. Are you familiar with the hydras in ancient stories?" She kept flipping through the parchment.

"Yes," Belyx replied like a child in school. "Once one head is cut off, two more take its place." Belyx knew where this was headed as her excitement faded.

"Precisely. If the leaders of the gangs are killed, they would only be martyrs to their causes and replaced by crazier proteges. In order to take them out, we have to dismantle their following. Like they are doing to us."

She was right. The people of Aikradal were relying on the crown less and less. With violence and uprising in every corner, it was pick a side or die and few citizens elected to die. "How can we accomplish this?"

Dara flipped to the correct page and her eyebrows shot up. "With this." She held up the scroll. "Our Leaves have received reports of a dangerous secret about Aikradal, and the gangs are hunting for it."

Belyx's heart slowed. What kind of secret would the palace be hiding? Besides the Order, of course. "What is it?"

Her grandmother rubbed her palms together as if trying to decipher a code. "I don't fully know. It could be our Order or something else entirely. It is a devastating rumor, and could cripple Aikradal as we know it."

Not knowing this annoyed Belyx and thought it even more shocking her grandmother possessed no other knowledge on it. "How can we stop this?" There had to be something, anything.

Her grandmother stayed neutral. "The reports mentioned a thief possessing the details of this secret, but it is hard to say."

"Hold up." Her grandmother paused, annoyance filling her eyes, but Belyx cared little. "Some common thief off the streets knows this deadly secret? How in the world?"

Her grandmother waited like a teacher in a disruptive class. "Yes. Aren't you listening, granddaughter?" Still confused as hell, Belyx froze, but Dara continued. "How he knows is unclear, but the rumors of his knowledge are too risky to ignore."

"I don't buy this. I bet the gangs are trying to fool us." It had to be. No way was her father hiding any kind of secret.

"Already ahead of you. I thought so too, but we lost the thief."

"You...of all people lost someone? What does that mean?"

Her grandmother pinched her nose. "It means he is in hiding, fled, or the gangs got him."

Which gang was the question? "How do we know he is still alive?" The gangs were not known for their mercy.

"Because this kingdom is still afloat. They would not harm him without the information." Like a feather, Belyx's heart lightened. She had a point. They had time. "Who has him?"

"It is rumored the Berserkers have a prisoner, but it may not be him." Belyx gulped. Of course it was the Berserkers. Sensing her fear, her grandmother responded, "I know. It may not even be true, but the Berserkers are relentless and will torture him blind until they get what they want and he is most likely not tough enough to handle the pain they give out."

"So, I need to save him?" Belyx cursed to herself. Some mission this would be. Save a thief who was in the deadliest gang's clutches. The recent excitement she had was packed up and gone now.

"Yes, and find out what he knows."

"I can't kill him?" Belyx would do whatever it took.

Her grandmother arched a brow. It was a stretch. "I didn't say kill. We don't execute innocents. He may know nothing, and this was a wild butterfly race, but we have to start somewhere."

Aikradal had no secrets, but she vowed to protect her kingdom at all costs. "I'm in."

Her grandmother smiled the smile she always did when she won, but she frowned once more. "It will be dangerous. On top of the Berserkers being vicious, this thief could also prove...difficult."

Belyx scoffed. "I can handle a street thief."

"Don't underestimate, Belyx." She pointed around the hideout, where a portrait of her mother sat on the wall. "Everyone underestimated us and look what we have done."

Belyx hated she was right, but a pilferer being deadly? There was no way in hell this old coot would give her trouble. If he was like any other thief, he would be a frilly, balding, smelly, old person. *Easy to interrogate.* "I guess it is a mission, then. How and when shall we do this?"

"I think tonight would be perfect." Dara went to grab more parchment, tracing the lines like a blade to flesh. "It is the Berserkers' weekly fighting tournament. There will be lots of people and many distractions. In and out, Belyx. Am I clear?"

"Always." Dara tilted her head down and gave her the "you're a liar," look.

Twisting at her sleeve, Belyx bowed. "I promise, grandmother." Dara nodded and Belyx cracked her knuckles. "Let's save this thief, then."

Five

"Deep breath. You can do this."

This was one of the first missions on her own against the Berserkers. She refused to fail, slipping into the manufacturing district of Aikradal. The Berserkers used an abandoned factory for their weekly fighting ring night. The council was aware of this, but the gang had too many people guarding it. It would cost the palace casualties they couldn't afford to lose.

Belyx stopped in front, avoiding the crowds piling into the building. The thunderous cheers bloomed from outside and the event hadn't even begun. Her mother made fighting for fun illegal, but after her death, they continued. People from across the kingdom flocked to witness the display of violence, while a couple competed for prizes of money and fame. It seemed harmless, although the people would never see the true destruction the Berserkers caused. *You are not here to stop them. Only save the thief.*

Careful to look as normal as possible, Belyx kept her hood down. If she left it up, she would be seen as an assassin. Sometimes she needed to be a random citizen of Aikradal. One who craved watching men punch the shit out of each other. The spying Leaves taught her this.

Belyx followed the crowds, studying the factory blueprints in her mind one last time. It sat behind a giant warehouse where the Berserkers did their operations. And now possibly housed a prisoner. The Order had intel about the hideout for a while, but her grandmother deemed it too dangerous to enter...even for them. She only sent Leaves to recover intelligence. Like the reason the palace never intervened, the Berserkers were a kill first, ask questions later kind of group. Was the thief already dead? Shaking her anxieties, she checked her person to make sure the poisons and blades were in order, praying she wouldn't have to use them.

A giant man with protruding muscles and tattoos circling his frame was taking everyone's money at the door. Being a princess, Belyx could've paid with no thought, but tonight, she was Doneque, the assassin. She never paid. A crowd of bustling drunk men made the perfect cover. Like training, she blended in with the foulmouthed, rough citizens and slipped inside. It was almost too easy.

One man made eye contact with her, but was too inebriated to care. Belyx ascended into the stands surrounding the ring. The fight would start soon.

A barrier enclosed the arena, which Belyx assumed was to prevent the fighters' variety of fluids from getting on the spectators. It was like an amphitheater of disorder. Various vendors sold snacks, so people could munch on sweet treats while men knocked each other's eyes out. Also, who would have an appetite with the putrid aroma of sweat and other juices floating about? Belyx gagged. Whoever did the cleaning should be fired.

Like an anxious kid, she waited in her seat. Once the fighting began, she would make her move.

A couple minutes went by and the people hushed. Below by the frigid looking arena, the leader of the Berserkers himself paraded to the center. Belyx's breath hitched.

Raul Fortan was what a leader of a gang known for intense bloodshed would look. His tall, muscular frame stood motionless in the center. He wore zero expression as the flame lights danced across his dark brown bald head. He had a good five inches on Belyx, but was nowhere as scary as the other man following him. His general, The Scorpion, perched a foot higher than Belyx. The onyx armor he bore matched the helmet covering most of his face. It was rumored no person alive had seen his face. The helm was in the shape of a bull and no doubt had blood on the horns. What scared Belyx more was what he held in his hands...a giant bladed spear, taller than him. The stories behind him, if he was a human, were sickening to think about.

Raul spoke, his voice boomed control and power. "Welcome citizens of this fine kingdom." The stands went wild with calls and he let it simmer, but not even a smirk crossed his face. "Who is ready to see some fights?" The crowds screamed once more. It pierced her ears, but she couldn't take her eyes off him; such a simple man, responsible for much anguish. "Reminder, citizens, that we represent a strength Aikradal holds dear. For years, this strength has been depleted from this great nation like a sickness. I hope to bring it back!" The Scorpion stepped forward and held up his life-taking spear, and the crowd quieted while Raul continued. "The first match, as you know, is a legacy fight against my number one champion, The Scorpion!" He motioned to the beast and the people cheered, as if unaware of how many citizens like them, he had gutted. "Now Scorpion, stand on your side and I'll let in our lucky fighter!"

Lucky was not the right word.

As the stands harmonized cheers, a burly man about six feet tall stalked in from the other side. His muscles rippled as he held his twin battle axes in his hand, but what made him unique was the long mustache sitting on his face. Despite his scary appearance, it would be his last fight.

"I present to you, Ulrich of Majeria!" Raul announced.

Ulrich stood, almost shaking as he lifted his jagged blades. He turned toward his opponent. "I will crush your bones, bug." His accent had thick vowels like those from Majeria. The spectators hushed while The Scorpion stayed poised, like Ulrich's jab was a slight breeze.

Raul took out a pistol and held it up to the roof. "I hope you have placed your bets. Remember, our challenger asked for this. Ready. And. Fight!"

The gun went off, and everything moved in slow motion. Belyx should go now, but even she was entranced in this fight. Ulrich's blood would most likely paint The Scorpion's armor.

The challenger charged The Scorpion with the confidence of a lion. The Scorpion stood, as if waiting for his daily kill. Once Ulrich neared, he struck the beast, but The Scorpion blocked and the clang echoed across the stands. Before Ulrich followed up, The general thrust a kick into his torso and he slammed into the ground.

Belyx held her breath. This would be over soon. The challenger crouched and let out what sounded like a battle cry and charged again. The Scorpion stuck up his weapon and, before Belyx could think, Ulrich was split in two, his parts spilling onto the sand. Blood and other entrails mixed with dirt as the Scorpion tore off his head, holding it up like a trophy.

Everyone cheered while Belyx gasped. Despite her skills of killing as well, this made her stomach recoil. She had no more desire to watch. At least when she killed, it was less gruesome. This was more animalistic, like The Scorpion craved it, like food. Raul approached the center as the workers cleared out the various pieces of the former challenger. "The Scorpion stays my champion! Now we move onto the main event!"

As Raul spoke, Belyx was on the move. She was behind schedule watching the blood bath. Circling the stands, she spotted the entrance to the warehouse, guarded by two Berserkers. *This will be too easy.* The guards were large as mountains, but even their muscled veins were not impervious to poison.

Belyx readied her bug-bite needle in senna, a laxative, and took a breath, putting on her best drunk face. The guards scowled at her stumbling. Just a drunk bitch, they would think. Slurring about her "desired love for The Scorpion," she ran right into a guard.

Which could have gone two ways, aggressive, or clueless.

Luckily, people underestimated a woman, and the guards helped her back to her feet, springing her trap.

"Ow! That damn bee!" she yelled, praying they would believe her. The guards ignored her ramblings until they both slapped their legs where the "bee" stung them. "I hate the bugs here!" the one with a protruding forehead declared.

"Me too," the other with awful breath said.

Large Forehead held Belyx still. "Please be more careful, ma'am." *Ma'am,* as if they were refined gentlemen now. At least members of this violent group respected women...Belyx wanted to roll her eyes.

Clumsily, Belyx pointed at them. "Ya got i-i-it." And hobbled away.

When she was sure they stopped looking, she dipped behind a wall and waited.

Ten minutes later found Large Forehead and Bad Breath retreating to the nearest wash room.

Belyx donned her hood and mask, rubbed her flower pin for luck and went right through the door, into the belly of the beast.

Six

If a thief was in the Berserker hideout, Belyx wouldn't even know where to start.

She was running out of time. If the fights ended, and she was still lurking in their warehouse, she would be dead meat.

Maybe her grandmother was wrong, and the thief wasn't here, or he died. Belyx cursed to herself and her grandmother for sending her on this assignment. She always claimed she was worried about Belyx's safety, but then sent her on a wild rat hunt.

The hideout was vast, with multiple floors and rooms spread throughout, and every door led to nothing but a blank room. Belyx guessed from the smell of cleaned blood, they were for training.

While avoiding the hallway patrols, she checked the rooms on the bottom floor. Her skin was coated in sweat and the dry air made her parched. The next room needed to have water, although she doubted its cleanliness. She opened the last door on the second floor to still find nothing.

The clock was ticking, and booms of Berserker footsteps came from the other side. Belyx's eyes stayed open as they passed. She would stand no chance against the herd. After it was clear, she ran to the top floor, scanning every doorway. Her eyes strained from the searching and the blood rushed to her ears. The Berserkers didn't radiate stealth as their stomps echoed for miles, giving her time to hide.

Her adrenaline surged as the next door Belyx tried was locked.

Weird. All the other doors were unlocked. This had to be the thief, or at least something equally important. Belyx sent a silent thank you to The God and used her lock pick to finagle the handle. The building was ancient, and this would be a stroll in the park. She wiped off her sweaty hands, but froze as a loud bang crashed from the distance. No brutes came as she kept her head down.

She continued her work and with a satisfying click, the door swung open. Her heart pulsed as she pushed through, closing the door behind her.

Eyes deceiving her, she blinked in quick succession. A hooded figure was bound to a chair in the middle of the room. The thief was literally on a golden platter for her. Well, she assumed it was the thief. He must not have heard her come in, for she stayed still and said nothing.

The thief didn't look intimidating, at least when he was sitting. Would he put up much of a fight? Belyx would be ready for his old thief tricks.

A gasp left her throat as she yanked off her hood.

He was the opposite of old. In fact, he was around Belyx's age, with gentle emerald eyes and a bed of dark curls resting on his head.

Nothing but a neutral expression was on his deep brown face. Belyx couldn't help but get lost in his sharp features. Why was a street thief this handsome?

Before Belyx debated what to do, the thief had her in a choke hold, with a blade pressed to her throat. The cold steel she knew all too well. She held down his arm, but he was taller and caught her by surprise. He held the steel closer as she spat, thinking of the ways to gut him. "Not one move," he said. His voice was youthful, but had the weight of someone who had been through hard times.

Belyx gripped his toned arm with her life, refusing to die like this. In one swoop, she fell back with her weight. He loosened his grip just enough for her to kick him back. Pulling out her knives, she turned around to find he had his up too.

She inhaled her calm and tried to be diplomatic. "We appear to be on the same side." Please be intelligent enough to understand basic reason. If he was a thief, his education was limited.

The thief kept up his knife, well it was hers. How did he steal it? "Put your blade down and prove it. I've had a rough couple of days." As Belyx studied his face, it was layered in fresh bruises. What had they done to him? The rawness of her neck reminded her he was dangerous, too.

"Why don't you put my knife down and come with me?"

He stepped a couple of inches back. "Wait, are you a girl?"

Belyx kept a straight face behind her mask. Did he just ask that? "The state of my genitals is not the pressing issue here." He scrunched his face at her crass remark. "What is important is we need to escape now."

He stayed still, blank faced. "No thanks. I have my plan. You may go. I appreciate the weapon, though."

Seriously? "You don't hold any bargain here. I saved you, so you listen to me."

The pilferer scoffed and smiled. His teeth were white as bone. Was he trying to charm her? It was a poor attempt, as she had seen spiders with more charm. "I freed myself last time I checked. Remember?"

He asked rhetorical questions like Madame did, only nothing would stop her from gutting him with no consequences. Belyx folded her arms. "What was your plan? Take on a Berserker in combat?"

He folded them back to mock her. Did he miss manners lessons on the streets? "Maybe. You don't know my plans."

Why was he acting like a stubborn ox? "You didn't have one, I'm guessing." Belyx was tired of this playful banter. The Berserkers would be done fighting soon. "Look. I was sent to save you. Who would you rather take a chance with?"

The thief's eyes gouged, his knife hand shaking. Had he ever killed before? "Why should I trust a poorly dressed assassin?"

Belyx ignored his jab and lowered her voice. "I am not asking you to. We need to move or we are both dead." Familiar Berserker footsteps stopped outside the door. "Anytime now." His looks were dreamy, but his brain was clouding them.

The thief braced the door. "We will never get out of here."

"I thought you had a plan?" Belyx rolled her eyes.

He held up his hands. "Hey, I usually do. I guess you can blame my head injury. What is your plan?" Now he wanted to hear it?

The pounding increased. "Do you know how to fight?"

"I can 'scrap around'," he said.

Four of them burst through, hungry for thief and assassin blood. Belyx knifed the nearest one's neck, and he went down like a giant sack of flour.

The thief engaged the others, but was knocked back into his chair.

Belyx dodged a couple swings from the other Berserker's club and lashed his inner thigh, blood spattered as he fell.

The thief screamed. The two berserkers had him pinned against the wall.

Guess scrap around meant suck at fighting.

Belyx vaulted over the chair and stabbed the closest in the back. The other turned, forgetting about her, and the thief kicked him in the soft part between his legs. A quick slice to his carotid sent him down.

Helping the thief up, she sneered, "scrap around, huh?"

He stood and wheezed. "In my defense, I was tired." He looked her up and down as blood dripped from her outfit that Freyja would need to clean. "Also, what are you?"

Under her mask, Belyx smirked. "Also, not important. There will be more. Let's go."

They rushed down the hallways of the upper floor. The Berserkers had the first set of stairs covered and Belyx searched for another. She debated jumping out a window, but the thief's falling skills were in question, plus there may not be a safe landing. It would be time to take her pick; death by fall or by group pummeling. The thief seemed to talk a big game with no follow through.

Like most men.

Berserker guards yelled as they rounded the corner. Belyx clutched the thief's hand and pulled him the other way. He followed with no protests, shockingly. Another door revealed a set of stairs. Without stopping, they launched down, taking multiple steps at a time.

"That's not good," the thief said, and Belyx agreed as Berserkers trampled up the steps right for them. Belyx needed to think fast. They were surrounded with nowhere to go and she couldn't fight through them, but she would certainly die trying, though.

"Follow my lead. This is tight quarters, but I have a plan to slip past them."

The thief crossed his arms. "What is it? An invisibility spell?"

Belyx flouted and took out a pellet filled with a gray powder. "I don't need magic." She chucked the ball down and the stairwell, filling it with a thick ash.

"Hold your breath," Belyx commanded as she took the thief's hand again and they dashed through the wheezing Berserkers and out onto the bottom floor.

Belyx's lungs cried for mercy, but they were almost free. The thief tugged her to the fighting area doors, but Belyx pulled back. "We need to go the other way. They are still finishing up the fights."

The thief recoiled, but something in his tiny brain told him to listen. Finally. "Is there another exit?"

"Through the delivery yard, but we need to move fast. Those goons will alert the place you escaped." Belyx motioned for him to follow, but he remained planted like a festering weed.

"Goons?" The thief said, snorting.

"It is an acceptable term, now, please." She grew restless at his lack of concern.

"What is your name?" He wanted to ask it now? Belyx debated leaving his sorry ass. With her luck, he would know nothing of the secret and this was a waste.

"Now?" Her senses were on high alert. Every creek and stomp set her on edge. They would catch up to them in no time.

He folded his arms like a toddler. "Guess you can go without me, then."

Fine, Belyx thought, but remembered the mission. She took out a dagger. "You don't think I could force you?"

"Try me." He stared her down as if she couldn't take him in a fight. Belyx had to pause and recall her discipline training.

Cursing in her head, she gave in. "Doneque."

His laugh had a slight snort that Belyx would have thought cute if a bunch of rhinos weren't after them. "I'm sorry, I'm sorry, but Doneque is no way your real name."

Belyx put away her knife. "It is my assassin name, and unless you want to find out why, move!" The thief still didn't budge and raised his eyebrows like she forgot something. "What now?" Belyx said, nerves jumping over hoops. He was going to get them killed, and he didn't even care!

"You know it is impolite to not ask someone's name too. Did they not teach you manners in assassin school?" Ok, that was Belyx's joke first.

She threw her hands up. "For all The God! What is your name?"

He cracked a smile that would have made Belyx swoon, but lives and missions were at stake, and she wanted this creep to hurry. "Enzo." Not what she expected in the least.

Belyx mocked his voice. "Is that your real name?"

Enzo ignored her and trudged to the double doors as if it was his plan. Her blood boiled, but Belyx chased after him, only to stop when a scream came from the other side. Belyx rushed in and her heart burst out of her throat.

Enzo, was being held up by The Scorpion.

Everything swirled in slow motion, and Belyx studied the area as if her life depended on it. Wooden boxes were stacked everywhere, and a lit chandelier on the ceiling was the only source of vision. If she lost the thief now, this mission would be for nothing and Belyx would be next. The Scorpion was a brutal fighter and what he did to the challenger earlier made Belyx's stomach roil. She couldn't take him down in a direct fight.

Enzo let out a guttural sound and tried to wrench himself free, but The Scorpion slammed his body into the ground. Enzo lay motionless. Hopefully not dead. Belyx guessed they still wanted him alive.

Belyx's legs took over as she sprinted for the far side of the room. The Scorpion walked after her, making it ten times scarier, especially with his eight foot spear in hand.

She climbed to the tallest box and made her way to the chandelier. The Scorpion lashed at the boxes she jumped on, trying to break them, but Belyx kept on moving. Her eyes stayed focused on her target, but the spear split through wood and sliced her leg. After jaw clenching pain, she safely landed on the last crate. Unsheathing her blade, she hurled her knife. The chain holding the chandelier came crashing down. The flames were sucked away with a peaceful hiss. Only darkness remained in the room to test how well The Scorpion fought in the dark.

Like a bird, Belyx leapt down, needing to find and save Enzo.

The room was silent and dark now, with only the breaths of the man/beast.

Belyx listened for anything alerting her as she crept around the boxes, checking every angle. If even one blow from the Berserker general landed, she would be killed. Her mission would fail and her kingdom would fall.

Belyx shifted around the corner, and her eyes widened.

The same heavy breathing filled her senses as it grew closer and closer.

She gasped as a giant hand tore through a box and seized her neck. The air took no time leaving her lungs as she tried to grasp at any molecule of it. Her head stayed fuzzy, but she remembered her training on being choked and held on, using her weight to pull down his meaty hand. Her wind pipe made a cracking sound. With only seconds, she used her other hand and sent a pin into his hand.

He didn't even grunt in pain, but released her. She hit the ground, controlling her coughs to prevent alerting him, fighting her lung strain. The Scorpion was onto her now. Where would she run with that bull after her? Zigzagging the opposite way, she ducked under the boxes. The Scorpion's footsteps gave him away with their thudding, and Belyx would know where he was.

Belyx's shaky breathing slowed as she rubbed her tender neck that would for sure need to be covered up. Her old ankle wound began to throb, which could be an issue, but not as much as Enzo lying around here somewhere.

Belyx reached for her venoms, debating on which ones would work on this demon. She pulled out a blade, but her stomach hitched as one of her poison pellets landed on the floor. It made a tiny sound, but it was enough. The boxes smashed in the distance and The Scorpion was approaching fast. Belyx surged up, picking a quick venom to coat her knife in and rolled, barely avoiding the charging beast. The Scorpion halted and twirled his spear around. With her steel, Belyx crouched down and propelled herself back before another spear strike nearly missed, vibrating the entire floor. Her blood and adrenaline reverberated in her ears.

At this point, who cared about the thief? She needed to save her own skin. The light from the exit came into view like a saving grace. Legs like fire, she hustled out. Death was not an option today. Screw the thief. She sent a quiet sorry for her kingdom and pushed for the escape. Would his secret die with him?

She was close, but fell when a heavy object slammed into her back. Belyx's vision blurred as she landed on her stomach, gasping for air. The massive weight of the lumber buried her and she winced as the splinters stuck in her skin. The Scorpion must have thrown a wooden box at her. He approached her slowly with his long, hungry blade in hand.

Belyx wailed as she launched as many knives as possible at him, but they ricocheted off his armor as if she was throwing paper at him. Her mask and hood had fallen down and her face was exposed to the beast. His dark vortex of eyes glared right into her very being. It wouldn't take much to determine these were the eyes of death. What took out this beast? The options dwindled as splinters of wood sank deeper into her leg. She tried to wiggle it free, but it was clamped like a bear trap. Mind soaring, when she was this afraid? None came as the Scorpion sauntered over, like he wanted to savor every moment of this torture.

Belyx would like nothing more than to soil his giant guts over the floor, but what scared her most was what kind of expression he wore behind the dark mask of his? These were the kinds of things she thought about before her death, which she prayed would be quick, but judging from his demeanor, it was unlikely.

"May The God rip your soul in two, psycho freak!" Yelling would have no effect on him, but she would have the last words this time. Although, everyone sort of did, since he never uttered a word.

The Scorpion wrung his hands around his spear as if he was a giddy kid about to get chocolate. Belyx searched for her smoke pellet, but it was out of reach. The beast lifted his spear up and Belyx shut her eyes.

Her blood would soon stain the floor.

Her mother flashed through her mind.

She had failed too, and Belyx would join her in the afterlife.

With a swoosh, his spear came down.

Belyx bit her teeth, but her head was still attached to her body. What happened? After opening her eyes, The Scorpion was turned around swinging his spear with fury.

She pulled up with her strength, ignoring the rapid pinching in her previously injured ankle, and pried her leg from the rubble. Standing sent a familiar pain up her thigh, but she choked it down like a rotten meal.

The Scorpion was too busy pursuing Enzo to notice her newfound freedom. Why did he save her when he had the opportunity to escape? In the dim moonlight coming through the rafters, Enzo dodged the beast's blows like the spear was a dancing partner. Belyx stood in awe, debating if she should help him. She took a step the other way and wracked her brain. Well, she saved him. It was only fair.

The Scorpion lunged and almost turned the thief into a skewer. He wouldn't be alive for long if she didn't help. She readied a poison blade and studied The Scorpion for any opening in his thick armor. Typically, the joints were exposed to provide a wide range of movement. That was her target.

The Scorpion struck, and Enzo crashed into more crates.

Belyx rubbed her rose pin for luck and charged. The Scorpion lifted his spear over Enzo like with Belyx.

She leapt and straddled her legs around the brute's neck. He twisted fast and tried to throw her off like a bull and she missed his armpit and lurched forward. The Scorpion tossed her off like she was a rag doll and Belyx slammed into the floor, back arching from the pain.

Through the ringing in her ears, the stomps grew closer. Belyx shook out of it and rolled as his spear struck down, just grazing her face. Adrenaline took over as Belyx stabbed in his eye socket. The hard blade sank into the soft flesh like a glove. He grunted as he whirled his arm and smacked Belyx away. Despite it being his fist, she was in a daze. The chill rushed throughout her spine as warm blood trickled down her head. The Berserker general's thuds followed her as she limped for the exit, and her body flew into more crates.

Why had her blade done nothing? The venom should have worked. This man was inhuman! The creature moved to her and halted, thick crimson oozing down his enormous frame. He charged for more warehouse boxes, destroying them along the way and flailing his arms like he was fighting a ghost.

Enzo took the chance and veered for the escape, leaving Belyx to witness the Scorpion fight the air, and she smiled, knowing exactly what caused it, the cobra. Good girl, Kali. He was hallucinating, which meant it had worked.

Belyx limped for the exit as well, gritting her teeth and praying no more Berserkers showed up. She had to use every ounce of strength to walk. Embracing the cool breeze of freedom, she caught up to Enzo.

In a dark alley, he had taken refuge, his breathing ragged. Belyx huffed and shoved him against a wall, knife to his throat.

"Enough games, thief. Tell me what you know about the palace!" She was surprised words came out as her lungs pinched.

He smiled, and Belyx cursed under her breath.

Seven

He crushed one of her pellets and the ashen powder sucked into Belyx's face. With watery eyes, she coughed and tried to snag any glimpse of him.

His heavy footsteps went right for the market. Belyx cleared her vision and ran after him, adrenaline keeping her going through her searing battle wounds. Enzo was fast, but Belyx would catch him. How come he didn't show more pain? Coward didn't even take any hits from the general.

Enzo bobbed and snaked through the evening crowds. Belyx did the same, ignoring the angry merchants' profanities. Enzo clutched some dirty common garbs and attempted to disguise himself. Any untrained pursuer would have lost him by now, but she was trained by the best. The thief, now in new clothes, rounded the alley and Belyx followed.

The thief was quick, but Belyx had his tricks in her mind now. He kept his hood on as he ran back to the South Market, but it had to be him. The thief bounced onto the roof and ascended it like an expert. His foolish mistake, as Belyx was the best climber in Aikradal. She latched on the wall and scaled it like a lemur, catching up to the thief and flinging her knife. It hit its mark, right into his leg. The figure grunted as he tumbled down.

Belyx straddled him and tore off his hood. She swore in a manner of ways. The runner was not Enzo, but a teenager, tears cascading down his bruised face. "Pl-please. Take what you want, but please don't hurt me. I am just starving!"

Releasing him, Belyx stood. From the clothes and unwashed aroma, he was clearly unhoused. Of course, other thieves existed in the city. The gangs made it near impossible for the palace to aid their citizens, leading to poverty and people doing what they needed to survive. What had her kingdom become? In the academy they discussed how amazing Aikradal was, being the first civilization formed after The Wakening and how it comprised strength. Belyx had yet to experience this Aikradal. Now it was a kingdom of fear and violence. The Order had their work cut out for them this time.

She let the kid go, flinging him extra coins and gauze for his leg wound, and meandered back to her perch. Surely, he would appear again.

Something snapped behind her, and she drew her knife, but nothing was there. Her breath held steady. Someone was here. She knew it.

Belyx circled like she was a mouse to a hawk. Was it the gangs wanting revenge for the warehouse? Her ankle throbbed, but they were no match. To comfort herself, she reached down to her venoms and gasped.

Did she forget them? She never did. But they were gone.

"Looking for something?" In the distance sat Enzo, swinging her venom pouch back and forth. "I wonder what these do? Maybe I should try them." He smirked and swung down from the short roof.

Belyx made a note to practice deterring pick pockets again. This was a whole new level of embarrassing. "Give those back, street rat." She held out her hand, praying he would test her. Just give me a reason.

"I'm truly troubled by your affronts. Yet you were the one who attacked a child."

"I thought he was you."

He put his hand to his chest, shaking her pouch like a sack of wheat. "I'm even more hurt. You would impale me?"

Sweat beaded down her neck. He would not get away this time. "Hand over my things and maybe we can talk like adults. Assuming you are one. "

Enzo shrugged and sniffed her bag, scrunching his nose. Why don't you try one, creep? "Talk?" He fluttered his hand at her. "You don't seem in the mood for talking. And usually on a date, people eat first. Just saying."

Belyx was glad her mask hid her blush as she tilted her head. The words of her grandmother came back to her. Pulling down her face covering, Belyx lowered her fighting stance, keeping eye contact. "Maybe dinner wouldn't be a bad thing." Thank The God no witnesses were around to see her acting like a brainless courtier.

The thief opened her bag and thumbed through her deadly items. "Well, I was almost impressed with your ability to be kind. We can try harder in the next lesson."

Her act faded fast. "What makes you think I can't?" The nerve of him was relentless.

Enzo looked her up and down like he was a judge in a pageant show. "Well, for starters, you're armed to the bones with eleven knives. That is an excessive amount, don't you think?"

"Twelve," Belyx corrected, but then sighed as Enzo held up one of hers. She may as well give him half of her weapons at this point. "I also know about the laced hair pin and the garrote. I'd assumed you'd be more careful about parading them around for us street rats to see."

Belyx raised her eyebrow, almost impressed. "Tell me what you know about the secret of Aikradal." Straight to the point.

Enzo clapped his hands. "I'd give that a high mark. No threatening words, even though you thought them."

Belyx crossed her arms and imagined his snarky head on a spike. Enzo tilted his head. "So, do you work for the palace? My guess would be secret king assassin or a Whisper."

Gagging, Belyx replied, "A Whisper? I look like one of them?"

He gave his hypnotic grin again. "Well, your hair, which I'm assuming is fake, is short, like how they wear it. It wasn't a far off suggestion."

A new wig was something she needed. "Well, what if I did work for the palace?" She had to tread carefully to not reveal herself. Keep everyone close, but far. Enzo stiffened up, his old macho facade fading as if he witnessed a ghost.

Belyx readied. He was about to run.

He chucked her pouch in the distance and sprinted the opposite way.

Belyx cursed.

Did this secret involve the palace? If yes, he would never trust her. Her admiration of him continued to grow at his diversion. She would never leave her venoms for someone to find and hustled after the bag. Perhaps she could still catch him? Luckily, he didn't have the best arm as she snatched the vials in a sprint and went after him.

The market bustled from the merchants packing up, and Belyx skimmed the crowd for anything resembling him. Think, Belyx. He may be clever, but everyone had a tell. Even the most notorious cons did.

An idea flashed in her head. The Scorpion struck him on his right side. His injuries would hold him back and he would have a limp. Belyx ascended to a shopkeeper building and searched like her life depended on it. Most people walked normally, and others hobbled from the wear and tear of a rough work-day. In the distance hobbled an "old man" with a cane, leaning a lot to his left. Enzo thought he concealed his tricks. He was gravely mistaken.

Belyx fell with grace and pursued her target. The old man "somehow" sped up with agility and precision. After all this work, Belyx refused to lose him this time, and she was on him like karma. He rounded a corner when Aikradal guards charged in the same direction. What were they doing here?

Captain Thomas advanced through the crowd, almost knocking Belyx over. The soldiers followed suit. Heat clung to her face. They couldn't be after him too, but her fears came to life as the guards besieged the thief and had him in chains.

Enzo groaned in pain as Thomas worked to secure a carriage. How did they hear about him? Did he have a good reason to fear the palace?

Belyx held her breath as Thomas approached Enzo. "You are hereby under arrest by order of King Terach. You will face trial and await your punishment. Including the Pits."

The spit in her throat dried. The Pits were used for murder and other immoral crimes. He was only a common thief. Enzo spat on the dirt, staining Thomas's pristine boots. "What crimes did I commit, handsome?" Still in turmoil, he couldn't resist throwing his sardonic words.

Thomas smirked and turned around. Aikradal citizens clustered to witness as well. "You are charged with treason against the crown. You hold information endangering the values of our kingdom."

Belyx squeezed her fists. How did they know? Did someone from The Order leak it to them? Surely, her grandmother would catch such disingenuousness. Although, was it a good thing? Her father could handle the threat and Aikradal would be fine. The thief's shortcomings and life of crime had caught up to him.

Her mission was done. It was helpful when other people did the work and Belyx deserved a break. He would cause her nothing but strife, and she had bigger things to worry about.

As Belyx slipped away, Enzo's screams echoed across the crowds. This was followed by a slam of the carriage door and Thomas commanding them to move out. Her grandmother would be proud of her for once. She imagined a warm embrace from her. One problem down and many more to go.

As the soldiers and crowd cleared, an image of Enzo's terrified face popped into her mind. His scared reaction when he found out she was with Aikradal danced like fire across her vision. Of course he would be. He was doing illegal things and only people who partook illegal things feared the palace.

She paused, the soft dirt scrunching beneath her. The carriage was on its way with the traitor, but this fear was something she recognized in herself. The same fear of losing the kingdom and the people she loved. *Like my mother.*

Enzo was a con artist. He faked any emotion to get what he wanted, but his panic was palpable. She had seen criminals in court. They dreaded getting prison time, but it was like Enzo feared them for another reason. Tears formed in her eyes. What secret was this? The thoughts were troublesome and she needed to brush them away and move on.

Stop! The work was done. She could go home now, enjoy her success. Taking one step forward, she paused, pivoting around.

Pinching her arm, she ran back to the carriage.

Whatever he knew, Belyx needed the information first. Her whole life had been about doing the right thing, no matter what the cost, but something tugged inside Belyx. If the thief made it to the palace, no one would see him again.

This was going to go down as one of Belyx's most foolish ideas ever, but like all of them, she faced it head on.

It was too late to back out now.

Belyx was about to betray her own kingdom for a common thief. Her head kept telling her to go home and forget, but something deeper in her said to find out what this secret was and why Enzo looked as white as a field mouse when he found out she was with Aikradal.

The carriage moved at a leisurely pace, with Thomas trotting behind on his illustrious mount. His golden hair flew free in the breeze as he wore a triumphant gleam. This would secure his reputation as a new captain. Belyx was about to tarnish his record, which Freyja would kill her for.

She readied her non-lethal venoms in case things became ugly, only needing to save Enzo and get the information. If everything went according to plan, no one would die. Belyx wished her grandmother were here. What would she say? Stay positive? You ninny, why are you betraying your kingdom? The last one was probably correct.

Belyx sighed and composed herself, vaulting for the nearest alley. The guard's horses rode in a square formation around the carriage. The animal did nothing wrong, but she had no other options. She readied one of her needles and crept closer to the side of the street.

The guards rounded the corner and Thomas's colt came into view. The crowds made the perfect cover as she stuck the steed in the leg. His mount panicked, almost tossing Thomas off. He tried to reassure it, but it galloped away with him still on.

The other guards halted and Belyx crouched for the carriage undetected. Amateurs. Belyx examined the simple lock and went to work. It would not take her long before Thomas's scared horse distracted the other guards. The poor sheep couldn't function without their captain.

The latch popped off with ease, but a guard saw her. Wasting no time, she flung open the door, and the thief tackled her to the ground. Of course, he had freed himself from his chains. Why did she even try anymore? They slammed into the hard concrete, her head ringing. Enzo straddled her and scrunched his face. Belyx had no time to explain as a sword came down on them.

Belyx bear hugged Enzo and rolled to the side, dirt flying from the sword impact. Belyx shot up and kneed the soldier's thigh and shoved him down, saying a silent apology.

The distraction wore out its course, for Thomas charged back. Belyx stood in front of Enzo as the guards surrounded them. She counted five, plus Thomas. This was supposed to be a quick rescue and now they had a full on brawl ahead of them.

"A mercenary fighting the crown, freeing his partner?" Thomas dropped from his horse and drew his long sword. "You are surrounded. You will both face The Pits for your treachery."

"I thought you were with them?" Enzo whispered to Belyx, and she ignored him, pulling out two knives. As much as she hated it, she had to face them. Her own people. Heart thudding to the beat of the breeze, she readied herself. Belyx didn't bother giving Enzo a knife, for he already had one of hers.

Thomas stared them down like they were a mark of a predator's scent. Belyx knew the look well. It was what he gave when he craved a match. "I don't get to fight such skilled opponents much. This will be great practice." He turned to his comrade. "Keep them alive." Time slowed as Belyx counted her breaths.

The Captain whistled, and the guards swarmed them. Belyx ran through to Thomas, not processing the upcoming duel. The Captain swung his blade at her head, but Belyx dodged and lashed at his non-lethal areas. Thomas blocked, proving to be more arduous, but Belyx had studied his fighting before. Thomas weaved every attack she gave and shoulder checked her away. His eyes widened and a familiar question came next.

"You're a woman?"

Belyx didn't give him time to think about it as she castigated him. He feinted every strike like she was a recruit with a training sword. With a breath, Belyx rolled behind him. His stalky figure was tricky, but she had him on speed. Belyx thrust at him and landed an elbow to his face. He recoiled, holding his now bloody nose.

In the commotion, The guards pursued Enzo. No surprise he would run like a coward. Thomas took out a second sword and waved them both around for show. "Take this as a warning, harlot. I may lose control and behead you and your boyfriend. Give up now!"

Belyx said nothing, for she refused to reveal herself through her voice. She raised her knives. Thomas smirked, a blotch of pursuit clouding his eyes, and attacked.

With every swing, she dodged and sideswiped with her knife. She lunged back, but he impeded her attempts. Her breaths spurred, but his did too. They both couldn't keep up this fight forever. He jabbed his sword at Belyx, but she eluded it, leaving herself open to a counterstrike from his other weapon. His blade moved true, and Belyx barely blocked as the impact rattled her to the ground, knives flying into the street. Now she was exposed. Thomas sprung, but she glided out of the way. Thomas over shot and Belyx ran behind him.

Thomas pivoted with finesse and smacked her back.

Warm tears welled in her eyes as the remaining guards enclosed on her. So much for Enzo. "We lost the thief, sir," one of them said.

Thomas spat blood in the dirt, taking a deep breath as if he was an old maid who lost a card game. "It will suffice. We have this traitor. Detain her."

The guards closed her in and she scanned for an opening.

One guard clutched her hood, but she twisted and elbowed his wrist. He grunted as he released, but two guards had secured her arms. She kicked one of them to the ground. The other kept his tight grip while Thomas and the others swarmed her like bees to honey.

Her knife was all she grabbed as her thoughts of being found out crept into her mind.

Vision blurring, she lashed at the guard.

He let go and at first; she thought she landed a blow on his arm, but he was closer than she thought.

Blood spattered.

Too much for an arm wound.

Belyx had struck his neck, his blood coating her hands.

The guard went down in slow motion and her senses rang. What had she done? Belyx couldn't contemplate anything else as she dodged Thomas's sword strikes and dipped between the other guards, running until her breaths called for relief.

And then she ran more.

After she was far enough away, she clambered to the ground. They didn't even try to catch her. Her hands sunk into her face as she slipped through closed shops. The Aikradal soldier's face kept circling her mind like venom in the bloodstream. She killed her own guard. Had she known him before? Did he have a family? Kids? Belyx retched into a corner, tears plummeting close behind.

Now the thief was gone too, which meant she had nothing to show for her betrayal.

Belyx slunk back against the wall, biting back a thick acid taste in her mouth. It was a full night now, the moon the only source of light.

A rock tumbled and Belyx hopped up, knife ready. The soldiers had found her.

Her suspicions were incorrect as one of her blades fell into the dirt. Enzo came out with his hands up. "I'm going to regret this," he said.

Belyx huffed. How could he ditch her? "I appreciate the help back there." Only a poison resembling her own left her mouth. She would gut this coward where he stood.

He shrugged. "I guess I wasn't much of a fighter." The wind swayed his hair as he stopped. It reminded Belyx of the boys who played at the beaches. Despite the messiness, it always fell back to normal. Each curl appeared to tell its own story as they gathered around his ears and forehead. "You aren't with Aikradal?"

Memories of her recent kill rushed her mind. "It's more complicated than that."

"I have lots of time." He sat down with no hint of running.

Belyx stayed standing, the ultimate power move. "What? No running this time? Lifting my stuff?"

He stared at the dirt for a while and looked up. His eyes were jade specks in the lunar light. A tinge of red swirled in them, like a dancing flame. "You tried to save me after I ditched you. Why?"

"Your fear."

"My what?" He arched a brow.

"Your fear. The way you ran from me. It was like you were so scared of Aikradal, you would betray common sense."

He chuckled. "Hey, I never betray common sense." Always a clown.

"That survival mode I see in myself. I don't know why, but I was hoping you would tell me." Flies with sugar. Flies with sugar. He had to tell her now.

Caution crept into the air. The guards would find them any minute, and every sound made Belyx jump.

Enzo twirled his thumbs in his lap. "I still don't know if I can trust you." His words cut like her blade, but she had to keep up the grace.

Belyx folded her arms. "Well, it's not like you're the picture of trust, either."

Enzo laughed. It was almost calm, like the night winds. "Well, you saved me from them, and maybe I can give you a chance and let you help me." Help him? The mission was to find out what he knew and be done.

"Help you with what?"

"I know Aikradal means a lot to you, but you have to understand, the secret they have is tremendous." Belyx gave an "I'm listening look," and Enzo continued. "The gangs are after a lost key."

"A key?"

"Let me finish," he said with humor and seriousness she hadn't seen in him. "This key unlocks a vault in the palace and—"

"The palace? What could be there?" Enzo tilted his head and Belyx sank back down. "Continue." Way not to expose yourself.

"This key unlocks something buried a long time ago. A vault of magical fae artifacts. Ones so powerful, if anyone possessed them, they would rule the continent."

Not the fae again! If her father knew of these things, why would he not use them to stop the gangs? "Where is the vault? Wouldn't the king have this key?" This was bigger than Belyx realized. She needed to find out posthaste.

Enzo stared off for a few seconds. "I don't know and it was rumored to come from the palace, but it may not be him."

"How did you learn out about this?"

"You're going to find this strange, but a witch told me." A witch? They hadn't been seen in hundreds of years. Before her people even settled onto the continent. Their legends were used to frighten children.

"There are no witches anymore, Enzo."

"You don't know what I saw. She told me there was a key that could unlock the powerful weapons of the fae. I do not know why she told me, but ever since she did, the gangs have been after me and the key. Hence why I was caught, and how I met such a charming assassin."

"But you don't have it or have any idea where it is?" Enzo shook his head. That was a fail. Now Belyx had more questions than answers at this point. Assuming the thief—Enzo wasn't lying to her. Thieves were notorious for those kinds of skills. Although, she was too.

Belyx sat down next to him. What would she do now? Helping him might lead to treasonous routes, and she already committed one of those acts today. If this key existed, Belyx had to find it. Not only to locate the truth, but to protect her kingdom.

"The gangs can't get it," Enzo added. "I can't see any of them ruling. The way they have damaged the streets I grew up on is sick. It used to be a thing of beauty, and now it is a place of fear."

Belyx pondered how living on the streets could be ravishing, but let it go. "I still don't understand why this 'witch' told you, and why the gangs were suddenly on your scent."

Enzo shrugged. "They can't rule, Doneque. None of them."

Belyx squinted. This is not making sense. This is a trap and I am about to spring it. She stuck out a cautious hand. "I'll help you find this, but you have to promise you won't steal from me again." Enzo went to reply, but Belyx cut him off. "And no running." It was a much needed mention.

He put his finger on his chin, like the ass he was. "Deal. As long as you promise not to kill me."

Belyx smirked, but held firm. "Deal." They shook hands like a twisted business arrangement.

Standing back up, Belyx offered him a hand, but he declined. "What is the first part of the plan?"

Enzo looked her up and down. "I would say a good nights sleep. You look for better a word, jejune."

Was he a walking word scroll? He was the one to talk. She had major preparations to do the next day and needed to keep hidden from the guard attack. "Fine. We will regroup and then meet at the markets tomorrow night."

Enzo stood up as well. "You got it, partner."

"Don't call me that." He was anything else. More like an inconvenient chore.

Enzo winked and ran off into the distance.

Belyx glanced up at the moon, jealous of its calming ability. Although, now nothing provided the same sort of thing. Either Belyx had just put forth the steps to make Aikradal better, or she just pushed the rock right on top of it.

EIGHT

U pon slipping onto her balcony, Belyx limped to the washroom. Her breaths quickened like someone was trying to steal the air out and her stomach was tied in knots.

She had never killed an Aikradal guard before. This would slip back to her grandmother. Would she be sent to The Pits for treason? It was too soon to tell. Belyx shed her sweaty layers of clothing and tossed her weapons on the floor, turning the tub faucet to the hottest setting and the steaming water filled the bath. A long soak called her name

"Belyx?"

What was Freyja doing in her room? "I'm fine," she shouted over the hissing faucet. "Just a rough mission!" Understatement of the century.

"Did you find the thief?" Belyx stifled a scream as Freyja came in.

"Sure did."

Freyja eyed her like she knew something, but Belyx kept her positive beam on and her handmaiden turned away. The monster was thwarted for now. "Well, get cleaned up and some rest, then."

Belyx shrugged. Freyja could always tell when something was wrong, but it wasn't like she was going to tell her she had to fight her crush to save a thief who may have knowledge of a key unlocking magical, deadly artifacts. It would be unwise. Word would spread, but Belyx had no reserves in her to handle such an emotional conversation.

The tub called to her as she plucked vials of scent oils. The stress relieving eucalyptus, lavender, tea tree, and more remedies Amenthya recommended. Pouring them in, Belyx slinked into the bath, buried by the calming aromas. She submerged and the still underwater paused the churning in her brain. At least for now.

After holding her breath, she floated to the warm surface and scrubbed herself. Blood pooled in the water and faded into the oils. Was it her blood or... the guards? Thank God Belyx learned to cry quietly. A lady never cried like a banshee, Madame would say. "Screw her," Belyx whispered.

After Belyx scraped and cleaned the grime from her mission off, she drained the tub and dried herself, flashing a look in the mirror. Who was she?

She was a killer. A killer who took innocent lives. All for a thief. A thief who was about as trustworthy as a fortune teller. Belyx took in her frame. Bruises smeared over her whole body like kisses from the devil. Going on like this would kill her.

An innocent man died by her blade. A man who swore an oath to protect her. She dressed in her silk night clothes, but forgot to take off her red color contacts, staring a moment too long. A mix of Princess Belyx and the assassin, Doneque.

An odd inkling rolled over her. As if they were the same person. No. They were different people. One did things for the good and the other killed. The tears came down as she gripped the sink tile and ripped off the contacts.

Her normal eyes were back. A quaint creamy hazel color like her mom's. The ones everyone adored and did everything right. The ones people wished were alive instead. If Belyx died, would anyone care as much? Of course not.

Sitting by the balcony was none other than her grandmother. "We need to stop meeting like this," Belyx said.

Dara came forward and lit a candle. The light shimmered in her sleepless eyes. "I assume it didn't go well?" She looked her up and down, most likely counting her injuries.

"You could say that."

"What happened? I was worried sick when I couldn't find you back in the hideout."

"I lost him." Those three words and a familiar sad girl appeared. One who was afraid to make any mistakes. One who had to live in the shadow of her effervescent mother and grandmother.

Her grandmother always said something wise, but Dara continued to sit on her bed, pressing the sheets. "It was true, though. He was taken by them?" She looked Belyx up and down again, and Belyx grew conscience of her bruises. "I'm assuming it wasn't a tranquil breakout."

Belyx shook her head. "The Scorpion was waiting." Her throat bobbed as his spear pulsed in her mind. She was lucky and thankful to be breathing right now.

Her grandmother spoke a hushed prayer in the ancient language. "He is a demon in a man's body. You are lucky to be alive. I'm assuming the thief died to his blade then?"

Belyx waited a beat, ready to share her news. "I saved the thief, and he told me what he knew." Her grandmother notched her eyebrows. "He said there was some key to a vault in the palace where fae artifacts were hidden."

"That is concerning. Anything with magic involved hasn't been seen since—well, thirteen years ago."

Belyx's original suspicions hit her like a carriage. "Did my father keep the items, then?"

"I hope not." Dara went to arrange Belyx's vases, her way of tamping down her anxiety. "The fae creatures were a peaceful tribe once, remember?" Belyx blinked rapidly, her throat drying. What came next was expected. "Until they killed your mother, of course." Her voice was laced with frost.

The once tranquil tribe lived in the Sehrlic forest, and controlled the powers of the elements. It was always a mystery to Belyx why they chose to kill her mother after being cordial with the humans for over 200 years. That event was a dark day in Aikradal's history, but her father handled it... At least, Belyx thought. If he did keep those artifacts, they would need to stay hidden, and Belyx would fight bone and foot to make sure it happened.

"If it is true. Do you think the gangs will use it?"

"We better hope not. If we think these gangs are causing a stir now, then having dangerous fae artifacts will bring a whole other multitude of problems."

Belyx wobbled in her shoes. Every step she took in this dark tunnel led to answers she didn't intend to face. "Well, it's only a rumor. It may not be true."

"I will do some digging, but in the mean time, you need to work with this thief."

Belyx took a couple of quick breaths and her grandmother eyed her like she knew. "I know your actions were accidental." Pursing her lips to block her tears, Belyx looked away, and her grandmother held her. "Things like this happen in war, my flower. It is hard to predict what choices we have to make."

Belyx broke down in her arms like a bursting mountain spring. "I just don't know anymore," she said through blubbering. "I killed a guard. A guard! No one from The Order has ever committed such an act!"

Dara scratched the back of her head. "Well, that wasn't always true." Belyx scrunched her brows. "My mother had to kill a couple guards who were crooked to secure our Order. It was necessary."

"Yea, except I did it to an innocent one."

Dara shrugged. How could she play this off calmly? As if Belyx's emotions and turmoil were a mere bug bite. "We can never know with these guards anymore. I have Freyja and the Stems looking into corruption from within. That will be our true downfall, not an invasion from gangs." Belyx gulped. More and more guards were switching sides for promises of wealth and fame. What guard would pull his sword on them next?

Belyx flexed her wrists, letting the still air calm her twisted thoughts. "I will find this key and destroy it."

She made a hmm sound and kept searching for more plants in need. "Do you know where to start?"

"No idea. I'm sure En—I mean, the thief knows."

She chuckled. "You can say his name, flower. I rather like it."

Belyx held back a blush, but it may have been too late. Her grandmother gave her a look like she was about to quiz her and braced for impact. "What group seems to know the most around this kingdom? Even more than us?"

That was it! And obvious too. She beat herself for missing the opportunity to have such a splendid plan.

"The Whispers." Their name left her tongue like a toxin. "I'm all over it. I am sure they know something. If the Berserkers knew, they would know more."

Her grandmother brightened, but went back to organizing her flowers. "Our kingdom is like these flowers. It is beautiful, but is sometimes overrun with disease and decay." She snipped a bud root with a fluid motion. "It must be cut."

She embraced her grandmother one more time. "I'm still conflicted on if saving the thief was a good idea. Maybe I should let this secret die."

"If more than a few know a secret, it can never die." She pulled away and stared straight in her eyes. Her warm blue eyes were filled with years of turmoil, yet shone bright. "You followed your instincts yesterday. Us Velena women have the best there is."

"What about the rest of The Order?" Belyx dreaded the answer. What would the others think of her?

"I have a meeting with them later. We will work on making sure Aikradal guards are nowhere near your assignments to prevent anymore accidents." The word cut Belyx. Just an accident. "The Thorns will remain off duty for a while. We can't risk them being caught either, or worse." All my fault. She made a note to apologize to the agents. Like her, they worked hard for their assignments and now they would be stuck doing Stem or Leaf jobs.

"I wish I could be there." She missed many meetings due to her other duties.

Dara stilled. "You are doing your part. The flower needs all parts to work in order to grow." Her grandmother stopped at the door. "Get some rest. There are ball preparations to make tomorrow. Try not to piss off Jewella. After that, try to track this key." She winked.

Belyx waved her grandmother goodnight and fell into the comfort of her soft sheets.

Amenthya would need to look at her again, and she would not be thrilled.

Her eyelids fluttered and for the first time in awhile, despite the worries clawing at her brain, she found slumber.

She was a Velena woman with an unmatched sense of wisdom and skill. Like her mother, she could do anything.

She shivered as a dark thought overshadowed her mind.

If her mother had such renowned intuition, then how was she killed so easily?

The next morning's council meeting made Belyx almost regurgitate into a flower vase.

"An assassin attacked you and your men and freed the thief?" Lord Kirk stroked his purple velvet lapel as if he was the most important voice.

Captain Thomas, who, despite the fight, looked better than Belyx did, shook his head. "I know what I saw. And she killed Garret."

Garret.

That was his name.

Belyx said a mental prayer to The God to protect his family.

Thomas stared at Belyx. How long had she been spacing out? "Care to answer, your highness?" Captain asked.

Belyx jutted her head. "Apologies. The palace will put together a nice service for him and make sure his family is compensated."

Kirk tilted his head down, while the rest of the council said nothing. Thomas only replied, "Sure." Clearly, he asked her something else. Could she do anything right? It was as if the panic in her brain set up camp and refused to leave.

Her father spoke up, thumbing the edge of his chalice. He started his drink early. His beard was now many shades of grey and disheveled. "Whoever this assassin is, I am putting a reward out for her and this thief. 10,000 gold for those who turn them in...dead or alive."

Belyx gulped, and Thomas stepped in. "Dead? You said we needed the thief alive?"

Her father's eyes grew more distant than they already were. "I care little for the lives of those who kill my men. Money will bring results." He sounded like a Goldfinger.

Master Jon opened his mouth, most likely to remind the king they didn't possess those kinds of funds, but closed it.

Kirk clapped. "Excellent plan, your majesty. Marvelous plan indeed. Worthy of—"

"He gets it," Belyx spat.

Kirk stuck his nose up like the child he was.

Belyx turned back to the council, thankful Freyja was able to cover her bruises from the fight. "What did the thief do?" Did anyone have information about the vault? One of them would have something she didn't.

The King scratched his stubble. "This thief, according to Lord Jaques's intel, possesses a dangerous weakness of our kingdom the gangs crave to use. Him dead will bury those secrets for the sake of our kingdom."

"Along with that incredulous assassin," Kirk added. Belyx held back a kick to his miserable shins.

"What sort of secret? What do we posses they could get? Does it have to do with the fae?" Did she ask too much?

Most likely, as her father squinted his eyes at her. "Please refrain from mentioning them, princess." He glanced at his advisors, and they turned a paler shade. They knew more than they said. *It is real. I need to find this vault.*

"The assassin is probably a Whisper member trying to infiltrate us," Jaques said. *That again.*

Thomas chuckled. "The Whispers don't fight with this style. They are cowards who spy and poison."

The king slammed his drink down, now empty. "Well, if it is another supposed gang vying for my kingdom, there will be hell to pay!"

Everyone quieted down for a beat. Jaques, the voice of reason, spoke up. "I'm sure the Whispers are just testing new tactics. The leader of theirs is crafty and changes with the tides. Who knows what she has planned?"

Kirk scoffed, but the King eased up. "You're correct. We need to focus our efforts on the Whispers. Any new reports I need to know about." *Same here.*

"Yes, your highness," Thomas said. He had nothing to add despite the obvious; The Whispers gossiped and used it against everyone.

Thomas made it to the end. "And we will get the printers on those reward posters as well. The thief and the Whisper won't even be able to sneeze without someone on their scent. I remember them both." He fumed for a second as if regaining himself. "No one disrespects my honor." Pushing out his chair, he stormed off. The rest of the council followed.

Belyx couldn't believe she was mistaken for a Whisper again. That was enough to make anyone nuts. It proved one thing; she needed to work with Enzo now. If not to save her kingdom, but to keep her family together.

She started to leave when her father stopped her, making her heart flutter. He was finally talking to her after some time. "Belyx, Madame Jewella expressed her concerns about the ball. Meet her at once in the main hall." *Nothing else?* He waved her off. "On with it. Madame Jewella is not one for tardiness."

"Yes, father." Gritting her teeth, she bowed and made her way to her oh so understanding teacher. It was time to face her fire.

Nine

Belyx did it.

Mouth stretching farther than usual, she pulled away from her immaculate silver and gold flower arrangements resting on the tables throughout the ballroom floor and the freshly pressed cloths fluttering like the winds of Majeria. How could they not feel welcome? Massive pillars lined with pearly garnishes emphasized Aikradal's strength and their best export, weaponry. A substantial reason to celebrate the hopeful aid from Majeria.

Although Belyx hadn't suggested the idea of working with them, she needed to prove herself to her father. Her duty as a princess always came first, despite whatever she had to do at night. Belyx brushed off dust from tables, taking in the lavish silk embroidered with intertwined arrows like a symphony of battle. But war was never beautiful.

"I do say this is quite illustrious," Lady Lim came in with her two cohorts behind her, wearing one of last year's gowns from Belyx's collection. The same one she said was "gorgeous."

"That's quite the big word, dear. Did you search for it all day?" Lady Maria, said jokingly.

Lim ignored her and fanned herself. "Oh, stop it you." She turned back to Belyx. "This ball for that island country will be so grand. Think any fellows will be there?"

"Looking to replace Lord Kirk?" Her aunt smiled from the back, winking at Belyx.

Lim threw her hands in the air. "My My! Not me, you old bats! This one." She thrust a manicured finger in Belyx's face, which was unladylike of her. "She needs a suiter, and what better way to unite two kingdoms than a marriage? That's what we used to do back then." The others stared at her. "What? I'm not the only one besides my husband who can throw around advice like rice at a weddin'. Oh, there I go mentioning those again." Her eyes fluttered at Belyx, and she felt the sudden urge to vomit. Engagement was the least of things on her mind right now.

Belyx prayed they would go away, but now the swarm had begun. "For the last time. I don't need a suitor Lim. I am content with me for now."

Lim scoffed, but Maria held her shoulder to ease her. "We know, princess. Apologies for our friend here. She forgot to take her beauty tonic."

"I never!" Lim went off to inspect more of the vestibules of the party while Maria followed. Her aunt Hannah stayed. "It truly is wonderful. Your father would appreciate it." Her voice was calm and soft. Who knew she had any relation to her father.

"You need to talk some sense into your brother," Belyx said.

Hannah laughed. "Does one talk sense into a bee for pollinating?" Belyx didn't laugh, and she continued. "Trust me, I've tried. But I think once the gangs are handled, he will relax." She brushed her palms like she accomplished a daunting trial.

Belyx sighed, trying to placate her mind about the undone details of the ball. "That seems like an impossible task as of late." Her aunt went to respond when Lim's screech echoed across the foyer. "That's my cue. I am sure she spilled something on herself." She bowed and left. Like a siren, her obligations called to her.

Before Belyx found time to unwind, Madame Jewella burst in, wearing a face less angry than usual. "Hmmm, not bad for once, princess. Although it shouldn't have taken the threatening to get you motivated to fulfill your duties." There it was.

"You're welcome, Madame." Belyx held back the urge to push her into the bouquets.

Madame circled the room, holding out handheld bifocals, as if trying to catch every blot of dust in her trap. "Fourth table is slightly uneven, but overall, pleasant work."

"I take it you will tell my father of my success?" She gave the fakest smile she could muster.

Madame cooed. "Ha. It will take more than planning a decent ball for me to start bragging about you to his majesty." Belyx rolled her eyes as Madame went through her checklist. "Food and drink?"

"All ordered and being prepared for tomorrow." Madame marked her scroll like a war dossier. "Entertainment?"

"The finest quartet in all the land." Madame humphed and dabbed the scroll with her ink, pausing and giving the "I have you now" smirk.

"And gift for Majeria? Surely we couldn't leave them without something as a token of their generosity."

Belyx's heart sank, but she hid her face with a smile. "All handled as well. No problem." She needed to talk to the metal smiths and fast. As if letting them have their weapon production wasn't a gift enough. Why couldn't politics be as easy as Thorn work?

Madame scowled as she scrawled her scroll, and Belyx wanted to mark her face with her blade. "Good. You are excused for the rest of the day, but I expect a full check tomorrow before the ball begins."

Belyx agreed and went on her way, making a note to take care of the gift later, but for now she needed nourishment and entered the kitchen to find a singing Cook pulling out a roast, smelling of garlic and rosemary. She set the steaming meat down and beamed at Belyx. "Hello dear one. Can I get you a snack? It is a little past lunch, but you've had a busy morning."

Cook raised her eyebrows as Belyx fell down on her table. "Why not?" She deserved to celebrate for her victory, no matter how small. With her recent failures, she made sure to relish in the successes. Cook placed down a bubbling plate of pastries, which Belyx devoured.

Cook snorted. "I take it from your mood, Madame Pompous didn't contort her shriveled face too hard at your work?"

Belyx swallowed a mouth full. "I believe she said, 'not bad for once.' What a win."

"Truly." Cook snickered and lathered butter and seasonings on the resting slab of beef. "It is nice to win sometimes. Especially with all you have gone through."

Checking to make sure no one was around, she whispered, "you heard too?" Cook eyed her a "yes, they did." "It was a reckless decision, but grandmother didn't even get mad."

Cook breathed out. "You will find you can get more outraged at yourself than others do at you."

Belyx's mind raced to Madame and her father. "I doubt that."

As if Cook read her thoughts, she responded. "Well, maybe some do, but your grandmother and I grew up in a different time with The Order. It was brand new and trying to solve corruption from within. The palace was not doing well either."

"Do you think it is still like that?" Belyx feared for her next answer.

Cook stilled and wiped her oily hands with a damp rag. "It is hard to say, flower. I know that since your grandmother hauled me in, literally, it has been better. I want to keep this attitude going."

The story of Cook was always a mystery to Belyx. No one had talked about it much, not even her grandmother. Cook and her were close friends until Dara became queen and then she left. After, Dara pulled her back in to help. Cook's fighting skills were as incomparable as her cooking. No one would dare challenge her on in anything. Before she retired, she was a Stem like Freyja and used more torturing tactics. As Cook pressed the roast, Belyx imagined it being a traitor and gulped.

Belyx opened her mouth to inquire more, but finished her pastries and stood. "Well, I have things to do before tomorrow. Thank you always, Cook. You mean a great deal to me." Death taught Belyx to cherish the living more.

Cook bowed with her plate of beef. "Be safe, your highness." She continued her duties as Belyx closed the kitchen door behind her.

How lucky she was to have such magnificent people. Nothing could stop the ball from going well now, and Belyx would receive the recognition she deserved. Once this was done, she would locate this key and preserve her kingdom. The storm clouds were parting and Belyx was ready for a new day of sun.

Waiting for night to fall and to meet Enzo, Belyx put on her robe and searched through the palace. If a vault did exist, she would find it. The castle at night was a strange and quiet thing. Belyx had often explored in a nighttime, but she never found a secret safe. Where would it be? Could it be in the kitchens? The art rooms? The weaponry? It would be some place hard to access. The schematics of the castle said nothing in the room stretched to anything.

May as well try the kitchen. She went downstairs and Cook had left it pristine as usual. Belyx eyed the ice box for a snack. Later.

Behind the kitchen sat the relic room, which hadn't been used in years. Belyx strode in. The only sound was her footsteps in the still night. Heirlooms of history rested in glass cases. The first sword of the original king, Jared Terach, poised in its display case. Sitting on a still pedestal was the first crown as well, which was only used for coronations of new kings. That won't be for a long time.

Belyx scanned the rest of the artifacts, holding back tears as she came across an all too familiar one.

There stood her family portrait. Painted weeks before her mom's passing. The last meaningful moment they had. Her father, bright eyed and happy, was donned in a velvet purple cape with his signature sword pressed to his side. Young Belyx wore a light green gown, a youthful face not yet aware of death. Her mother was different. Jewels encasing her bodice outshined them both as she had on a matching lavender silk dress; a face of a true ruler, not a thing out of place. Her father moved the painting from the front entrance after her passing, as too many painful memories were caused by it.

Something about the calming presence drew her closer, and she went to touch it when a person appeared behind her. She stifled a scream, but relaxed.

"Princess Belyx. What are you doing up at this hour?" Lord Jaques was wearing his own night clothes, carrying a steaming cup of tea and a small novel. She had never seen her father's advisors in this state of comfort. Although she was thankful it wasn't Lord Kirk.

"Restless." Princesses visited strange rooms at night, right? "I just needed some late night pick me ups."

He laughed harmoniously as he looked her up and down. "Princess duties proving to be difficult, young one?"

Belyx rubbed her neck. "More than you know." The dark hallway grew quiet as Jaques kept up a neutral expression and then motioned for her to follow into the kitchen.

"Your night has sprouted in luck." He giggled again. "I know the perfect pick me up for a sad princess, and I may have left her a bite." As they entered, a tray of semi-fresh croquettes sat on the table. Belyx's stomach roiled as she grabbed the buttery pastry and plopped it into her mouth. It wasn't the cure, but it delayed the pain.

She swallowed loud and debated her lack of princess-like behavior. "I needed that."

Jaques gestured for her to sit. Belyx questioned saying no, but maybe he could advise her. He was an advisor after all and sometimes sided with her in council.

Gorging on more croquettes, she sat while Jaques swirled his tea. "It wasn't easy becoming an advisor to your father." He paused. "No disrespect, of course." Her father wasn't simple as well and she admired his honesty. An example of what an advisor needed to be. Not an ass kisser like Kirk.

"I understand."

He smiled, showing some of his crooked teeth. His modest upbringing prevented him from receiving proper dental care, but it beamed all the same. "I am still surprised to this day your father selected me. I was a poor boy from the outskirts of Aikradal with barely any experience, but he noticed my people skills."

"You call Petrovkan the outskirts?" It was a bad kingdom, but it was far from Aikradal.

"Yes, of course." He drank his tea, and Belyx sensed his need for privacy. Belyx recalled his story. It was the opposite of Kirk's. Kirk was privileged and taught by the elite. What Kirk had in battle strategy, Jaques had in politics and social awareness.

Hence why he wasn't an asshole like Kirk.

Jaques continued. "My family was taken from me at a young age. I had to be raised by strangers and fight for everything I have. It seemed hard at first, but it taught me a lot about myself." Everyone from Petrovkan had these kinds of stories and it made Belyx sick to think it was still a kingdom. Belyx ate more croquettes in silence. Part of her knew she had never had a rough life, but another felt she was also unlucky in other ways. The pressure of ruling could make anyone snap like a twig in a storm.

Lord Jaques broke the silence. "Anyway, enough about me. What happened to you? You're up at this queer night and clinging to food for comfort. That tells me something is wrong."

"Nothing." Belyx needed an easy lie. "Just Madame Jewella being difficult as always."

"Oh, that Madame. She will never get a book published, by the way. Not with the content I've read." Belyx snickered. Madame tried writing on the side and Belyx feared to read anything from the mind of that woman.

Belyx fiddled with the crumbs, thankful she stayed up talking with him. "I also worry about my father. His grief has never faded. Do you think it will?"

Jaques thumbed his tea cup. "It is hard to say. I would love to expect he will improve, but thirteen years is a long time to wait for someone to reform. I dread for this kingdom. The walls are closing in like a viper to prey."

"The gangs are too powerful." Belyx shuddered at the thought of being under the rule of one of the four gangs.

"Indeed," Jaques said. "I pray King Terach will find his way out of the darkness, but in the meantime, the council will have to handle things and help him make rational choices." Jaques had to talk him down many times, and Belyx thought her duties were difficult. Belyx clenched her fists, remembering how Jaques still voted against her for the ball. As if sensing it, he said, "I'm sorry I voted against you yesterday. I know Majeria is precarious, but we are at an impasse we can't navigate."

Belyx crossed her arms. "It's fine."

Jaques chuckled. Normally, Belyx would be mad, but he had a way of diffusing emotions. "It isn't. I have seen what Majeria's princess says to you and it's horrible, but heed my words, child. Harsh words can only strengthen."

"Easier said. I wish I was a powerful influence, like my mother."

Jaques paused. He never knew her mother, but his face grieved the same way her father did. Even her reputation was impactful. "She sounded like a noble ruler. I heard only positive things. Like I knew her personally."

Belyx stared at the dim candle lit in the kitchen. The way it danced on the waxy tip reminded her of life and how it moved around rapidly. People died and people were born. People would save and people would kill. They were just beings trying to survive... until their flames burnt out.

"Princess. May I share something with you?" Belyx rubbed the inside of her palm. What new ground breaking thing could he possibly say?

"Sure."

"The council didn't want to tell you, but you are eighteen. You should know more." Belyx jutted her head at him. Could this be? "The secret the thief has does involve the fae."

Belyx faked surprise. "What?"

"The thief stole a key which opens a vault filled with their powerful artifacts."

Her father lied to her. To her face! After all she did for him! "Why are you telling me this?"

Jaques stared into the distance. "I had a sister once." If Belyx recalled this, she felt bad for not remembering. "The gangs killed her ten years ago and I can't let this thief give them more power."

"I have a feeling the thief would have given it to them by now if he had it," Belyx said in a neutral tone.

"Oh, he has it." His voice rose, and this was the first Belyx had seen him in such a heated state. "Which was why I sent the guards once I knew. We can't let the gangs get it. They will take over and I will continue dispatching guards after this thief and assassin until the key is returned." Fear laced his demeanor, but some other emotion hid behind it. Almost revenge like, but his sister dying would play into it, but wouldn't he want to defeat the gangs who did it, not some thief?

"Thank you for telling me Jaques." She placed a hand on his and he nodded at her.

"Please don't tell your father I told you. He is very upset since it went missing."

This was a new development. Her father lost the key too. "How did it go missing?"

Jaques shook his head. "No one knows, but it had to be a bribed noble or something. No one even knew where the key was hidden."

"I pray they don't get it, Lord Jaques." For more reasons than one. She was tempted to wake her father right now and eat into him about trust, but she held it back. Jaques would only get in trouble and she needed more people on her side more than ever.

He stood and bowed. "This has been a remarkable conversation, your highness, but I must withdraw for the evening. I have a big day coming up. With Majeria's visit looming, I need to find ways to woo them. I believe you have some planning to do as well?"

Belyx sighed. "Good sleep, Jaques."

He left, and she fidgeted with her empty plate, trying to ignore her throbbing muscles and brain. She put her dish in the sink, and staggered up the stairs. It was time for her rendevous with Enzo.

TEN

Enzo was late...

Instead of becoming more agitated, Belyx took the extra time to check her appearance in a nearby puddle. The frequent drizzles provided a crisp clean air throughout the kingdom. Belyx admired rain and how it could wash the troubles away. *Someday.* She already checked herself in the mirror before she left, but once more wouldn't hurt. It was always important to present the part of an assassin, and it had nothing to do with the handsome thief she was working with. *He can't be trusted. Stay cool. You know what you need to do.*

A small fraction of Belyx prayed this key never existed and she could move on with dismantling the gangs, however she planned.

After a few moments, footsteps pattered from the alley. Belyx clenched her knives to slow her heartbeat, but it was only Enzo approaching. With no limp either. He already recovered from the injuries he sustained. Did he use a secret remedy like her?

He came into the moonlight, wearing a loose-fitting shirt and common trousers. He acknowledged her as he munched on street food. It was nearly past twelve, and they agreed on half-past eleven.

Belyx folded her arms like a scolding grandmother or teacher. She knew plenty of those looks. "You're late."

Enzo took his last bite and wiped the crumbs on his tan tunic. His sleeves were rolled up, revealing a series of flower tattoos. Such markings were unclean for royals, but the intricacy of the artwork leapt in bounds. "Well, I had things to do," he responded with his pleasant as ever tone.

Belyx caught her rolling eyes. "I thought this was important to you?" She tired of others not taking tasks as serious as her.

"I have a life, you know. What do you do? Kill small animals at lunch?" *Ouch*.

"Many things, but I prioritize and am on time to meetings, no matter how clandestine."

"You make this sound like a sumptuous convention. What are you, a noble or something?" Close to it.

"None of your concern, thief. I have information on how to find this key."

"Always business with you. Not even a how was your day? I'm offended." Enzo smirked.

Belyx tilted her head down and gave him a "stop wasting my time" look.

Enzo held up his hands. "Ok, The God, what is your special intel?"

"Don't make fun of my intel. It was rather troublesome to learn," Belyx lied.

Enzo folded his arms. "How did you get it?"

"It's a secret."

"You seem to keep a lot of those." The dimples on his pointed chin wavered.

Belyx blinked rapidly. "What group of people always knows everything that goes on around here?" God, I sounded like my grandmother.

Enzo opened his mouth and closed it, finally shutting it. "No way. How will we locate them?"

"The Whispers are pretty easy to spot, but hard to follow. They look alike to mirror their leader." Belyx cringed at the thought of such creepy followers.

"It is messed up," Enzo said. "Like this book where the evil minions dress the same and—" he paused at Belyx's blank stare. "Not a reader I see."

"I try not to waste my time with make-believe worlds when the one I live in needs service."

"But it can be a pleasant escape. Especially the romances." Now Enzo was losing it.

"You read romance novels?" Belyx meant for it to sound less judgmental, but it was her default at this point.

Enzo feigned offense. "What? A burly man like myself can't enjoy a nice slow burn, 'oops, there is only one bed' love story?"

Belyx blushed, but scowled to counter it. "I didn't say that. I meant with the thieving. I thought you would have little time for such activities." Sensitive thieves were a thing now. Interesting.

"Actually, books are the only things I don't steal. The library here is amazing." Belyx thought of her grandmother, who created the process of borrowing literature and then returning it when people were done. It proved to be successful. Some citizens stole the books, but most made it back in one piece. "Very refreshing to know you have a piece of conscience."

Enzo scoffed. "You think I go around stealing anything I want all day?"

"Kind of?"

Enzo paused and squinted his eyes, as if studying Belyx. "Why do you help Aikradal? You're obviously not working for them since... you know." Was that a jab at her recent kill?

"That was an accident, but people can do things out of the goodness of their hearts, Enzo. You should try it."

He crossed his arms. "I'm not buying it."

Belyx shook her head, a wave of irritation growing like a rash. "As I stated before, not all of us go around taking what other hard-working people earn. Now, can we please get on this mission?" It was too early in the evening and Belyx had little patience remaining

Enzo blew out a long breath. "Fine. Where do we start then, leader?"

Belyx motioned for him to follow as they crept their way through the market area. The night life began to grow as people made their final shopping decisions. The metal smiths, wood smiths, jewel smiths, and bakers were closing up their shops. Once they did, the real fun would begin.

"I'm sure you know what the Whispers look like?" She turned into her tutoring grandmother again. They walked side by side, his hand brushing hers. Was it an accident? His calluses sent twinges of heat through her arms.

"Short bobbed hair, skinny features, always looking like they are petrified?" Enzo replied.

"That's it." They would be there. "No problem. I've seen them around. They aren't too frightening."

Belyx recalled how they had almost infiltrated the palace and The Order. "Don't underestimate them. They are deadlier than they seem. Information is a weapon, too." This key was a living example.

"After dealing with the Berserkers and their actual weapons, I'd hate to disagree with you."

Belyx shot him a piercing glare. "Keep focus and stay on the lookout."

"So you don't like books? Like at all?" Not this again.

Belyx side eyed him. "Focus. Please."

"I'm just wondering." He held up his hands. Belyx frowned at the lack of accidental touching now. "It seems a lady of your caliber would like to end a night of killing with some nice slow burn romance."

She took the bait. "I just don't get the idea. Some of those love stories are unrealistic, like people who hate each other don't magically fall in love to make a point. It makes no sense and those adventure novels are even worse. The women are always in danger and forget to wear clothing."

He stared at her with a blank expression, as if finding the right words to say. "Well, as you determined, the real world sucks, and a withdrawal is nice."

"Whatever." Belyx needed to shift back to the task at hand. Whispers were around, and she knew it. The closing markets provided the best gossip. She glanced from the butcher shops back to the jewel smiths. The older ladies made the most detailed designs, and any person wearing them looked lavish. It was a shame thieves like Enzo ripped them off. The butcher sharpened his blades. No one messed with his shop. Although, who would steal rotting meat? Starving people.

A family with multiple shouting kids circled a pastry stand, the children giddy, begging for the sweets. The mother tried to wave them away. "We can't afford it. Some other time." Their collective cries broke Belyx's heart until Enzo went over and gave them each a coin. The mother thanked him and he came back to Belyx as they devoured their dessert.

Oh, to be a kid again, Belyx thought.

"What?" Enzo caught her disbelief stare.

"Nothing." He probably stole those coins.

She continued to study the markets as an elbow to her side took her out of her stupor. "Doneque, there!" Enzo pointed and sure enough, a tall woman with short blonde bobbed hair sat outside a bank window, most likely listening for idle shipments or money orders.

"We need to play this carefully," Belyx whispered as she bent down. "One false move, and we lose the chance to find their lair." Knowing how they operated. They could discover they were watching, too.

"Wait." Enzo blinked twice. "I thought we were going to interrogate her?"

For the first time, Belyx almost laughed at his words. "The Leader's minions know nothing. Their only duties are reporting things. It is best if we infiltrate their hideout." The Leader ran a tight ship that would be hard to stow away on.

"Are you sure that's a good idea?"

Belyx narrowed her eyes. "I thought you said they weren't intimidating?" This thief kept getting better and better.

"Well, doesn't mean they aren't full of surprises! Their hideout could have traps and such." He truly was something else. His sniveling confirmed he was nothing but a coward.

As usual, Belyx would need to take the lead. "No worries. You can stay back and I will get the location of the key." She preferred working alone, anyway.

Enzo stuck his arm out, blocking Belyx. "No way." Why would he care if she did it by herself? Don't trust him, Belyx, no matter what.

"Fine, but right now, we need to focus." How many times would she have to say that tonight? "This clone won't be there for long."

After a while, the Whisper moved and Belyx tailed her. Enzo followed, after almost falling asleep. His face was soft with dreams and his slight snore Belyx couldn't help but listen to.

Enough!

The Whisper crossed through the housing area, always checking over her shoulder for followers. Luckily, Belyx and Enzo had similar training and crept with the shadows. The Whisper suspected nothing as she slithered right into the industrial district of the kingdom and continued another couple of miles south toward the coast.

The Whisper paused a second, staring at the moon and pulling out her scroll, most likely filled with the latest gossip. She whispered to herself as if rehearsing for a performance. "Ok, ok. I heard the bank owner had money orders in. Shipment is next week, wait. Two weeks." She shuffled through her scrolls like they were on fire. "Two weeks. Two weeks. Ok. Time to go in." Taking a deep breath, she hastened into an abandoned salt mine stationed at the edge of a shore cliff. It was disbanded for distribution issues years ago. Majeria imported salt never tasted the same again. The gangs seemed to frequent these isolated areas. The Order should check on those.

They kept their distance on the agent, and Belyx's lip quivered at the peeling infrastructure of the facility. The moist breeze wore away most material, and this one looked like it was going to slide into the sea.

"What is the play?" Enzo asked.

"Play?"

"You know. How do we get in there?"

"I was gonna try the front door." Belyx smirked, giving Enzo a taste of his own sassy manner.

Enzo stuck up a hand. "Ok, A, not cool. B, aren't you petrified of them?"

"You keep eating your words here." Belyx's eyes were going to stay up in her head all night. "We climb in through the side and neutralize any threats. Plus, I don't even see guards."

"It is a wonder they haven't been destroyed by another gang since they can't even protect their lair."

Belyx eyed him. "What are you, an advisor now?"

He shrugged. "I dabble."

She arched a brow at his generic clothes with no weapons hidden beneath. Clothing that would catch easily. "Also, are you sure you want to wear those on this task?"

"Sorry, I don't have the money for whatever unpronounceable fabric that is. I bet you live in the upper housing ring near the palace."

"What makes you think that?" She studied Enzo, careful not to reveal herself.

"All your materials, the knives, the snake venoms. Which, by the way, terrifies the daylights out of me. How can you get the snakes?"

"Well, I start with feeding them thieves and they do my bidding."

Enzo blinked and shook his head. "Anyway, only someone with a steady flow of coins would afford your clothes. Does your father know you're out cutting throats and conversing with street rats?"

"Does yours?" Belyx retorted, and Enzo closed his mouth, staring ahead, breathing harder through his nose. Belyx must have struck a sensitive spot. "Come on."

Enzo stayed silent and accompanied her down the shaggy path as they crouched around the side in case of any hidden guards. They approached a fractured window and Belyx knocked on it twice. The hinges groaned. Despite the Whisper's moving in, they had made no repairs. She leaned her ears up to it to detect any conversation.

Nothing.

She motioned to Enzo and shifted the window open. Enzo entered first and Belyx followed behind.

From the windowpane, the whole inside was vacant, not a Whisper in sight. Belyx scratched her head. "They must be hiding in an underground bunker or something." They took a tip from the Order on that one.

"What an idea," Enzo replied. Belyx shot him blades as she vaulted down, rolling to catch her fall. The place had only outdated equipment and dust. The Whispers didn't work up here. Enzo slid down a scaffold pole as Belyx scanned for any disguised doors.

Belyx walked around the vicinity. "We need to find something that seems out of place but isn't." Smoothing off surfaces, she tried the floor for any sort of hatch, and checked behind tool shelves. This damn warehouse had no entrance. Where did the Whisper go?

"Here." Enzo stood next to a fake, disheveled portrait on the far wall and pulled it open. With a reaping groan, the massive portrait opened, leading to stairs descending into a lit area.

The hideout of the Whispers.

How did Enzo locate it with such haste? Belyx made a mental note to inform The Order and palace of this. Even with the shortage of Aikradal guards, a full attack here would end at least one gang. She thanked The God and continued to go down when a swishing sound reverberated by the window.

On instinct, she tackled Enzo to ground and a metal projectile sank into the wall.

The Whispers did have guards. Belyx bolted up, holding up her own blade as another flew at her. She pivoted around a steel pillar and the projectile bounced off. Someone or multiple someones were up on the rafters. With caution, Belyx stuck her head out, but no one was there.

A board creaked behind, and she crouched. A figure in all black launched a kunai her way. Belyx eluded it and sliced the assailant, sending them down in an instant.

She yanked off the attacker's hood to find a short-haired woman with a scar on her left cheek.

A Whisper.

She had a variety of throwing blades on her. Belyx had no time to investigate more when Enzo let out a scream. Tossing the dead Whisper down, she dashed over, spotting Enzo in combat with a similar dark figure. Were there only two?

The attacker's fighting style followed the fighters in the kingdom of Petrovkan, mimicking a dance more than a fight. Enzo threw a quick attack, but she moved like a ballet dancer and swept him down. Belyx unsheathed one of her blades and launched it right into their heart.

Enzo leaned on his knees, breathing hard as he wiped the dirt off his shirt. He had a gaping tear in the side, which oozed thick blood. Belyx studied the assailant again. Her knives were dipped in myrtux, a terrible drug causing heavy convulsions, similar to foxglove. They took a page from her poison book, it seemed.

"She didn't stick you with this, did she?" She shot a worried glance at Enzo. The timing of the toxin varied, but he wouldn't have long.

Enzo shook his head. "I nicked it on the splintered wood there. Why?"

Belyx held up the blade. "They coated it in poison."

"No wonder I thought you were a Whisper."

Belyx frowned and set the weapon down, keeping her senses open for any more attackers. "I use venom on my blades. Poison is too unpredictable on weapons. But, what's scarier is they are evolving. The Whispers didn't use to fight like this. They mainly listened and retreated."

"Well, maybe they save the fighting to protect their base from, you know, meddling thieves and assassins."

"True, but why only two guards?" Perhaps she shouldn't send the guards here. Based on their fighting, the guards would stand no chance. Enzo shrugged and Belyx glanced at his wound again, which had already started to close. "That healed fast."

"It wasn't too deep." Enzo moved into the secret entrance without even flinching.

Belyx handed Enzo a blade, but gave him a "you better not lose it" look. "After you, I guess?"

"Into the belly of the beast." Enzo replied as he accepted the steel, leading Belyx down the dark stairwell.

Eleven

The Whisper's underground bunker spanned for what seemed like miles. The tunnels had intersecting channels like a twisted maze. Finding the lair was the simple part. The hard part was locating where they operated.

A few Whispers went through the labyrinth. They moved quick, like they were on a schedule and if they didn't follow, they would lose a toe. Belyx had never encountered their leader, Sewek, but rumors were she ran a strict system. Anyone who veered off from the program was dealt with. It was like professors and their students. The level of intimidation would require a gentle but aggressive touch. Sewek would be dangerous. The Whispers were a sneaky group, but the way they fought earlier sent earthquakes through her chest. Could they handle an entire room of them? Enzo and she barely took out two. The rest better be listeners only.

They reached what looked like the center, with more tunnels breaking off. Art pieces and tapestries from different kingdoms lined the walls. Sewek had a multi-cultural taste in decor. "How did they build these tunnels? There are hundreds of them and they lead all over!" Enzo said as he sipped from his water pouch. How long would this tunnel go? Belyx rubbed her eyes and drank some too. The walk was endless. If they found this place, it would be a fight.

"They probably blackmailed miners into doing it. They have a reach over the kingdom and beyond."

Enzo shook his head. "I think we underestimated them."

Belyx sneered. "You mean you did?"

"Details. But you seemed confident, saying they couldn't fight and such. Wrong."

"I was uninformed," Belyx replied as she continued down the path, plotting her escape, which would not be easy based on the tremendous number of intersecting twists and turns.

"I have a feeling like we are being watched," Enzo cut in to the rocky silence.

Belyx waved him off. "Don't be paranoid... Look!" In front of them sat a massive metal door with various latches and gemstones laid on it, like the entrance to a secret palace. The gems were real, and each one was placed with care and detail. It rivaled the Aikradal castle in design.

Multiple figures burst out of the shadows, dressed in black leather, holding short blades. The Whispers were here to greet them. "What is your business with our all knowing, most beautiful leader?"

Another spoke, smiling wide across her makeup coated face. "Our all knowing leader has been expecting you." They denoted with a similar pattern. Her teeth clacked from the chill sliding down her back.

A different one blinked twice and added, "our alluring leader will see you as long as you relinquish your weapons here." She motioned to the well-polished ground.

Belyx eyed Enzo, and he shrugged, throwing down his one knife. Easy for him. She had more to lose, but agreed, putting her knives and venoms in the same place. She had no trouble killing with her hands as well.

The four clones left the items, casting a quick glance at each other, and knocked on the door in a rapid succession. The room remained silent, except the breathing of the acolytes. It was calm, but unsure. A series of clicks and the giant doors flew open. A scent of lavender and honeysuckle floated throughout the room.

One of the Whispers prodded in front. "Introducing our intelligent and all knowing leader. She has magnificent ears throughout the land. No one can rival her information and power. We present to you, The Future Queen. Sewek

Bera." Belyx did not enjoy the title. Her stomach felt like she consumed her own poison. Enzo grabbed her hand, but she pulled away. The fear would not make her do irrational things like find comfort in him.

The floor was laid in intricate tile with silhouettes of feminine figures dripping in jewels, and not a speck of dust was in sight. If running a vicious gang didn't work out, interior decorating was an acceptable alternative for her.

Sitting at a monstrous desk stacked with scrolls was a towering figure of a woman. She had her back turned to them, fingering through her parchments deliberately, like they were on her time now. The same dark-haired bob style was on her head. Each hair was perfect, like it and its whole family were threatened if it faltered. This look must have inspired the others. Her assistant, Orlena, glared at them, wearing a blonde version of the style and standing a couple inches taller than Belyx.

"Why is this still incomplete?" Sewek wasn't talking to them. She held a scroll to Orlena, who turned a bright shade of beet.

Orlena kept a bow, not catching any eye contact. "Apologies, your all knowing. I'll send out a group straight away." Her voice wavered.

Sewek didn't respond as the twitchy assistant grabbed the scroll and crossed past them.

Belyx coughed. She didn't have all night. Enzo widened his eyes at her bad manners.

"Took your time getting here, I see." Now she was speaking to them.

Belyx stepped forward. "You knew?"

Sewek stood and Belyx's spit dried. She had to be at least over six feet tall. The tallest woman Belyx had ever seen. Her face was another thing for worry. Sewek's needly nose pointed right into Belyx's soul, with facial features as sharp as a blade, and her deadpan expression could scare away any demons in the room. Suddenly, Belyx was a child again, being berated by Madame for not walking well enough. Belyx's posture increased as if by habit.

Sewek gave a silent chuckle. "You do know who I am, right? Leader of the greatest information gathering group in all of Keyica. I knew you were following my girl from the start. Don't worry, she was dealt with for her insolence." Sewek was one of those who lived for rhetorical questions. A most pretentious place.

Belyx hid her fear. Who knew someone elicited more intimidation than the hulking Scorpion? The way Sewek presented herself made an entire army bow down. "Then why would you let us in, if I may ask?" She fought fire with fire.

Sewek glowered and studied Belyx from head to toe, staring over Enzo like he was nothing. She pulled out a scroll. "Enzo. Common street thief. Raised himself after the death of his mentor, Ren." That struck a chord in Enzo, for his body sank down an inch. "You've been hustling ever since, until, the pathetic excuse for a group caught you. Now why is that?"

"I thought you knew all?" Enzo chided. Belyx elbowed him. Even Belyx didn't know how deadly she could be.

Sewek's eyes widened. "Do not challenge me with wits, vermin. You possess no weapons. Body and mind."

Enzo sat up straighter, as if her words fueled his fire. "I can assure you I have no problem with either."

"Doneque." She pulled out another scroll, ignoring Enzo like a fit-throwing toddler. "We have little information on you, despite taking down various gang movements throughout the kingdom. If I had to guess, I would say you work for the palace."

"Wrong." Belyx held her stare. Any inclination of lying would reveal her identity.

Sewek put up a hand. "Did you know it is obscene to interrupt?" Belyx closed her mouth and Sewek waited, as if to enjoy the attention they gave her. "But you saved this thief from the palace guards and even massacred one, so tell me, who do you really work for?"

Belyx folded her arms. "Myself."

"Interesting." The Whisper leader made notes behind her desk. She traced a long bony talon along the top of the finished wood. Her hand had one ring per finger coordinating with her ivory colored pantsuit. Despite it not being a formal event, She wore heeled shoes and they clacked as she walked as if to declare her ever illustrious presence. "I don't believe you, but it is disturbing. I abhor not knowing details." The Leader sat down and began to write on a scroll. Belyx could slaughter her right now if she pleased, but this woman had everything planned. Any attempt would risk her or Enzo's life.

Sewek pulled out something and Belyx gasped, staring down the barrel of a pistol. Enzo stepped in front of her without a thought. Why did he do that? Sewek chuckled, setting down the gun. "Interesting as well. He has feelings for you. What a shame I am going to play a part in such tragedy."

Belyx tried to push Enzo away, but he held firm. Blood rushed to Belyx's face. Why would he show his hand? "Never. He is just a dumb thief." She ignored Enzo's grunt. "Now tell us where the key is. Unless, of course, you don't know all?" This game was hers to win.

Sewek wrote in her notes, smiling down like she just composed a masterpiece. "Foolish assassin. Of course, I know where the key is. The complication is, I will not permit it to you."

Belyx took a step forward, hands clenched. She would fight with all she had for it. Sewek eyed the pistol on the desk, as if daring Belyx to take it. "You think you can get up here before I open fire? Come on. I've studied your technique. Although impressive, it is still lacking. But, if you want to try, Be. My. Guest."

They stayed in their standoff. Belyx could make it before she fired. Enzo gripped her shoulder and shook his head. Even he thought it was foolish.

Sewek put the gun away, as if to tempt her further. "I would listen to your beloved. He just saved your feeble life."

Belyx ignored her comment. Focus, Belyx. "What do you want, then? Stop wasting our time."

Sewek tilted her head like a banshee. "Isn't it clear? I want to rule this kingdom. The king has neglected us for far too long. He knows little of what goes on. Haven't you ever heard of 'knowledge is power?'"

"It comes to mind," Belyx replied. It sounded like something Madame Jewella would spout.

"The king is already in a weakened state. Killing him would be a bore." The thought of her dad's death sent dryness through her throat. "I would assign you to kill the tramp princess, Belyx, but that would be way too difficult for the likes of you two. I tried." Belyx clenched her fists and said a quiet thanks to Freyja. "Besides, the princess is so incompetent at ruling. Even if she did take over one day, she would fail even worse than her deplorable father." Breath, Belyx. She will get hers one day. "Since the royal family is handled, I propose to take out a rival gang. One who has been a thorn in my operations for some time, the Berserkers."

Enzo stepped forward now. "You want us to end the Berserkers for you? How do we do that?"

Sewek drew a blade and jabbed it into a wooden snake statue on her desk. "Cut the head of the snake and the rest of the body falls." She glared. "Bring me Raul Fortan's head and the location of the key is yours."

Belyx's muscles sank. This would prove to be harder than she planned. Raul Fortan would be a formidable kill, but doable. Despite her reservations, Enzo answered before her, almost too eagerly. "We'll do it."

Sewek's lips curled into a satisfied grin like she won an award for deception. "I figured you might." What did she mean, Enzo would? Belyx glanced back at Enzo and raised her eyebrows like, are you sure there isn't another way? Enzo also displayed a gratified smirk. This had to be a blood feud. She knew he was held hostage by the Berserkers, but what else did they do to him? Did it have to do with the dead mentor of his?

She turned back to Sewek. "Won't he just be a martyr? Cut off its head and two more grow in place?" The words of grandmother were helpful again.

Sewek waved her hand. "I'm not familiar with that one. Explain why." *Some know it all.*

"Raul dead won't end the Berserkers. Someone will take over."

Sewek coughed a low chuckle, like she refused to laugh. "Raul is the only one with intellect in that conglomerate. You think his invalid guard dog he has can rule after him?"

She had a point, but Belyx wouldn't give her the satisfaction of a win. "You never know, but..." Belyx had to think about this, but they were running out of time. The longer this key remained in the wrong hands, the closer her kingdom was to ruin. "We have a deal, it seems." She swallowed to lubricate her parched throat.

Sewek clasped her talons together. "Perfect. My friends will show you out." The clones entered as if on cue and lined up in rows. Friends? Belyx and Enzo went to walk out when Sewek called them again. "Oh, and remember, don't underestimate us or try anything. It will be the last thing you do, assassin and thief."

They kept moving, side eying each other like, "What did we just get ourselves into?"

After the clones released them down the long stretch of tunnels, giving vague directions on how to exit, Enzo and Belyx didn't utter a word to each other. Belyx stayed a few paces behind Enzo, the awkward scuffling of feet filling the space. Why wouldn't he talk to her? She knew why she was ignoring him, but how dare he accept a deal without talking to her first? Leader Raul would be heavily guarded and they both almost died the last time they went up against The Berserkers. Enzo carried something on his shoulders and Belyx planned to discover it.

"You were eager to end the Berserkers in there." Enzo's face stayed neutral. "I know they hurt you, but what made you agree so fast." Still nothing. He kept walking. It was the least he had ever said in the short time Belyx had known him. "Did they do something else to you? What did Sewek mean by dead mentor? Who is Ren?"

Enzo lurched to a halt and faced Belyx, the green in his eyes distorted in slight tears. "Someone important to me. Someone who saved my life. You wouldn't get it, working alone." She did, but she followed along. People in rage needed space. Some needed it for thirteen years.

Enzo turned back around and wiped his tears on his sleeve. "The Berserkers killed the one friend I had in this blasted kingdom. I have no problem ending their leader, so help or don't." He was thirsty for revenge like her, and he would steamroll anyone who stood in the way. A feeling told Belyx to share something about herself, but she couldn't risk exposing too much. Other people's identities were at stake too and she would never forgive herself if anything happened to The Order.

Belyx caught up to Enzo and put a palm on his firm shoulder, but he flinched away. They both continued hiking in silence until they approached one of the many exits. After this walking, Belyx would need a rest.

The exit led to a secret door in an alleyway by dumpsters meant for factory sewage. The putrid scent of raw materials hit Belyx like a sucker punch. They hastened to a more covered area, planning their next steps.

Belyx sighed. "I think this task is too dangerous. We will never defeat them."

Enzo sat on the dirt and munched on dried meat, offering Belyx some, but she declined. He continued eating in silence for a few moments. Belyx prayed this would be enough time to simmer down and think about this ludicrous scheme.

"We could kill him if we worked together. I know it is possible." He swallowed a heavy gulp, helping himself to more.

Belyx wanted to rip her wig off and show him everything to make him feel better. Surprised at how she cared for him. She was becoming the women in those frivolous novels. "We barely made it out of their warehouse before. What makes you think we can break in, kill a skilled and protected leader, and then escape?" Flashbacks of The Scorpion drowned her mind. The way he split anything with his bare hands and the way he slow-walked to his victims. Belyx shook the concerns away.

Enzo finished his food and stood up. "Like I said, you are welcome to stay, but I am going to try."

This was a new level of annoying, even for him. "If you were sure, why didn't you try this until now? Why wait for a deal with Sewek?"

He stared into the distance. The breeze made his dark curls flutter in the night sky. "I have been planning it, but I never had a skilled killer to help."

Belyx crossed her arms. Why was she about to do this? It was sharing time. "I know what it is like to lose someone, too." Enzo looked at her own tear-filled eyes and she prayed the contacts would remain. "The need for revenge solves nothing. It will start a never ending string of violence. If we go after The Berserkers, they will not stop until we are buried. That is what Sewek plans on."

Enzo plopped back down, turning away to hide his tears. Should she hug him? No. They were barely partners, not friends. "Then how do you propose we get the location from Sewek? One does not cross the all-knowing one, Doneque."

Belyx smiled. "I think there is a way to fool the all-knowing one."

Enzo smirked for the first time in a while. "Oh yeah? How do we fool her wannabe majesty?" This banter sent Belyx's heart up her throat.

"She said to bring her Raul's head." Enzo gave her a look like he knew where this was heading. "I know a place where they keep many kinds of heads and can alter the appearance of one."

"Sounds like you have done these activities before?"

"Once or twice." She smirked back, watching him squirm.

Enzo's face grew into a grin. If Belyx were foolish, she would think he wanted to kiss her, but she would chop off his adulthood if he tried. "I knew our arrangement would work out."

"Bullshit. I had to practically beg you."

"Not how I saw it." He winked.

Belyx laughed, but turned her face straight. This was business and she refused to let her feelings eclipse her goal of preserving her kingdom. Once this was over, they would go their separate ways. She would go back to princess duties and he would go back to lifting items in the markets. A princess and a thief had no means to be friends, and the assassin would be the only persona he knew.

Belyx snatched a piece of meat from Enzo. He went to protest, but waved her off like the smart thief he was. She stood and held a hand to him. "Get up. We need to act quick if we plan to pull this off."

TWELVE

"So, that's the plan?" Enzo stared in front of the mausoleum with wide eyes, like he witnessed a spirit eat his whole family.

"What? Scared of some corpses? When we die, our souls go to The God. Dead bodies are nothing to be nervous of." Belyx paused and turned her head. "You follow The God, don't you?" Some people didn't believe in Them, but most weren't around Aikradal. Mostly, the non-believers comprised the naturalists, the fae, and the ones who believed in the old ways.

Enzo coughed. "No, I do, but the idea of lifeless flesh still grosses me out."

Belyx made a tsk noise. "Ok, so the priest works at night, but he takes his smoke break, which is in fifteen minutes." Tobacco was addicting in these parts.

"Got it," Enzo deadpanned.

"What? No sassy remark? These corpses have you rattled." Belyx had to poke fun.

Enzo side eyed her. "I'll be fine. Just, umm, don't get too far from me?"

Belyx rolled her eyes, but shot him a shrug. "Deal."

The priest left at around the time Belyx said. This wasn't her first time breaking into a morgue...and she hated to recall it.

They broke into the door with ease. Enzo offered, but Belyx did the honors, as this was still her mission.

The chilled air swirled around them and Belyx rubbed her arms for warmth. Enzo seemed unfazed. He must be used to living in the cold. They piped in icy air from underground to preserve the bodies for burial, after being processed by the priests of course. Belyx couldn't help but glower at Enzo's fear. She had killed enough people to never be afraid of death. A part of her wanted to grab his hand. Fool.

They glided across the marble floors, with only the faint sound of their breaths. The dead were always quiet. They turned the corner and slipped into a room marked "Body Storage."

"Here it is," Belyx said, rubbing her chilled arms. If corpses hit above a certain temperature, they began to rot and the sight and smell weren't pleasant.

Enzo gulped. "Why do they even keep these things around?"

"They are used for studying what makes us work. It was against The God until the regions agreed it was actually The God's intention to study them."

"How convenient." The blasphemy wasn't appreciated. Although he was already a thief, how moral could he be? Belyx's own killing latched onto her mind, but it was different. It was for the greater good of her kingdom. Stealing was always wrong... besides for stealing a body. For the greater good, Belyx.

Enzo opened the door, and they went in. The bodies lay on tables, covered by thin white sheets. The air didn't move an inch, as if a presence loomed. Nonsense. The God handled the souls. Spirits were only in stories.

Enzo shuddered again. "This place reminds me of a novel I read about dead people crawling from the ground and eating everyone."

"Really? With the books again?" Belyx uncovered the first couple of covers and almost lost her lunch at the gangly faces. Those wouldn't do.

Enzo turned his eyes away. "Never mind. It had a weird plot twist, anyway. An overused trope."

"Trope?"

"Like a theme, such as friends to lovers, or..." he put his hand to his chin. "A love triangle."

Belyx wanted to heave from something other than the bodies. "Love triangles. So childish."

"People eat that up." Enzo pinched a sheet and lifted, only to set it down, his dark complexion morphing into a paler shade. "I enjoy it."

"Any self-respecting person, especially a woman, should never find pride in choosing between two different people."

"It's not about how 'self-respecting' they are. It's about the conflict." Were they debating books in this dingy place? This had to mark as a new low, even for Belyx.

"My life has enough conflict, thank you very much." No bodies matched any resemblance of Raul. This would prove harder than she thought.

Enzo gagged at a burned victim, his whole body melted. "Well, what do you do for fun?"

Should she tell him? Don't. "I write, umm poetry." Too late.

Enzo snorted, which faded from Belyx's glare. "What is funny?" Why did she reveal such a crucial detail about herself? What a waste of time and now this ruffian was going to judge her.

"It's just ironic. A deadly assassin writing about spring flowers and soft candies."

Belyx scoffed. "Poems about other things exist. Especially darker themes."

"Sounds odd to me. Care to read some?" The green-eyed thief wiggled his eyebrows at her as they sifted through more stiff bodies. Belyx prayed the conversation would die like them.

They were running out of time. "Can we focus, please? Raul is difficult to replicate, but if we can just find a dark-skinned, bald head, that would be—"

"Found something!" Enzo pointed under a sheet and Belyx nearly knocked him over. The body of a middle-aged man was sprawled like he was in peaceful slumber and he resembled Raul. She took her blade and, like a slab of cheese, carved the neck clean off. "Ok, now I can throw up," Enzo said.

A loud bang came from the entrance. Belyx dove into the hard marble.

"Who is there, sick bastards!" The scraggly priest slammed the door behind him. He would be easy to subdue. Belyx took out a knife, but Enzo shook his head and motioned for her to wait. What could he do about it? Steal something? Sass him to death?

Enzo stood up and Belyx gripped her dagger tighter. "Hello kind sir."

"What are you doing here, immoral beast!" He wasn't wrong.

"Apologies," Enzo said, taking out a bag of coins. "Can I persuade you to look the other way? Just wanted to see my dead mother one last time."

Although crass, maybe it would work. No way would a pristine man of the faith accept such bribes from corpse thieves.

The old priest stopped and considered. "How much?" And Belyx slammed her head against the floor.

They exited the body storage, Enzo whistling with cheer. Belyx ate her words. "Nice thinking," she said under her breath.

"Not everything has to be handled with venom and blades."

Belyx folded her arms. "I don't always do that, plus I was just going to knock him out."

Enzo shrugged. "Sometimes people can be dealt with in less painful ways. You should try it next time."

Belyx clenched the skull in her hand, ignoring Enzo and strutting toward her next destination. Like he should give her advice. He knew nothing. "Where are we going?" Enzo huffed as he ran after her.

"My way of doing something besides killing." She couldn't hide the acid in her voice.

Enzo stayed silent for once and followed her. Reaching the place, Belyx knocked on a decorated mahogany door, praying the owner would answer. A couple of pulses later and an older looking woman answered, holding the door partway. Belyx waved with her fingers and her grandmother's old friend frowned, wrinkles grouping on her copper-toned face.

"You only come to me when you need something, Doneque." This wasn't wrong, and she made a note to visit in less dire circumstances whenever that would be.

Enzo snuck around Belyx and stuck his hand to Ponka. "I'm Enzo. Nice to meet you." She curled her face at his gesture.

Belyx pinched her nose in embarrassment while slapping his hand away. "Apologies for him. He is a complication." She ignored Enzo's scowl.

Ponka looked over at both of them. "In." She held her hand up at Enzo. "Not him."

Belyx whispered to Enzo. "Don't take it personally. She doesn't trust men. Stand guard and I'll be right out." Did it lesson the sting? Most likely not.

"Do your thing," Enzo said with a straight face. He seriously needed to get over himself.

Ponka's home was as Belyx remembered. The decor consisted of ancient paintings lining the black walls with various artifacts from other regions scattered throughout, but also in the same place as last time. As Belyx entered the supposed common area, she was hit with the faint scent of ginger and tea. Why was it always tea?

"Set down that." Ponka pointed to her jumbled desk as she prepped the boiling water. The station was lined with plaster, paint, and many shades of coals.

Belyx set the head on it. "I can't be too long."

Ponka glared at her like Madame Jewella, as if to say, "I will take my sweet ass time."

"What do you require of me this hour?"

Belyx swallowed to wet her dry throat, suddenly craving the gross tea. "I need this head to look like Raul Fortan, leader of the Berserkers."

Ponka didn't even question the request as she came over and placed down Belyx's half made tea. She drained it, choking down the bitter leaves as Ponka inspected the head. "What have you gotten yourself into now?" Her concern was always refreshing.

"Nothing too bad. Aikradal in danger. What's new?" Her attempt to lighten the mood failed with a side eye.

"Say no more." Ponka took to work, brushing her dark bangs from her face. Her deft fingers handled the paints and coals along the severed head. "Aikradal has been in danger for a while." Belyx had to agree with her words. The threat loomed closer and closer to the gates. But she would save it. Ponka turned the head, keeping a keen eye on her precision. Her eidetic memory meant she didn't need a painting of the person. If she saw them once, they were locked in her vault. They needed these skills in The Order, but she dare not ask again. Like Cook, Ponka's involvement in The Order was requested, but Ponka agreed never to work for them again... At least directly. She still assisted now and then, but Dara only gave her minor missions.

The loud silence filled the room until Ponka chuckled, unlike her. "Who was the man out there? He was cute."

Belyx turned to the side. "Just some thief who has a similar goal as me. Who most likely will betray me."

Ponka flipped the head upside down, swishing the neckline to perfection. "Your mother had such different dreams for this place. Your grandmother too."

"If only I could do what my mother did." Ponka kept painting. The head began to produce Raul's arduous features. Ponka's skill was unmatched.

"You have feelings for this thief." It wasn't a question.

Heat stuck to Belyx's cheeks. How could she say such blatant slander? "Absolutely not! He is impossible to work with, he is stubborn, and he always has something snarky to say." The list could go on all night, but she had no time.

Ponka completed the last touches on her masterpiece. "No potent feelings are pleasant. Remember that, young one." She raised the head like a gift and Belyx stowed it into the bag.

"I owe you one, Ponka." She always did.

Ponka gazed out her window into the moonlit sky. "There won't be enough time, I'm afraid." How positive. "Fight hard and remember one thing." She took Belyx's hand, Ponka's dry hands scratched hers. "Use your mother's intuition.

It will save you." There it was again. If only intuition came with a parchment of instructions.

Belyx gave a close-lipped smile and slipped outside to find Enzo leaned against a wall with his arms draped over his chest like a gown. "Who was your trusting friend?"

"Someone from the past. Don't worry about it." Belyx pulled out the head, now resembling Raul Fortan. "And the best cosmetic artisan in all the region."

Enzo ran his fingers along it, not averted by death anymore. "Think Sewek will believe it?"

Belyx shrugged. "I hope so. It is our only chance."

Enzo shuffled his feet. "I may have tipped the scale in our favor."

Belyx held her breath. "What did you do?"

"Sewek and her crones are clearly watching us, so I caused a scene near the Berserker hideout. That way, Sewek hears about an attack." He was brilliant. Why didn't Belyx think of that? Way to go, Belyx. Let the thief outplay you.

"Good thinking." Belyx replied as she stowed the head away.

"Any reason that lady doesn't trust men?" Belyx ignored him. He didn't deserve the story and Enzo took the silence as an answer. "Well, not all men are wicked, you know."

She side eyed him. "I realize."

They continued in solace through the hidden alley door. Ponka's words kept haunting her. Was Aikradal un-savable? She clenched her fists, taking a chance it could be saved. The key would be found and eradicated. No matter how much power it unlocked, Belyx would shield her kingdom. This was the moment she had been training for.

Before they reached Sewek's lair through the twists and turns Enzo seemed to remember well. He stopped Belyx, his face gloomy. "Look, Doneque." His green eyes peered into her own. "No matter what happens in there..." He paused, as if to reflect his words. "I have your back."

Belyx quaffed. Did he mean it? Only time would truly tell. She agreed, but said nothing else.

They knocked, and the door opened, as if to their tomb.

Sewek ignored them and continued writing on her desk. They turned in their weapons to a Whisper out front and she took them with shaky hands.

Belyx tossed the head onto Sewek's scrolls like a sack of fish, but she discounted it and kept scribbling.

After a beat, Sewek unfurled the bag with her menacing, but manicured nails, nodding in approval. "I take it he wasn't too challenging? Did you execute his guard dog as well?"

"He wasn't there," Belyx lied. The important thing when lying was to pull from truths.

Sewek pursed her lips. "Very lucky for you. I'm sure he will find some hole to bury himself in. But overall, I am impressed." She snapped her gaunt fingers and two of her followers came in with a tray of steaming liquid. Sewek hardly glanced their way as they set it in front and poured the water into three porcelain cups. They served everyone and retreated out.

"Let us drink to a job well done and an interesting alliance." With her eyebrow raised, Sewek took a sip. Enzo followed suit, but Belyx trusted no one. She put it to her lips and let the tea rest. Should she have told Enzo not to drink? He would be fine. Sewek believed them, plus Belyx hated tea.

Sewek sat back down and printed something on a script. "Here is the location of the key. Now I hope we can come to an understanding you will never set foot in my domain without my summons again... And trust me, I will know."

"No worries there," Belyx replied. This place gave her the creeps, and she planned to let The Order or Aikradal guards handle it.

Sewek wrote for awhile longer before her assistant, Orlena, shuffled in, avoiding eye contact with Enzo and Belyx. The assistant leaned down and whispered something in Sewek's ear. She ceased writing and set her pen down like a delicate leaf. "I would like you to tell me more about how you took down the mighty Raul? Was it hard? I can imagine the struggle."

Enzo's cheeks reddened and Belyx's palms sweat, but she would not show her hand. "We are on a time crunch ourselves. We will just see ourselves ou—"

Enzo made a choking sound and fell to the floor, his breaths wheezing. Belyx looked at Sewek and then back to Enzo, a sinking pit in her gut growing. Enzo tried to get words out, but none came. His body shook as blood dripped from the corners of his mouth. The tea had been poisoned, but why? Her vision stilled.

Sewek always knew.

Belyx hustled to his side as he convulsed. Only myrtux or foxglove would cause these symptoms. He only had mere minutes to live.

Sewek stood up and shredded the scroll of the location. "You think I didn't know you would betray me? Foolish to think you could fool someone as all knowing as me." Orlena smirked behind her, widening her eyes in pleasure.

Enzo vomited onto her well stitched rug. Soon he would be dead and she would be to blame.

Without thinking, Belyx launched her cup of tea at the Whisper leader, trying to ignore Enzo's groans. She would pay for this.

The porcelain missed and shattered behind them. The assistant pulled out a blade and lunged for Belyx, but she dodged like a fly and struck the center of her long legs. She grunted and released the weapon. Belyx snagged the dagger and held Orlena, only to be facing Sewek's pistol again. "Tell me what the poison was, or I'll gut your crone."

"Crone?" Orlena gasped as Belyx inched the steel closer, drawing a slight trickle of blood.

Sewek didn't even blink. "I see you didn't drink my concoction. What told you it was laced?"

"Not trusting people. Especially false idols. You were going to poison us no matter what. You believed us. Orlena had just told you. Admit it, we fooled your scrawny ass."

Orlena struggled, but Belyx held her firm.

Sewek's face grew beet red. "I knew about it before and you can't prove otherwise!" Belyx enjoyed her squirming like a worm. Sewek's face changed back to her normal pale tone. "I know your lover is still dying." Enzo stopped thrashing. The beginning to an end.

"What did you do? Take the antidote before?"

Sewek stilled. "I underestimated you, mercenary, but no matter." She peered at Enzo and grimaced. "That stain will never come out. Oh, well." A smile developed on her pointy face. "We could stall here and let your friend die, or you can leave and never come back. Kill Orlena. I have hundreds just like her, eager for a spot next to me, the future queen."

Belyx tried to drown out Enzo's gasps. Death arrived at his door. She could run and find the key on her own, but her memories shifted to him saving her from The Scorpion and how he promised to have her back.

I never made that promise. Belyx had never worked with anyone before. The clock ticked by like sludge in her mind.

Enzo began to shiver again like a drowning animal. He had less than a minute. Belyx sucked in every breath she had, steadying her lungs.

In one move, she shoved Orlena forward and ducked. The pistol shot missed, and Belyx knocked the firearm out of Sewek's hand. She screeched, taking out her own blade and swinging, but Belyx worked too hard to fail now. After dodging the blows, she elbowed Sewek in the largest target on her face, her nose.

The Whisper dropped her weapon and stumbled backwards. Belyx snatched the nearest object she could find, a hardcover book, and struck the tall whisper leader in the face. Her body slammed into her bookcase and she lay still. Books had uses after all.

Sewek's desk was organized like a crypt keeper's as she rifled through the contents. Come on, antidote, where are you? Enzo would be dead soon, and it was her turn to save him. The world around her blurred. The ringing in her ears settled as her hands shook. She exhaled as the antidote for myrtux and foxglove came into view.

Enzo's breaths flatlined. If Belyx gave him the wrong one, he would perish. If she gave him both, they would counteract each other and he would die. The two poisons mimicked symptoms, but the difference was dots floating in the victim's eyes.

She smacked Enzo. "Enzo. Did you see dots when you went down?"

He turned his head to her, but his mouth hung open with only lifeless eyes. The once vibrant green was now a pale grey. He couldn't answer her and she would need to guess. Her training on poisons now proved useless in this encounter. She closed her eyes and prayed as hard as she ever had. "Please, our parent. Give me a sign for the correct choice."

Belyx chose one and pried it down Enzo's purple lips.

Enzo was gone.

But then his eyes fluttered open like he had just woke up from a nightmare. "Do-Doneque?" His voice was hoarse from the vomiting and coughing. Belyx embraced him, tears racing down her face. His weak arms brushed her back. "I would—wouldn't think you c—cared so much." He coughed in a frenzy behind her.

Leaving Enzo to recover, she rushed to the desk where Sewek and Orlena remained unconscious and scoured the remanence of her shreds.

Enzo pushed himself to a sitting position. "Did she write it?"

Belyx shook her head. "She just wrote about how amazing she is. She never intended to let us leave. You shouldn't have drunk that tea."

"How was I supposed to know?"

Belyx kept rifling through the compartments of the desk. There had to be something. "This is why you stick to thieving and I'll be the killer here." Enzo barely trusted Belyx, who saved him, and yet he trusted this sketchy cult leader. It was a fluke he survived this long.

Enzo's eyes widened as Sewek started to stir. "I'll grab our things, take care of her!" Enzo leapt up and out the door.

Belyx took Sewek's knife and held it to her throat. Her eyes slugged open. "Bitch," Sewek spat.

Belyx grinned. "Save the compliments. Tell me where the key is and I'll consider letting you keep your fingers." Sewek seethed as Enzo came back. "Enzo, hand me the dried up white petals in my pouch."

"You wouldn't dare!" Sewek's eyes darted back and forth.

Belyx grabbed the bag from Enzo. "Oh, you've heard of hemlock? I hear it is dangerous with virtually no cure, unlike what you used on gullible over there. Now tell me what I want to know. Key. Location." Would Sewek die for this information? If so, it proved to be way more dangerous than Belyx originally imagined.

Please give it up. Belyx shoved the poison closer, and Sewek shook. "Fine. Fine! It's in a Goldfinger vault in the northern housing area."

Belyx carefully gave the hemlock back to Enzo and inched the blade to Sewek's face. Belyx should do Aikradal a favor and fix it? "How do you know this?"

Sewek glared at her. "The key was taken not too long ago from the palace, and it resurfaced. The gold-blind Goldfingers are holding it for something. Most likely trying to blackmail the palace." Had they succeeded? No one would stoop this low... or would they?

"We were trying to get it ourselves, but we heard this trash." She side eyed Enzo, who stuck out his tongue. "Stole it and those nasty Berserkers caught him first, and I wasn't sending in my friends to save him, but low and behold some street-walker assassin shows up and does it for me. And the fool doesn't even have it!"

Belyx fought back the tingle in her limbs. "Who gave it to them in the first place?" She rotated the blade right at her long throat.

Sewek licked her drying lips with a cocky smile. "No idea." In a swift motion, Belyx slammed the hilt of the blade into Sewek's temple, sending her back to the ground. Belyx stayed upright for awhile, contemplating her words. Who would betray them? Was it Lord Kirk? The Masters? Lord Jaques? They wouldn't risk something that dangerous being handed over like items in a merchant stand. Someone else was behind this.

Enzo grabbed Belyx's hand. "Who from the palace would steal it?"

"I don't know, but we need to continue with this plan and retrieve it." Belyx's ribs constricted in her lungs.

Enzo gathered the rest of their things. "We need to proceed. We can break in tonight and steal the key."

Belyx caught back her tears. "You're right. Let's go."

They took off through the same tunnels. Nightfall had passed and the cold air traveled around the near empty street. The upper housing district was north. If everything went according to plan, they would be finished with this turmoil tonight. Too many clues led back to the palace, and it was like a snake suffocating her. Belyx had things she needed to confer with her father. All this time she was running all over trying to stop this secret and a person her father trusted may have stolen the key. What kind of trusted worker did that?

Music vibrated from a distance. What kinds of people partied at this time? A soothing song slithered into Belyx's brain. It reminded her of the lullabies her mother used to sing.

The world hushed as if someone had wrapped a soft blanket over her head.

She was floating.

Enzo shouted something, but it was white noise.

Her vision blurred and then drifted to a lulling light.

Thirteen

Pounding music filled her head.

Dancing lights and sweaty bodies were like specks around her.

Belyx twirled through the ballroom, drink in hand. The party guests were dressed in flawless clothing, from chiffon gowns to silk suits. She put her hands through her dark wig and pressed her fingers along her velvet dress to the beats of the song.

She felt like a princess.

Wasn't she a princess?

A handsome, green-eyed gentleman locked eyes with her. By the end of the night, his lips would be hers. Responding to her cues, the man came over. He spoke, but Belyx was too occupied with her dancing to listen. The melody swept her off her feet like she was a swan gliding over a moonlit pond.

She could go anywhere she pleased.

She was free.

The man gave up, and the song finished. Her brain craved another beverage. The bar was run by a tall dark-skinned man who refilled her goblet with red liquid. It tasted like fruits and treasure. He winked as Belyx placed a couple of coins in his palm.

Belyx sipped the chilled drink as she moved around the dance hall, wondering who their decorator was. The skyline was crusted in gold and crimson specks, illuminating every woven pattern. The labyrinth paintings of magical creatures spanned across the walls and candles on the ceiling were floating in midair, as if by magic. In the ballroom's front was a band dressed up in fancy black suits, playing a variety of instruments ranging from the violin to the harp. Their tunes could assuage bulls.

Belyx paced over the milky black and white tile floor when a shorter gentleman bowed, kissing her outstretched hand. "Welcome gorgeous, to my party. I am your gracious host, Scandeni Dergo, leader of the Cabarets!" He held his arm up in an elegant gesture. His electric blue hair was unlike anything Belyx had seen before. It stuck up in points along his head and turned his brown eyes deeper. Who was his make-up artist?

This group rang familiar, but she couldn't quite grasp it. She returned the praise. "Doneque." Was Doneque her real name?

He waved his hands in the air like a performer. "Magnifico! What a splendid name!" His accent couldn't be placed. It sounded Petrovkan with the subtle vowels, but it was too eloquent. "I hope you enjoy your time. Please stay as long as you like. Lovely Doneque. It is not often I find a lady with such piercing crimson eyes."

"Like the color of blood."

He made a moaning sound. "Delicious."

Belyx blushed. "I am known for my danger." Why was she flirting with him?

Scandeni cooed. "What a lady. Well, I must return to my guests, but find me again if you want a more intimate tour of my party palace." He kissed her hand again. Party palace indeed. The Aikradal palace needed this and more. Who was their princess?

What a shame for an empty cup! Belyx went for another refill when the curly haired man from earlier cut her off. "Doneque, we need to leave" Where was the fire?

Belyx snickered. She was having too much fun to go anywhere. He should leave, whoever he was. "No thanks, but make yourself useful and take my goblet?" She placed it in his calloused hands and stumbled over to the bar where other fine noblemen were conversing.

One turned to Belyx, a hungry look in his eye. "Well, look at you. I have never seen such striking red eyes." He stroked her back and his buddies giggled, getting used to this feeling.

"What a charmer," Belyx said as the bartender topped off her glass. She devoured half of it and snorted, clinging to the charming man. His hand slid lower and lower until the green-eyed man grabbed him by the lapel and thrust him into a chair, his weight breaking it in pieces.

Belyx slapped the emerald-eyed man across the face. How dare he ruin her fun! She went to strike again when he clutched her hand. Her quick reflexes slowed and she couldn't pull away. "Doneque. This is dangerous. Let's go." This again! The man released Belyx as she bit his hand and ran away from the creep, signaling guards near the entrance.

"Help! That man over there is trying to stop me from having a grand time!" She pointed right at him, and he sprinted for the other end. The guards chased after him. Bye loser.

"I ain't seen you around here," a strange voice said behind Belyx. Another guest with odd hair approached her, tapping her bright teal party shoes. Instead of blue locks like Scandeni's, it was cotton candy pink and shaved on one side. She wore a matching silk pantsuit and her scowling face was fully painted. Her thick accent mimicked Scandeni's.

"Doneque."

The woman peered closer. "Roxette Han. Scandeni's assistant." Her face was brushed with shimmering rose and orange blushes, but something boiled under her fresh face. Belyx wondered if she was more than a helper to him. Roxette licked her white teeth and shot Belyx daggers. "Nice wig, but around here, we show our authentic selves. Take it off doll."

No use arguing with the host's next in command. Belyx needed to be herself to enjoy this party. She went to remove her wig when a chair slammed into Roxette. The assistant squealed as she hit the ground.

The dark skinned man dashed into Belyx. What was his problem? Why couldn't he leave her alone? She kicked the man in the shin and took out one of her blades and went to plunge it in his stupid neck when he gripped her arms. Belyx tried to yank free when a searing heat tore across her body and straight to her head. Strobes of her whole life cracked back to her like a storm. Her father and mother, her grandmother, The Order, Freyja, and now, Enzo, appeared by magic. Memories of good and bad tap danced in her brain.

Belyx ripped the blade away from Enzo. Where was she, and why were these people dressed up? Why was she dressed up? The band kept playing, despite the armed guards surrounding them. Scandeni Dergo's eyes met hers. The leader of the Cabarets, a dangerous group known for enticing guests to party the entire night until they joined or perished. She gulped. The enticement worked, and she was lucky to be alive. The Order had never been able to infiltrate him before and now Belyx stood in the presence of the threat.

Scandeni prodded over. Enzo held his blade up, as did Belyx. "How in The Mother did you break my trance?" Mother? Who was that?

"Let everyone go. Your games are sick, Scandeni." Enzo gritted his teeth.

Roxette let out a high pitch chuckle, dangling off Scandeni's shoulder. "Remember Enzo, you were the one who wanted to join us ages ago."

Belyx turned to him. "What?"

Enzo stuck up his hands, shooting a pleading face at Belyx. "I had nowhere else to go! But once I found out what they did to people, I was out."

Belyx stayed rigid. How could he even think they were a wonderful group to begin with?

"Can this lover's quarrel wait?" Roxette said. "I say we capture and gut them!"

Why did everyone think they were lovers! Scandeni kissed his assistant, and Belyx gagged. "I couldn't agree more, my truffle. Guards. Take them!"

The guards closed in, armed with long spears encrusted in gemstones. Leave it to Scandeni to be extra. Belyx took out another knife, thankful she had them under her dress. The closest guard lunged for her, but she spun away from the spear and stuck him in the throat, taking his weapon and cracking it in half. Despite the uncountable amount of alcohol in her system, her senses kept up. She used the pointed end of the spear and subdued another guard.

Enzo faced the two guards at once. Belyx went to help when Roxette cartwheeled in her way. Her acrobatics explained the pantsuit. "You have ruined our party! You will pay!" She twirled her wooden stave around before launching it at Belyx. She blocked the attack with her spear, following with a body check. Roxette backed up and twirled the staff. Blocking the strike again, she took a step forward, heel palming the assistant in the chin. Her slender frame launched back.

Roxette coughed up blood on the polished tile. "Who even are you?" She tried one last effort to hit from below, but Belyx avoided the strikes. Roxette had zero form, making it a quick fight. The assistant left her staff out too long, and Belyx stepped out of the way and sent a knockout kick right into her painted face.

Enzo took down his guards, grabbed Belyx's hand, and they dashed for the exit. Scandeni watched them run out without a fight. He wasn't much of a fighter, it appeared.

The cool air assaulted them as they escaped the dance hall. It was a run-down dwelling in the trade area. How did no one think to check this? Right, the supposed trance.

Once they were far enough away, the harmonious music died out. Belyx halted to catch her breath. Her lungs were a campfire. "What happened in there?" Belyx asked between gasps. Chunks of time were missing from her memory. Was it a drug she wasn't aware of? She would need an antidote to free the other people.

Enzo panted hard like a dog in a sweltering day. "I don't know how."

"You worked for them. You should know. It was a drug. What is it called?" Belyx couldn't tamp the flame in her voice.

Enzo glared at Belyx. "First off. It was a long time ago, and I had just lost my mentor and needed a group. I figured they would fit since Scandeni used to be a con artist, too. Second, how would he have drugged us from outside?"

"Well, magic only exists in witch stories."

"You know the rumors about him, right?"

Belyx did recall, but they were outlandish. "There is no way Scandeni is a male witch. Witches are only female."

"Therefore, you need to read more." Enzo stilled his breath. "Sometimes they are born male with the witch's abilities and they are sent off into the twisted rivers to die, but some survive and do evil shit like Scandeni."

Belyx gazed at Enzo. "How did you pull free of Scandeni's drug or spell or whatever, then?" How did he free her, too?

Enzo shrugged. "Must have been the antidote you gave me. Maybe it affected his drug." Enzo stood up, brushing his pants off. "Well, if we hope to get the key, we better get moving."

That was a dodge. Was it magic or not! There had to be more to why he survived it and how he freed her. "Thanks anyway. I don't even want to know how I acted."

"You were actually kind of fun." He went to hand Belyx's knife back, but she waved him off. "I don't think I had seen you smile since we met. You were having a great time."

Belyx chuckled. "Well, maybe I should have stayed there since I'm so droll all the time."

"I didn't say that." Enzo's stare lingered at Belyx. Sincere. "I just meant it was good to see you have fun." Why would he care about her having fun? Only people who cared for each other did that, and she did not care about him. He had only gotten her into trouble with his recklessness. Belyx wanted to ask more like how she wore this lovely dress, but the sun fractured across the sky and she launched into a panic.

What time was it? The party felt like minutes, but it went on all night. "I have to go!"

Enzo grabbed her arm before she could leave. "Wait."

Belyx yanked away. "I'm serious. I have a day job! Damn those Cabarets! We were out all night!"

She turned to run when Enzo replied, "Princess duties?"

Belyx's mouth opened to a new level. "How? What? When?" Did this mean she needed to kill him now?

"I sort of had suspicions you were royalty by the way you addressed people. Your verbiage comes from only those with a palace education, and also the second night we met, you whispered to yourself and said your name." How did he hear her self pep talk? His hearing must have been stellar.

She couldn't hide anymore. As Doneque, she had never had to converse this much with someone. Her missions were quick and simple and now she understood why. Even princess Belyx bled to her assassin persona.

Daylight was in full force now and she had to go. "Please don't tell anyone."

"I would never, but I would eventually like an explanation."

"Deal. Later tonight?"

Enzo nodded. What was his expression? Was it regret? Sadness? Anger? She fled into the daytime town before a bigger threat materialized, being caught not in bed.

FOURTEEN

After she slipped through the guard towers during the day, which proved to be rather difficult hence their names; she had to crawl through the garden and wait for the ground patrols to pass before climbing up onto her balcony.

Freyja was inside her room and yanked her in, pointing to the door as Madame banged on it. "Princess. Every woman gets their moon cycle and can work just as hard. Now hurry it up or I will get someone to bust down this door. Where are you, servant girl?"

"Handmaiden," Freyja whispered under her breath as she shoved Belyx in the washroom. "Princess. You need to move. I bought you some time telling her it was your moon cycle, which was close to the day anyway, but Madame is not patient. You're lucky I discovered you gone first. I am late for my duties." Some timing Belyx had.

Belyx rushed out of her clothes and changed into something more princess-like while trying to straighten away her flat wig hair. Freyja marched over and proved her worth as a handmaiden, practically ripping her hair off with a comb. Freyja worked her magic on her, enjoying Belyx's pain. "Updo front will have to do."

"Thanks Freyja." Belyx's head stung.

She cracked a slight smile. "Tell me about it later, but you have a ball to get ready for tonight." A sinking pit hit Belyx's stomach. The damn ball. That was just what she needed. The Cabarets sounded nicer and nicer by the minute. Waving Freyja away, Belyx opened the door.

Madame charged in like a bull. "My my. A princess never sleeps past the sun." She judged her up and down. "You look horrendous. What kind of handmaiden did they give you? I will inform your father of her insolence."

Freyja coughed in the bathroom to announce her presence. (like it would make a difference) and Belyx twirled her hair in her fingers. "Apologies. My moon cycle seemed to get me today. I'm sure you know the feeling." Madame had most likely not had a cycle in years.

Madame frowned and pulled Belyx by her arm and she winced as it was still sore from her night. "The ball is relatively ready, but we have some last-minute concerns to handle. I expected you to be well rested, but it seems you will have to do your best."

"Yes, Madame." Belyx kissed any chance of sleep goodbye. For the rest of the morning and afternoon, they spent the time running around, checking on the requirements for the ball.

Cook had prepared a whole platter of Majerian foods. Belyx's stomach wrenched at the sight of the seafood. Things swimming in the dirty water should never be consumed. Although they were set out like a work of art. The dead fish almost looked happy to be eaten.

Inka and Onka bowed as Belyx walked by, finishing the light touches on the artistic decorations. She shot them an awkward smile for what they had to do, but it was immaculate none the less. This needed to go well.

The flowers were left arranged attractively on the tables, and Belyx had to dust them off and straighten others. The blue lilies they imported would impress their rival kingdom. Belyx brushed off her hands and headed back to her room for a much earned reprieve, but Madame found her first. "What happened with the entertainment?"

Belyx almost slapped her head. They had to come set up and do a sound check before the ball. At this rate, they would be late and the ball would not have music in the beginning. "I will send a messenger to them right away." Maybe they would be faster?

"You better. A lady never forgets a task, no matter how small."

Belyx's eyes were too tired to roll.

Once she sent the messenger, telling him to hasten, she crept into her bed-chamber and passed out before her head hit the pillow.

"Princess!" A blurry vision of Freyja stood above her. Belyx groaned as she pulled herself up. She had one of those dreamless sleeps she wished she had more, disturbed as Freyja shucked multiple gowns to the bed. "We need to get ready. The ball begins in a couple of hours. Majeria arrived early, and you missed welcoming them. Madame was not thrilled."

Belyx stretched. "Yeah, what is new?" Everything was going wrong already, but if she didn't have this rest, someone would have been murdered. They should thank her. Freyja pushed Belyx to the washroom, where a bath was prepared, with tea tree leaves and rose petals floating inside. It had been a while since she had been pampered. The dirt and grime were difficult to scrub off her body, but soon her skin was silky smooth.

Freyja helped her out and began fixing her hair. "So, mind telling me why the mission went late last night?" Belyx's eyes watered as Freyja pulled Belyx's locks into a tight braid.

"The Cabaret's captured us. I was under their weird spell or drug most of the night."

Freyja's eyes enlarged. "You are lucky to be alive. They aren't the scariest in theory, but those parties can be lethal. People never return. How did you escape?"

"Enzo, I mean the thief saved us." She tried to stifle her blush, but her fair skin hid nothing.

"Oh no. I know that look."

Belyx swallowed a lump. "I do not have a look. We are just working together." Barely.

"In my experience, working together can lead to complicated feelings."

Freyja was a fool who spoke nonsense! "He is just a common thief. Nothing is special about him. A princess could never date such a person."

"But an assassin could." Belyx didn't respond as Freyja finished her styling. It was refreshing to see her hair back to normal again. The burgundy lock fell like perfect snowflakes. "Ok, now the face. Let's start with those bags under your eyes."

Belyx swatted Freyja's arm, and they laughed. She missed regular princess duties and the occasional nightly outing, but Doneque was creeping closer and closer to her royal life, and she needed to stanch it down again. "I'm worried Freyja."

Freyja applied some deep coal to her eyes, making the hazel color pop. "Afraid of what?"

"The kingdom. Everything. I don't know what to do. It is falling on my shoulders."

Freyja took a breath and pulled away, checking for blemishes. "It can be hard, especially with what we are facing out there, but you have to remember, you are not alone. The Order is here to help you. Always."

Belyx kept the thought of Enzo knowing about her down. Nothing would stop him from bringing down the whole Order if he pleased. He wouldn't, Belyx. He wouldn't. A tinge of guilt struck her. How dare she say she was alone when she had many helpful people right here? "You're right. I was just being paranoid, as usual."

Freyja leaned in and applied some blush. "I usually am. Now stop moving your face so we can finish. Then, get you into a dress suited for a princess."

Belyx tilted back and closed her eyes. She had what she needed to do well at this ball and win aid from Majeria. Once the party and the key were taken care of, nothing would stand in the way of her saving Aikradal.

Belyx adjusted her shoe before entering the Great Hall. The party had begun and she found it trouble to breathe. Earn the aid. Be nice.

The king and queen of Majeria couldn't make the trip, and of course, they sent their prodigy of a daughter and detested rival of Belyx, Princess Vivienne Rochenda. As Doneque, her battles were straight forward, kill and slip away. Here would be a battle of wits and batting eyelashes; The style of fighting she loathed. She took one more calculated breath and smoothed her shimmering long blue gown. A lighter cerulean sash with a material popping in the light wrapped around her waist. Majeria's colors were as matched as possible for the remarkable occasion.

Belyx entered the room and thanked the guards. The ballroom bustled with a multitude of people. Nobles and servants from Majeria and Aikradal alike milled about. Her father's advisors sniggered and cooed with Majeria's, talking about strategy no less. They were dressed in traditional Majerian garbs. Instead of the silks and chiffons Aikradal wore, they had dyed cotton that didn't stick due to the humidity. If they tried to wear leathers or silk, it would bunch up. She had discussions with doing international lines, but Madame found it killed their culture to branch out.

A rapid symphony came from the band. They arrived early thankfully, and the guests had music. The crisis was averted was for now. The partygoers danced the traditional jig Belyx had forgotten. It had twists and turns and jumps. She longed to join, but the hosts seldom participated. Work had to be done.

Cook's food table was spread with a variety of seafood dishes ranging from stuffed salmon to blackened shrimp, and it was flying off the trays faster than Cook and the other "servants" placed it. Belyx took a bite of a slimy clam and curled her tongue. Although, thanks to Cook's skills, it slid down her throat with ease.

The pillars bore the sigil of Majeria, the fish, to honor Aikradal's esteemed guests. That should jostle favor to receive their assistance. With their support, Belyx could focus on the key and who stole it. The less she had to do, the better. No thinking about the blasted key tonight. She had a goal to accomplish.

Belyx turned around and tried to retreat, but it was too late. Lady Lim and Maria came right for her, dressed in Majerian colors as well, although Lim combined the colors of both kingdoms. Who knew she was creative? But should purple and blue ever be mixed? "I say, this party is bigger than a storm in the field." Lim sipped from her almost empty drink flute.

"Slow down, dear. Wouldn't want Lord Kirk to drag you back to your room... Again," Lady Maria smiled as she nibbled on a pastry.

Belyx couldn't contain the knot in her stomach, and they weren't helping. "If you'll excuse me, I have to talk to more guests."

"Kiss ass away!" Lim went to fraternize or scare other Majerians while Maria followed, trying to keep her in tow.

She circled the ballroom and bowed at her guests, holding her breath for her encounter with Princess Perfect. Her father came into view and was actually smiling. That grin hadn't been seen in years, but it was only a mask for his kingdom.

Belyx stopped and readjusted her hairstyle. It had to look exact, for her father was conversing with none other than Princess Vivienne. She tittered like a chatting bird as she flicked one of her three golden braids back. Her dress was immaculate, with shimmering teals and blues interweaving like a suspenseful battle. Suddenly, Belyx's own gown dimmed in comparison. The King caught her eye and motioned her over. Putting on the fakest of her smiles, she strode over; let the war begin.

"My beautiful daughter." That was new. Her father was capable of turning on the flatter like a courtier. "You remember Princess Vivienne from Majeria? It has been awhile, right?" More like two years when she "accidentally" ripped

Belyx's dress and "spilled" punch on her, while making it like it was Belyx's fault. She totally forgot about it.

Princess Vivienne bowed to Belyx, but kept her eyes wide open, moving to embrace her. She searched for a heartbeat, and sure enough, she was still human... barely. "Princess Belyx. What an honor it is. You look so grown up from two years ago and I cherish your dress. It is... comfortable."

Her father bowed his head as he gave Belyx a quick "behave" stare and headed off to another group of Majerians to smooth them over. Vivienne waved away like he was going to war and pivoted back, shooting her a blinding smile. "Delightful party. It is nice to see some effort around here. I liked how the children helped you decorate. It is so... quaint."

Belyx's nails dug into her palm. "Only the best for our guests, princess."

Vivienne cooed. "I have to say, that cook of yours knows how to assemble an array of palatable food. I almost didn't have to spit it out, but that is how I stay thin... you should try my methods sometime." Her leafy eyes fluttered, displaying her sharp as knives cheekbones. Belyx wanted to hug her stomach after the chide, but she didn't need to be a lifeless twig. Her own confidence was enough. "Are you even synched? What modern bravado you have?"

The way she said modern was not a compliment. Her mother made synching optional for the court ladies, claiming natural bodies shouldn't be buried. Belyx always felt comfortable in her skin, but around Vivienne, she was an imposter in her own home. "Well, I have nothing to hide here. Usually, common criminals partake in that," Belyx replied with a smile.

"A princess always does everything for appearances." Ok, Madame. "I guess you do things differently here." Vivienne grabbed a glass of wine from Inka, who scowled when she turned around. The Majerian princess took a sip, grimaced like it was vinegar, and set it down. "Anyway, we know why you've invited us here. It seems you have a little uprising problem. Sad, your mother could always handle that sort of thing."

Belyx gritted her teeth. "My father is doing a fine job. It is overwhelming at the moment." Defend and deflect.

Vivienne laughed as if the fate of their kingdom was a comedy play. "Oh, Belyx, you can't actually be serious. Your father looks like he hasn't seen sleep in years and the way he tries to act like everything is fine, so tragic."

Belyx stepped closer to Vivienne. Doneque would wrap her head around a pillar, but a princess's weapons were her eyes. Madame Jewella's advice cringed in her head. "He has a lot to deal with, but we are doing fine. The gangs are getting weaker."

"Oh?" Her eyebrows rose. "It didn't look that way on the way in. The streets were so atrocious, I had to burn my travel dress. I should make you reimburse me for it, but it appears money is tight right now."

"We are fine." Belyx had little self-control left in her.

Vivienne muttered a profanity and bit on a salmon skewer, making a face like she just ate vomit and tossed it on the floor. "You are drowning, Princess. Soon the tide will be so high, you won't be able to swim out and guess who will swim past you?"

Belyx tired of the sea metaphors. "Really original, but I swim fine." Care for a race?

"I can tell." Vivienne eyed her up and down. "Try to get some sleep. We can see it in your eyes." She did a quick scan around the room. "I would work on my party planning as well. This is adorable, but it was a stretch to call this event a ball." Vivienne retreated before Belyx could retort, most likely to people more important.

Belyx spotted a knife nearby. One throw and her perfect posed body would fall like the rest beneath her. Huffing, Belyx downed her drink, receiving an odd glance from one of the Majerian guests. Was he a noble? No. He was Belyx's age, perhaps younger.

"May I help you?" Why couldn't she be as carefree as in the Cabaret party?

"She is mean to me, too." Weird confession right now. Upon closer inspection, he looked similar to Princess Vivienne, with the same striking blonde hair and angular face bones.

"Yeah, well, I am sure the extravagance of your kingdom makes up for that." The alcohol was loosening her tongue. "I wasn't aware she had a brother."

"Cousin." She would almost think him handsome, had he not been related to that witch.

"How unfortunate."

He stepped closer. If he tried anything, he would lose a hand. "You need to help us," he whispered.

Help them? They had to this ball so they would aid Aikradal. "What do you mean?"

He shifted as Vivienne glared at him and retreated.

Belyx rolled her eyes. One of their fancy ships must have sunk or something. She downed another drink, the alcohol lightened her head, and she planned to socialize some more. The Majerian nobles were receptive to reasoning for aid. They better convince Princess Fire-breather to help.

Her father calmed the music and stepped up to the stage. "Welcome, honored guests!" His voice boomed like a ruler. It was still there. "I would like to make a toast to our ally kingdom, the renowned Majeria!" Everyone clapped. Even Belyx had to play a part in the facade. "And I would like to thank the radiant Princess Vivienne for coming all this way on behalf of her parents, the king and queen. It takes great responsibility to accomplish such a task and we pray you are feeling celebrated enough for your efforts!" Vivienne's smile grew like a mold as she waved, no doubt choking down the wine. "Please accept this gift from Aikradal to you. Bring it in!" Belyx jutted her head toward the opening of the door.

This idea of hers would seal the deal. A few of the guards heaved it in. The metal and gears sang like a battle cry. Not many kingdoms had them, and this would aid Majeria for years to come. "This is our newest model of ballista and our best protection weapon. Take it as a token of our bond."

Princess Vivienne approached the stage, and the applause grew. "Thank you, King Terach, for your hospitality tonight. We in Majeria honor the bond we share and hope The God provides virtue to our kingdoms." She bowed to her father, and he kissed her hand.

"Enjoy the rest of the evening," her father said, coming down and gesturing the music to resume.

Belyx loathed the way Vivienne fake accepted a gift. Belyx had to swing a couple of deals to get it ready and Vivienne would likely throw it in the river.

The comforting face of her grandmother beamed, munching on a shrimp. Belyx bowed. "What an event, huh?"

Her grandmother set down her shrimp. She was wearing a chiffon blue gown, the bottom spinning down to the floor. "It truly is. You organized it thorough-ly."

"Do you think it will be enough to get help?" The hitch in her voice gave away her genuine fear.

"Only the meeting after will tell. Are you working tonight too?"

"Yes," she whispered. "We found the location of the thing."

Her grandmother scoped the room. "Be careful. This is growing into some-thing treacherous."

"Don't worry, grandmother. I will preserve this kingdom."

Her grandmother rubbed her cheek. "It is not an effortless task, flower. I pray it works out."

"It will." It had to.

"Now, Go enjoy the party. I think I will retire. Old bones and all." She winked.

Belyx bowed, and her grandmother dipped away, wishing Freyja were here, but she patrolled around the outside with the Stems, stopping any threats that would dare ruin the soon to be alliance.

Her father approached her, wearing a hopeful look. "Belyx. Princess Vivienne and her advisors are ready to discuss terms."

"Already?" It was almost too fast. Maybe Vivienne grew a heart after all.

"Yes, now move. We need all the charm we can muster." His voice lifted. It was a side she hadn't seen of her father in awhile.

They greeted each other in the room next to the Great Hall. Advisors Kirk and Jaques were waiting with Vivienne and her two council members. Belyx bowed, and the king stood in the front. Vivienne met eyes with her advisors and they nodded. "We have our terms for the aid." Did they just agree?

"We will do anything," her father replied. Belyx's palms sweat. Majeria's first advisor stepped up. He was a scraggly man with wispy gray hair and a sunken face. "We agreed if Majeria sends our troops to irradiate your gang problem, you will abdicate all power to Majeria. Which includes taxes and our laws. You may keep your name, but you are officially owned by us." What? Wasn't being in charge of weapon production enough?

Her father would never consent to such terms, but her father's face stilled. "I accept." Lord Kirk and Jaques whispered in his ear, as if telling him to consider it, but he waved them off, fuming. This was the end. Who knew something worse than the gangs invading. She would never bow to them.

Belyx couldn't control herself any longer. "We are a powerful kingdom. Our citizens would never stand for such actions. We demand better terms. Weren't our weapons enough?"

Vivienne scoffed and her advisors stood in silence like she was the queen and not a princess. "You clearly don't see the level of threat your kingdom is in. We are the ones risking our lives. The gangs could go after us next. We need to make sure your kingdom understands this and can pay us back. Also, your production isn't great. We get our supplies for cheaper and have no use for yours." How did they swing that?

Belyx stormed over, ignoring her father's glare. "True allies don't make others abdicate for them. We refuse to be ruled by you." Her tone wavered. There had never been a war between kingdoms, but this could be the start.

Vivienne darted her eyes to the king. "Well, good thing you don't make the decisions around here."

Her father huffed. "Princess Belyx. You are acting like a spoiled child." Vivienne smirked slightly and Belyx tightened her fists. "Leave this meeting. I will talk to you later." Little would stop her from murdering the Majerian bitch and her advisors.

Only her father would. "Father, we can't do this. By The God, we are going against what we stand for!"

The King slammed his fist on the table and Belyx shuddered. "I am King Terach to you right now and you have no say. You do nothing for our kingdom. You can barely fulfill your princess duties, and you are always distracted by your selfish endeavors. It is you who doesn't care." He stuck a finger in her face and that was it. They shattered her like a glass, and tears welled in her eyes. She couldn't even look at Vivienne, who relished every second of this. She dropped her head down. Maybe he was right. She was a failure. If only she could tell him about the Order and what she had done and what she planned to do, but that would ruin everything.

She sucked in a breath. "Fine. I'll go—"

A scream shot from the ballroom, and the music ceased. Belyx and the others rushed over. What had happened? When they entered, the guests circled around something. The king and Belyx pushed through to find the still body of a Majerian guest. The one who spoke with Belyx earlier, Vivienne's cousin. He was too young. His eyes were bloodshot and lifeless. His body was as still as ice.

Vivienne shot out a piercing hollar and knocked Belyx over to him. "Who did this?" she yelled. "How could you let this happen?" Her finger went right through Belyx. It was poison that killed him. The signs were obvious. "My cousin! Who is responsible?" Vivienne cried, almost rehearsed, but Belyx had no time to look as the guards crossed through.

"A note," Thomas declared. "It's from The four gangs threatening any of the Majerians who help Aikradal." When did the gangs ever work together?

Princess Vivienne sank to the ground, hands shaking. "Deal is off. We will no longer be aiding your kingdom. You couldn't even keep my people secure at this ludicrous party. My mother and father will hear of this." Her father stayed back, surrounded by his guards.

How had Freyja missed this? More importantly, how could Belyx let this happen?

The guests cleared out after a questioning by the guards. Belyx listened in, but found none to be suspicious. The gangs had never killed on the grounds before. How could they have succeeded now? Especially with Aikradal and Majerian guards working double time. Her mind went to a betrayal, but she wouldn't dare open that can.

After they left, The Majerians headed home despite being offered a night in the palace. Princess Vivienne spouted it was unsafe. Her work was wasted.

In her room, Freyja entered in a frenzy. Tear marks stained her painted face. Belyx went to comfort her friend, but she held up a hand. "Don't, my lady."

"Cut the act. What happened? Are you ok?" Belyx's hands still shook.

"I failed my job again. If it were you and the king, I would jump off this balcony."

"Don't say things like that. You are the best protector."

"Don't patronize me, Belyx!" Belyx blinked rapidly, taken aback by her handmaiden's anger. "It could have been you. I checked everyone there. There was no gang activity."

Belyx found it strange at the opportunity to kill her father or her and yet they chose a lowly cousin of Vivienne. "It was almost too perfect."

"What, like it was staged?"

"I do not know, but I know Majeria almost had us joining their kingdom in exchange for protection, and I don't see why Majeria would stage something to ruin it."

Freyja tilted her head. "You think Princess Vivienne would slay her own cousin? I know you hate her, but even that is a stretch."

"You're right. I don't know. How did the gangs work together?"

She turned and pinched her nose. "It makes no sense. I've studied these gangs for years and they would never attack together."

"I feel the same way, but desperation makes us do unnatural things. What have Inka and Onka said? Aren't they in charge of monitoring the gangs?"

Freyja shook her head. "I already asked them. They said there was no sign." She went to walk out the door. "I need to investigate more. I won't sleep until I find out how they squirmed in."

Belyx knew her headstrong friend would never still. "Do you need help?"

Freyja gave a slight smile. "You have your own mission tonight."

"I could cancel."

"We all have our duties, Princess. This one is mine."

Belyx acknowledged her protector as she left the room and changed out of her ballroom clothes. Night had struck, and she trusted Freyja and the other members to handle this. Right now, she had other priorities and with Majeria out of the equation, destroying the key was the only way to save her kingdom.

Fifteen

"The gang infiltrated the ball and poisoned some random from Majeria?" Enzo sat on his perch, snacking on some hard meat.

"Well, he wasn't a random," Belyx said. "He was Princess Vivienne's cousin."

Enzo brushed off his hands. The bright moonlight glow emphasized his clear skin as he wore a tighter shirt, showing off his slim physique. "It just seems peculiar for the gangs to do something teamwork like. Majeria's help would make it harder for them though, so maybe?"

"That's the thing too. Princess Vivienne didn't seem to care about retribution for his death. She wanted to leave, but if my cousin was killed, I would want blood." Although Belyx was dressed as Doneque, it was a foreign feeling for someone outside The Order knowing who she was. The vulnerable string tugged at the back of her mind. Would Enzo betray her? A desperate person would make a thick coin for such information. She wasn't arrested yet, she was safe for now.

"Why do you come out at night killing vile people for the kingdom? Does anyone else know?" She dreaded the question. Belyx would never reveal The Order, but she had to dance around the truth. "I was trained by my grandmother who did the same thing as princess and it has passed on since her mother."

Enzo scrunched his eyebrows. "That is kind of weird. How did this start?" Stop asking questions!

Belyx sighed. This would prove difficult. "Her mother hated seeing Aikradal in chaos and fixed it herself. She received training from this Majerian man who knew combat and such."

"What about the poisons and snakes?"

"That too."

"What's his name?"

Belyx threw her hands up. "One thing at a time. We only just met. What about you? What made you become what you are?"

Enzo rubbed his palms together. "Well, my family was stolen from me in a raid thirteen years ago."

"Wait." Belyx counted his age in her head. "You were on the streets at five?"

Enzo cringed and blinked rapidly. "Sure was. Ren took me in and cared for me. They showed me the art of the con, but then they were caught by The Berserkers and... you know, the rest."

Belyx grabbed his hand, and a singe of heat crept to her face again. Like in The Cabaret party. "Losing that many people in your life must make it hard to trust others."

He arched a brow. "You think? Now you know why I didn't just trust the mysterious hooded female coming to my aid. A Whisper I might add." Almost smiling herself, Belyx hit him and his expression changed. "Did the fae really kill your mother?"

Belyx chewed her lip. Of course, these questions have always crossed her mind. "That's what my father told me. It is strange because they had always been a peaceful society, but I guess it was an act. I'm glad my father did what he did. They were dangerous." Although it remained unclear how her father bested the threatening creatures, Belyx didn't need an answer.

Enzo clenched his fists and relaxed them, staring at Belyx. "Me too." They stayed silent for a while, blinking at the empty streets. Enzo's story spoke to Belyx. Flashes of an innocent five-year-old boy crying in the thralls and saved by some thief went through her head. How did he survive at such a young age and how did he survive the Berserkers over his mentor? She was tempted to ask more, but he was distraught about it and she let it go.

"Alright," Belyx said, standing. "Let's get into this vault. Have you identified the house?"

Enzo shot another incredulous look. "Who do you think you're talking to? Of course. It's a large white one north of the housing district. Very fancy and many, many guards."

"Do you think the leader lives there?"

Enzo shook his head. "I think it is presented as worker's housing."

"With that many guards?" Enzo shrugged. "How did my father miss it?"

Enzo put a hand on her shoulder, which she didn't swat away. "He is going through a lot. I can't imagine being king right now."

"It is my vision to rule Aikradal, but we need to make sure there is one to rule." Talking to Enzo came as natural as venoms and her poems. It was familiar. Belyx couldn't understand how a person could frustrate and flatter her at the same time.

Enzo led her to the perimeter of the house. He wasn't lying about the plethora of guards surrounding it like a compound. The metal gate expanded ten feet in the air, with a guard monitoring carriages passing through. This was no mansion, but a mini palace.

"How do we get in there?"

"Have no faith?" Enzo half smiled again, bringing color to Belyx's cheeks. "The guards change at random times, but the south entrance by the rock garden is pretty accessible. We have to scale the wall."

Belyx could handle it, no problem. "Sounds easy enough. Do we know where the vault is?"

Enzo wrinkled his forehead. "I checked schematics for the homes at the library and there are ten rooms total." Belyx wished she had seen it. The location of a safe would be pivotal to design and logic. Thanks Princess lessons.

"How are the rooms laid out?"

Enzo shrugged? "Why does it matter?"

"They would put the vault in a location that is safest and some rooms are more secure than others." She rolled her eyes like it was obvious.

"I was gonna ask how you knew, but then I remembered... princess... anyway, the layout is two stories with three rooms on the bottom floor and seven on the top."

Belyx cursed. The vault would be upstairs and she hoped for fewer options. "How are the seven rooms spread out?"

"Two in front and five in back, with the five in back divided by lavatories. The leader would know a thief would try the back, so it had to be in one of the five in front."

Belyx buzzed at his smart answer. He continued to prove himself. "Right, it will most likely be a study and hidden by, or under, something."

"Well, sounds like we each check each front room and go from there."

Belyx pinched her nose. "Easier said. I have a bad feeling once we get in, there will be too many guards."

"Then what do you propose?" His mockery radiated like his idea wasn't good enough.

A guard marched along the edge of the gate and waved off someone getting in a carriage with a promising individual, Chancy Markwater, the bookkeeper for the Goldfingers. She recognized him from his tall lanky form and brown side part. He also had a finger size mustache above his tiny lips.

The driver whipped the horses, and Belyx beamed, turning to Enzo. "I have the perfect idea."

Sixteen

This wasn't the first time Belyx stared down the barrel of a pistol.

Although six seemed a little excessive.

The bookkeeper, Chancy, sneered as his goons surrounded them. The warehouse was filled with illegal products spacious enough no one would find out if two people were gunned down. "Nice plan," Enzo whispered to her, and she shot him daggers in return. How was she supposed to predict the carriage led to an enormous storage quarters loaded with Goldfingers? She had faced these pretentious fools before and she would do it again, using Enzo's tactics this time.

"You know. I have more coin than you think. I'm sure we can work something out?"

Chancy pursed his mustached lip. "Oh, give it a break, worm. We have more money than the palace. Your contribution would be nothing more than a drop in the sea." He stuck his wrinkled finger at them. "Shoot the peasants." The "peasants" comment was sort of rude. Leave it to a group of entitled thugs to make a princess feel destitute.

The men cocked their pistols and Enzo seized her hand, heavy with sweat. She refused to die here. In one swift motion, she released a smoke bomb and a thick cloud of mist enveloped them.

Gunfire sounded, leaving Belyx and Enzo to find cover. Now was her chance. Rolling from the vapor, she subdued a nearby Goldfinger. His body plummeted with a grunt. Another coughed like a pompous weakling, and she disarmed his firearm and cracked his skull with it.

Chancy hustled the other way, fleeing the fight. Belyx picked up her steps after him. He turned, pistol aimed straight for her and fired, but she evaded it, cursing as she tripped into some fruit boxes. The cold juices trickled over her face and clothing. The berry scent would never wash out.

More gunshots exploded as Enzo bobbed and weaved around the other goons, knifing them in return. He observed Belyx's style well. She wiggled her way out of the mush and caught sight of Chancy barreling into a carriage, their only source of information about to escape. A prayer comforted her as she aimed her blade for the reins, trying not to hit the horses this time. Her knife sang true, and sliced the ropes, leaving the stallions unscathed. Chancy pointed his weapon out the carriage and sent a barrage of bullets her way, but Belyx bolted behind a bannister, the wood splintering from the shots. Unsheathing another blade, Belyx waited for his gunfire to cease. It took ten seconds to reload the pistols.

Her mind calmed as she counted. As soon as he stuck the pistol out of the window to fire, her knife sailed and knocked it out of his hand and Belyx dashed for carriage, praying he didn't have a backup weapon.

Chancy opened the door, but Belyx kicked the door closed, slamming him back inside. The driver swung a cane down, but Belyx moved to the side and pulled the driver down with it. He slammed into the ground and Belyx delivered a knee to his face.

She yanked open the door and brought a knife to Chancy's throat. He held his hands up and shivered like a puppy in the ocean. "Please. I'll tell you any-thing, just don't hurt me!"

"Don't worry, I won't be long." This would be easier than Belyx thought.

He sang like a canary. "The key is in a vault in the study. The code is a latch combination." He motioned the design. It was a triangle with three slashes through it.

Belyx dragged him closer, smelling his alcohol sweat. "Thanks for the coop-eration in all this. If you're lying, I will take off your hand. Good luck counting the extorted money without it."

Chancy gulped. "I don't even know why you or Leader Caprash IV cares about some antique key. He said it was a family heirloom, The God."

"How did he get it? It belonged to the palace," she asked, careful not to reveal too much.

"How do you think? Our influence stretches through the pathetic royals."

This confirms a traitor, but who? It is Kirk, most likely.

"Who?"

Chancy refused to answer and Belyx knocked him out, binding his hands and feet. She left the carriage to Enzo, charging in, huffing like a messenger. "You get the information?"

"He spilled everything. Although Caprash told him the key was a family heirloom and someone from the palace stole it for him. Does that make any sense?"

Enzo shook his head, still winded from the fight. He took out four of them on his own. Such a wonderful influence on him she was.

Belyx rolled the guards over. "We will put on their uniforms. We can load the other carriage with these shipments and they will let us in the front door."

They changed into the uniforms. Belyx grimaced as it sagged on her, but he was the smallest Goldfinger there. She tied the loose fabric with a belt in hopes of it not falling off her, especially in front of Enzo.

He, on the other hand, looked ravishing in his stolen uniform, like it was made for him. The silk lapel hugged his muscles and the fit outlined other exceptional assets of his. This was the most dressed she had seen him. "What?" He must have noticed her staring.

She turned away, rubbing her arm. "Nothing. You just look, ummm..."

"Sexy? Dashing?" He cracked a smile.

"I wouldn't say that." Was she blushing? "Anyway, let's hurry. I can't risk coming in late again."

They sat on the carriage and launched the fixed reins. Who knew Belyx's sewing would ever come in handy out here? As they entered the dark streets of

Aikradal, it would have been romantic if not for the disguises and the carrying of smuggled goods. Everything was in those boxes. Ranging from produce to weapons. What surprised Belyx the most was the Majerian glass and fish. Did the Goldfinger's deals stretch to Majeria? Did they know? It would be ironic if the gangs infested them next.

The storm clouds gathered the sky like an important meeting was taking place. "You have a parasol?" Enzo asked. "I'd hate for such a fancy lady to get her toes wet."

Belyx fake laughed as she rubbed one of her knives. "I always liked the rain here."

"Try sleeping in it. Not fun."

Forgetting once again that Enzo lived in these streets, Belyx looked down. "I'm sorry you didn't have a true home."

He waved her off. "Home isn't a place. It's more like a mindset. Home was always where I felt the most comfortable, whether it be in an inn or an alley. As long as I stayed true to myself, I was happy...and also with a good book."

Belyx admired his attitude. Here she was complaining of her double lives of luxury when other citizens barely had one life. Enzo and many people of Aikradal deserved better. "Did you know other people who lived on the streets?" Was it ok to ask?

He clenched the reins. "Lots of great ones. Most never make it because of crime, hunger, or..."

"Or what?"

"It's nothing."

"Clearly it isn't." She locked eyes with him, refusing his answer.

He blew the loose strands of hair from his face, as if what we would say would be worse than what she already knew. "Guard violence." *Ok, that was.*

Belyx's cheeks reddened. Had her soldiers hurt people living on the street? "I had no idea they did such things. I always assumed they wanted to help the people." Of course they didn't. Everyone had a price. A motto she would continue to remember and one that would always be a threat to her kingdom.

"It wasn't all the time, but sometimes the guards had rules or urges and they would take it out on people like me." Why was he making light of such a grotesque thing? How could something bad be happening under her father's rule? The king was a kind man who made sure everyone was protected. *He didn't know this. Lord Kirk hid it most likely.*

"I hope I can put in a word and change that." Her throat dried. Was it her place to say?

"Thanks, Bel—I mean Doneque." She almost told him to call her Belyx, but he was right. This was separate from the palace. They were two different people. Belyx was prim and poised, whereas Doneque stalked the night and killed to protect her kingdom. Which one wanted to hold Enzo's hand, however?

Relinquishing control, she ignored her inhibitions and put her hand on Enzo's. He didn't pull away, glancing at her. "This is nice."

"Do you have to comment on everything?"

"Sorry, it's ingrained in my personality." He was silent for a bit. They were almost there, but a small fraction of Belyx longed for five more minutes. *Go slower, horses!* Enzo did a weird coughing thing with his throat, then he surprised Belyx. "After we get the key and such. If we live, of course." His rambling was like a buffoon now. "Would you want to, umm, I don't know, do something more fun?"

"More fun than infiltrating gangs and almost dying? I don't know if it exists." She possessed sarcasm too and let herself smile in front of him. His cheeks reddened, which was hard to see under the night sky. The oh-so-confident thief was nervous.

He choked up a laugh. "Well, I mean you can't beat certain death, but no. Like something else less deadly?"

Belyx's brain was on red alert. Was he asking her out? Like in the plays and the bad novels he read? This would crash land. A princess and a thief didn't go on dates. She stuck to pleasing the kingdom, and he lifted items. It was the way the world should be. Everyone had a place, and they needed to stay there.

Her mind trailed in its own world as she let him sit too long on this. Would he change his mind? Doneque certainly could have some fun with a peddler. Fun never hurt and oh, how she missed fun…Less life-threatening fun. "Sure." One syllable sealed her fate, but now was the time to focus.

The mansion's illustrious gates came into view and the key was locked inside. The guards at the gate waved them through with barely a thought. Fools. Some security they had. Maybe they should have just snuck in.

They were attended by other Goldfingers who unloaded the crates and organized them in rows, most likely to be taken out again to sell. One taller woman with a scroll shot them a frightening look. "Where are the tomatas?" Her accent made the o sound like an a. Her painted eyelashes towered over her lilac eyes as she blinked at them in rapid succession. "And also, where's Chancy? He was suppose to be with yous."

Enzo leapt down to her level and extended his winning charm like a blade. "He had to stop and take care of something for Leader Caprash IV. He wouldn't say." Even Enzo created his own accent similar to hers and it took everything in Belyx not to stare openmouthed.

The lady blinked more and Belyx went into her character. "Also, the tomatoes had a minor mishap. Can't trust anyone anymore, am I right?"

The woman hardly acknowledged her as she kept her feline focus on Enzo, which Belyx envied. Was her performance that bad?

"Majerians always sending us bad stuffs." She sighed as Belyx attempted not to curse. It was Majeria smuggling things this whole time? No wonder they didn't care about the weapon production! This needed to be reported to her father straight away. To think they almost became a part of them! Although, how would Belyx inform him?

The lady analyzed the products and scribbled in her scroll. "Report to Leader Caprash IV, the both of yous. I ain't got no time to babysit incompetence." She leaned into Enzo, too close for Belyx's comfort. "It sometimes helps to blame Majeria or the partners on the job." Belyx admired her brazen attitude since she was standing right there. Her self-control wavered. *Stay in character.* The lady sent them away like they were children and Belyx tightened her fists, but Enzo grabbed her hand as they went through the wide double doors.

Belyx swore to herself as the immaculate entryway led to a stream of fancy ornaments marking the foyer. Golden statues of animals gawked out at them with vases filled to the brim with various flowers. The silk tapestries and curtains put the Aikradal palace to shame. Were all the gangs knowledgable interior decorators?

Another tiny lady behind a desk, wearing small glasses, greeted them as they walked by. She chomped her tobacco like a cow. "What can I do you for?" Her accent was similar to the other lady's. Where did they learn such dialects?

Enzo leaned forward, eliciting no response from the secretary as if she wasn't wooed by his charm. "We were instructed to see Leader Caprash IV straight away."

She sucked her tobacco and rolled her eyes, fingering through a group of scrolls with various times scrawled on them. "Phoebe is gonna get me beheaded one day, I swears. She always does this when he is in his study, working. Like I make a whole master schedule and who follows it? Nobodys."

"Phoebe can be a real hard ass," Enzo replied, and the lady's previous mental shield fell as she blushed. Belyx felt a tightening in her stomach again. *Jealously was not fun!*

"I'll send you boths up, but please knock. Sometimes Mr. Caprash has mixed company, if you catch my breeze."

They both nodded, and the secretary eyed Belyx. "Red eyes. Where did you get those, sweetheart?"

Belyx blinked, unsure of what to say next. "Posha Apothecary south of housing. Great cosmetics." She gulped, praying the lady wouldn't pry further. *Why did I leave them in?*

"Alternative. I like it. Thanks doll." Belyx gave a close lip smile and followed Enzo as they ascended the marble staircase.

"Nice one," Enzo whispered.

"Shut up and focus, please." Belyx adjusted her loose uniform as more Goldfingers passed them. How many patrolled this fortress? Caprash was always a paranoid man.

Belyx and Enzo circled the upstairs until they found the adorned doors leading to the study. Before they even knocked, a well-dressed female came out, counting the coins in her velvet purse. She bestowed them a wink and trotted ahead.

The thought of what had just gone down made Belyx shudder. Caprash definitely wasn't doing his taxes with her...not that he did those anyways. Enzo rapped on the door twice before a husky voice told them to come in.

The dry aroma of alcohol and tobacco wafted in the air upon entering. Unfamiliar drug odors were present. As they stepped on the lavish alpaca rug, the leader of The Goldfingers sat behind a polished cedar desk adorned with golden statues. They were not fake either.

Leader Caprash was a sight. He wore an undershirt where his enormous arms poked out. She prayed he had on trousers underneath, especially after what just went down. It was surprising Caprash still had energy for those activities.

Caprash was the oldest of the leaders and his thinning grey comb over did not help his case. His age meant nothing, though, as he knew how to trick any system involving money. His power and influence caused many inflation problems in her kingdom.

"Business at this hour?" He scowled as he poured himself another drink. The amber liquid pooled softly at the top. "I prefer my visitors in the night to be like her, if you know what I mean?" The leader smirked at Enzo and Belyx fought the urge to heave. Caprash motioned for them to sit while Belyx scanned the room. Where was the safe?

Enzo shot right to the point, and Belyx thanked The God for his charm. "Phoebe said to report any dangerous cargo from Majeria and I can tell you the tomatas looked like corpses."

Caprash spat a smoky spittle into his trash and lit his cigar. The scent assaulted Belyx's nose as she tried not to recoil. "Those Majerian fuckers think they can outwit me? No thank you. I will fire all of them and hire new ones. It is simple." His dark eyes traced over to Belyx. "If you don't like someone, sweetheart, you just replace them like carriage wheels." He hacked a couple of laughs and flipped a coin at Enzo. She scrunched her eyes at the cheapness of the gesture. "Thanks for reporting this to me. If you see Chancy, tell him I must speak with him. Now, back to work! You only get a five-minute break, and I believe this counts since you were sitting." He chortled into his kerchief, now browned.

Belyx stood, trying to ignore his lingering gaze on her bodice. "Say," he said. "I don't have many females in shipping. What is your name, gorgeous?" Belyx needed a long, soapy bath just from his attention.

She used her smile as a shield. "Theodosia of Petrovkan, sir Scarsdale."

He pounded back his drink and wiped his dribbling chin. "Stick around if you'd like. I have plenty of coin." Enzo's eyes widened.

Belyx reddened at Enzo's shocked face. "I have an early morning, sir."

Caprash jostled the coins in his bag as if weighing his options and finally grinned, his teeth matching his brown desk. "Well, if you change your mind, I am here, darling." How many pet names could one throw in a meeting?

Belyx bowed. Did they even bow to each other? She left with Enzo, shivering in her uniformed boots. "He seemed like a well-respected guy," Enzo cooed, also trying not to retch.

"Real classy." Belyx tugged at her loose collar, waiting for when she could end this charade. Once they were in a quiet location, Belyx said, "There was no safe in there. Chancy must have been lying."

Enzo shot her an "I caught you" look. "Not observant, are you?"

Belyx snapped him a look? "I beg your pardon?"

"He had it under his desk." Enzo tapped his foot on the floor. "The finest place to hide anything. Rich people don't mess around."

A tingle of stupidity berated her for the miss. "Well, that is new."

Enzo shrugged. "Next time you are with your father, look under his desk. I bet there is something. They also hide things behind elaborate paintings like the Whispers. It is obvious and offensive to us thief rats." He wiggled his eyebrows at her and she ignored him.

"I'll pass, but anyway, how do we break into it?"

"Well, I was thinking wait until he goes to sleep and then—"

"Hey! No messin' about in the hall. Back to work!" A large dark-skinned man with a giant pistol in his holster hurled them a glare of death. These people really meant business. He must have been a manager.

"Sorry boss," Enzo replied and went to led Belyx away when the "boss" stopped them again.

"She can assist the kitchen. You are needed in unloading. We need all the muscle we can get, even if it is lacking." Belyx wanted to snort at his jab, relieved it was Enzo's turn to be prodded like her.

Enzo opened his mouth, but closed it as Belyx said, "Sure thing. Sorry, sir." Shooting Enzo a bolstering look, she headed for the kitchens. She had time to kill, anyway. Caprash's schedule said he went to bed in an hour. How hard would the kitchens be?

They were hard.

The room bustled with cooks and servants milling about. It almost resembled Aikradal, minus the safety of the Order and Cook's hilarious jokes. The head cook in there, Jacquelin, had a thick Petrovkan accent and barked orders like they were children. Belyx couldn't even introduce her fake self before someone was throwing dishes at her.

"The workers are done eating and we need these washed up for the morning," Jacquelin ordered, the black kohl under her eyes vibrating. She stood a foot shorter than Belyx and yet she was ten feet taller, waving a metal spoon around like she was going to beat someone with it. Belyx shook as the servers slammed the plates into the sink. The time and the pile of crusty dishes encroached upon her and Belyx needed to hurry.

Dishes were not something Belyx ever did, but she found them utterly relaxing. The way the warm water slipped between her fingers as the pungent scented soap crept into her nostrils. It gave her time to think and reflect. Belyx considered doing them more often. Madame Jewella would piss herself.

The harder stains required more work, and Belyx's arms wavered. *What in The God did they eat?* The leftover soggy food grazed her hand, and she gagged.

Ok, maybe she wouldn't do this back at the palace.

The clock struck eleven and Belyx wasn't even half finished. Jacquelin bid everyone a good night and glared at Belyx, threatening her life if the dishes weren't done by morning. Belyx gave her best smile and continued until she was alone. Forgetting she would not be there in the morning, she dried off her water logged hands and hustled past the foyer and up the stairs. As she reached the hall, a set of hands grabbed her. Without thinking, she jabbed the assailant in the throat.

She gasped as Enzo doubled over, sucking up air as quietly as possible. After a couple hacks, he sneered at Belyx. "Why did you do that?" Belyx put her fists on her hips. "Why would you just grab someone in enemy territory?"

He couldn't answer as footsteps pounded from the stairs. She helped Enzo to his feet and slipped behind a pillar. The Goldfinger guards exchanged playful banter as they paraded by. Belyx exhaled and realized how close she was to Enzo now. No space existed between their bodies, and hers heated. She couldn't help but marvel at his solid pedigree pressed against hers. His muscles brushed her under his thin frame. They traded a glance and Belyx fled the bannister without even checking if it was safe, forcing her cheeks to return to their natural color.

Enzo came out, kneading his neck. "If I bruise, you pay for my cosmetics." He winked.

Belyx motioned for him to follow. "Come on. Caprash is asleep by now and I am growing more and more anxious in this place." Belyx cursed as two guards stood outside the door, proof something important *was* inside. *Brilliant, Enzo.*

One guard was short and fat and the other had a beard older than Belyx. This would take some effort to break into. In the past, Belyx would have given them a dose of cobra venom and rushed in, but Enzo had a point when it came to subtlety.

"Your move," Belyx said.

Enzo flipped his hair in return. "Easy come, easy go." He trotted over to the men guarding the door, who paid him no mind. "Looks like it is that kind of night," Enzo said with his fake accent, making Belyx swoon slightly. "Me and my partner have come to relieve you. Take the night off. Buy a drink for me, eh?"

The fat guard eyed Enzo up and down like he was an animal being trained. "We were told and paid to stay here all night. Nice try. You are not swindling our promotion, kid." Belyx's heart stopped.

The bearded one spoke too. "You ain't getting a cut from this pay either, now you can run on home to daddy." Enzo's face tightened, but he retreated to Belyx.

She crossed her arms. "I thought this was a breeze for you."

"It's not my fault! These guys respond to gold, not words," Enzo whispered.

Belyx pulled her needle point from her person and coated it in venom. "Leave it to me then."

Enzo grabbed her arm. "This is dangerous. Maybe we can pay them?"

"These guys are making more than we have. It's time for my way." Belyx pushed forward, preparing her trick. She walked by, pretended she was clumsy and stuck the tall one. He would go down soon. Shorty snagged her wrist before she could get to him and shoved her away.

"What the?" His hand went for his pistol when Enzo tackled him to the ground, subduing him. The bearded one went to scream, but Belyx separated his throat, blood spraying the once lavish walls. Enzo glared at her as she went to open the door to find it locked.

"Check for a key," Belyx said.

Enzo fished the pockets of the guards, cursing to himself. "I knew this wouldn't work."

"My trick always works!" More footsteps thundered down the hall. Enzo jingled the keys in his hands and tossed them to Belyx, who creaked open the study door and dragged the bearded guard's body in while Enzo grabbed the fat one. She shut the door, only to hear muffled noises from the other side. They would see the blood soon.

Enzo pushed the desk over and lifted the rug off to find a hidden vault with a trace combination. Belyx hated and loved how right he was. She rushed and input the combo, praying Chancy was telling the truth or they would have a fight on their hands.

Sweat clung to her brow as she worked the complicated pattern. Whatever this was, Caprash put forth a lot of effort to keep it protected. A satisfying click came from the lock and she pulled it open, revealing a shimmering key about the size of her palm inside. She snatched it, marveling at its simplicity. It looked like an ordinary key, with two prongs and a coin shaped hole at the top. The only thing intricate about it was it was well shined despite its age. Its etchings were foreign, but it must have been wear and tear. How could something this small create this much trouble?

Belyx pocketed it and gasped as guards screamed on the other side of the door. Instinctively, she raced to the window. If she jumped right, the fall would cause minor pain, but Enzo would need to follow, despite his apprehensions.

Belyx grabbed the golden statue of a lion on Caprash's desk and flung it, shattering the window. Enzo halted. "There is no way I am jumping!"

The door cracked. They were coming. "It's here or there!" Belyx cleared the glass and leapt with her might. The world slowed around her. She aimed for the soft spot below and hit her mark, letting the impact course through her body, which would need to be checked later...

"Jump!" Belyx called up.

Enzo stared over the edge. The noise of the Goldfingers grew louder and others would hear too. He needed to move. Should she leave him again? Before she considered further, Enzo was crashing on the ground in front of her, head bobbing. Was it that hard? She yanked him away as gun shots whizzed by. The outside patrols were onto them. Good thing pistols weren't the most accurate weapon.

Belyx and Enzo dove behind a bush, letting the gunfire ricochet. Wood and metal splintered around them. "Have any other brilliant ideas?" Enzo screamed between shots.

Praying, Belyx pulled out a knife. "Fight and get the hell over that wall!" She stuck her head out to over ten guards firing and rushing their way. They couldn't fight them all. The fence was the only way out. It was a weaker steel, despite the wealthiness of the area. Caprash didn't want to spare any expense. *You should have!* The stables were nearby, and Belyx turned to Enzo. "Do you trust me?"

The gunshots grew closer and closer. "I don't think I have a choice," Enzo replied.

Belyx took it as a yes. "Follow me!" They sprinted to the carriages, bobbing and weaving to avoid becoming holed cheese.

A stable-hand came out with a shovel, but Belyx hooked her legs around his neck and slammed him down. Enzo, already figuring out her plan, prepared the horses in the carriage. "I sure hope this works!" Enzo said as Belyx secured the remaining knots. The guards circled the corner, it was now or never. He mushed the horses, and they charged for the gates. The Goldfingers fired, but they missed their marks.

The carriage was at full speed to the gate when a bullet clipped the steed and it went down, launching the carriage right into the fence. It dented as Enzo and Belyx went flying.

Belyx rolled to stanch her impact and something in her shoulder clicked. She ignored it as she helped Enzo up and lobbed a knife at one of the guards, sending him down.

Enzo was ahead of her and climbed over the broken fence. Belyx threw knives at every Goldfinger she could and ran. The stable lady (Phoebe?) from earlier appeared in front of her, pistol ready, but Belyx sidestepped out of the way and struck her with her own firearm, feeling satisfied.

Once she vaulted the boundary, Enzo pulled her aside as more gunfire followed. Would they follow them? She kept up with Enzo as the deafening shots faded. He knew the streets better than anyone and could escape.

After it quieted, Enzo let go of Belyx's hand and tumbled to the ground, catching his breath. Belyx bent over and lost her meal into the wall.

Enzo offered Belyx his bloody hand, her heaving subsided now. "Ok, I think we could use a drink."

SEVENTEEN

Before any celebration, Belyx had to address her wounds. No one went unscathed jumping from a two-story house, getting shot at, and thrown from a moving carriage. Enzo had his own bruises and whined profusely.

"Ouch. That stings!" Enzo winced as she applied herbs to his bullet grazed arm.

"It will hurt a lot worse if infection sets in." They both hid under a prodigious embankment, checking that no rodents lurked around. He was shirtless and Belyx's sudden urge to trace along his chiseled frame clouded her vision. She rubbed the medicine on, taking her time on each crevice, but nothing could stamp the heat in her cheeks. Sitting up made her shoulder throb. Amenthya would need to put her mysterious paste on it later.

After she bandaged up Enzo, she tossed him his shirt, turning away as he dressed. A pit in her throat formed. "Drinks, you said?"

Enzo stood and moved his arm in a circular motion. His loose top rose a little, revealing a muscled stomach with a patch of dark hair tracing down. *Close your mouth, Belyx.* He would think she had swallowed a moth. "I know just the place," he said with a cheesy smile and pulled Belyx up. "Are you sure your shoulder is ok?"

It stung, but a drink or two would abet it. "I've been through much worse. Let's go already." Doneque wanted to have fun.

Out of the places Belyx partook in drinking, this one took the prize for the dingiest. Multiple patrons mulled about, proclaiming their conquests to impress the other men or the female servers. Others were out cold on the benches inside and in the thralls outside. Belyx had to step over a snoring oaf just to enter. The floating dust in the air and the odor of feet and fermentation made her choke. A princess would never be caught dead here. Good thing she was not a princess tonight.

"The Drunk Pony?" Belyx grimaced at the crass name of the establishment.

"Don't knock it till you try it." Enzo led her passed an almost naked man mumbling incantations to himself. He glared at Belyx with a fire in his eyes, but Enzo kept her moving. They squeezed through the sweaty tavern rats to the front of the bar. Her clothes would need to be scorched later.

The bartender was drying a glass with a dirty rag when he caught sight of Enzo. "Enzo! How are we today?" The bartender stood shorter, with thinning brown hair and an overwhelming mustache taking camp under his hulking nose. He bore a scar on his left eye, and Belyx wondered what his story was.

Enzo tossed him a coin. "Two specials, please. For me and my friend here."

The man eyed her, but not in a creepy way, more like an approval way, assuming this was a date, too. "Beautiful friend you have there, Enzo." He chuckled as he pulled out two pint glasses and filled them with a thick brown liquid and chopped up what looked like an onion, tossing the rank pieces in.

Belyx stood straight faced as he set them in front of her.

She held the glass and went to smell it when Enzo stopped her. "No. Just drink it. You'll thank me later." He waved the bar keep off, and they searched for an empty table, finding a quiet spot near the billiard tables and dart boards.

Belyx eyed them. She hadn't played billiards in ages. Enzo took a giant slug of his drink and wiped his mouth. "You play?" Shaking her head, she sipped more of the liquid. It wasn't bad. "What, no billiard tables in the palace of yours?" Enzo smirked as he downed more of his glass.

"Yes, but there is never any time. I haven't had a nice outing like this in a while. It's refreshing."

"I take all my dates here." He laughed at her frown. "I'm kidding. But I love to just chill here with a great drink and read. It makes the whole living on the street thing enjoyable."

Belyx gripped her steamy cup and slugged more of the sweet onion liquid, surprised at how such a combo worked. "What is your favorite book?"

A dark brow rose and Enzo sat up like a toddler hearing his favorite story. "Why? Are you gonna read it?"

"I didn't say that." What had she done?

Enzo's finger circled the cold glass and parts of Belyx craved his mouth. "If I tell you, I request you let me read one of your poems."

Belyx almost spit her drink out. "No, no, no. Off limits. No one reads those."

"And why not? Too much blood and violence?"

A fake laugh came from Belyx's mouth. "No. It's personal." A hulking man chanted at his victory in a game of darts, chugging the last of his ale and tumbling to the ground.

"Well, I get it with the whole personal thing, but my favorite book is The Dancing Flower." His cheeks reddened. "I enjoy the mix of action with romance and great plot twists like..." He paused, and did the thing he always did when he was about to say something stupid, and his hands sank in his lap. "Sorry. I'm not gonna spoil it."

"Come on," Belyx neared the end of her drink, wanting more, among other things in front of her.

He shook his head like an advisor. "Nope. It is against the rules to spoil a book."

"Well now, I guess I have to read it." She leaned forward, inhibitions stifled from the alcohol.

His lips twitched up. "Well, I have a copy at my place."

"Is it stolen?"

He put his hand on his chest, feigning offense. "We talked about this! I would never steal a book! I take food and clothes, but never something sacred.

Although, I may have bought it with money I stole. You will never prove it, though!"

Belyx snorted, dribbling her beverage down her chin, and wiped it with haste. *How unladylike!* Enzo kept giving her his subtle grin like he couldn't care less about traditional things like that. "I thought you lived on the street. How do you have a place?"

"I work for an innkeeper on the north side and she lets me rent a room for cheap."

"That must be nice. Why didn't you tell me earlier?"

"When you grow up without a home for so long, permanence is relative..." He wiggled his eyebrows. "Maybe I should write poetry." Their stares lingered way too long and Belyx wanted nothing more than to trace his cheek and kiss his full mouth.

"Play you a game?" Belyx said to slice the tension, as she started racking the billiards table. Enzo followed. "Thieves break first." She tossed a billiard cue his way, and he caught it, rolling his eyes.

Rolling her eyes was her thing first.

He sent the white ball into the loaded triangle, and the game began.

Enzo leaned down to the take the shot and Belyx couldn't help but gaze at his muscular legs leading up to his backside. He finished the move, and she jerked away, taking her turn. Was he looking at her the same way?

After Belyx celebrated her victory (by one ball), they stumbled out of the glamorous bar and trudged back to his place. She needed his book, and a promise was a promise. "Ok. Ok," Enzo said while chuckling. "You hate seafood. Why?"

"Not funny. It has a weird texture and tastes slimy!" He busted out laughing and Belyx shoved him into a wall, holding him for a second too long. His face stared into hers and kissing him would be easy, but she was feeling playful, and released him, walking on ahead. "Well, at least I'm not scared of heights."

"I am not scared of—" Belyx lifted a brow and his face lowered.

"What gave it away?"

"Back at the Goldfingers? You took ninety years to jump."

"Ok, it was like ten seconds."

"Ninety years. I'm pretty sure I'm ancient now."

Enzo shoved her, but she pulled him back. In their clumsiness, they slammed into a brick wall, grasping each other's arms and falling down, laughing like drunken miners.

Belyx's cheeks brushed with his and their mouths lingered, and like fire, they connected.

It was haughty at first but stilled. The heat nestled into her senses as they flowed in an even rhythm. His lips were shockingly soft and a trace of stubble on his upper lip tickled Belyx, only making her shiver. He tasted like the sweet onion drink, but a more potent floral flavor came through. How she knew what it tasted like was beyond her and she didn't care!

They pulled away and Enzo's face glowed. Walking away, he turned his head and gave a close-lipped smile. How dare he leave her in this state like a tease! "My place is this way," he called out. Belyx followed, and it was silent before Enzo clutched her hand. For a moment, they were a like a normal couple. *Princess who?*

"I never thought my rescuer would end up kissing me," Enzo said as they walked. She stepped slower to make the time last longer.

"I thought you said you saved yourself?"

Enzo shrugged. "Well, I think I could have taken those Berserkers by myself. Who knows? Jokes aside." *Shocking words, he spoke.* "I'm glad you were there."

"We make a surprising team." Although it was a foolish endeavor, she longed for his lips again. Like a hunger she needed satiating.

Enzo led her into a modest inn, decorated with flowers and various knick knacks. It possessed a quaint and welcome aura despite the cheapness. Decadent things didn't always mean better.

The patrons were like the ones at the bar, but by this time, they were more subdued. The innkeeper worked tirelessly, wiping the sweat off her brow, cleaning the released contents of a customer's liquor on the floor. Belyx shot Enzo a look and couldn't imagine doing such laborious work. The dishes were enough!

They squeezed their way upstairs, and he opened his door. The room was smaller than Belyx's washroom, but Enzo made it homey. His small desk was piled with books. He had a decent sized cot with more books on the bedside table. How many things did this man read? Despite the size, something about it reminded her of home, and Belyx never wanted to leave.

"It's not a lot, but it's mine for now." Enzo waved his hands. "Care for a grand tour? There is a standard and deluxe package, but the deluxe costs extra."

Belyx folded her arms, stifling a smile. "By how much?"

"Not much." Winking, he pulled Belyx into him, their lips meeting like they were apart for too long. They would never make such a mistake again. Teasing her fingers along his solid back, she pulled him tighter into her. He let out a whimper as Belyx smiled against his mouth. Her tongue went in and he greeted it like a guest, returning the favor. She could go like this for hours, but messing with him was more fun.

She pulled away, letting the heat linger above them. "So, that book?"

Enzo adjusted his trousers and glowed on the way to his desk, and then handed it to her. The cover was pristine. Although Belyx wasn't much of a reader, she appreciated the designs. Across the leather front sat a cluster of circling roses and, in the center, a blade piercing through them. Belyx looked at Enzo's tattoo again, and it resembled it. "Wow. You even got a matching tattoo. That is dedication."

"I could say the same for your pin. Why a rose?"

Belyx sucked in a breath. Should she tell him? "I admire the imagery of the rose. It's sweet, but can cut someone if underestimated. Kind of like me."

"You think you're sweet?" He howled as she nudged him.

"No, it's just living this double life can be heavy, but the rose reminds me of the duplicity between sweet and deadly." Did she quote the Order's motto? Yes, but he didn't need to know.

He traced the pin and stared at her for a beat. "The bed also has room for two, but it will cost extra."

What was the time? Belyx couldn't stay late again, but Enzo's face had this giddy expression, like someone finding out they were getting a kitten. Her goosebumps danced. Freyja would cover for her. What was the worst that could happen?

He pulled her in. "Ouch," Enzo said. Clearing her throat, she shucked off her knives, along with the key, eying it before placing it on the nightstand. The door was locked, and no one was breaking in here. Plus, she had hearing like a fox.

Their kissing continued like hungry animals and as if in slow motion, they fell to the bed. He was gentle and respectful of her body, asking if it was ok and if it felt good. Belyx accepted it with open arms and legs. The weight of his frame soothed her bones, and she wanted more of him. The fire was ignited.

Taking the lead, she removed his clothes, and he did the same, peeling her leathers off. But he was going too slow! Although Belyx hadn't done this often, she knew the logistics and what she enjoyed. Belyx debated removing her wig, but left it on. *Only Doneque can do this.* Their bodies became one as they fluttered into the night, letting time stand still and exploring parts of each other.

When they were finished, Enzo held her close, and she exhaled, closing her eyes. Her kingdom would soon be saved after she destroyed the key, and now she had someone she could call hers. The assassin and the thief. It sounded like a plot from one of his books. This wasn't fantasy, though. This was real. Belyx traced her fingers over his back before giving him one more kiss, his curly hair tickling her forehead. She turned around and fell asleep to the subtle heat of Enzo's hands rubbing her body. For once, she was safe.

The warm trickle of sunlight crept through Enzo's room. Belyx grinned to herself as she reached for the person who she shared a bed with last night. The bed was empty. Still half asleep, she shrugged it off, her grin emulating more. He was most likely grabbing morning pastries and coffee. She covered her face with the itchy pillow and plotted to get at least another hour of sleep. When was the most recent time she slept this well?

Her mind traveled to what Freyja was thinking, or if anyone else found out. Maybe she should dip out early, to be sure. Freyja worked hard and deserved a break. She would leave a note for Enzo and buy him any sweets he wanted tonight! The key would be handled and she could go on another date with him. It had been way too long since the previous one...a couple hours.

As her back relaxed, she imagined the key and her grandmother's face when she brought it in. No one would doubt her anymore. She saved Aikradal's secret, but too bad her father would never know. He wouldn't believe it, anyway.

Belyx opened her eyes, curious about the details of the key. With her being caught up in the moment the night before, she hadn't been able to study it more. *Those markings were particular. Were they from this land?*

Like lightning, she sat up, heart pounding as her breathing hitched.

This couldn't be happening.

Bolting out of bed, Belyx flung open the nightstand drawers.

Nothing.

No. No. No!

Belyx scanned the room and scratched the empty wall. The floors were bare and the messy desk was vacant. Enzo's things were gone as well. On the now desolate ground was the book he gave her, The Dancing Flowers. She grabbed the hardcover, barely able to hold it with shaky hands. Why would Enzo do this? There had to be a reasonable explanation. Did he leave somewhere and he would be outside waiting for her? *That was it.*

Her fingers numbed, holding her belongings and his book. "There has to be a reason," she kept saying to herself.

With wobbly knees, she collected her stuff and went down the narrow stair-case. Enzo was nowhere in sight, only some men getting their early morning alcohol fix and travelers munching on a cold meal. Belyx pushed past them, ignoring their dirty stares. She didn't have time to check herself in the mirror and regretted it.

Outside, the cloudy skies threatened to cover the gorgeous sunrise, threatening rain. It seemed fitting as she held the book and her items tighter and tighter until it left an imprint. Where was Enzo? Why would he do this? Tears welled in her eyes as she roamed through the housing district, keeping her sights straight ahead, refusing to even acknowledge anyone else. She felt as though a flame was rising inside of her, burning and burning, until it seared everything in its path. Belyx turned into an abandoned alley and fell to her hands and knees, scattering her things across the ground.

Not caring if anyone heard, she whimpered. The tears ran like a river through the alley and onto Enzo's book.

The book! She snatched the novel and flitted through the pages. Enzo may have left a clue. They were empty, with no notes or any explanation of his betrayal. Page after page, she ripped and shredded, crinkling each leaf until it was no more, tossing them in the air, letting them fly away in the morning breeze like her happiness.

She gritted her teeth. Enzo had tricked her. He fooled her into helping him and stole the key for himself. Why would he want it? Maybe he made a deal with another gang.

Or did someone else want to take over Aikradal? *It had to be Majeria!* They must have payed him quite a price. Thieves were the same. Why didn't Belyx see it earlier? Blood trickled as she pinched her skin. Enzo used her, and it would only be a matter of time before she watched her kingdom fall.

The reason was superfluous, Belyx failed. Aikradal's secrets would be spilled, and it was her fault. She was a failure, letting a stranger infiltrate her feelings and revealing the one thing she held dear, her identity, and then he wielded it to steal the one item needed to save her kingdom from ruin. No matter the secret, the gangs or Majeria would take advantage and stake their claim against her father and he would fall.

Belyx grasped her head, watching the thick clouds suffocate the sun until no light remained. She imagined Enzo's face and no more tears dropped, anger steaming from the puddles. As she slipped back to the palace, Belyx made a vow to The God that if she ever saw the treasonous piece of filth again, she would separate his lying head from his lying body.

EIGHTEEN

Freyja stood by the door with her arms crossed, scowling as Belyx slumped in. Normally, Belyx would say hello, but she skulked right to her bed, face down, regenerating her lost tears. Enzo had hurt her worse than anyone, putting a vice grip on her trust and shoving it into blades.

"Belyx? What happened?" Freyja's scowl lessened, noticing her demeanor. "Did you find the key?" Belyx shook her head in her pillow. How would she tell her what had happened? It was too obvious. She gave her heart to a stranger, and he smashed it. "I'm sure you'll find it," Freyja said reassuringly. "I'll bring you some food." Freyja closed the door and she thanked The God as tears fell again. Pulling the sheets closer, she let her eyes shut and fell into a deep sleep.

Her grandmother woke her, face painted and dressed as usual. "Flower..."

One word and she spilled. "He betrayed me, grandmother." A supposed trusting guy had burned her.

Dara shook her head, looking out over the balcony. The morning sun had set, swirling in a mix of colors. A tray of cold food sat by her side. Freyja must not have wanted to wake her. "It's complicated, depending on others. Sometimes people are not always who they say. It is always best to move on and focus on what matters."

"But I don't have the key!" Her voice was raw from crying. "What if it gets into the wrong hands? Why aren't you more worried about this?"

Her grandmother shrugged. "The key may have been a big deal or not. Who is to say?"

Why didn't her grandmother share her burden? "Everyone. The gangs have been fighting nonstop to get it and use it. You were the one who assigned me to this!"

"I know." Dara sat down. "Rumors can be a dangerous thing. Why do you think the Whispers use it as a weapon? It is as sharp as a scabbard and cuts deeper."

"The key was well guarded. We almost died, Grandmother." If it was no big deal, then the Goldfingers would have let it go. Belyx flipped over, but her grandmother stuck a hand on her shoulder.

More tears streamed as her grandmother rubbed her back. "Wait before you go level ten. What is your plan to remediate this?"

"Find the thief and gut him for the key." Sounded simple enough!

"I didn't train you to kill people for revenge. Ponder this and decide what to do next. Take your time too. It may surprise you what you can solve right in front of you."

Belyx pulled away, not in the mood for her grandmother's toxic positivity. Dara, giving up, stood. "The Budding is tonight. The of age Seedlings are looking forward to your presence. It starts at midnight." *The Budding.* Hers was not too long ago. It was when she became a Thorn. Dara hosted it once a year before the change in season. "Please come. It may clear your head."

Things with the kingdom had been hectic. It had a chance of cheering her up. "Maybe," Belyx replied in her covers.

"Enjoy your day off. Try to work on your poetry. We all need a release in this stressful environment." Dara left the room.

Belyx reached with her free hand and ate a little of her food. The cold sausage and biscuits slid down her throat; she didn't savor it, but her body craved the fuel. Stretching her hurt shoulder, she rolled out of bed, remembering to see the healer, but she would wait.

Something else needed to be done. She sauntered over to her desk and pulled out a blank scroll. Now, what words rhymed with lying bastard?

By the end of the day, her phrases poured on the page. Although she hated to admit it, writing her concerns helped. This was the first step to moving on. Her poem sat in front of her, reading it kept her still heart beating.

A bond out of convenience
A spark starting as soon as it stopped
You were the flower I thought I needed
I picked you from pain and it bloomed
There would be no dance with this flower

Belyx rolled up the parchment and stowed it away with her other completed works; getting out her knives and sharpening them with fury. Night would take its sweet time, but when it came, she would search for Enzo...and make him pay.

But first, she needed to address an untreated wound. Her shoulder throbbed as she pulled on more decent clothing and descended the palace, praying Amenthya was still awake.

NINETEEN

"*N*ow explain what happened again?" Amenthya oozed her paste onto Belyx's shoulder, removing the bandage the traitor put on her.

"Crashed a carriage. No big deal." Belyx was too tired and depressed to say anything more and she wished Amenthya would drop it. Luckily, she did and finished wrapping the wound.

"Anything else, princess?"

Belyx planned to go out again, but she didn't care. "Not at all. Thank you again."

"Be safe." The healer stood to freshen up her ingredients.

Belyx retreated to her room, wound still tingling, and changed into her Doneque garb. The Budding ceremony needed their princess.

"What a group of Thorns this year," Belyx said to her grandmother as the two chosen girls passed their Leaves tests on disguise and stealth. The amount of potential in the Order was astounding. It rivaled Belyx's own stealth skills, but Leaves needed it more, for they were not the killers. *Unlike me.*

Dara bestowed the heavy breathing, former Seedlings their rose pins, whispering to Belyx, "You ain't seen nothing yet."

Frala, a girl with a shaved head and a surprising knack for wig making, stepped to her grandmother. "I, Dara Velena, grant you rank of Leaf. May you provide the Order with crucial information and continue our services to the kingdom. Do you accept?"

The recruit nodded. "It is my pleasure to honor us, and I am ready to start training."

Dara motioned Onka to step forward. "Onka will be the Petal in charge of you. Have any words, Onka?"

Onka shuffled up. "My training is not easy, but like other successful Leaves, it is your duty to surround yourself with the kingdom and learn its ways. We start tomorrow."

Frala accepted and rubbed her shiny pin, now attached to her person. *I remember when I earned mine,* Belyx thought.

The next Leaf received her pin and Inka's demands were short and sweet. How she trained them when her speaking abilities lacked was beyond Belyx.

"Alright!" Dara announced. The younger Seedlings sat in the training room, rocking on their mats. The Budding trials were a yearly tradition they looked forward to watching. "Let's bring out the Thorn nominees!" She eyed Belyx, a nod to her own test last year. Belyx recalled it vividly.

"We are going to make you a Leaf. As the princess, I don't want you in any danger."

"Grandmother. You said I could try for Thorn! I want to help my kingdom!"

"Belyx. We talked about this. Thorns put themselves the most in danger, and I can't risk losing you.

She protested by sneaking into the Thorn trial, risking consequences, but she proved herself that day, determined by the fighting spirit of her mother; to do the things she did. Protecting her kingdom every day was something she would lose her life for. *And I still am.*

The three nominees stepped up to the center of the training area. The tests were fierce. A Thorn had to be quick and think on her feet, but also know when to leave a fight. The girls were still. The one on the left was Cressa, with a mess of blonde locks on her head; Always saying her hair was her good luck charm.

The middle girl was Shawna, a shorter recruit, but moved like a monkey in speed.

The far right girl was who Belyx was most skeptical about, Addie. She had wavy red hair with a similar fiery spirit. Her anger and impulse control worried Belyx. Although she was one to talk.

"The first test is stealth," Dara said. "Like Leaves, you must infiltrate the target area. The target will be on the other side. A smart Thorn fights as little as she needs. Other Order members have posed as guards and you have a specific doll to bring back. You have five minutes to return it, or you fail."

Belyx gulped. Failure meant they had to be a servant for life and if not, they were given a reasonable sum to go elsewhere. Not many failed, and some who did tried to expose the Order out of spite, but they were handled. Not everyone was cut out for this life. *It must be easier. Never to worry about anything and live life as a simple woman.*

The recruits sped like the wind across the mock corridors. Dara designed them to mimic mansions and such. Cressa ducked under every crevice and waited for the "guards" to pass by. She made it to the doll with no trouble.

Shawna beat her and everyone. Her speed was unmatched and even better in a scuffle. She had a near fail, but the guard moved on.

Addie proved more difficult. In the last room, she lost patience and had to subdue the guards. They went down, but it took her time. If she was to make it, she would have to push through more on the way back. Although unconventional, she succeeded and threw the doll in front, panting.

Dara jutted her head at the recruits. "Well done. Although some used a little less than desired tactics, but it worked. Now for the final test."

It was ironic how they spent years training in their field to pass two little tests. "The last test is a fight with weapons. Sometimes, it isn't about who loses, but how they fight. There can be a positive side to failing as long as you survive. Raise the platform!"

The Order members grabbed a pulley and yanked it. The once grounded circle in the middle of the room elevated. Heights reminded Belyx of Enzo and how he would hate this. She bit her lip. How dare she think of him!

The recruits each had to pick a wooden replica of any weapon. This was where personal style came in handy. Belyx had chosen the fake knife, shockingly. It was an uncommon choice, as most went for the flashy or heavy weapons, but knives had a sort of finesse to them.

Dara spoke once the Seedlings climbed to the raised platform from her own watching perch. "Now, remember the rules. Use your weapons and skills to knock the others off the platform. Fight hard. You can still be selected for being knocked off." She turned to Belyx, who had been defeated after taking out two nominees. She cried after, thinking she had failed, but her grandmother helped her up.

"You did it, Flower. I'm sorry I doubted you."

Belyx clutched her pin as her grandmother finished with the other rules. "Ready!" Cressa swung her nunchucks. The chain in the middle sang with anticipation. "Set." Shawna twirled her twin wooden blades around with the precision of a tightrope walker. "Go!"

Addie moved, choosing to remain weaponless, a bold choice there. Would she be able to pull out off? She said weapons were cheap and a true fighter used her fists. She also made fun of Belyx for using poisons and venom, having other choice words, but everyone had their own style that worked for them.

Cressa and Shawna dueled. Nunchuck met wood as they exchanged blows. Cressa was too focused to notice Addie grapple her to the ground. Shawna went to knock Addie off when Addie spun, kicking Shawna back. Addie smiled before Cressa rolled up and nailed her clean in the jaw. The crack shook the arena. Addie gritted her teeth and was back up, blood trickling down her face.

Belyx knew her anger. The emotion from loss. Addie had lost her parents and baby sister to a Berserker raid two years ago. She trained with the Berserkers to learn their style and tried to fight The Scorpion. After her defeat, she was paralyzed on her left side, digging through the garbage for food when the Order saved her. Amenthya worked her skills and six months later, she was walking and training, vowing to be a Thorn to rid the streets of murderers.

Her grandmother was weary, for revenge was never the answer, but her skill was nothing to be ignored. As evident from the fact she just knocked both recruits back.

It had been mere minutes, but time slowed in a fight. Cressa and Shawna tried to double team Addie, landing blow after blow, but Addie refused to go down.

Belyx recalled her own challenge. She took down two of the four other Seedlings with ease. Then, Belyx was determined to prove herself, loving the chance to win. The others ganged up on her, too.

Now Addie faced the same. Dara gave her a look and Belyx kept a straight face.

Addie reeled back, about to fall off as the other two recruits were relentless, and came at her. Three person fights always shifted to one versus two and Addie was the "lucky" one, about to face a similar fate as Belyx did. Her feet dangled off the edge with no hope in sight when Cressa made an error; she swung her nunchuck across and Addie's eyes widened. She snatched the wooden swords from Shawna and yanked her over. The problem with winning was the over confidence. They were too caught up with the intense breathing and blurred vision from the excitement and Addie knew it. Using both of their weapons against them, she rotated and flung the recruits off. The girls thudded on the soft mats, cursing.

Applause roared from the Seedlings and Belyx.

All three received their rose badges.

After Addie did, she shifted to Belyx. "Thanks."

Belyx tilted her head. "For what? You did it yourself."

Addie laughed, rubbing her soon to be bruised shoulder. "Last year, you stood up for yourself and showed what this organization is truly for. You inspire us." Addie attached her pin to her body and joined the others.

Belyx was an influence on these recruits. *Some influence. All I do is fail.*

Belyx recalled the night she received hers.

"You may fail at times, Belyx, but as long as you can get back up and try again, the Order will prevail."

Rubbing her pin again, Belyx wished her mother could see her success. The twenty Seedlings stole glances at her; The princess who also passed the Thorn trials. She waved at them and they gleamed with excitement. *I should train with them again,* Belyx thought.

"Thank you for another great Budding." Dara announced. "I hope you enjoy your new roles. And Seedlings," she turned to them as they displayed wide eyes and innocent faces, "be prepared for next year. Off to bed!"

Everyone else hummed goodnights and Dara stretched her arms. "Well, I believe we have a lively couple of days coming up with the holiday and training new recruits."

Belyx almost slapped herself. Wakening Day was coming and that meant many preparations had to be arranged. "She's right. Madame Jewella may actually spit acid if I screw this one up." She hugged the women goodbye, taking extra time on her grandmother; needing to cherish the time she had with the ones she loved. The fresh recruits were helpful, but they also provided another thing...a future for the Order.

TWENTY

"The tapestries don't go there, they go at the entrance." For once, Belyx was the one barking orders at the servants, feeling slightly bad, but Madame Jewella fell ill and now Belyx had to be the one to make sure everything went right. As much as she hated Madame's judgmental attitude, an extra set of eyes wouldn't hurt. *Just pretend it's a trial.*

Cook came out with samples of baked goods. A princess never indulged in too many sweets...Belyx sampled them, forgetting she missed breakfast in her haste. "Delicious," she said with a mouthful of crumbs.

"I asked which one," Cook replied curtly.

Belyx paused mid chew and swallowed. "Oh. Why not all?"

Cook's frown morphed into glee. "You got it, princess."

"Thank you!" Cook shot her a concerned look, no doubt about her uncharacteristic enthusiasm. No matter, she had more work to be done.

"Captain. We need guards covering the corners and flanks. We can't risk a breach like last time."

Captain Thomas marched over, radiating extra positive energy, wiggling his eyebrows. "Have no faith?" Freyja made a scoffing noise from far away, and Thomas inflated a smile back. Something had definitely happened there. *Good for her!*

"I'm serious. Despite the turmoil right now. We need this holiday to increase morale. The citizens get to attend this ball, which means more chances of infiltration." Not all citizens attended, of course, but mainly the influential ones. No matter, they could still be compromised, and she refused to take any chances.

After Thomas agreed, she sauntered over to Freyja, admiring her effort. "The stars look good."

Freyja eyed her. "Decorating is not my strength." One fell as if on cue. "Damn these stars. Why did they show the settlers the way to Keyica? Why not like one enormous light or whatever."

"Okay, now you are sounding ridiculous," Belyx laughed.

Freyja stuck the star back up and glared at it to stay. "Whatever. The God statues are here. Where do you want them?"

A few servants carried in a massive statue depicting a powerful man and a powerful woman. The God. Man and Woman. All things. All people. There was even an energy in between for those who didn't identify with any given gender as The God represented all individuals of Keyica.

Belyx said a silent prayer and instructed the movers to put the marble statues in the front. Wakening Day was the day to honor Them and how They led the original settlers to this great continent.

She thanked the movers and stepped onto the podium, where the history of the land would be shared. She adored the story of how the settlers fled from The Old Place, Morag. The people were being killed for turning against The Idol, a cruel being who made everyone follow a certain ledger, but the rebels discovered The God's teachings and gave them the wisdom to flee. Many people perished along the way, but it was remarkable how they discovered Keyica and made it their own. Everyone across the continent would celebrate this momentous holiday.

An empty decorated table glared at Belyx. The fae used to sit there. They were always invited and although Belyx was young, she could remember them vividly using their cool elemental powers to help decorate and how she would play with their children. Her favorite part about them were their pointy ears and unique arm tattoos. She pushed the memory back. They betrayed Aikradal and killed her mother. How could such a peaceful people turn to murderers? It proved no matter how nice someone appeared, they were always hiding betrayal.

Belyx took in her progress. The holiday was tomorrow and everything was ready. The royal table was ebbed in silvers and blues, while the guest tables shimmered in sapphires. As the only time citizens could attend, it needed to be special. If this holiday went well, they would see Aikradal as a well respected and striving force. They would fight against the cowering gangs and Aikradal would be peaceful again. Despite wherever the key was, it didn't matter. If the people respected Aikradal enough, no fae power could snap them.

Screw Enzo. He was a fool to think this key would end her kingdom. Her mind raced to the recruits who passed last night, the hope shimmering in their eyes. They were the future, and Belyx would make sure they had one to look up to. She prayed to The God one more time and went through her checklist.

Her father and his two advisors scowled at Belyx for her late arrival. Lord Kirk made a tsk noise before speaking. "Well, now that we are here, we can begin." *What a tireless tripe!*

"Apologies," Belyx said with her fakest etiquette. "Planning an entire holiday party by yourself can be a daunting task. Especially when no one offers to help." She showed teeth and batted her eyelashes with fury.

Kirk scoffed and opened his scroll. "Well, I am afraid your work may have been a waste. I motion to rescind the holiday."

Belyx's water glass almost slipped, but she caught it in time. "Excuse me? Absolutely not. Aikradal needs this I—"

"Belyx, watch your tone in these meetings," her father warned, and Belyx sank back down, folding her arms. "Continue your reasoning, Lord. Council is listening." Here he was, taking his side again.

"Yes, very well. This party has diminished quite a bit of sums and we believe it should be spent on other things...like taking down these gangs."

Belyx stared at Kirk and her father to make sure he was done before she could speak. "You know as well these gatherings increase morale. Let the people be proud of us again. If they believe in the crown, then they will fight for us against any temptation."

Lord Loser snorted. "This isn't a fairy tale story. The citizens of Aikradal care little about morale. They want these gangs arrested and to continue with their lives. I, for one, agree."

Belyx was about to smack him when Lord Jaques stepped in. "Belyx has a point, though." He gave her a wink. "If the people see we are continuing things as normal, then they will feel normal. Stick to battle strategy, Lord Kirk." It almost pained her again to lose the key. Jaques wanted it too. To stop the gangs after his sister's death by their hands. *I'll never be able to tell him that I lost it.*

"Stick to ass kissing, Lord Jaques," Kirk replied, licking his teeth, although a hypocritical statement.

"Enough!" Her father leaned in. "If we cancel, the people will sense our fear. That would only cause worry and gossip. My daughter and Lord Jaques are correct. The party will continue as planned."

Belyx shot a snarky smile to Kirk, who folded his arms. "Let's hope there aren't any complications like the last event. It would be a shame if more people perished because of us...again."

"Is that a threat, Lord?" Belyx ignored her father's glare. "I am curious why you always disagree with everything helpful."

Kirk scrunched his nose. "Preposterous. I am the only rational one here besides his majesty." The council frowned at his blanket statement. Master Jon wiggled his mouth rapidly. "This council needs rational thinkers. The last thing I want is to be a slave to the gangs."

"You would make a fine one." Belyx felt a sense of pride at her remark.

Kirk leered. "Princess, with all the respect in the kingdom, I have been doing this long before you were born and plan to for awhile, so please save the childish squabble."

Taken aback, Belyx turned to her father for help, but he stared ahead. "Well, I am smart enough to spot a traitor and if I were queen, I would investigate you."

"Which we hope isn't for awhile, right princess? Now, who sounds treasonous?"

The table banged, her father fuming. "I will not have this in my throne room. We all want what is best for the kingdom. Let's at least try acting like it. The holiday will go on." That was a win in her eyes. *Finally!*

Belyx tilted away from Kirk, fighting the temptation to test her venoms on him. *What a blithering fool!* Kirk smoothed his lapel. "Let's move onto the next order of business."

Belyx groaned as the meeting dragged on for the rest of the day.

Afterward, she sank into her bed and debated going out and searching for Enzo, but he could wait. Belyx needed to prepare for the holiday tomorrow and despite how traitor Kirk felt, the citizens needed this, and Belyx would do what was best for her people.

The crisp sound of horns graced the morning sky. Wakening Day was here, and the celebrating had begun. Upon arrival from Morag, the settlers had a grueling, cold season. They almost didn't survive, but The God gave them courage and strength and they prevailed which was why everyone celebrated it before the turn in seasons.

The weather had chilled and Belyx held her robe closed as she stared out of her balcony. Captain Thomas was riding around, organizing the guards for the holiday. He waved at Belyx, and she smiled back. Why couldn't everyone be as dedicated as him? In his chivalry, she almost forgot their duel a month ago. Another mistake for nothing. She should have let Thomas gut Enzo and it would have saved her the trouble.

"Close the door. It's cold." Freyja's tired voice came from within the warm room.

Belyx rolled her eyes and closed the door. "I know Majerians hate the cold, but aren't you used to this by now?"

Freyja wrapped herself in a bundle, writing with fury on her scroll. "Never. I swear the cold season hits faster than anything."

"I don't mind it. The hot season is too sticky."

"Agree to disagree." Freyja kept writing.

"What are you working on?"

Freyja set down her pen and giggled. "Oh, just ideas for scents. Don't laugh, but I've been taking a candle smithing class."

Belyx grabbed her parchment, grinning at the ingredients. "A handmaiden, protector, and a candle smith." How she found time was beyond her. "I can't wait to smell these!"

"Well, I am experimenting. Thomas is friends with some artisans and they showed me some tricks." Her voice trailed as she looked down at the ground.

Belyx raised her eyebrows. "How is that going?"

Freyja blushed. Even through her dark complexion, it broke through. "We are just talking, but I am hopeful. We plan to spend a weekend together after the holiday. I wish we could attend together, but we are both working..."

"Well, I would say not to worry, but we need all hands on deck tonight." There couldn't be an incident like with the Majerian ball.

"Don't I know it," Freyja sighed. "It's time, isn't it?"

"I could get ready myself, you know." Belyx went to the washroom, but Freyja intently followed as predicted.

"Oh no. If you mess up your looks, it comes down on me and I have a role to fulfill, Princess." She smirked.

"Making me not ugly?"

Freyja sat her in the chair and started her bath. "Impossible." She splashed Belyx.

Belyx squealed. "Save it for Thomas!" This earned her another splash, and before she knew it, they were both soaked and laughing. Belyx toweled off her body. "Ok, now I think we need to get ready."

Freyja pushed her wet braids from her face. "Agreed."

The party was nothing short of vast. Every citizen of high standing was there, waltzing and conversing with one another. The council worried about the turnout due to the gang threat, but maybe more people believed in Aikradal than they thought. Or just wanted an excuse to party.

Belyx greeted her guests. The dress Freyja picked out for her was stunning. The long, infinity chiffon purple material hugged her body like a warm embrace and ruffled down to the hem. Her high heels would kill her feet by the end of the night, but she survived The Scorpion; surviving painful shoes would pale in comparison. It was only one night.

Freyja was working overtime as the guests thronged in and Belyx was instructed by her father to acknowledge the patrons. Of course, this made Thomas loom over her as if Freyja wasn't already near. Despite Belyx being trained to kill, having a protector around was comforting, especially in giant, unknown crowds.

The citizens were dressed in an array of clothing. They wore silks, tweeds, and other expensive fabrics as they graced the ballroom. Everyone devoured Cook's platter and Belyx shot Cook an "I told you" look, and kept conversing with her guests.

"I must say, Princess, you are stunning." An older lady dressed in an emerald encrusted gown said. She reminded Belyx of her grandmother. Why did old people radiate such exuberance?

"It is my pleasure. The citizens of Aikradal make this possible." She wore her most diamond gleam and went to embrace the guest when Captain Thomas pulled her back. *Right, no touching.* One knife strike and it would be over. Everyone was a potential threat.

"Apologies ma'am. Gotta keep the princess safe." The older woman waved it off and started conversing with her friends. The hordes finally settled and Belyx downed a glass of sparkling wine. "Tired yet?" Thomas asked, sporting his shining crossed swords insignia on his sleeve.

"We just haven't had this many people in awhile, but it is turning out well. I couldn't be more proud of our kingdom. How are things around here?"

Thomas shrugged. "Nothing too unhinged. A few protesters are out front, but they are minor."

A twist developed in her stomach. "Protesters? What about?"

He arched a brow. "None of the worrying, please. It is handled. They just don't agree with your father's rule. You know, tainted blood. It usually is farther away, but they have crept closer."

"They have to be gang members. Arrest them." Why wasn't he more worried?

"Sadly, I can't arrest them on hunches. We have a sharp eye on the—" Another guard pushed through and whispered in his ear, and he rolled his eyes. "Drunk fight out front. Be right back."

Belyx gave a half smile and scanned the party, sharing pleasantries with the guests and palace nobles. The party had just started and yet the urge to crawl into her soft bed hit her like a wagon.

After the drink flow slowed and the food table lessened, her father marched up to the podium, surrounded by his guards. Lord Kirk and Jaques poised behind him, Kirk wearing his usual scowl. "Attention citizens of this precious kingdom." Everyone quieted down. She had barely seen her father tonight. "I would foremost like to thank the people of Aikradal." Everyone's faces shifted to a happy gleam. "Without you, this kingdom would not exist."

"I would also like to thank my daughter and your princess, Belyx." She waved as more people applauded, fighting the red rushing up her cheeks. "I know our late queen would be proud of her." The room hushed, and King Terach cleared his throat. "Let's not forget why we celebrate this holiday. Our freedom to worship The God!" Everyone held up their glasses and Belyx swore The God statues smiled.

"Morag oppressed our people, and we fostered the courage to flee from trouble, following the stars The God spread out for us. We landed, and the harsh rains gave us fruitful crops and supplies for this kingdom, the first kingdom to be formed." He stayed silent for a beat, looking down. "Despite the forthcomings and challenges we battle, we must remember what our sigil of the crossed swords means. It means we fight those who would dare threaten us. We are the strongest kingdom in the region and any who threaten the crown will answer directly to us." For the first time, her father smiled. Were those tears in his eyes too? With his hand, he motioned Belyx to the front. She paraded up, waving to the still crowd. What was her father doing?

"Every year, I carry the sword across the room as a symbol of our strength and offer it to The God. Tonight, I would like my daughter to fulfill this, to symbolize the fight for this kingdom and region. Your future queen." The words caressed her like wool. He believed in her.

The priest, dressed in his silver ceremonial robes dragging behind him, guided everyone in a silent prayer, spoken in the ancient language before the arrival. Belyx enjoyed the way the syllables danced off the tongue. Dead languages had these effects.

He finished, and handed Belyx the ancient blade, almost crying as she received it. The carving on it read, Fight For All. The blade was heavier and imbalanced, but it was brought from the original settlers. She held it up, and the crowd shifted, making a path for her. Her father embraced her and whispered, "I am proud of you." After, her tears threatened to smudge her kohl. For years, her father had shown nothing but demise and despair, but now, he was a whole different person. And here they were, celebrating a glorious holiday. Hope became a possibility.

Belyx marched through the crowd while scanning for threats. Attacking an armed princess seemed like a risky move, but the gangs weren't always rational. Where were Captain and Freyja? She made it to the statue and stuck it in between the man and the woman, saying a thank you to Them. They had blessed her people. She needed to do more and made a vow to keep preventing any threats to them. This marked the beginning of the end to chaos as hope filled like lungs of air. A new day full of possibilities was upon them.

"And now," her father said. "Enjoy the party and remain strong!"

The music resumed and Belyx released the breath she held. What an amazing moment she would remember forever. Her father always did the sword ceremony, and now it was her turn. She was a princess. No terrible thief would ever change her.

"The second appetizer was my favorite, but the eighth had quite a story to tell." Lady Lim conversed with her Aunt Hannah by the tables, and Belyx couldn't help but snicker.

"Why sound like a food critic now?" Her aunt sipped her drink.

"Goodness' sake!" Lim threw her hands up. "I am a consumer. My opinion and money matter the most!"

"Oh? Lord Kirk's money?" her aunt replied.

Belyx listened on as Lady Hannah slayed Lim with words and it made her hum to herself. Although Lady Maria ruined it, coming to her aid as usual with drinks in hand. They would sleep well tonight.

The party neared its end point when a gigantic crash echoed from outside. Her father's guards were already on him, but through the panic, Belyx snuck out to see. Was it the harmless protesters or the gangs?

As Belyx stepped off the main floor, someone yanked her back. She turned and realized it was Freyja. "What are you doing Princess?" she said still holding her arm. "You are supposed flee from trouble, not toward it. Now go back."

Belyx ripped her arm free. "What happened?"

Freyja rolled her eyes as if she knew she would not win this fight. "Some violence against the guards broke out. A few brutish men tried to get in, but Captain and I are handling it."

Clearly! "Let me help too."

Freyja arched a brow. "It will be over soon by the time you get ready."

Belyx stepped forward. "I can go now." Fighting as a princess was possible too.

"You would reveal your skills and—"

Another bang rumbled the room.

Freyja bolted out and Belyx went to follow when a couple Aikradal guards blocked her.

"This way, princess." One guard ordered. Belyx wanted to fight through them, but Freyja was right. She knew her place, and that was keeping the Order secret safe. Thomas and Freyja could handle whatever it was. *Like they did with Majeria?* The thought brought her discomfort.

Her father hugged her the moment she entered safety. "Belyx. Stay out of there! What were you thinking? If some lout slithered in here, he would turn you to pulp."

Belyx wanted to reassure him it would be the other way around, even in her heels, but she sunk her head down. "I only wanted to see."

"It's alright. Your mother also loved the action." Belyx knew he wanted to say, "and it got her killed," but he held his tongue.

The noises calmed, and the guests waited with everyone else for the all clear. Belyx couldn't stop fidgeting with her dress and wrinkled a part of it. Inka and Onka were nowhere in sight, either. Of course, they would help with the rest of the Stems. The new ones had quite the introduction to the job and Belyx was forced to sit there like a helpless swan, praying everyone was fine.

Her grandmother squeezed her hand and fluttered her eyes, as if to say, "the Order is handling it." After a couple aching minutes, Thomas and his guards emerged covered in blood and dust.

Belyx's father rushed forward. "Report Captain."

Thomas wiped his brow. "It was a minor attack, your highness. Only a couple of guards were injured, but we pushed them back."

"Who did this?" Her father's voice stilled.

Thomas handed the king a note covered in God knows what and Lord Kirk opened it, loving to stick his enormous nose in everything. He cleared his throat. "Your claim of strength is a lie. We will come for you all..." he paused and turned white as a sheet. "We will slaughter your men, enslave your women, and turn your children to our cause. Your strength is limited and your head will be on a pike by the main gate. Sincerely, Raul Fortan, Leader of The Great Berserkers." He gulped.

King Terach sank low, grasping his heart. The heat in the room increased as he stomped his foot down. "I must meet with my council about this. Everyone else, off to bed." He turned to Belyx. "Especially you."

Belyx wanted to offer her services, but Dara pulled her away. "I'll get her to bed, your majesty. No worries." Her father was already out the of the room when she replied.

Dara helped Belyx back to her room as if she couldn't get there herself. "Tonight was the closest they have gotten," she said.

Belyx gritted her teeth. "I'll gut them."

Dara shut Belyx's door. "I will wait here for Freyja while she is cleaning up this mess. We halted a major threat tonight."

Belyx sat on her bed, too shaky to change. "I should have assisted."

"It was not your place. You would—"

"Have exposed us, I know." Belyx took a breath. She hated snapping at her grandmother. "I just feel helpless sometimes."

Her grandmother chuckled. "No. You have the urge to be involved and assist all the time, like—"

"My mother. I get that a lot."

"I was going to say me." Belyx stared into her grandmother's eyes, almost detecting a trace of unease. "You have to be careful and know you aren't alone. As Belyx, you are a princess. Your disguise is when you can fight. Never forget."

She nodded, and the door flew open to a panting Freyja. "Berserker bastards." She slugged down the water Dara handed her. "We thwarted this one. Our guards almost couldn't handle them. We need to be on major red alert now."

"Agreed." Dara replied. "I need to check on some things, but no leaving tonight, Belyx. Freyja will keep watch. I'll have Cook get you coffee."

Freyja clicked her tongue. "On it."

Belyx went to the washroom and grunted. "I was going to search for En— I mean the key tonight."

"Well, too bad," Freyja said as she plopped down on the desk brandishing her knife. "The Berserkers are in a ravenous mood. We can't risk being caught."

Belyx reluctantly changed into her nightclothes. "I've survived The Scorpion. I can handle a couple of low life brutes."

"From what I heard, he almost tore you in two. It is best to play it safe."

Belyx rolled her eyes as she removed the paint on her face and undid her hair, wincing at the pulls. She slammed her brush down. Leave it to the gangs to ruin her party. Her father was finally happy, and like a candle, the feeling was blown out.

Once Belyx slipped into bed, she plotted what she would do to the gangs and no one would hold her back.

After feigning sleep and making sure Freyja was gone, she launched out of bed. She pulled out her spare leathers and wig. Belyx would never be a princess who sat by idly. The Berserkers were too close to her home tonight and her only chance at ending this was the key. If she couldn't find Enzo on her own, then she knew just the group who would.

TWENTY-ONE

On her way to the Whisper hideout at the beaches, a group of people gathered around a peculiar individual in the street. Was this a fight to interrupt?

Belyx frowned as it was no brawl, but a storyteller. She was an older woman around her grandmother's age, with salt and pepper braids outlining her pale skin. The wrinkles hugged her body like a cocoon as she waved her tawny fingers about. Although she wasn't a witch, she reminded her of them from the stories.

"Gather. Gather," she declared to the spectators. "Let old Rhin Vyx tell you a tale. A tale of the witches and the fae." It was said like a curse, more than an invitation, but the people stood intrigued and dropped coins into her hat. Belyx slipped through and did the same. The lady acknowledged her and continued her wild gestures.

"It was the beginning of time. Long before the humans arrived. There lived two tribes who are not around today...the Fae... and the Witches." The way she spoke lured the crowd in like a siren song. This was definitely for show, but Belyx enjoyed hearing the stories of the time prior to humans landing in Keyica.

"These tribes lived in harmony, worshipping their gods, following only one simple rule; they were forbidden to fall in love. This went on for centuries until, as predicted, they did. The Queen of the witches, Ulo Lenix, and the king of the fae, Oak, crossed paths." She paused for dramatic effect. Belyx was surprised the people wanted to hear these tales, as it was taboo to speak of the creatures, especially after the death of her mother.

Everyone's eyes widened like acolytes listening to a sermon. "They continued their affair awhile and nothing happened. Maybe the warning was a hoax...not! The gods sent down an individual called The Original, a being so powerful, he could use every power of nature." This was not anyone Belyx was familiar with. How did one person have so much power? The God would never allow such things. This was just a story, fiction. "He came down and cursed the tribes, banishing the witches to the twisted rivers and the fae to the forest. The lands were arid and they had no way to interact. This caused a rift between them and war broke loose. Some tried to escape the continent, but the banishment affected the Sea of Kifalia as well. Much like you all, no one was able to leave." Such blasphemy turned Belyx's fingers to ice. She was taught the Sea of Kifalia wouldn't let anyone sail away due to The God's will to keep the people safe. The only exception was Majeria, and they sailed their goods to other kingdoms.

Belyx pivoted to move on when the woman continued. "It is said over time, the curse will grow stronger and stronger, until the land is so dangerous, it will kill all who inhabit it...unless—" She looked around the mass and gazed at Belyx like a shivering young child. "A person can unite the witches and fae again. This is said to break the curse. For what started it shall end it once more. Remember, the next disaster that sweeps through...is the start of the end." Cackling, she shook her bag of money. The crowd asked meaningless questions and Belyx wanted to roll her eyes.

"How can they be united if the witches are extink?" a little girl asked.

Vyx curled her lips into a smile. "Well, it is said they aren't extinct. In fact, I am a witch. Let me show you." The people backed up as Belyx readied her knife. The storyteller came forward and pulled a flower out of the girl's ear. She shrieked, but the assembly and Belyx relaxed. Nothing but a stage trick. Was she the circus witch who told Enzo about the key?

The woman answered more questions and performed more circus illusions, making the kids grin, but soon, the night fell too thick and everyone cleared out.

The crone collected her things as Belyx followed in the shadows. Where did this woman come from and why was she spreading such stories?

Belyx needed answers, but as she crept after her, the lady turned with deftness and Belyx grasped her knives.

"You are a special one. I can tell."

A loud bang interrupted and made Belyx jump; she rotated to see what it was. After nothing, to her surprise, Vyx was gone. Belyx rushed to the streets, but she left no trace.

A shiver protruded down her spine. Was Vyx a witch or just a crazy old lady? *Fool.* Witches haven't been seen in ages. Focus on your task.

Belyx hustled, wasting enough of her time for the evening, and trudged her way back to find the Whispers.

The beach had a way of holding memories. The sand may get washed away by the chilling tides and calm gusts, but something held people's energies there. The footprints were nothing but empty shells. Belyx related to the emptiness as she let herself sink into it. How could she fail so badly? Belyx shook her negative thoughts, for they were only blocks to her goal. She would find the thief and get back the key, winning her grandmother's approval and with luck, getting the bastard's head for her mantel.

The only people who would know of his location hid straight ahead, the Whisper hideout. Belyx recalled the near death experience in vivid detail. Enzo's writhing body on the floor, begging for release, and Sewek's smug face like she had won.

Head throbbing, the idea of turning them in crossed her mind, but after the betrayal and then the attack, the palace didn't have the resources to invade the Whispers. No matter how weak looking, they were crafty and couldn't be trusted.

Readying her knives and venoms, Belyx burst through the front entrance. Stealth was not an option here, as the fresh black mamba venom coated her steel. She wasn't messing around this time and would kill them for Enzo's location.

Scanning the room, no hidden assassin attacked. *Strange.* Had Belyx slain their only guards. Every corner she passed bore nothing but dusty factory materials, and she had to stifle a cough from the musty air. The painting was in the same place as before, and she pried it open, turning fast to catch any sneak attack, but no one did.

Belyx headed down the corridor, twirling both knives. Her memory was fuzzy of which twists to go down, but she would take the entire night if she had to.

A creak, and Belyx shifted. Nothing. *Where are they?* She circled around, counting her breaths. What game were they playing?

After awhile of walking, she reached the fancy hall and gasped. The ornate tapestries once clinging to the rocky walls were gone. The door remained, but as Belyx suspected, nothing was in there.

The Whispers had fled, but to where? Sewek must not have trusted Belyx to keep their location a secret. *Smart.* Belyx pounded the empty wall, sending a shock up her arm. Her only chance of finding Enzo was obsolete, like a crumbling building. Falling to the ground, she cried into her knives. How could she have been this stupid? *Again.* She pleaded with The God to help her, but there was no sign. Why did she always worship something who didn't aid her? *Don't be blasphemous. They assist in more ways than you know.*

Defeated, she trudged back, but turned around once she hit the beaches, with the distinct feeling someone was watching her.

"Who is there?"

No one answered, as if an assassin would. She kept going when a loud clang in the distance caught her attention. The sand muffled her footsteps as she snuck to the top of the hill.

It was a boat leaving the shore. Was it Majeria? It had to be, but it bore no fish flags, only a solid black one, which made her stomach swim. As Belyx edged closer, groups of people were huddled together with their arms down. They were chained. *Slaves.* Belyx unsheathed a knife. This would not stand on her beaches. The Whispers were a fail, but this would suffice as something.

The slaves were being led by four figures. They must have been Goldfingers, trying to bring back slavery to Aikradal. *Not on my watch.* Four Goldfingers would be too easy.

As they shoved the slaves toward a concealed carriage, Belyx's feet planted to the ground.

They weren't Goldfingers.

Three of them brandished shiny armor with twin sword insignias on the shoulders. They were Aikradal guards walking with...

No. It couldn't be.

Master of Coin, Jon Gyra, walked among them. He had a hood on, but she knew his stature and caught a glimpse of a wrinkled face. He was a traitor, but was he the same one who stole the key too? It had to have been. The Goldfinger assistant said they had a double agent and she should have seen it. Of course, the Goldfingers had a hand in the Master of Coin.

Desperate to get answers, Belyx flung a knife for the nearest guard, recalling the last time she killed one, but stamped it down. *Traitors should die.* As the blade struck, she left no time for the others to yell as she took down the other one, following with a strike to the final guard. Her breath stilled as she recognized him as one of the guards she chose months ago. He *had* fallen to temptation.

Master Jon stepped away, pistol raised. "You can't have the slaves, Whisper!"

Before Belyx moved, he fired, and the bullet grazed her arm.

Reeling in a hot pain like no other, Belyx attacked, disarming the old man and slamming him to the floor. With shaky hands, she prepared a blade in viper venom; a useful way to interrogate someone. "Please, I'll pay you whatever!

Please let me live! They are good slaves!" he screamed so loud, anyone around would hear.

Her blood steamed as she finished coating her blade. "How can you pay me? I thought the palace was short on funds?"

Master Jon's eyes widened. "How did you...?"

She cut his arm, and he screamed. *Payback.* "I have just cut you with painful viper venom. It causes severe fever and convulsions until your heart and lungs slowly quit." Master Jon's breathing quickened and she took out another vial. "Blood from an infected horse is the only known cure. Tell me what I want to know and it is yours."

Master Jon gulped, his face already flushing from the effects. "Sure. Whatever it takes!"

"Good. Now, who are you doing this for, and why?"

He writhed more than normal and a tinge of fear rolled over Belyx. *I may have given him too much.* "The palace ran out of funds years ago. I had no choice! The Goldfingers knew and offered me a deal. To turn a closed eye to the illegal shipments and they would give me a cut. I only used it to keep the palace afloat." That explained how they could afford things despite the crippling budget. He was involved in the illegal trading the whole time. She had little time and needed to ask her next question.

"What about the key?" she asked and he gave her a blank stare, and she stabbed a knife into his leg. He screamed as the slaves murmured behind them.

"The Goldfingers paid me to steal it from his majesty!"

It was right around the time her father started to be more agitated and depressed. "Why didn't the Goldfingers use it?"

Master Jon coughed blood. He would spew his last breath if he didn't spit it out. "Caprash didn't care about ruling as long as he controlled the crown's money." Which he did. By keeping the Master of Coin under his finger, he had the freedom to do anything he wanted and if Master Jon tried to pull out, they would tell her father he stole the key and he would be sent to The Pits for treason. Caprash may have been a sleaze, but he was an intuitive thinker.

Belyx turned to the slaves. "What about them? Where are they fro—"

As the rain poured, Master Jon's whole body shook as he scratched at his throat. Belyx moved with the antidote, but his flailing swat it out of her hands. Before she had the chance to chase it down, his body stilled, eyes bulging out of his head. His old age was a factor she didn't consider. The next plan made Belyx curse. She wanted him to stand trial, but now it will look like he was murdered.

That's it! His corruption needed to stay hidden. If the people found out the Goldfingers were working in the palace, they would riot. This way, the narrative would change and make him a martyr. As much as she hated it, it would work.

The shivering slaves backed away from Belyx, but she held up her hands, blood dripping down her wound with the rain. "It's ok. I'm here to free you." She used her princess voice, and they stilled. Belyx worked their manacles and after they were freed, one approached her. He was tall, with tawny skin and tufts of dark hair sprouting on his head. He bowed and pointed to his heart. These were the slaves who couldn't speak. Their stories were well known throughout the kingdom. They were raised with no form of communication to limit rebelling, but they found their ways. People always created methods to fight back.

Belyx bowed and wished she had the ability do more and gave them the rest of her coins and prayed they would find a sense of freedom in her kingdom, but with the way things were going, nowhere was safe anymore.

She hustled back home with no Enzo or key, but saving those eight slaves had to be enough...for now.

Before Belyx went back to her room, she remembered her venom was low, and after a night of betrayal and failure to find the key, she needed something positive to lift her spirits. The make-shift wrap for her wound would hold for now.

The Order hideout was quiet in the middle of the night. Belyx crept down to her gardens to check how her lovely snakes were doing. Belyx almost smiled as her belladonna was growing in groves. Her fertilizer she tried had worked. She harvested its blood red petals and crushed them into her pellets.

Afterward, her snakes ate with ferocity. "Sorry. I am a little late. Saving the kingdom." If her Viper, Jay, could talk, she would curse her out. What a life to be a snake? No duties or responsibility to deal with.

"Ok. Venom time."

The extraction process was relatively painless for them, and Belyx couldn't say she hadn't almost died before. She mastered the most comfortable trick, using a long tube, and a hollowed fruit from the Sehrlic Forest called the Jinpox.

After getting venom from three snakes, she moved onto her old gal, Gwyar. The black mamba slithered with the speed of a slug out the tube. Once its head poked out, Belyx held her breath and grabbed her head. The snake squirmed, but opened its mouth and bit into the hollow fruit. She pressed down and let the venom seep into it. Afterwards, she helped Gwyar slither back. The snake struggled with tremendous effort. "How long do you have, old girl?" Black mambas weren't common and trying to replace her would be difficult as well as sad.

Before she left, something caught her eye. When an attempt kept failing, it was hard to look at, so she often gave up on her unhatched egg, but tonight was different and her mood would change for the better.

The dormant egg had hatched! Her hands shook as she pulled out her parchment, detailing the appearance of the little guy, or girl. This couldn't be happening. She thanked The God and apologized for doubting Them. *This snake could be a game changer!* It was as tiny as a feather, but it had the oddest texture to its green skin. Minute spikes frilled at its edges like leaves. Pen in hand, she took note of this. *I have never seen a snake like this before.*

It must have been hungry! How long had it been? Belyx shook her head at her negligence, giving the hatchling some insects.

As it ate, Belyx's heart was filled with a newfound hope. Everything grew old and died, but were also born just the same. This egg proved one thing after her failures.

Maybe things were looking up. And maybe she possessed the pieces to do well.

Even with a throbbing arm, Belyx still managed to climb up her balcony. As soon as she opened the door, a hand grabbed her by the hair and shoved her in. She screamed, preparing to fight when she put her hands down. Her grandmother, wearing dried tears, glared her down. Freyja stood behind, arms crossed.

Belyx had done it now. "You better have a good explanation for this. What happened to don't go out tonight?" Her grandmother's usual positive tone was out the window.

Sopping wet and pruned, Belyx trudged by her to change. Her grandmother grabbed her again, but Belyx broke free, recoiling at her bullet wound. "What is your problem?" Belyx gawked at her grandmother, the most angry she had ever seen her.

"What, you think you can take on the gangs now? You think you are above us?"

Belyx's feelings burst out the seams. "Well, someone had to do something! I refuse to be a princess who does nothing."

"You fool." Belyx reeled at her grandmother's insults. "You can't save everyone and take care of Aikradal yourself. Do you know what would have happened if you died?" The silence festered, knowing the answer. "There is no other heir! And then the gangs are that much closer to attaining the crown! I will not sugarcoat this any longer. Losing you would be the last strike in your father's life. How can you be so selfish?"

Her grandmother's words made sense, but Belyx's feelings were past sense. "How can I be selfish? I risked my life for my people. Mother would have done the same!"

Dara pointed a finger at her, almost as if to slap her. "Don't you dare bring up my daughter! She died because of these reckless beliefs. She went against advice and trusted the wrong people, risking too much and look what happened? The kingdom fell apart!"

Belyx lashed at her grandmother, forgetting she was a skilled fighter, and she put Belyx in an armlock, slamming her onto the bed.

Belyx replied through her teeth. "Mother didn't deserve you. You were a terrible mother, letting her die!"

In a flow, Dara released her. Belyx would regret those words, but her grandmother needed to hear them. Everyone needed to leave her alone! It was silent as Dara shuffled to the door. "I pray you find peace, but consider your training and assignments halted until further notice." She slammed the door.

Desperate, Belyx looked to Freyja for reassurance, but there was none. "Sometimes, you make my job difficult."

Refusing to stop her tirade now, Belyx tightened her fist. "Then quit! Go make your trashy candles in our taken over kingdom! What is stopping you? Aikradal is going to shit! May as well get out while you can. At least you have a choice! I am stuck here to die with it and frankly, that time is coming!" She launched her words like knives, wanting to feel normal again, but it didn't help.

Freyja shook her head. "We all have a choice." Freyja walked to the door. "And I made mine. Take care alone, as usual." Her door slammed shut too.

Belyx took her night stand and flung it against the wall, letting the pieces scatter. She tore off her uniform and stabbed it repeatedly. In shambles, she fell face first into her bed, not even drying off.

213

Twenty-Two

The next couple of days, Belyx feigned illness and avoided everyone. Madame Jewella scorned her through the door, shouting things like a "princess can't afford to be ill, for she has too much to do."

Belyx had a few choice words in her head to reply, but just replied an apology like a civilized princess.

Freyja brought her food for every meal, avoiding eye contact, and Belyx debated apologizing, but what would be the point? Freyja was free to leave.

She tried to cope with her poems, but the only poetic things she got down were "I hate my life," and it didn't have a creative ring to it.

Once she forced her body up, she went through basic knife techniques in her room, envisioning a few select people in front of her. She slipped and nicked her cheek like an amateur. She hustled to the restroom, holding a damp cloth to it, sighing in the mirror. The bags under her eyes had bags and her hair was tattered and sticking out like she wrestled a bear. Her skin shone with grease, which now bore a cut. The gunshot left a purple mark where it grazed her. It was time to see Amenthya, dreading it, as her grandmother likely told everyone her failures. Although her arm hurt, it needed to wait.

A bath sounded like the best solution, but after submerging in the soapy liquid, the suffocation flooded back her shortcomings. A traitor had been amongst the palace and she was too clueless to notice. If she hadn't been obsessed with the key, her other in house problems would be fixed.

Belyx let out her frustration. Luckily, her screams were muffled underwater. Defeated, she yanked her head up, drained the water, and slumped back into bed, unable to sleep without nightmares. Who was she fooling, playing the part of princess and assassin like this? She dreamed of a simpler life, but dreams were a fool's journey.

Her grandmother never checked up on her in the following days. The things she said to her grandmother cut deep, but she wasn't the only one to blame.

It had been almost a month since Enzo betrayed her and there had been no sign of an attempt on the supposed vault. She scowled at her plates of food, only eating when her body ached for nutrition. This was how it was, and she was alone now. Even her father never stopped by to check on her "ailment." How was the kingdom doing? Obviously, no one had taken over. The council had the power to handle things without her

After inspecting her arm, the gash spewed a white substance, evidence of an infection. If she wanted to keep her limb, it was time to bite the knife and visit Amenthya.

"I assumed you would have just left the cream on my door?" Belyx tried to be coy, but Amenthya exhaled out of her nose, focusing on her task.

"You won't get sympathy from me, princess."

"I didn't ask for it." Everyone was mad at her. It didn't matter anymore.

"I screwed up, Amenthya." She still didn't respond, but Belyx needed an ear for her vents. "I've lost a lot of people lately. My whole family is dwindling and many of Aikradal's citizens are losing hope."

Amenthya squeezed her bruised arm and Belyx pulled back. "You know no loss."

"Excuse me?"

"I wasn't finished." Her eyes bore into Belyx's and she wanted to knock over her plants in outrage. "Until you are the last one left in your family, you still have hope." Belyx closed her mouth and Amenthya continued. "My whole family was slaughtered to make me obey. I could have killed myself in response."

"I'm sorry. I didn't know." She knew Amenthya had no loved ones, but never the entire story. Her throat tightened.

"Instead of quitting, I stayed. Loss is a part of life, but my secret to healing is never giving up on your dreams and never giving up on doing the right thing."

Belyx took her arm back, sitting in silence for a beat. Amenthya went to her plants and mixed more cream. "I admire your courage, princess." The comment made Belyx's ears perk up. "We need more bravery. It reminds me of your mother."

What a ride to be berated and then adorned? "Thank you." Belyx bowed and retreated to her room. She had apologies to give and ways to save the kingdom to plan.

TWENTY-THREE

A strand of hair fell from Belyx's attempt at a decent braid. She huffed and stuck it back in the clip. It was times like these when she missed Freyja's steady hand, as well as conversing with her friend. Day broke, and Freyja had not brought in her food yet. After the night Belyx had, she was ready to apologize, and she hoped her protector/handmaiden would forgive her for the deplorable things she said. *She would, as she always did.*

Belyx rubbed the now eggplant color on her arm and applied her powder concealer, but it turned into an even worse dark lump. Another thing Freyja took care of. She thanked The God Freyja didn't quit as she was the most dedicated Petal in the Order.

Her grandmother also deserved an apology. Despite her harsh words, her grandmother worked hard to make sure Belyx was prepared to rule one day and how to handle any threats.

Belyx finished the tiresome effort of her hair and face and picked out a simple peach gown. Today, she would leave her room and grace everyone again while catching up on her missing work. No doubt Madame Jewella had been keeping track. Even her lecturing sounded refreshing after a week of seldom contact.

One place came to mind where she felt most at home and had an escape from the drama; the gardens. Flowers were special as they went through a variety of conditions and yet would still bloom; while other flowers, the slightest set back would wilt them away. It was like people...and lately, Belyx had been feeling like the latter.

Belyx grew lost in this perfect space. The rows and rows of sweet-scented aromas lifted her mood like a steady climb up a building. The shrubs had withered from the cold season, but her grandmother was diligent and revived them. *Like she did with me.* With her notebook in hand, she headed to her favorite writing spot.

The breeze nipped at her, but anyplace was better than her congested room. The lack of people around shot a wrenching sensation in Belyx's gut. Besides for the guards, everyone else was inside. The frigid weather had a way of making people retreat and she expected to be caught and report for her duties. May as well enjoy the quiet. Belyx skidded out of the pathway when the main gate tumbled down, shaking the earth below.

Where were the alarm bells? Belyx was on her heels to see what it was, and gasped as Aikradal soldiers ran down from their towers to fight the supposed threat.

Belyx gulped and slowly stepped back. The people who broke down the gates were muscled, brutish, and craved violence.

The Berserkers had broken into the palace and made it further than on Wakening Day. Didn't they ever quit?

They should have never gotten this far. Sweat clung to Belyx despite the chill. The palace was too far to make it back in time, so she slunk back into the gardens. Every sound made her flinch as she pulled the secret hatch and went down where other Order members were training.

"Princess," one young Seedling said. "What's happening? We heard the crash!"

Belyx couldn't control her breathing. "We need to send out the Stems. The Berserkers are here. Where are Dara and Freyja?"

Echos of terrified screams circled the room. These girls were about three years her junior, Seedlings like she was. She was in charge now.

"We don't know, Princess," another said, much younger than the last. "They said they had to pick up supplies from the markets today." *By The God of course, the one time they left.*

Multiple cries came from the back, but Belyx hustled to them. "It is all right. They won't find us if we stay here. I am sure other agents and the guards will handle it. Make sure you have a weapon, in case they find you." Some of these girls had just arrived and had little training in invasion situations. *I have to be strong for them. No more will die on my watch.*

They armed themselves while Belyx found a sharp blade for herself and assisted the younger ones. "Ok, now help me push these tables against the door." The few who weren't panicking helped her stack them by the hatch entry. Belyx figured it wouldn't hold the Berserkers, but it would slow them enough. "Now, get down everyone and don't make a sound." The Seedlings obeyed and waited and waited.

The silence only made it more grueling as Belyx's neck prickled. How long could they last down here? Many questions flooded into Belyx's mind like poison. Where was her father? How did they break in? What would happen when her grandmother and Freyja returned? She held a couple of girls' shaking hands. They were new to training and the Berserkers would eat them alive, or worse, sell them back to where they were rescued. These girls had never seen freedom or the light of day. Now, Belyx's former problems paled.

Belyx's hand numbed from rubbing the ground. She couldn't just sit here. Something needed to be done.

Anything.

Her grandmother's words of not solving everything came to her mind. Dara, Freyja, Cook, Captain Thomas, and her father were out there. They had them covered. Her job was to stay alive and protect these girls. They would survive today.

Belyx didn't know how much time had passed, but the screams and sounds of cracking stone grew louder and louder, it vibrated through the walls. Had they infiltrated the inner palace yet? If they did, her father's chamber had a panic room where they would be well hidden. Images of her family and friends' dead bodies planted in her mind. She knew the way The Scorpion fought and he would behead them in seconds.

Belyx counted to ten. Everything would be fine, but she wished she was out there, helping. She regretted not changing into Doneque when she had the chance.

She stood. Why was Princess Belyx less capable of fighting? Dara was wrong. She didn't need Doneque to take on this threat. Princess Belyx had knowledge of politics and negotiation, as well as a quick wit. The Berserkers wanted the throne, sure, but Belyx had the skills to reason with them. They couldn't last forever in this hideout, even if it was well hidden. They would be caught or starve first and it was only a matter of time. Belyx squeezed her thighs. *No more hiding.*

Belyx trudged with a new found confidence to the entrance and crossed the tables.

"Princess, Wait!" the older of them said while the others gave her worried glances.

"Stay here and if we are taken, use your training and get out of here." She clasped the older one's hand. "What is your name?"

"Lavender, Princess." The youthful face hadn't been hardened by experiences, like most of them.

"Lavender. What rank do you hope to pass next year?"

She coughed. "Thorn. Like you, princess."

Belyx smiled, taking in her younger self, hoping to do more for her kingdom. "Start now. Take care of the Seedlings and kill any who try to hurt them. There should be plenty of food for awhile. Do not save us if we are taken, understand. We need the Order to stay alive. Swear by The God." Like Belyx would listen, but this was different. An entire generation was at stake.

"Princess." Her voice wavered, and Belyx saw herself in her; A girl excited and full of life, changing over time with harsh experiences.

"Swear it!"

Lavender stood taller. "I swear it, your highness. But what are you doing?"

Belyx walked up to the hatch door. "Not hiding anymore, that is what."

Belyx regretted her plan as soon as she stepped foot on the gardens. The grounds were a desecrated mess. Statues of previous rulers were shattered, the ponds were broken, and trailing fires burned across the pathways. It took everything for Belyx not to scream, but she had to keep it together.

The smell of death and battle wafted in the air. A scent Belyx knew too well by now. The next best thing would be to make sure her father and the others made it out. Starting with the panic room, she snuck in through a secret kitchen entrance. This came in handy often when Belyx wanted a snack after a night of doing Order business.

As soon as Belyx poked her head through the kitchen storage entrance, a loud bang protruded from the other side and muffled screams followed. Belyx stayed put, clenching her knife.

"What is this woman?" A man said before the same voice grunted, following a sound of broken glass. Belyx's fear lifted like a breeze, and she opened the door to Cook walloping Berserkers with a frying pan in one hand and butcher knife in the other. Despite her age, her size matched theirs as she kicked one into the stove and set his face ablaze. She wasn't alone as Inka and Onka fought back to back. Inka with her bull whip, lashing enemies like she was a beast tamer; and Onka slamming one in the face with her studded baton.

Cook's eyes widened. "Princess. What are you doing here?" She struck a Berserker in the neck as she asked.

The plethora of gang members in the room turned their heads and eyed Belyx like she was a piece of gold. "Get her!" one yelled, and they swarmed Belyx. In this still moment, it was too late to go back and hide.

Inka and Onka moved like gazelles from their positions and subdued the charging brutes, but too many filled the kitchen. Word would spread she was here.

Belyx backed up and screamed as a Berserker grabbed her hair. She tilted her head back and slammed it into the Berserker's nose. The enemy let go of her and Belyx struck his neck with her blade, blood spurting over her once pink gown.

More enemies approached and Cook was too busy taking on five of them in tandem to help her...and Inka and Onka were overrun too. Belyx kicked one in the groin and lashed his neck, but one snatched her hair, slamming her face into the table. The force made her head shake, and he pulled her back to slam it again when Belyx grabbed flour from the bowl and flicked it back. In his coughing fit, he released her, and she slew him.

By that time, Cook, Inka, and Onka had dealt with the others and helped Belyx to her feet. The slam left an aftermath headache Belyx couldn't sway. "What in The God, you stupid girl?" Cook struggled for breath as she wiped blood off her apron, which wasn't her blood. "Wherever you were hiding, you should have stayed there!"

"I had to do something." More dots blurred her vision now. "Where is my father?"

"In the safe room, like you should be. Inka! Get the Princess to her father's bunker."

Inka rolled her eyes but went to lead when Belyx brushed her away. "No, I want to help. I can negotiate with them. They can be reasoned with."

Cook pinched her nose. "Does one reason with a raging bull?"

Belyx would not stand for this. This was her home to defend. "We can beat them. I've seen what they can do."

"We have a plan. Your grandmother and Freyja will return and handle this. We have them held up at the front of the palace doors. There is no way they are—"

A loud crash proved her wrong and Belyx took this chance and slipped away, ignoring their protests as she hustled for the entrance.

The fighting had only just begun.

What was once an elegant foyer was now a massacre. The Aikradal guards noticed Belyx and retreated to her as she climbed to the top of the stairs, about to make another terrible mistake.

"Stop!" Belyx's voice carried as she imagined a powerful queen speaking down to her enemies.

Someone from the Berserkers came forward like a hungry dog, and the guards backed around Belyx.

"What is the little princess doing here? Come to give us knitting lessons?" a Berserker said while the others howled.

Be strong Belyx. "No. I come in place of my father to negotiate a deal. The time for fighting is over. What do you require and the crown will accommodate?"

The Berserkers chuckled and Belyx clenched her fists.

"We always want a fight! Don't you know us at all?" one of them said.

A guard stood next to her, shaking in his armor. The same recruit she hired months ago. His red locks bringing back the memory. "Princess, we can hold them if you hide. Hurry."

Belyx counted about ten of her guards, and six Berserkers, but she did not know where The Scorpion was. Should she run and cower? *No.* "This kingdom has been in debt to your strength." The Berserkers displayed puzzled glances. "Aikradal would be blessed to have fine guards as yourselves. It is an honorable position, filled with dignity and respect."

One Berserker spat. "Leader Raul says we would be treated like kings. What could you do?"

"The one thing my mother promised. To remain strong. The people need hope again and you represent that." She played to their egos and it *would* work.

Slow applause came from the distance and Belyx's face reddened at Raul's tall frame entering. His men carried Captain Thomas behind in tatters, throwing him to the ground. "Riveting negotiation skills Princess, but what you don't understand is *we* are the strength of Aikradal and we will shed the weakness of the crown."

Thomas, bloodied and bruised, locked eyes with Belyx and he shook his head as his face hit the marble. A stomping sound boomed and Belyx's blood stilled when The Scorpion traipsed in, his armor and spear coated in Aikradal blood. *We meet again,* Belyx thought.

"Raul!" Belyx yelled, trying to control the trembling in her voice. Seeing Thomas on the ground and what the Berserker said earlier ignited an idea in her mind and it might just work. "If you are as powerful as you say, then put up your best fighter against ours."

Raul's men were watching. They loved a good fight and he couldn't refuse. The only danger was if Thomas could handle it. *He could handle anything. He had to.*

Raul's giant head curved up as he sneered. "Who do you wager?" She had him.

Belyx looked down. "Captain Thomas Beckert."

Thomas stirred on the ground, shaking his head. Raul glanced at him and motioned his men to unchain him. The Captain limped over while the others laughed at his slowness.

Raul brushed his palms. "I choose The Scorpion." *Surprise.*

Thomas made it to Belyx and leaned on her. "Please. I can't."

Belyx held his hand. It was cold to the bone. "You have the skills, captain. You can prove yourself. Show the other men you can lead. Defeat this beast."

"Are we going to start?" Raul's voice echoed. "I grow impatient with your glacial decisions."

Belyx raised her hand and Thomas turned to the leader. "He is in."

The Scorpion stepped to the center of the foyer as his men backed away. The once decorated embellishments would now be a place for blood shed.

Thomas took his sword and twirled it around, a confidence Belyx had seen in him before, growing like a flame, ready to engulf the threat.

"Ready!" Belyx yelled, catching a bubble in her throat. *Please, Thomas.* "Set!"

Everyone stood motionless. Thomas and The Scorpion eyed each other. Only one would make it out alive.

"Go!"

Their blades matched. Despite the massive size of The Scorpion, Thomas held his own. He dipped below the Scorpion's wide strike, coming up on his other side and swinging his sword across the beast's back. The armor sang, and The Scorpion swung a hand in return, just missing Thomas.

Come on, Thomas. If I can do it, you can.

The other Berserkers cheered when their champion sent a thrusting kick right into Thomas's chest, sending him and his sword flying. Belyx stepped to help but caught herself. This was Thomas's fight. Everyone here had a job to do.

Thomas rolled out of the way as The Scorpion stabbed the ground, each strike cracking the concrete. He was a machine and Thomas was running out of tricks. Readying on his knees, Thomas sprang forward, retrieving his blade. This was his last attempt to save his kingdom.

Thomas deployed a barrage of attacks at the champion, but they were barely bug bites to The Scorpion as he blocked and struck back. The Captain ducked right as the blade grazed by his head. *Go for the legs, come on.* She used to observe him train the others, and he always instructed to find an opponent's weakness.

As if he inscribed her thoughts, Thomas stayed low and lashed at the ankles of the Berserker. This did little, but Thomas dodged every move The Scorpion threw at him. Had he ever faced an opponent this rugged before? Thomas's chest bobbed, he wouldn't last much longer.

Belyx contemplated her words. "The armpit! Hit the armpit! And then the eyes!" People would question her knowledge, but even a delicate princess had observant abilities.

In a flash, The Scorpion and Thomas looked her way. The Scorpion's face was hidden, but Belyx had the distinct idea she just marked herself. Being that she attempted the same strike on him months ago.

Thomas took advantage of the beast's intense stare and swung his hilt right into his helmet. The Scorpion reeled back; the floor shaking from his size.

An almost guttural growl came from deep within the Berserker general as he charged Thomas, his spear ready to claim heads. Thomas dodged and parried with elegant precision. He was a fighter, and he was winning. The Scorpion's body thrashed. Thomas maneuvered and shimmied as The Scorpion tried to skewer him. Belyx detected a hint of a smile in Thomas as he launched his sword in The Scorpion's armpit.

The general sank as Thomas yanked it free, dodging a counter strike and following with a stab to his eye. The other Berserkers jumped out of the way as The Scorpion plummeted towards them.

The general convulsed on the ground, unable to move, but much alive. He stayed down. Raul's champion was defeated...for now.

Raul leaned over to his champion and whispered something in his ear. The Scorpion twitched like the undead and pushed himself back up, blood trickling down his iron mask, ready to fight more. Only something inhuman could survive such an onslaught.

"We are done here," Raul said to Belyx's surprise and his henchmen cursed.

Thomas's knees wobbled as he kept a straight face, now covered in dirt and blood. His once golden locks were now soiled with the same substances.

King Terach came down from the steps, out of his safe room, giving Belyx a look he had never given her before, admiration. "We still have strength yet, it seems," he said.

He let the Berserkers leave per the agreement, but Raul never stopped staring at Belyx like he would return. *Let him try.*

The other guards helped Thomas to his feet. "Sir, are you alright? No one has taken down that beast before!"

"I'm fine. I'm fine." He waved them off and met eyes with Belyx, a new fire burning in them. Nothing thankful, but something filled with anger. *He is just in shock, Belyx.*

As Thomas limped back inside to hopefully a healer, a soldier whispered to another. "You know, if someone defeats the Berserker champion in the fighting rings, they replace him. Can you imagine Captain in such a role?"

The soldiers snickered, but Belyx found nothing funny.

TWENTY-FOUR

"I was late, wasn't I?" her grandmother asked as she came into the trashed foyer with kingdom guards behind her. Freyja walked with them, pretending to be a normal bystander.

Belyx forgot why they were fighting and sprinted to hug her grandmother, and never letting go. "I thought I lost you."

Dara pulled away. "I am not defeated easily. I am very proud of you, flower."

"You mean you aren't mad?"

"How can I stay mad at the one thing bringing me joy?" She frowned at Belyx's bruises, most likely plotting the Berserker deaths as well.

Dara embraced her again, but Freyja folded her arms, sticking her nose in the air. "Freyja?" Surely her protector forgave her too. "Look," Belyx grabbed her protector's hand. "I've made errors in judgement, I know. But I would be nothing without someone like you by my side."

Freyja eyed her up and down. "Also, to do your hair and makeup because those choices were a crime on their own."

They enveloped in one another, but not too long as work had to be done.

The rest of the day was spent cleaning up the mess the Berserkers caused and dealing with the next steps. The palace was unrecognizable. The tapestries hung in tatters and the statues of the former rulers lay in rubble as bodies of Aikradal soldiers and Berserkers stained the marble floors. To think the same room held Wakening Day a month ago.

Belyx shook her head as she scoped out the perimeter. She should take a break, but today was the closest they were to losing the kingdom. The outside of the palace resembled an earthquake. The saddest was her grandmother's rose garden; now depicting the aftermath of a hoard of birds tearing through it. Her grandmother was meeting with the other Petals to discuss the attack and how to increase their defenses. Another invasion would cripple the kingdom.

Belyx wanted to attend, but knew she had things to do here. Plus, she was no Petal. She didn't deserve the honor. Would she ever? Aikradal showed great strength today, but would it be enough?

A guard had betrayed them. It was the only way the Berserkers could have gotten in. A problem this deep would take time to fix. Taking a breath, she would start with the guards who stood by.

Belyx went to see Amenthya, whose eyes bore thick black clouds. She had about twenty guards and other palace dwellers in her wake. Amenthya barely acknowledged her when she entered. "Need a hand?" The wounds she received were fine. A princess always put her people first.

Amenthya handed Belyx her paste and bandages as a silent confirmation, and Belyx worked down the line of soldiers. They looked as young as she and others older than her father. Although the guard's numbers were dwindling, they remained, and she would always honor those.

Members of the Order nodded at Belyx as she nursed their injuries. They were the driving force behind keeping the Berserkers back and deserved the gratitude. Speaking of, where was Captain Thomas? With his injuries he sustained from The Scorpion, it was no easy feat. He would come for healing soon.

The rest of the line went by in quick succession. Belyx studied Amenthya as she helped the workers with such precision and care, as if they were her own personal patients. Despite the vast number, she made sure everyone was healed. They would recover from this and be ready to defend Aikradal again. When Belyx finished the last person, she handed Amenthya her concoction. "Not bad, princess. Maybe you can train to be a healer if Thorn doesn't work out." She was kidding, but it still slipped off her tongue as a jab.

"No one could replace you. I'm just glad we didn't suffer too many casualties." Belyx's throat tired, but a princess never quit till the job was done.

"One is still too many, I'm afraid." Amenthya stacked up her pestles and organized her gauze. "You assisting here helped morale. I understand what Dara sees in you."

Belyx waved her off, checking to make sure no one was around. "Hardly. I'm a screw up who keeps getting myself into trouble and I don't know how I can rule when I can't even find a person who stole a key."

Amenthya passed her a cleaning rag and took a deep breath. Why was she so somber? "You will do greater things than you know. I can feel it."

Belyx didn't want to believe her. She feared bad things were coming and danger peered its ugly head on the horizon. "I hope you're right."

With a swoosh, Amenthya preserved the last of the paste. "I usually am."

With the ominous statement, Belyx retreated back to her room, where her items lay scattered and destroyed like a storm came through. Belyx began picking them up when her father came in. Surprised, Belyx stood taller. "Father, what do I—?"

He held up his hand. "You did a crazy thing today." His tone was softer than she anticipated.

"I'm sorry I—"

"I wasn't finished." Fishing in his pocket, her father pulled out a bracelet. "You did what your mother would have done. There was no way she would have stayed hidden, either." He walked over to her bed. Were they having a serene moment? This floating feeling was new to her. "This was your mothers." Belyx took the bracelet. It was purple and silver with smooth orbs interwoven through the crossed sword design.

It cut into her hand as she squeezed it tight. "I keep hearing that, but I'm not her."

Her father, no longer wearing his king mask, took a long sigh. "My daughter. Living in her shadow is what we both have in common. It was evident today we have many things to correct. I trust we can start together." *Thirteen years.* It had been thirteen years of nothing and finally her father acknowledged her progress. "I would like to hear your ideas from now on. Anything we can do. I realize we have to try new strategies if we are to defeat this threat."

"What made you change your mind?"

Her father rubbed his beard. "When I was in the bunker." He coughed. "What kind of father stays hidden while his daughter negotiates with the enemy, putting herself in jeopardy. I hid like a coward. You are the true hero to this kingdom."

Belyx's cheeks softened. His smooth words were calming, as if it was the one thing she was waiting for. Although Thomas deserved the true thanks. He was the one who bested the beast. "It was reckless. I could have died and ended the Velena line. I should have stayed."

"No." His voice carried. "We were nothing but stagnant statues to be broken. I admired how you used their egos against them, and it worked. Our captain prevailed."

"Did you expect him to?" It was a risky move. What would have happened if Thomas lost? Belyx shuttered at the thought.

Her father stared at the floor. "You needed to try something, but you gave me the courage to do better now. Sometimes recklessness is important. It can get matters done most people wouldn't even think about." He stilled, hands shaking. "But promise me you will be more careful in the future."

Belyx was speechless as she embraced her father. His mighty touch brought back visions of her and her parents playing in the warm gardens. The room filled with laughter and joy. If only it never ended.

But it did, and he walked to the door, his king face returning. "Council meeting in thirty? Why don't you let the maids handle this? I will see you soon."

Fighting back tears, Belyx replied, "I'll see you there." The door closed and Belyx rubbed her new bracelet to her chest and fell into her bed.

"Foolish girl," Lord Kirk spewed as he leaned back in his chair, dismissing her as usual.

"That is enough, Lord," her father replied. "Your princess will be heard and we will implement her plan. Now please continue."

Belyx took a breath, mentally shooting Kirk a rude gesture. "We need to pull our funds together and recruit the citizens of Aikradal to assist us."

Jaques scribbled in his ledger. "I tolerate the plan, but as stated earlier, it could put people in danger."

"People are already in danger. I mean, look what happened to our Master of Coin." They found his body earlier. The story was he had been taken by the Goldfingers and refused to do their bidding, dying for the crown. The thought of him as a hero cut her deep, but it had to be done. *For Aikradal.*

Belyx twisted her mom's bracelet, a calming addition to her wrist. "Ever since our queen was killed, everyone looked up to us about what to do next and we failed them. It is our duty to let them fight for their kingdom. All of them." She made eye contact with her father. "It is what the queen would have done."

The king put his hands together. "Alright, Lord Jaques and Belyx, let's draft a proposal and Captain Thomas, I need your top-notch training for these citizens."

Captain Thomas sat far away with his arms crossed, staring at the wall. Belyx wished he had a chance to rest a bit before this. "Yes, your majesty."

Kirk scowled. "This is perilous and more citizens will join these gangs more than ever now!"

"They already have," Belyx said. "And as the advisor, you must be supportive of our decisions from the council." She blinded his too small eyes with her smile and Kirk huffed.

Lord Jaques clapped his hands, unrolling a new blank document. "Let's get to writing."

Belyx's fingers heated as they began discussing ways to use the people of Aikradal to help fight this problem. Since no other kingdom would provide them aide, they had to do it themselves. The flyers would go out tomorrow and things would change.

Late into the night, they finished the draft and signed off on it. Even Kirk did, and Belyx relished at his pain. She felt like a palace sized weight was lifted off her shoulders...to finally have a say in council.

As she hastened back to her room for a long earned sleep, Thomas grabbed her arm and pulled her aside. The grip stung a little, but he released her. "Captain? Are you ok?" Belyx tried a sympathetic approach instead of breaking his wrist.

"You are hiding something." His breath reeked of booze, his face only inches from hers. Belyx puffed her chest and inched closer to him. Why was he acting like this? "What do you mean?"

"I figured it out after my fight with The Scorpion." Belyx's throat burned. What did he find out? "You know more things about fighting and combat than you let on."

Belyx almost sighed in relief. The Order was safe for now. "I just observe the soldiers sometimes."

Thomas averted her gaze, clenching and unclenching his fists. "How did you know to go for his armpit?"

Belyx thanked The God she prepared a rebuttal. "A princess can be observant."

Thomas grew closer to her with his overpowering frame, and she detected the faintest hint of a scar on his cheek from when he fought her. *Well, Doneque.* "I am the Captain of the Guard." He paused. Should Belyx respond? "I don't need the weak figurehead princess who fucks up even the littlest of tasks helping me in battle."

Belyx shuffled her feet, looking for an escape. What had come over him? Belyx opened her mouth to reply, but he put his fist next to her face. "I am the Captain. I defeated The Scorpion and I shall continue to show Aikradal's lost strength."

"We are strong," Belyx trembled as Thomas backed away.

"Mostly," he replied, turning back into the dark hallway.

Trying to shake off whatever happened, Belyx hustled to her room. Why did he act that way? He was just tired from the fight.

He will be fine tomorrow once we implement my idea. Belyx glowed. "My idea," she whispered.

To a pleasant surprise, Freyja and her grandmother were in her room, standing arm and arm with grins on their faces. Word traveled fast.

Dara waved. "I heard your father actually accepted your input. It was an excellent one."

"It's no big deal." Belyx knew it was.

Her grandmother stepped closer. "At the Order, we fix minor problems; Security threats, crime issues, but as a princess, you are fixing big issues like these gangs."

Security wasn't a small thing, but she agreed. "I'm just glad father is returning to his old self." Whatever that may be.

"Oh, flower." Her grandmother sat. "He will never be the same as he was and neither will I. Look at how powerful your mother was." Did her grandmother just say something negative?

"But things are looking up," Belyx added.

Freyja arched a brow. "Look at you, the positive one. We were attacked today, and you are saying things are better."

Belyx shrugged. "What can I say? My father needed the push. I am looking forward to the adjustments." Dara and Freyja eyed each other. "What is up with you two?"

"Shall we tell her?" Dara said to Freyja. *Tell me what? Please don't be bad.*

Freyja smiled. Thank The God. "We are recruiting more girls from around the kingdom into the Order."

Belyx raised her eyebrows. "What?"

Dara clapped. "Yes. It is time we expand this operation. I can't say I came up with the idea on my own." Belyx pointed to herself and her grandmother's face confirmed. "Your idea to recruit the citizens is what we needed, but I will need all the help I can get. What do you say? Work with your old gran to train young girls to defend this place. Maybe even becoming a Petal? Well, you're still too young, so perhaps a mixture of Thorn and Petal."

Despite the horrible day, it shifted to a better tide as her grandmother trusted her to lend a hand to expand The Order. It was what she hoped for. "You want my help?"

"Yes, granddaughter. You proved today you have what it takes to lead."

Freyja squeezed Belyx. "Can you believe it? There will be more people like us."

Dara went for the door. "It will be tough and they will have to be trusted with this secret, but nothing great was ever easy. Freyja, come draft a plan with me."

"Yes, ma'am," Freyja said, mock saluting. Belyx started to follow, but Freyja stuck out her hand. "Rest, princess." She winked. "You deserve it."

Normally Belyx would protest, but she had enough drafting of plans for one evening and bid them both goodnight.

Once she closed the door, Belyx went out to the balcony. The moon light had started to pour in and the cool breeze tickled Belyx's cheeks. Despite the events of today, Belyx proved she possessed the skills to face down any threat, including the intense Berserkers...And the council. She shut her eyes and said a silent thank you to The God and her mom, forgetting for a while about the betrayal from the thief.

TWENTY-FIVE

I n the dark night of the shaded forest, the red-haired former queen trailed through it with only a torch for light, outlines of the trees dancing like a parade. Queen Abigail kept looking over her shoulder as she traipsed along the rough nature trail, taking care to not make a sound on a branch. She was on mission and no one would stop her.

The woman stopped as a shadowy figure appeared. She bowed, keeping her torch light up. "What is the report?" she said with a voice as soft as velvet.

The figure came into the light. He was dark-skinned, with pointy ears and leaflike tattoos covering his whole body. "My agents have spread out as far as they can. They are catching onto us. How shall we proceed, Abigail?" His voice was sweet like fruit, but carried heavy authority.

"Send in more. We can't let them get away with this. They are selling people," the queen replied.

The fae man turned away. "Some here think this is too risky and oppose our agreement to the settlers."

Queen Abigail stood tall, not wavering, her face fading in and out of the fire. "The fae have been helpful in every endeavor. Surely they can't withdraw now, since we are so close."

"Dark magic threatens us. They intend to harm this place if we interfere. We magical creatures must remain neutral in conflicts."

"You wouldn't say such things if your kind were being sold."

"I understand you have a daughter to think about, but we can't risk our lives. I fear for *your* safety." The fae spoke with respect, despite not being under her rule.

The Queen of Aikradal threaded her fingers in her leathers. "I would never force you to do anything. I will have the Order take over from now on. Bring your tribe members home."

The fae bowed and Abigail kissed his hand, his face bore fear and determination as he turned and hustled back.

Belyx awoke from her slumber. What a weird but vivid dream? What was her mother doing with the fae? If she was working with them, why did they betray her? The time was only an hour past midnight. She settled into bed and tried to sleep more to make sense of it. Dreams were not real, it was only her racing thoughts.

She jolted up, sprouting the best idea. Her father must have some kind of information on all this. *I need to find out more. Doneque needs to have a word with the king.*

Jumping from her bed, Belyx changed into her assassin garb. "I need you now," she whispered to it.

On her way up to her father's room, a sudden movement caught her eye and bolted down the stairs. It was most likely a Leaf, but Belyx had to be sure. The figure moved fast as they trailed down the steps, and Belyx had to speed-walk to keep up. *If it is an intruder, I should yell, but if it's not, I'll look crazy.*

The hooded person flew through the kitchens and into the art room, as if sensing Belyx was near. She pulled out her knives and charged in, but it was a dead end. She frowned. No one was there. Where did they go?

After scanning the room, something seemed off by the family portrait, as if a faint breeze was coming from it. With shaking fingers, Belyx rubbed along the frame's edge, giving a slight pull, but it didn't budge. The figure must have gone somewhere else. She turned to look elsewhere when a chill slithered down her neck.

With a closer look, sure enough, the draft did come from behind the portrait. How had she or the Order not know about this? Unless her grandmother was keeping secrets...again.

She felt the back of it and ran into a hook-like latch. With a click, the portrait creaked open. Checking her back, her knives, and her breathing, Belyx entered the passageway. The drop in temperature made her shutter as she shut the portrait.

As she crept down, the blasphemous statues of demons confused her. Was a secret cult living right under her home the whole time? Her father would have a fury about this. Any movement set Belyx's teeth in feel like ice as her knife stayed ready to gut the hooded person...or thing sleeping here.

The passageway sunk deeper and deeper as the darkness grew. A torch sounded like a missed idea about now and she cursed at her lack of preparation, but a faint light shot through the end of the tunnel. Where did it lead?

Belyx slipped and her face met concrete as she rolled down the stairs, trying to stifle her grunts. When she landed, her muscles ached, but a bright room shone before her. It was as big as the main ballroom floor, with lit torches and stalactites surrounding the area. More demon and weird looking men statues circled the room as well and Belyx had a distinct feeling they were following her movements.

Now thankful for the torch lights, no matter how creepy, Belyx gazed around the room, but found no other door. Belyx went along the sides, peering for any crevice of a passageway.

The statues had teeth the size of daggers. Belyx recalled these from the stories of who The God had to fight to claim this land. Someone clearly felt like The God wasn't for them. Unless they built the palace over an old shrine from before.

The room was silent and reeked of metal dust. As she examined a torch, it wasn't burned down. *Like they kept replacing it.* This was no old shrine, but was it constructed and maintained? Someone from the palace had to have worshipped the demons. It was most likely Lord Kirk. If anyone would worship blood sucking demons, it would be the blood sucker himself.

After traversing the room, Belyx sauntered to the middle and studied the floor. Ornate marble depictions of people being eaten and, worse, graced the design. The floor was smooth, with no trace of a switch or trapdoor. Belyx sighed and considered heading back. *Tell your father and let him see it. And about the intruder.*

With her decision set, she marched back where she came when the lights went dark as if a gigantic monster blew them out. Belyx's senses heightened.

She wasn't alone in this room.

Someone or something lurked about. *The trespasser!*

A creak sent Belyx's attention to the left as it prowled closer and closer with human steps. Belyx struck out, whatever was coming underestimated her night fighting skills.

Knife sliced flesh as the assailant grunted. It sounded low and male, but oddly familiar. It ran, but she chased the attacker, following the faint footsteps. Her head slammed into a wall, and she stilled.

Shaking her headache, she held up her blade and returned slowly to the middle, ignoring the ringing in her ears. She had snagged a piece of whatever it was.

After a few minutes, the lights came back, and the creep stood right in front of her.

To her surprise, The person, clad in a black hood, was who she never thought she would encounter again.

There, panting and holding his cut arm, was none other than Enzo.

Rage was the only emotion Belyx could fathom as she recalled the stories of people who suddenly lost their minds and went on a killing spree, waking in a stupor with blood on their hands.

At this moment, Belyx understood that.

She lunged. Her blade was steady in hand, going for his heart. His traitorous heart. Visions of saving him for the first time invaded her heated blood. Her laughing at the jokes he made. And worst of all, the kiss. The kiss sealed his fate. It wasn't even the fact he betrayed her, but that he did it after toying with her emotions like she was a doll. She refused to be his toy in a box, and he would never treat her or anyone the same again.

The problem Enzo faced by betraying Belyx was she spent her free time thinking of the ways she would slaughter him like the vile fish he was. She smiled as she envisioned his lying guts splaying the floor.

Where was she? She didn't care. Enzo in front of her was what she cared about, and her blade was ready. The details could be sorted out later. Was he talking? No explanation would save him.

Her blade struck his flesh again as he screamed. He evaded most of her strikes, but she was an animal thirsting for blood. She lashed and lashed and he tried to push her back, but the knife met his hand again and his face pained. Belyx took pleasure in it, reminded of her anguish the last month. The attempt to run was futile as Belyx grabbed his shoulder, preparing to jam her steel into his throat, but he sent a quick elbow into her jaw.

Reeling from her pain, Enzo went on the offensive. He swiped at her with yet again, her knife, but Belyx laughed to herself. Blades were her game, not his. After evading a few strikes, Belyx knocked his blade out of his hand, and kicked his groin and he doubled over on the ground.

Her emotions cleared, and the pulsing in her ears paused.

"Belyx." He spat out blood. "Please. I can explain."

Belyx knelt down and jammed her blade into his thigh. He screamed louder and Belyx cared little if anyone heard. Let them come and see the traitor.

"Sounds like my screams the morning you betrayed me." Going to plunge again with her knife, Enzo rolled out of the way, kicking her back.

Enzo hobbled up. "I had no choice! You don't understand." The blood trickled from his leg, but not bad for where he was stabbed. *I need to aim better.* Did Belyx want explanations? As much as anyone, but in this moment, she had already thought of everything and none were adequate enough.

Belyx screeched as she went into another frenzy. Enzo tried to block and run, but Belyx's assassin training came full circle as this would be a kill she relished. Enzo went left, she went right and did a fake out with her blade, diving to the ground and sweeping his feet out from under him. He grunted as Belyx straddled him, recalling a time when they did something similar that night.

"Nothing you say will save your life, traitorous bastard."

Enzo grabbed her arm as she plunged down. He had the strength, but she had the angle. Belyx snatched the blade with both hands and seethed as she put her weight down. Enzo moved slightly, and the blade nicked his cheek. A miss would not happen again. Enzo wrapped his legs around her and pulled, but Belyx elbowed his open leg wound, and he released her.

Belyx slapped him and a release took over her body. With a balled fist, Belyx pounded his face, over and over again, ignoring his cowardice pleas and the fire of pain in her knuckles.

After the fifth hit, Enzo sunk down, eyes blinking and nose bleeding. Belyx snatched her knife from her leg holster and stuck it to his throat. Enzo opened his eyes and the deep green sank into her soul. The source of where his charm came from.

Shaking her head, Belyx pushed the blade further, but stopped. Her mother's face flashed into her mind. Was she a killer? Did she kill like this? Like a flicker, her grandmother's words echoed in her head. *Although we are trained to kill. It does not mean it is the right thing.*

Her breaths quickened. For a month, she had dreamt about this. About seeing Enzo again and severing him limb from limb, but as he lay there, Belyx couldn't do it. He was troubled, like her. The thief who liked to read and wanted to read *her* poems. Her hand shook. It was a lie, *Belyx. Kill him now. He deserves it.* Belyx raised her hand.

Enzo stilled, closing his eyes.

Belyx screamed and plunged down.

The knife clanged into the marble next to Enzo's face, her tears pouring onto him. Grunting, she shot up and walked away, folding her arms, sniffling like the sad princess she was.

Enzo sat up and stared into the wall. After steadying her breaths, Belyx faced him. "Ok. You have five minutes to tell me everything."

"The first thing I want is for you not to freak out on me again." Enzo pressed part of his loose sleeve on his knife wound; his face was already swelling from the strikes.

Belyx crossed her arms. "Time is ticking."

Enzo sighed. "I understand why you are mad, but once you hear what I have to say, it will become clearer." Belyx didn't believe him, but she held the cards. Even though she spared him, it didn't guarantee his life. "I don't know how else to say this, but I'm fae."

Belyx's eyes shot open. "What now?" Was this one of her reasons in her head? *Not even close.*

"Fae. I'm sure you learned about them?" Belyx folded her arms and lifted her knife. "Right," Enzo continued. "I'm not human, I'm fae."

Belyx couldn't believe what she was hearing. The fae were wiped out for betraying her mother. Why did she not catch on earlier? "Prove it." Acid spewed from her mouth. If he had anything to do with her mother's death, she would gut him with no more stalling.

"I can't, but I can tell you I'm a fire fae. See?" He tilted his arm up and the covered part of the flower tattoo showed tiny flames. Anyone who knew could see it. "I had to cover it up because, you know."

"I don't. Was it the fact your kind killed my mother?"

"That isn't true." His tone changed, like one of a wounded child.

Every conversation they had flooded back to her. Was anything he said real? "Not what I heard. She built up their trust, and they betrayed her."

"Again. It wasn't true. We are peaceful creatures. Why would we kill a person who respected us and kept us a part of their culture?"

"Domination? Everyone wants power. Anger from settling on your land?"

"This is why people need to read more. Our gods prohibit us from being power hungry. We are humble and tranquil. If we wanted to kill the humans, we could have done it when you settled here over 200 years ago. Also, you didn't settle in our forest. We didn't own any other part. Seriously, do you own history books?"

Belyx gasped, recalling a fact about the fae. "Wait, how old are you?" Almost wrenching as she waited for an answer.

Enzo grimaced. "Gross! I would never do things with you if we weren't in similar ages of maturity. I am technically thirty-six," detecting Belyx's scowl, he changed tones. "But fae mature half as fast as humans, so I'm eighteen. It is weird your mind went there first."

"Well, how was I supposed to know? You practically spew lies."

"I'll allow that, but besides aging, we are also immune to witch enchantments." Belyx gasped and Enzo responded. "Yes, that's how I escaped from Scandeni's curse."

This was coming down on Belyx with too much force. "Well, then explain how you broke my curse. I've never read that." She hadn't read much, but he didn't need that information.

"The tidbit about not reading doesn't surprise me. Because of the negative propaganda, our books were destroyed. Trust me, I looked. Besides, I don't know how I broke you out, but it was like my immunity rushed in and saved you." So it was a curse...not a drug.

"What about your ears?" Belyx slammed her common sense for asking this.

Enzo rubbed his lobes. "I have to cut them short every couple days and yes, it is painful." *Good*, Belyx thought.

"That explains how you healed quickly the other night." Belyx shuddered. Fae recovered faster than humans.

Enzo stepped closer, but Belyx stuck out her knife. "The feelings I had were real. I felt terrible about what I had done and how I couldn't do anything during the Berserker attack."

"Wait. You were there?"

Enzo circled his feet around the ground. "I sort of saw you, and I used the Berserker attack to sneak into the castle. I tried your father's study and that had nothing, so I went to try another place." That's when I caught him. *He could have slit my father's throat. He got past the Stems too.*

"Wait, why do you want the fae artifacts?" Enzo's face said it all. "What does it actually unlock?"

Enzo clutched his right pocket, a tell of where the key was. "My trapped family and tribe."

"All of them?"

He coughed. "The fae weren't killed the day after your mother died. Your father did something...else."

What did her father do? He would never do something unprecedented. Sensing her tension, Enzo said, "he cast a kind of spell and locked my tribe away, using the key."

"A spell? So now my father is a witch?" Was she a witch, then?

"Well, no, but I think the reason this shrine is, um, the way it is is because he made a deal with a dark force. He could never have killed the fae on his own. No offense, we are a powerful group and would have protected ourselves successfully."

Belyx laughed. "Really? That is ridiculous. My father was not a coward and would never use magic. How did you survive, then? I guess you are slippery after all."

Enzo frowned. "I was off exploring, and when I came back, everyone was gone."

Belyx felt a tinge of guilt for bashing him, but his lying didn't ease his case. "So that was how you ended up on the street? Didn't you think to ask anyone for help?"

Enzo stared at the ground. "Hate spreads like wildfire. When I came into Aikradal, signs and protests were everywhere, claiming to kill the fae."

Belyx's heart sank. "I'm sorry Enzo." He shrugged. "But how did you learn about the key? The truth. Still some circus witch?"

"Yes."

"They don't live around here, Enzo." She failed to mention the potential one she met on the street, but she was just a pretender, no more.

"Oh, they are around and I would fear them." Belyx held her tongue, and Enzo continued. "She told me about the key and how there was a way to break the curse on my people."

"And you trusted her?" He was as stupid as Belyx for trusting someone.

"If there was a chance to bring your mother back, would you go to the ends of the continent to do it?" Belyx closed her mouth, tired of putting her foot in it. "But she never told me how she knew of this key and right after, the gangs started targeting me like a weird coincidence. All of a sudden, this rumor of fae magic came up, and then I was caught. You can only slip away so many times when four powerful groups are on your tail."

The emotions Belyx faced tonight had the power to level mountains. "Why didn't you tell me?"

Enzo chuckled. "Fair enough. I was going to until I found out who you were. Also, the way you spoke about the fae was unsettling. Would you trust you after?"

It made sense why. She was the king's daughter. The man who took his family. It became clearer, but still twisted like a complicated poem. "I guess not."

Enzo grabbed Belyx's hand, and she went to pull away, but stopped. "My feelings for you grew, but I had to think about my family. So, I took the key and intended to free them right away, but things turned sour." Enzo froze. "The witch came back and tried to take it. She fought hard and injured me, but I escaped."

"How did you get away?"

He shrugged, but eyed her. "Ok, no more lies. I found Scandeni, and they protected me until I was healed enough to go. I had to escape them too when they trapped me, but as I said, his spells don't affect me."

Belyx wanted to scream how foolish it was to trust the Cabarets, but admired his honesty. She would have done anything to free her family and survive. "So you have fire. Show me."

"I told you, I can't. Our powers have requirements, but basically, if we don't use them for a long time, it fades away."

"Why didn't you use it often? Never mind." Belyx imagined a panicked Enzo too afraid to try his abilities, not even risking a spark. "You can't use them ever again?"

Enzo stilled. "Never." What a feat, to have such great power and lose it forever. Belyx understood as well as anyone what it was like to hide. Although Enzo had to do it for survival...

Wasn't she doing the same thing? "To be honest. Before I would have done anything for my kingdom." Enzo's eyes twinkled in the torchlight and his face narrowed. "I thought the key was just for powerful artifacts. Who knew it was something this evil? Why would my father lie about it?"

Enzo shrugged, and his mouth parted. "I understand the duty to your kingdom, Belyx. You can stop me, but just know I am going to fight for my tribe as well."

Belyx looked the thief up and down. His face was more stubbly and his hair had grown an inch or two, with the curly strands hanging in his face. This man she both hated and loved was pure.

No, Belyx. He betrayed you and left you alone, crying. Wouldn't Belyx have done the same thing to save her loved ones? She gripped her knife. With all her power, she swore an oath to the Order to uphold the values of Aikradal. Enzo was a threat to them and to her kingdom. The day when she was eighteen and passed the Budding trials was the best day of her life. Her pining and grieving had ended, and she finally had an outlet for her pain. Kill for Aikradal. Enzo proved he was untrustworthy, but Belyx couldn't help but notice the similarities.

In one swoop, tears rolling down her face, she threw the knife.

The metal clanged on the stone as she hugged Enzo, praying he wouldn't stab her in the back with one of her knives. He embraced her in return, his breathing steady and safe. His citrus and salt smell ignited a familiar warmth in Belyx.

Belyx pulled away. "Let's save your tribe." She would regret this, like with saving him, but she couldn't let an entire group suffer. Although she needed to be cautious. Lying was still a possibility.

"Well, your guess is as good as mine where to find this vault." Enzo said.

Belyx scanned the floor again and noticed a crevice was arched in the outline of the gruesome design she missed earlier. "It appears a trapdoor opens here, but I have no idea how it opens. There has to be a mechanism, like how the torches went out. You did that, right?" Enzo shook his head and Belyx's throat dried. "Ok, well let's hurry then." A powerless fae and an assassin would be no match for a demonic force.

Enzo and Belyx stalked around, trying for any loose switches or threads. Would it even be easy to find? The torch lights twinkled across the intricate paintings of vile creatures eating humans. Did these creatures still exist?

On first glance, Belyx would've missed a crucial detail, but after a second look, she quivered. "The torches."

Enzo turned his head. "What?"

Belyx's fingers rubbed over the curved details of the light vessels. From far away, they looked like normal etchings, but the snakes twisted upward, as if slithering away from the ground. The torch wiggled as she pressed on it and with a snap, it rotated upside down. The flame crawled through the snakes and traveled back up to a new flame on the top again. "Flip them. Enzo, flip them upside down."

Enzo beamed as he maneuvered each torch, and Belyx went down her line. There had to have been one hundred of them stretching along the upper edge. Belyx climbed a crumbled staircase to get the rest and Enzo did the same. After a beat, they had finished.

At first, nothing happened. Belyx and Enzo rushed back down to the center, waiting for a miracle to happen. Rubbing the sweat from her brow, Belyx sighed. "Why didn't it work?"

Enzo pushed forward. "Now, who is the genius?" Belyx waited with impatient glaring until he put his foot over a slight divot depicting a serpent wrapped around a soldier. "Those who defy him are strangled by snakes," he said as if rehearsing a proverb and stepped on it.

The floor cracked and groaned as it slid open, as if the people on the bottom were being caught by the monsters. It never intended to be a benevolent sign. Belyx had to step out of the way not to fall through. Now in front of them was a steep, dark staircase, with torch lights trailing the way down as if by magic. With a gulp, Belyx rubbed her sweaty hands on her bodice. "Let's go."

Enzo froze. "Whatever we find down there, I want you to know I care for you a lot, and I hope this works out."

He had said these promises before and they almost died then too. "It will. It will." Belyx had to doubt her words. She took a step down when a loud voice sent chills up her spine.

"Halt, thieves."

Belyx turned, dreading every second of the encounter.

A figure stomped over, armor and chain mail clinking. When he came into the light, Belyx knew this would be tougher than she thought.

He unsheathed his enormous sword, glinting with gems...As a king's weapon should. "I will make you both pay," her father said.

Twenty-Six

B elyx's legs felt like they were stuck in sludge. Her father, her own blood, had his sword drawn and was out for their heads. Before Belyx reached for her knife, her father charged, holding his blade to Enzo's throat with deft-like precision. "I would advise against that, assassin."

She moved her hand back as Enzo's eyes filled with terror. Belyx gave him a reassuring look. Her father was concerned about intruders, nothing else. He never cast a curse.

His weapon pressed harder on Enzo. "So," the king said. "This is the thief and assassin who laid waste to my guards. And now you are here to steal the magical artifacts." He was still lying.

Enzo pushed the king away, but her father swung his sword for his head. She launched her knife and knocked the steel away. Enzo backed to Belyx, but her father sliced his weapon for her now, his own daughter. With her blade, she struck his and it flew out of her hand. He slammed her into the wall with his mighty strength. Would she have to subdue her own father?

King Terach moved fast in his armor, striking at them. Enzo jumped one way and Belyx the other. She took out a venom to immobilize him, but he forced her back. Blades at the ready, she lashed with ferocity. But her father was trained. He blocked every strike. Spinning, her father slammed Belyx with his hilt and her ears rung as she hit the ground.

Enzo sprung on the king, knocking his sword away. Belyx picked it up as Enzo was thrown into the rocks. The king moved to him when Belyx lurched in front, holding his weapon. "Stand down, King." She lowered her voice, praying he wouldn't recognize his daughter's.

Her father stood in a fighting stance, as if he was going nowhere. She could take him out without killing him. *I just need to get to my non-lethal venoms.* Belyx swung the blade in an arc, but her father worked his sharp footwork and knocked her in the face, tearing the sword from her grasp. He followed with a deft slash and cut her leg. Tumbling forward, she knifed his calf, but his armor protected him. With sheer force, her father kicked her stomach, and she doubled over, grunting in pain.

Lying on her back, she pulled out the venom she needed, but her father stood above her, blade to her chest. "Not too tough now, are you, killer? Who do you work for? The Whispers? Berserkers?"

Belyx couldn't find the words as she eyed her father, staring into those deep hazel eyes resembling her own, cursing at the fake contacts she had on.

"Just tell him!" Enzo yelled, but her father whacked him in the face with his hilt.

"Now I will ask again." His sword dangled over to a dazed Enzo. "Who do you work for?"

Belyx bit her tongue, the king's sword mere inches from Enzo's heart. She had to do something quick. His steel hovered up and Belyx screamed, "Stop, Father!"

The blade stayed in midair as her father scrunched his eyebrows. "Belyx?" He stumbled back. "It can't be." Enzo rolled out of his reach.

Belyx removed her hood and wig, letting her burgundy strands cascade down to her neck. "It's me."

Her father looked away, gripping his sword tight. "Not my daughter." He pointed. "You are an imposter!" Before he could lunge at her again, Enzo stepped in front, taking an armored forearm to the head and landing in the rubble.

Why was he acting like this? The king came at her, and she held up her hands. "The last thing mother said to us was 'I love you both more than the stars and the entire sky.'"

Her father halted in his tracks, his jaw clenched as he twisted his hilt like a towel. "It can't be. Belyx, why? How?" After he asked, he fell to his knees in agony. "No!" he yelled. "No! I can't! She is my daughter!"

Who was he talking to? Belyx went to him, but he lashed his sword at her. "Stay back! It's not safe!" Afraid to face what came next, Belyx stopped.

He ceased his sword swinging and slowly rose as if possessed, glaring at Belyx with unfamiliar eyes. "I must honor him. We made a deal. I'm sorry, daughter."

"Are you crazy? I am your blood!" Tears welled in her eyes. She wished Enzo was awake to see this.

He shook his head. "You were never supposed to find out. It was supposed to be fixed!"

"What did you do?" Belyx's throat dried as the words spewed. What had he done? "You preached power and unity! Did you make a deal with a demon?"

Her father cracked his neck. "Not a demon, a being. A powerful being. With the power to bring back your mother." His words stung. "My wife."

"You can't bring her back! She is gone!" Could this be real? Nothing existed that had the power to do what he said. *Would you do anything to bring her back?* Enzo's encouragements radiated in her mind like a festering wart. She refused to be tempted.

Her father spat, stomping the ground. "She was everything to me! You hardly even knew her!"

Belyx recoiled. How could he say such things? Her mother was as vivid to her as anyone. "Who did you sell your soul to?" Her blade was readied. Her father was not the man she once called father anymore. He was a monster.

The King of Aikradal laughed. "I tried hard to be a good father and keep you safe and here you are gallivanting as a treasonous assassin. Who trained you?"

Your wife's mother. "Myself." Her lie came out prepared.

The king skulked close to her, breath reeking of death. "You will not lie to your king!" He slapped her face, his hands cold and raw. "You have betrayed your kingdom. And traitors must die."

A new heat pooled around her fresh bruise, letting her killer instincts flow like the river. She couldn't kill her father. "I am no traitor! I have saved Aikradal and have been fighting the gangs. While you did nothing, I kept them off our backs." Her father fumed. "I even found your key and was going to destroy it until I learned about what you did to the fae!"

Her father was wretched. "Those vermin murdered the queen. They had to pay!"

"Don't you see, father? We were tricked! They didn't kill mom. Someone else did! Enzo is one of them and you took his family!" She regretted outing him at the moment, but her father had to understand.

Her father's face turned to Enzo like a wild animal. Belyx messed up this time. "If he is fae, then he must die!" Her father pounced on the unconscious Enzo.

Before Belyx could think, her hand went to her knife and threw. The blade met its mark and her father went down. He gasped for air, holding his bloody side where the armor split. "Wretched girl!" He spat as his blood stained the demonic floor.

Belyx kicked his sword away and pressed his hand on the wound. He made a guttural sound almost inhuman like. "You are blinded by hate, father. I can't believe you did this. This is against The God and what They stand for."

"Belyx?" Enzo shifted awake and sat up, taking in everything.

"Get to the vault. Save your tribe. I have a mess to clean up."

Her father grabbed her hair and yanked it back, but he didn't try to kill her. His voice shook as alcohol protruded from his breath. Did he drink this much to cope? "Kill me. Kill me, please. I can't do it anymore." The king's tone changed to weak and desperate, but murdering her father was not an option and she wrenched away.

Her father pulled out a small jeweled knife, and held it up to himself, but Enzo slammed his face with a torch and he went down.

"Now you know how it feels," Enzo said as he threw the torch down.

The king was still breathing as she rolled him over. "We need to free your family. My father is under a dark influence. Maybe using the key will break it." Belyx hoped she was right. This couldn't be him. *It couldn't be.*

Enzo helped her restrain her father, and they rested him against the wall. The king's face was as pale as a scroll and recessed in, as if something was eating away at him from the inside. She forced a minor sedative down his throat to make sure he couldn't break free as well.

Enzo grabbed Belyx's hand and they took a torch, hurrying down the steps.

"I can't believe my father did this. It's vile. How could he do this to our kingdom?" Belyx kicked the dirt as they treaded through the catacombs, which had nothing but darkness and decay. Where was this door?

Enzo sighed. "People do wild things when they are grieving. I would have done anything to get Ren back." Ren, his old tutor. The one who taught him how to live on the streets. "I realized I could have followed my emotions and killed the Berserkers after they killed them, but it wouldn't have brought them back."

"Yea, that's what stopped you."

Enzo glared at her, putting his hand to his chest. "Did you just make a joke? At me?"

Belyx rolled her eyes. Despite the severity of this moment, Enzo's presence was a comfort. She gripped his hand, and he held tighter. "I'm scared of what will happen next. Once this secret surfaces, I can't watch Aikradal fall."

"I think helping me will give the people peace of mind. You'll make a great queen." He swallowed, realizing the time would come sooner than later.

"Not like my mother, who apparently died by another threat. It's like the crypt opened again."

Enzo's hand squeezed hers. "I won't let anything happen to you."

"I thought I was the one saving you?" Belyx almost smiled.

"I think we are even on that count, and maybe I won't save you." He looked into her eyes. "But I will fight by your side."

Belyx dreaded her next statement. "Do you think your family and the others will be the same?" Enzo cringed. *Nice one, Belyx.* "I mean, being trapped somewhere for thirteen years could take a toll on a person's mental state."

Enzo stayed silent, and they continued walking. It was like with each step; they were nearing hell itself.

Enzo stopped. A door the size of a giant stood in front of them, its exterior coated in gold with snake designs on the side and, to Belyx's relief, a key hole near the bottom. "Looks like an important door to me," Belyx said.

Enzo rushed over, barely able to take out the key from his pocket.

Belyx kept back. The whole thing could go wrong, and she wanted to be prepared. She rubbed her blade in viper venom, not taking a chance on potential demonized fae. Would Enzo fight with them if given the choice?

Enzo stuck the key in the lock.

The silence absorbed the room but the faint beat of Enzo's heart. He would finally see his family. Belyx wished her mother was in there too, but things never worked out how she hoped. Enzo twisted the key and with a clunk, nothing budged. With a hard twist, he grunted from the effort, but the door stayed shut.

Belyx tried it. "Why won't it work?"

Enzo scratched his head with fury. "This makes no sense. It should have worked! She said it would!" Belyx held back telling him a circus witch was not a reliable source.

"We can go ask my father. I will do whatever it takes."

Enzo slammed his fist into the door and kept it there. "I will burn it down. I can do it. Please! Please!" He banged the door harder and harder. "I will not fail you again! I should be in there with you!" Tears stained his bruised face. The bruises Belyx gave him. She reached for him, but he pulled away. Shaking back and forth, he fell into Belyx. "I thought this would work. It has to. It has to."

He sank lower and Belyx rubbed her hand along his strong back, carrying his pain and resentment—similar to her father's. "It's not over yet. It has something to do with the spell."

Enzo sniffed and looked away, his soft puffy eyes gazing into her own. "You think so?"

Belyx grabbed both of his hands. "Enzo, despite our intentions the last couple of months. I know one thing, we work well together. We took on the four gangs and made it out alive each time. If that doesn't show skill, then nothing makes sense in this world."

Enzo stilled, and fell into Belyx again, his sweet scent clinging to her. "How do you always have the right thing to say?"

Belyx pulled away and bowed. "A princess always has a way to please her subjects."

He snorted. "I have to say, I don't miss the horrible wig."

She smiled as she touched her head, truly herself for once. "Maybe it can retire for a bit. I never thought I would ever be exposed like this."

"Around me you can." Enzo kissed her, a mix of tears, salt, and possibly blood filled her mouth, but she didn't care what it was. She was the one with him. A heat she never knew she missed.

Breaking the perfect moment, Belyx headed back to the entrance. "You stay here. I will have a word with my father."

He shook his head. "You will not go up there alone. The door isn't going anywhere."

"You sure?"

"With my life, we finish this together. Plus, I can't let you face your father alone."

Belyx nodded, and they trudged back. Those creatures would be freed tonight. Not only for Enzo, but for her people. She would be the change she wanted to see.

Once they reached the top of the steps, in which Belyx contemplated ways to squeeze the information from her father, she paused.

Her father wasn't where they left him. Enzo and she drew their weapons, scanning the area. Only the sound of flickering flames filled the room.

"Those won't be necessary," another familiar voice of the night said.

Belyx's heart danced its own rhythm. Her father was standing now, still restrained, but someone held a knife to his throat. A person Belyx never thought would ever betray them.

Someone she trusted the most.

The curse and how to free the fae were now the least of her problems.

His advisor, Jaques, wore a devilish smile, tracing her father's face with the blade. "We have much to discuss it seems."

If Belyx had to face anymore surprises today, she would launch herself into the Sea of Kifalia. Her father was still drowsy from the poison, but Jaques held him up with impressive strength.

"Which gang do you work for, traitor?" Belyx still couldn't fathom it was him.

Jaques responded with a guttural laugh. "My dear princess. I would never serve such filth." His voice was different from the Jaques she had known. How did he keep up his act this entire time?

Belyx continued her stare as if in an intense chess match. "Then who do you work for?"

Jaques growled and waved his knife around. "What makes you think I work for anyone, being just a pitiful advisor and all?"

"You aren't. Are you?" Enzo said, receiving a glare from the supposed advisor.

"No. I'm not." He pointed his blade out, hand still as water. "I would never stoop so low. I was once a powerful being, trying to live my life when this oaf played with dark magic." Her father groaned. "You just couldn't stay out of the fae's business. You had to use them as a scapegoat like they would ever be capable of murdering Abigail! Well, I have other plans now." The name came out casually, like he knew her.

"You'll never be king!" Belyx's voice flared. What was happening in her court? First the Master of Coin, and now this?

Jaques shook his head. "You were always a presumptuous bitch, trying to fix everything. Trying to prove yourself." He spat on the ground. "You are nothing like the queen and you never will be!"

"You knew my mother?" She faltered slightly, but Enzo's presence calmed her.

"She loved the fae. Unlike him." He pointed his blade back at the king, who started to stir.

"You're fae?" Enzo asked.

"Wrong again." Jaques put his knife down. "I'm something better than your putrid slime of a race." He growled, cackling to himself as his body shimmered an iridescent glow, waves of bright colors surrounding him.

An explosion shook the room and his once slight frame grew taller and taller until he passed Enzo's height. His hair shifted to a stark white and his same pale eyes reflected the fire.

Enzo gasped. "A male witch." *Like Scandeni. How many more walked amongst them?*

"For once, you are right." Jaques's voice changed to one with a lace of evil. "We males are born from those ground kissing witches every day, and what do they do? They cast us out like pigs to slaughter, without the decency to end us themselves. Cowards." He swirled energy around his palm. "But little did they know of our abilities. I can shape shift into anything I want." In an instant, he shifted back to advisor Jaques, and then Belyx, and after, a shorter woman with dense wrinkles and stark white hair.

Enzo cursed. "You were the circus witch who informed me about the key!"

Jaques switched back into his original, gangly form. "You catch on quick, but you were more slippery than I anticipated."

Belyx related too much. Enzo shook his head. "You nearly killed me for the key! Why not steal it yourself?"

Jaques laughed. "Why try to find something when a desperate fae trash will do it for you? Surely you follow the same mantra as a common thief. I told you and then I gossiped to the gangs about bullshit magical artifacts so they would kill you!"

Enzo retreated, but Belyx stepped in front. "You said you were acquainted with my mother." He kept dodging the question.

Jaques eased his body, as if taking in a new outfit. "I used to disguise myself as a fae to protect my identity. I only knew a life of hate and pain. Then the queen of this acid hole showed up, asking for the fae's services around the continent. Queen Abigail differed from the rest. She didn't fear the fae. She gave them a purpose."

"What do you mean?" Belyx tried to mask the terror in her voice.

"She would use the fae to spy on other kingdoms." It was like in her dream. What was her mother up to?

"You didn't kill her?"

Jaques spat, "Of course we didn't! The fae cherished her!" He still lumped himself with the fae.

"Then who did?" Enzo asked.

Jaques sneered. "Who do you think? It was humans. You bunch always kill each other like a chore. It was probably someone from that cesspool, Majeria."

Not Majeria again. "What? Why would they betray us?" Belyx asked.

Jaques admired his nails. Her father had to wake soon. The poison wasn't strong. "We found out about their illegal smuggling rings and brothels and they were trying to bring them here!"

Bile rose to Belyx's throat as she fought the urge to sit down. "Why go after us, then? Why not go after them if they did it?" Belyx swore to The God if Princess Vivienne was involved, she would gut her.

"I wanted to, but the fae were peaceful and boring. They refused to avenge your mother." He turned to Enzo. "Your pathetic kind can't do anything." Enzo lunged, but Jaques held the knife closer to her father. Even though he didn't need to, he stopped, as her father meant little to him. It was for Belyx. "I almost convinced them to when the illustrious and haughty King Terach invaded our forest and took them in a blink of an eye."

Enzo stilled. "How did you find out about the king's secret?"

"Witches are far more superior. I had my eye on the Dark Tome for a while with an intent to use it, so it was no surprise when the bitch's father took it." Enzo gulped. What was this Dark Tome? Jaques chuckled, as if sensing her confusion. "Oh, how uneducated humans are. Your thief trash knows, but I will explain to you, simple-mind." Belyx went for her knife, but Enzo held her calm. "The Dark Tome was given to the fae by the witches as a peace offering when the fighting ceased. The fae kept it well hidden. Even I couldn't find it. Then, King pathetic gets it and uses it on them. Fools."

"Humans can't use spells. How did the king do it?" Enzo asked.

"Oh, they can." The king groaned, shaking. Belyx needed his help soon. "If they make an agreement with an outside force. Your father received help from a dangerous being." He *was* telling the truth.

"Who?" Belyx asked.

Jaques shrugged. "It goes by many names. All are true and rotten." Jaques tapped his foot. "His price though." He tilted his long neck at Belyx. "In order to trap the fae, he needed a powerful spell. He handed over a piece of his life to make the key work. As long as air passes through his lungs, the key won't unlock shit."

"No." Belyx choked back tears. What had he done?

The king's eyes jutted awake. "What? Belyx. What is happening?"

"Can it!" Jaques slammed his head, and he went down. Belyx gripped her blade. One throw and he would go down. "Also, I am not the pathetic one you call 'Jaques.' My true name is Aydevko, Master of Shapes."

"Scary," Enzo said with sarcasm.

Aydevko hissed. "Quiet you inbreed! You're weak, just like the pitiful advisor!"

Belyx stood in front again. "What do you want with the key, then?"

Aydevko smiled. "To do something they should have done a while back. Eradicate the humans."

Belyx shook her head, tears building. "My mother would never agree with this."

"They killed your mother!" His voice rose. "All humans do is fight amongst each other for fun. I mean, look at the gangs. They are the product of a failing society, and I want to shed this tumor from the world. Humans have no place here anymore."

Belyx related to his pain. If she found out who killed her mother, she would slay them, too. The look on the shifter's face screamed loss and hurt. A searing blight Belyx and her father were familiar with.

No matter what, she wouldn't go down her father's path. Enzo's wise words of moving on fought in her brain like a saving life force. "Aydevko," she said in a soft tone. "I lost a mother, too. I lost someone I knew well, but also not at all. Let us help you. We can investigate Majeria together and bring them to justice."

"No!" His voice twisted with darkness as it echoed off the drab walls. "I have waited far too long to have a princess slime tell me what to do. As you said. When she passed, you were barely a child. You didn't know her like me! You didn't...love her like me."

She took a shaky step back. "You loved my mother?" Belyx prayed her mother didn't feel the same way towards him.

Flustered, Aydevko reeled back. "She would have been mine if it weren't for this horrible man." He pointed at the passed out king again. "She would have loved me more."

"My mother was too honor-bound to fall for your pale ass!"

Aydevko hissed. "You don't think I knew! But I have a long lifespan and the King would've died before her and we could've been together. I could find a spell to make her live forever. It would be fairytale worthy."

Enzo stepped up. "You can't bring someone back from death, but you can make someone immortal? What kind of magic is this?"

Aydevko arched a brow. "You will mind your tone around such a sacred item, vermin." He kicked her father forward and with a snap of his fingers, a book the size of his palm appeared. It was moldy from age and its edges were fraying. "This holds power beyond your wildest imagination and I plan to use it again today!" He chuckled. "I've been searching this palace thirteen years for it. Thirteen years! I had to create that pathetic advisor to infiltrate the palace."

Belyx scowled. "It was you the whole time!" Images of the kind Jaques, who joined after her mother's death flooded her mind. *It was him.* Her skin felt paper thin. It was a ruse.

Aydevko stuck out his tongue. "Yes, he was one of my better characters I created I guess, although I should've killed the other advisor years ago. I would have saved you lots of trouble."

"What do you mean?" Lord Kirk was bad, but not any traitor against the kingdom.

He shook his head. "You are clueless. Kirk worked for the Whispers! He was Sewek's errand boy!" He cackled. "It was so obvious. The way he kissed the ground she walked on. Lucky for you, I recently stained the entryway with his blood. Consider it a parting gift."

Kirk dead didn't phase or upset Belyx, although the traitor thing needed to be confirmed. "Whispers don't recruit men," Enzo replied.

"That's how she fooled you. She made you accustomed to a pattern and broke it to trick you. He fed everything to her on a diamond plate! Sewek was the only one smart enough to rule. You should have killed her when you had the chance, assassin."

"So you have been watching us? When did you figure out who I was?"

Aydevko grinned. "During the night of your groveling. I saw you sneaking in one night and it resembled the assassin who saved the thief. Then I caught you snooping around. Who knew you were on the path for the key as well. Which was a bonus."

"Why not reveal us to help your plan?"

"You were not my concern. Although I still don't know nor care about how you are well trained. I'm sure it's that infernal old bag you call a grandma. She was hard to read indeed."

"My grandmother was more honorable than you, snake."

Aydevko reeled his pale head. "Snake is not an insult. They stalk the ground and are the apex predators. People flee before them! I will have what is mine!"

Her father woke and lunged at the witch, but Aydevko was too fast and stabbed him in the side. Belyx threw her dagger, but he caught it like a ball and held it to her father's throat. "Death by his own daughter's blade. Poetic."

"I'm sorry, flower," her father's voice was more of a whimper now. "I only wanted our family together again. You make me happy and you will make an excellent queen, just like your mother."

The world buzzed throughout Belyx as her head swirled with a heavy torrent. A ringing of alarm wailed in her ears. No. No!

Belyx lunged forward, but it was too late. Aydevko, in one quick motion, slew her father, blood spurting from his neck. His body slammed against the marble, along with Belyx's happiness. Going to strike, the witch vanished. She whirled around and gasped as he appeared behind Enzo. "Look out!"

Enzo turned in time as Aydevko lashed at the thief. He dodged and struck back, but Aydevko was relentless. Belyx's feet stayed glued to the ground as Enzo avoided a few of his blows and knocked him away.

Aydevko winced in pain, but chuckled a throaty laugh. "You aren't the only pickpocket, fae." In his hand, lay the key. Belyx growled to herself. He had what he needed now for whatever his plan was. Aydevko held up the object. "With this, my plan shall be—"

A crack and the key flew into the air. The key moved back with the whip and the recipient caught it in their manicured hands. Aydevko growled, showing teeth.

Dara kept a straight face as she pocketed the item. A battle skirt with tight leathers underneath replaced her usual fancy clothes and she had her hair wrapped in a crisp braid. Belyx had never seen her grandmother dressed like this.

Dara glared down the witch. "It seems you have taken something that isn't yours, Aydevko." She turned to Belyx and Enzo, a twinkle of hope, but also fear fused in her stare. "You messed with the wrong family this time."

Twenty-Seven

Standing tall, her grandmother faced down the witch. "Well, it seems this night is just full of surprises. What an advisor you are." Her grandmother kept a neutral tone, as she did in most conflict.

Aydevko scoffed, stepping over the king's corpse. Belyx prayed she would gut him. "I figured you had something to do with this assassin princess motif. How many more are part of your little club?" He spoke to her as if she was a child.

Dara stood firm, unrelenting as she taught Belyx. "Many more. And they are on the way, shifter. Fate was not on your side this time."

"What gave it away?" he said with no hint of surprise.

"I've witnessed you sneaking around the library and into the king's private quarters. At first, I didn't know what it was for, but you aren't as covert as you think. I found your journals on the missing key and how a thief had it. Thanks for the tip."

She knew the entire time. Why didn't she tell her?

Aydevko mock applauded. "And then you sent your pitiful granddaughter to retrieve it. How witch like. Getting other people to do your work."

Belyx turned to her grandmother. "Is it true? Were you aware the whole time?"

Dara shook her head. "I did not know what the key was truly for. All I knew is it contained kingdom shattering power. Little did I expect it was a heartbroken cast-out-witch looking for the trapped fae."

Aydevko growled. "They didn't know what they were missing. To exclude someone just based on their gender! Preposterous."

"Join the club, shifter." Her grandmother's voice matched his without a hint of fear. "You couldn't be excluded. That is why you joined the fae and clung to the first person who gave you the time of day. My daughter."

"You." He pointed at Dara with his sickly talon. "She didn't deserve a mother like you. Controlling and overly positive. Queen Abigail never spoke highly of you. She let me know how you refused to investigate Majeria despite the evidence of their immoral schemes!"

If his words sliced her grandmother, she never showed it. "It is against the agreement between the kingdoms to meddle in each other's affairs. I tried to tell her it was a dangerous idea and look what happened." The things her grandmother never told Belyx came to light. At the moment, Belyx had a hard time deciding who to be more angry at; her father, Dara, Aydevko, or herself.

"You couldn't protect your own daughter. What makes you think you can protect a kingdom?" His words struck like steel. "Your little group had the power to infiltrate any kingdom it wanted. Majeria is selling children and working with the Goldfingers! How could you not care?"

Dara readied her stance. "I don't fret about things out of my control." She gazed at Belyx. "I can only prepare the ones I love to defend themselves when the time comes. I'm sorry, flower. I did not know the extent of what your father had done."

Tears jumbled in her eyes and Enzo reached for her, but she pulled away. "I love you, grandmother." Despite her anger, it was true.

Her grandmother smiled, but Aydevko fake retched. "Boring! Enough of this tripe. Hand over the key or I rip it from your saggy corpse!"

Her grandmother launched a whip strike at the shifter, but he moved like a shadow and dodged it, heading right to her. Dara winked at Belyx and flung a smoke pellet on the ground. In seconds, the room filled with a thick fog.

She felt someone grab her hand and slide the key into it. "Run," her grandmother whispered.

A forceful gust pushed through the room, and the ash cleared. Belyx ran toward the entrance, but Enzo grabbed her. "My family. We can't leave."

Belyx went to protest when Aydevko jumped at her, only to be yanked back by her grandmother's whip. He seethed as he broke free and she bolted for the trapdoor when a field of energy materialized in front of it. Aydevko shook his head, Dark Tome open in hand.

Dara gritted her teeth as she lashed him, but with a snap, her whip turned into a serpent. Her grandmother let go without even a scream and it slithered away. Belyx only watched in horror.

Aydevko sauntered to her grandmother, darkness swirling around him. Dara pulled out a pair of twin blades, the steel glinting in the torchlight. Aydevko closed his tome and two black swords appeared in his hands as well. "I've studied every weapon, hag, and for longer than you."

Dara stilled her head. "It may be true, but I have enough skill to rid the world of your darkness."

"Your move." Aydevko paused, as if facing a lion. They stared each other down and Dara glanced Belyx's way as if to say goodbye. Aydevko pounced at her grandmother, swords flying like a wheel, but Dara blocked every strike with care, only striking back when her opponent had an opening. Aydevko moved too fast and Belyx struggled to keep up, but her grandmother did with ease.

Aydevko shifted right and nicked her grandmother in the hand. She flinched in pain, but kept up the defense. Belyx couldn't stand and let this happen. Taking her blade, she went to her grandmother, but a force pushed her back. "This dance is only for two, sweetheart!" Aydevko yelled as he parried Dara's strike. Their skills were a match.

Belyx stepped back. When a familiar hand reached into her pocket, she tried to stop it, but Enzo was already running down to the trapdoor, key in hand. "Enzo!"

"No!" Aydevko shouted as he launched a stream of darkness for Enzo, but he rolled before it struck him. The shifter went to run after, but Dara took the opportunity and sliced his arm. Aydevko screamed as he stumbled backwards and Dara went for her necklace, Belyx's mother's necklace, and Aydevko jumped on her in a fury. Belyx was only a captive audience, being forced to watch as her grandmother faced a nightmare.

The woman responsible for her training and success was battling for the kingdom, proving she was the true mother to Belyx. The woman who helped raise and train her. Nothing made Belyx more thankful at this moment. The things her grandmother sacrificed weren't for nothing. Her mother was great because she had a great mother. Dara had been with her from the beginning and she would defeat this threat.

Aydevko moved with a flurry of quick slashes and knocked a sword from Dara's hand. Dara stepped back and pulled out a small blade to replace it, with a ruby encrusted on the hilt. This dagger had been passed down for generations, reminding the Velena women to remain strong in dreadful times. Her grandmother's words were like a peaceful song being played in a pristine garden.

Dara fought Aydevko with everything she had. He would strike her and she would strike back. Belyx prayed to give her grandmother strength. As if on cue, Dara disarmed the shifter and knocked him to the ground. Aydevko tried to stand, but she pulled out a garrote and twisted his arm back, slamming his face into the wall. His tome fell from his pocket and grandmother reached for it.

Belyx screamed at the knife Aydevko held behind his back. Snakes struck true, and they struck fast. Her grandmother turned to Belyx, eyes widening as she plummeted to the tile, Aydevko standing over her.

Emotions blurred. First her father, and now her grandmother.

She charged the shifter, but once he snagged the Tome, he sent a cloud of energy, knocking her into the stone. The entire world shattered around her as she struggled to move. *Come on. Come on.* Her muscles refused to work as she lay helpless, like a wilted flower, unable to absorb up its own water.

"Foolish." Aydevko laughed, glancing between Belyx and her grandmother, a pool of crimson flooding beneath her. "To think mere mortals thought they could take on me." He clicked his tongue, turning his head at Belyx. "You watched your grandmother fall just like you will watch your people fall." In a snap, the blades, venoms, and poisons flew out of Belyx and smashed into a lump. "These are mere mortal weapons." His spit hit the tile. "Have your goodbye. I have a plan to fulfill." With an evil spring in his step, he went down the tunnel.

Belyx's legs wobbled as her blurry vision returned to normal. *Go after him! Go after him!* her thoughts screamed at her, but her mind only took her to one place; where her dying grandmother lay.

How could she go after Aydevko when her grandmother swam in her own blood? *Enzo would handle it,* she tried to reassure herself as she squeezed her grandmother's chilled hand. Dara stared at the ceiling, a slight smile forming on her face. Why was she happy? She failed trying to stop Aydevko.

"It's all my fault, grandmother. I screwed this up." Tears plummeted down Belyx's face, blurring her vision and she dried them. She would treasure the last view of this amazing woman. Belyx tried to roll her over to fix the wound, but her grandmother stopped her.

"Flower. It is too late for me." Blood trickled down her cracked lips.

"We have to try! We can't give up!" Her hands shook underneath her grandmother's.

Dara coughed up blood, splattering the floor and Belyx in it. "I am immensely proud of you. I should have seen this coming. If it is anyone's fault, it is mine." Her voice struggled to spew the words.

Belyx's breaths wheezed as she cursed with no end. "No! We have to try! Please!" She kept trying to help her grandmother, but like a tree, Dara planted herself.

"Stop. You will be queen and run the Order now." Her grandmother avoided Belyx's eyes. "Your first duty is to defeat Aydevko."

Belyx wanted to hide away, to never ever step foot in the palace again, but she had to. It was her duty. "I don't have any experience on how to do those things." Her body went limp. "I can't rule an entire kingdom, plus the Order. You did all of it."

Dara turned. "You are more like your mother than you know." She coughed more thick blood. Dara's time was slipping away like drops of rain on the concrete.

"How can I defeat him? He has immense power I can't touch. I'm only human."

Dara's shaky hand grasped at the necklace around her throat. The one of The God, with two swirl designs and in the center, contained a small vial. "Poison for magical creatures. I've had it in case they tried to go after you. Little did I know the truth. No one is what they seem. Remember that." *It was hidden in there the whole time?*

Belyx took the vile, it held no more than an ounce of poison. "Will this work?" Her heart thudded in her chest. She couldn't stop this, but her grandmother had the skills to.

"I pray it does. The God will watch over you. Aydevko's tome carries his power. Separate him from it." Her grandmother shook and convulsed. Belyx had the urge to turn away, but she kept eye contact and never let go of her hand, refusing to until it was over. After her grandmother stilled, she managed one last smile. "Save the kingdom. Change the people's attitudes. You can, flower. I know it."

She handed her the ruby blade from under her clothes. How did it not get taken? "fae made," she choked out. The Fae were immune to witch spells. The metal refused to obey him, and it would be his end.

The time passed was unknown, but she treasured her grandmother's grip in hers and then, as if a torch went out, her grandmother released.

Belyx sat there, eyes closed, sucking in slow breaths while the vile pinched her palm. Enzo needed help below to stop Aydevko. He claimed two of her family members tonight, but the count would stop there. No one else she loved would die to his hand.

Belyx took one last glance at her grandmother's body. She was peaceful and yet troubled. "This is for you and everyone here." She took the fae blade and opened the vial; Tiny purple droplets fell onto it. This poison was something Belyx had never seen before, but she trusted her grandmother. Yielding was not an option. With a prayer to The God for her grandmother's safe travel to the afterlife, she stood, trying not to fall on her shaky legs and sheathed the knife. Doneque would end this. Her wig and hood were on as she headed down the steps, ready to take on the witch who murdered her family.

Twenty-Eight

Belyx couldn't count on her blades or venom this time. She had one blade and it would be enough. With her shoulders held high, she stormed the tunnel, praying she had the strength to take Aydevko down.

A yell from Enzo increased her pace and once she hit the clearing, Enzo was slammed against the door, out cold.

Aydevko turned toward his new opponent and sneered. "Princess. Or should I say Doneque? I can't tell which is which I'm afraid. Can you?" He looked taller and more menacing, ready for a fight.

"Drop the key. You have taken too many of who I love tonight." Her voice wouldn't wobble. She would stare down the monster and defeat him. *Like my grandmother tried.*

Aydevko laughed, making her throat burn. "You poor dear. It must be hard to lose all you hold precious. Oh wait. I know exactly how it feels. Maybe we can work out a deal?" His fingers twisted around his tome like it was the only thing giving him power. "Help me fulfill my plans, and I will let you and the fae live. We can stop the fighting right here. Let the humans get what they deserve. What do you say?"

Normally, this would be a straightforward choice for Belyx, but she gave her falsest smile. "No." The words left her mouth quick and Aydevko reeled back.

"Not even going to think about it? Pity. I don't give too many chances." A flash of darkness traveled through the air, but Belyx leapt behind the stalagmites, avoiding the blast.

Keeping low, she crept around as Aydevko destroyed the rocks.

"You can't hide forever, assassin! Give up!" More dark energy soared from his fingertips, but Belyx dodged the blows, moving from rock to rock to keep her position hidden. She had the advantage this time.

I just need to stall him until the Order arrives. If she could inject the poison in him beforehand, that would be a bonus, but even her grandmother struggled with such a task. Taking mind of the weight on her feet, she snuck closer and closer to the witch.

His bolts were scattering rubble across the room and she would run out of hiding places soon. Belyx kept her heart still as she slowed her breaths. After she rounded the corner, she pulled out her poisoned blade and closed the distance. The faint charcoal scent radiated as his back was turned. She swung down, but a burst of energy knocked her back.

Aydevko smiled like he found his prey and sent more blasts her way. Belyx evaded them, feeling the death radiate off it, like the happiness was leaving the world. She lunged back to Aydevko and reached for the Tome, but Aydevko kicked her away. Stumbling, she caught herself, only to be greeted with a cold blast. Her fears rushed into her head like wind as she slammed into the nearby rubble. *Stay down. Stay down.*

Aydevko hummed as his footsteps grew near. Belyx's body shook with images of her friends and loved ones dying, but her mother's face wiped the fear away. "Foolish girl. When will you learn?" Each footstep he made was an opportunity to quit, but Belyx refused. Eyes closed, she waited for the moment to strike.

Her hand grasped a broken stalagmite and, in one blind swoop, launched it at his head. It met its mark as Aydevko screeched. Like a panther, Belyx kicked the Tome right from his grasp. Going for her knife, she lashed at him, but he was too fast and parried the blade, sending a counterstrike into Belyx's face.

Holding her hands up, her vision blurred.

Aydevko cracked his neck and pulled out his own short blade. "I think I'm having déjà vu. Do I have to kill another Velena bitch tonight?"

Belyx shook off her pain and twirled her steel. One cut was all it would take. "Your move, traitor."

"It is you who is the traitor, young one." Aydevko went down and swiped at her legs, but she sidestepped back. Once she went right, she sent a thrusting knee into his side. She wanted to attack more, but kept up her defense like her grandmother would. Aydevko came back with a vengeance, swinging his steel around his body.

Despite his supposed training, knives were her territory. After evading a few blows, Belyx elbowed Aydevko in the face. He shook his head and Belyx struck again, but he dodged and slapped her across the face, laughing as she rubbed her raw cheek.

"You're pretty deft, but naïve. It takes years to get this skilled and look how it still turned out for your old gran."

He baited her, and it worked. Belyx's face seared as she threw a flurry of strikes at him, but of course he was ready and maneuvered every one, sending a piercing counterstrike into her face. Warm liquid trickled down her head, but it wasn't enough to stop her. Taking a breath, she reeled in her anger, replacing it with something better—love.

"Was it that easy to take you down? You humans are too sensitive. How will it feel when I rule and kill every human? You don't want at least some humans to die? Like Majeria? The kingdom who killed your mother?"

He had a point, but it would cause too many deaths of innocents. Revenge never was the answer. "You seem to be the sensitive one, wiping out an entire race because my mother didn't love you back."

Aydevko clicked his tongue. "Nice try, but I won't fall for your hook." Belyx went to respond when Aydevko was on her again. "I tire of chat. Let's dance!"

His quick strikes were hard to time, but Belyx had faced worse. He was nothing but an unhinged thing with anger issues and it would be his demise. After a couple of lashes, she faked left, and went around, and Aydevko stepped off balance. This was her moment to attack as his arm lay open and exposed. She sent the blade down, cutting his flesh.

Aydevko spun in the air and clocked Belyx with his heel. The ground collided with her face, but she had won. The poison would work and he would be no more. Sitting up, she spat blood, smiling. Aydevko sighed. "What are you smug about?"

Struggling to stand up, Belyx chuckled. "For an omniscient being, you are pretty clueless." Her voice grew confident. "You fell for my trick." She held up the empty vial. "Poison for magical creatures."

Aydevko's face turned blank in fear, but then, like water to ice, it changed to an enormous grin. "Do you think you are sneaky? I smelt it on your grandmother when she stepped foot into our fight. I knew she would give it to you in her dying breath."

Belyx wanted to cry, but he was bluffing. He was trying to keep face before his death.

Like a second skin, Aydevko peeled the knife cut away, throwing the remnants in the distance. "Snake skin spell," he mused. "But I admire your ability to land a strike. I figured you'd have to work extra hard for it."

Belyx released her fury and charged at him, screaming. A deeper slice had to do the trick, perhaps in the neck! She attacked, but couldn't stick a blow. Her muscles cried out for relief as she stabbed at him, but in one quick redirection, he took the poisoned knife and thrust Belyx to the ground.

Wincing at her side, watching this creature loom over her, she spat, "Fine. Kill me. I won't go down without a fight."

His eyes wavered as if deliberating something and turned to the passed out Enzo. Her eyes widened. "Or. I try this little concoction on your fae lover over there? I'm sure he will cherish it." Aydevko absorbed the poison from the dagger, forming a glowing purple energy orb fluttering in his hand.

Not another one. No one else!

Belyx found strength she didn't know she had and launched herself in front of him as the power released from his palm and it slammed into her.

At first, Belyx felt nothing, but then, everything. A warm sensation pooled at her center and black curtains formed in her eyes. What little feeling she had left in her hands touched around the wound. Hot blood spilled from her while her vision stilled.

How could she have failed like this? She sacrificed herself for a thief...the kingdom would fall and she would no longer be queen. Her fingers trembled as her body floated up to a faint light and in a snap, it fell.

The last thing she heard was a crack, and the world went dark.

Twenty-Nine

A fae boy loved running in the forest.

His day started when the sun came out and would end when it went down. The boy felt the wind in his hair as he ran as fast as possible through the trees, timing the seconds in his head.

Running was his favorite activity. His father had just loaded his nap sack with freshly baked berry scones, enough to last him the entire day. His other father gave him pallets of paint and brushes in case he felt inspired. The boy never did art, for he was too busy sprinting.

The Sehrlic forest spread north of the kingdom, Aikradal, and stopped right at the Dath Mountains. It was the biggest place to run! Today, the boy turned and went straight up toward the River Thex, an ancient stream ending their boundary to the Desert of Polakaz. He spent his days near it, nibbling on warm biscuits and tossing stones in the moving brook. This was where he felt safe to use his powers. His fathers told him he had to be careful to use them in the forest, for if it burned down, the gods would be angry and punish him.

Standing by the safe water, he sent a spark flying into the air. The heat leaving his body felt incredible, his cheeks absorbing sun like fire. He needed to release his flames every day or his power would fade. Part of him loved his ability, but another was afraid of it. "You are the rarest of the fae," his father would say. "Fire and water fae were special. Not like your father and me. A nature and wind fae." Part of him wished he was just like them. Someone who had the appearance to blend in, but he received only fearful looks from his tribe. Why couldn't he stay invisible?

After his power release, he would do more running and head back to camp for dinner and games with the other kids. It was his turn to be it on his favorite game, Spring the Tree.

His fathers' favorite activity were the nightly performances, which involved singing, acting, and dancing. The cast would dress up and perform the history of Keyica, when the fae and witch tribes lived in harmony until the witches tried to take over. The boy wished the witches weren't evil like the stories. He wanted everyone to get along and not fight like the humans did.

That day, his father told him to stay out till dark...the boy wanted to anyway, but the words from his father kept echoing. "Stay out today, Enzo. The day is yours ok?" Enzo nodded and ran off like his usual self, but his father gave him an extra long hug. "Say bye to papa too, ok?" Enzo always did. Why did he make such a fuss about it today?

After saying bye to his fathers, he went off and filled his day with his typical running and practicing his abilities.

When he returned home, no one was there. He called and called for hours, but no one answered. Enzo searched the entire night, but nothing. His family was gone.

It's your fault.

You should have been there.

You let them die.

You could have saved them.

The boy screamed and screamed...and never stopped.

Enzo woke in a flurry, nothing but the cold ground beneath him. The last thing he remembered was getting blasted by Aydevko. Belyx's screams were the last thing he heard in time to witness her hitting the floor, and Aydevko standing above her. *No. Was Belyx dead? She died for me, then. Even after what I've done.*

"Oh, you're awake. Just in time." Aydevko sauntered over to the lock and inserted the key. Enzo charged the witch, but with a snap, a burst of energy shot him back.

The lock clicked, and the massive doors swung open. Already waiting on the other side were the fae, his family. Images of him as a boy playing with them crawled to his mind. A mass of his tribe stood there, confusion and pain lining their faces. He couldn't help but look for his fathers who were nowhere to be seen. The fae refused to come forward, as if skeptical of their newfound freedom.

Aydevko held out a hand. "They have refused to take revenge on the humans, so I will make them!"

"They are immune to witch magic!" Enzo's breaths hitched. Aydevko had to be aware, right? All his life searching and here the fae were, in front of him, yet in the moment, he wanted his tribe to remain hidden.

"Some witch magic does work, but it leans more demonic." Aydevko snapped his fingers and dark energy swirled. "How do you think this pathetic oaf of a king trapped them here?" Enzo hadn't thought of that. *Of course, demons played a role.*

The fae backed away slowly, refusing to fight back. They were thin like they had barely eaten and their sunken expressions bore no trace of happiness. Aydevko smiled. "Now is your chance, thief. Look what the humans did to your kind. They locked them up like cattle and threw away the key. Your tribe did nothing wrong. Join me and we will take this land back for the creatures."

Enzo hated his words, but he had a point. The humans had only shown him hate and violence. Someone who didn't show malice. Someone who didn't do what the humans did. Someone who understood and helped him even after he betrayed her.

Belyx. She showed humans were able be good, like any species. Enzo tightened his fists, looking for a power no longer there. "You're gonna have to fight through us. We fae are strong, we are kind, and we will never do your bidding!"

As Enzo's voice grew, he frowned as Aydevko applauded as if he gave an elaborate show.

"If you're done, I would like to cast this spell." He began speaking incantations. They slithered through Enzo's ears like a soothing song, but one of death. A wrenching black snake coiled in his mind. *Fight it, Enzo. Fight it.*

A picture displayed him doing horrid things to humans. He was burning their homes and slaughtering their children. *They deserve it.*

No, they don't.

They do.

His voices were at war with each other. They were torturing him.

Choose me.

Choose me.

He couldn't. Just couldn't. Belyx flashed before his eyes. What would she do in this? She fought her own father and her grandmother died for *him*. He refused to play along in this game. Aydevko had to be stopped to free his family.

Eyes shot open, Enzo launched up, but Aydevko and the other fae were gone. Belyx remained on the ground, and he wanted to stay with her, but he had a job to do. He took her knife, admiring the fae handy work.

At the end of the stairs was something Enzo was not expecting. Servants and maids were fighting against his tribe. It must be the Order Belyx's grandmother spoke of. The fae had a hint of red in their eyes. They did not know what they were doing and were tempted like Enzo. Why was he the only one who had beaten the spell? *Once again.*

The women battled hard despite the fae's elemental powers. Enzo rushed over to a familiar woman who finished knocking a wind fae to the ground. She was taller, with dark skin and intense braids. She must have been Belyx's handmaiden, Freyja.

With a hunger in her eyes, she charged for Enzo but he held up his hands. "I'm on your side! They are under a curse!" Would she believe him?

The handmaiden lurched to a stop and looked him up and down, as if contemplating his demise. "A curse?"

"Yes. The fae mean no harm. Please don't kill them." Freyja folded her arms and opened her mouth to respond when a gust of wind blew the maidens away. Afraid to look, Enzo gulped. It was his father, Thano.

Enzo rushed to him. "Father! Stop!"

Thano glared with crimson eyes, preparing the air in his palm. How could he attack his own son? Before he could, Freyja snuck behind him, which was impressive considering a fae's keen sense of hearing, and slammed him into a wall by his thick red hair.

"Only knock them out! They are under a curse!" Freyja yelled, and the purple wearing Order members switched to less lethal tactics, fighting with precision and honor, similar to Belyx.

His other father, Gink, rushed Freyja as if taking revenge for his mate. Freyja gritted her teeth as his father entrapped her in vines and the other fae surrounded her, ready to kill. Enzo pushed through them. They must have assumed he was on their side.

"Sorry, father." His father tilted his head, but Enzo took a rock and struck him, his large body plummeting to the ground. The vines lowered and Freyja continued fighting. This was an entire tribe of fae. There was no way they had the skills to defeat them, especially normal humans.

Enzo knocked out a few more and made his way to Freyja. "We can't get through this, you know."

The handmaiden hit a fae in the face with a staff, and Enzo was pretty sure he knew them. "Well, where are *your* fancy powers, then?" She was already agitated with him. Belyx must have spewed choice words about what he did.

Enzo tried to find his power, but it was like a dry well. Years of not using powers cost a fae all their abilities. "It doesn't matter. We need to find Aydevko. The spell is in his book. If we take it, we can beat him."

Two blonde twins fought side by side, but were launched into the statues by an air gust. Freyja dodged a water bullet and bent her staff into a bow, launching an arrow and striking the wind fae in the leg, sending him down.

The fae overwhelmed them. Enzo lashed back with his knife, but had a hard time subduing his tribe without causing lethal injuries. They needed a new plan, and fast. A larger woman in an apron grabbed a fae by the throat and tossed him like a chicken into the wall. She took on two more at once. Whoever trained these women did a thorough job. It was probably Belyx's grandmother. He gulped. *Who died for me.*

More fae swarmed the area, but Freyja and a few other members held them back before a large fire blast encased them. Enzo ran to help, but an ember seared his hand.

A fire fae had trapped them. It was Pyne, an old friend of Enzo's. There weren't many other fire faes, and they bonded from their rarity. Now he was about to kill everyone.

The vortex surrounded the women, and Freyja stepped in front, willing to go down for them. *Like Belyx.* Even in death, she would fight it head on. Belyx was lucky to have such a noble handmaiden.

Enzo climbed to the fae, only to be throttled by flames. The embers scorched his skin but he wouldn't give up.

The women in the inferno screamed and Enzo searched for any power in his well, any ounce of a spark. *Come on. Come on.*

He fought against the emptiness in his well. The fire was there and he would find it.

The fae and maidens dueled with all their might as bodies of both lay over the area. All this bloodshed and this carnage could have been avoided if he used his power to free them thirteen years ago...instead of retreating like a scared boy.

Heat clung to his face. The fire fae would swallow them up soon. Tightening his fists, Enzo approached the fae, his former friend, now under the spell of a witch. The fae launched another stream of fire, but Enzo held out his hands. If his fire wouldn't come, he would force it out. The blast pushed him back. His whole body boiled, but he stayed, screaming through the swirls of embers. He would not die this way. One step after another, he trudged through the blaze. The fae's fire would not last long as his power would dry up. He couldn't burn him.

When the fire grew too hot and Enzo's feet begged him to stop, he choked it down. This needed to end, for his family, and for Belyx. The fae pulled his flames back and he rushed through, tackling him to the ground, and slamming his fists into his face. The vortex lowered, and the trapped woman ran over. Enzo stood, whispering an apology as he left the sleeping fae.

"Aydevko is on the surface," Enzo said.

Freyja cracked her neck. "Then we get to there. Are you ready?"

Freyja charged with the force of a lion, her bow/staff in hand, knocking back enemies. The thought they would heal when injured calmed Enzo.

When fighting at the top of the stairs, Enzo tried to reach for his flames. The hits of fire didn't affect him, but he was unable to create his own. He bared his teeth. If this was the time, it was now. "Freyja!" A blonde maiden called, carrying her twin.

Freyja stomped on an enemy's foot and elbowed him in the jaw. Enzo struck him from behind with his hilt. "How's Inka?"

The blonde sister shook her head. "She has seen worse. She will be fine. We are pushing them back, but a strong magic user up above is wiping us out."

Freyja cursed. "By The God if he makes it to the streets, he will slaughter anyone in his path."

Enzo didn't know why this group was formed, but they fought with purpose.

"Thief," Freyja pointed to him.

"Enzo." Why did this thief label keep following him?

Freyja eyed him down like she cared less. "Our plan is to push through this mess and charge the shifter. What should we know?"

"Take his book. It is his power," he said again.

"Then the plan is to get the book. Onka. On my side. Enzo." She paused. "I don't know what happened with Belyx, but right now, we need you and whatever skills you possess. Can you do that?"

Onka grabbed her sister's whip. "I am borrowing this, sis." She kissed her sister's cheek and stood still, ready to fight.

Enzo gripped his knife. "Let's go."

They ran up, dodging the elements and helping others. Too many girls littered the ground, no match for the powerful fae.

Enzo grasped a nearby fae and slammed her face into the stone. Freyja followed up with a jump kick to another while Onka subdued them with her baton. A fae launched gusts of wind for the twin maid, but she whipped her baton and it struck his wrist. As Enzo rounded the corner, he clubbed a fae's face with the hilt of the blade and he tumbled down.

The entrance painting was in view. *This is against the gods. Come help me now. I have forsaken you by neglecting my gift. Please give me one chance to restore it. Your people are in danger of their own actions.*

Enzo hadn't prayed in a while, but he needed to try something. If they reached Aydevko, he wouldn't be able to defeat him without his fire.

They passed through the painting, and the main floor of the palace was a bloodbath. The Aikradal soldiers fought against the fae, killing them. Enzo's gut sank, as they didn't know about the spell. A soldier went to stab one when Onka's baton hit the sword out of his hand.

"Whose side are you on?" the soldier chided her, but the fae jumped up for revenge. Enzo stepped in the way and he lashed him in the arm. They hit the ground, and Enzo knocked the fae out.

Onka came to his side and blinked at him. She saved his kind. Humans were capable of more.

Freyja caught up to them, covered in blood, though not her own. "Where is the creep?" As if to answer, an explosion cracked from the entrance and they raced to find Aydevko throwing maidens and soldiers into walls and various statues. He was floating, his snowy white hair swirling in dark energy.

"Onka, the book," Enzo said.

She pulled out her sister's whip. "Way ahead of you. Distraction, please."

Freyja nocked an arrow and fired for the shifter, but it rebounded off his energy and he veered like a hawk. "Fae thief. You did make it. How's princess worthless?"

Freyja fired another arrow, but he grabbed it with a shadowy hand and chucked it back. Freyja and Enzo rolled as the impact slammed by them. The armored soldier's display came alive and swung at Enzo, but he parried the sword with his knife, stepping back. He gasped as Aydevko flew close to him, raising a dark hand to strike, but an arrow knocked him away. "Insolent whore!" he yelled as he launched multiple beams for the handmaiden.

She leapt to dodge, but it shattered the wall near her and the shards crashed into her face. Freyja lay helpless and Enzo cursed, jumping out of the way from more falling pillars. How much more did this castle hold?

Aydevko cut him off as he veered around the corner, his magic swirling like a cape. Enzo called and called for his power.

Please give me one ember to combat his energy. Just one!

Aydevko swirled his hand when a long whip snatched the Tome from his other. He plummeted to the ground and Enzo readied his knife. Aydevko landed, but even without the Tome, he put up an impressive fight. Dodging Enzo's strikes, he twisted his arm behind his back, snagging the knife and cutting Enzo's wrist. Enzo's posture stiffened as Aydevko launched a kick into his face. He flew and hit a pillar, dazed.

He pushed himself up, hoping Onka was far away, but a scream came from the top of the banister as Onka fought the Aikradal soldiers. Aydevko raced for the stairs. "The book!" he shouted.

A guard pulled his sword from inside Onka and she fell with a thud, blood pooling around her body. The traitor guard threw down the Tome and Aydevko soared into the air again, throwing guards and female assassins away.

Enzo dashed behind the rubble as Aydevko continued his fight. He needed a plan and scanned Aydevko for any weakness when an idea hit him. The Tome was anything that could be stolen, like gold or jewels. A distraction was the perfect ploy, like how he was taught by Ren.

The ideal moment was close. His stomach twisted. He wasn't a thief, but who he had to be. *Last time.*

Aydevko lowered himself down and blasted more allies away, their numbers dwindling. Enzo was close, but Aydevko would notice. The gods must have listened. A woman around Belyx's age ran for him with dual swords and lashed at him. He tried to strike back, but this maiden had skill. Her short blonde hair stilled in the fight.

The maiden put up such an attack; he didn't see Enzo replace his book with a fake. Enzo sprinted as quick as his legs let him, trying to ignore the dark energy radiating from the text. The entrance to the castle was in sight. Once he hit the streets, he would be home free.

A gust of wind throttled him and he fell forward, his face eating marble. He sat up when his father, Thano, stood in front. Enzo clutched onto the Tome and tried to stand back up, but a vine snatched it from his grasp. His other father, Gink, snatched it in his hand. Tears streamed down his face. "Fathers! It's me! Your son! Look inside yourself! WE can stop this together!"

They held blank stares at him. "Yes! So bad! Not any worse than the humans." Aydevko walked over, blood on his once clean outfit. "Pathetic. You deserve to die for your priorities. You think the humans would save you after this?"

Enzo inhaled, letting the despair from his thirteen years of hiding sear his skin. Losing his family, being homeless, losing Ren, meeting Belyx, losing Belyx, and losing his tribe again. He would not let it happen.

Deep in the pit of his power, a flicker of a candle grew and, with each spew of hope, it shifted brighter. Despite the limitations of his powers, he would *never* stop trying. The gods had not abandoned him.

"Belyx would save us." Enzo huffed.

Aydevko laughed, dark energy churning around him again. "She would leave you the second she could save her kingdom. You are nothing." But she didn't. She had the chance to do it, and she didn't.

Enzo smiled. A fire. A blistering one, like a phoenix, ascended toward him. He felt it now. Its warmth provided him comfort after many chilly nights on the street and he refuted it. But it forgave him; like Belyx did.

A spark formed on his finger tips and he grasped the power.

As Enzo raised his hands, Aydevko clapped and swirled Enzo in the darkness.

THIRTY

Belyx's blood felt like it was encased in an icy cocoon, trying to free itself as her limbs betrayed her, unable to move. Was she in the afterlife? Maybe joining her mother wasn't a bad thing.

And her father and grandmother...everyone she ever loved was dead or would die soon. She had to give up. No matter where Belyx was now, she didn't care. Her will to get up faded from her grandmother's death. *Let Aydevko kill the humans. They deserved it. They trapped the fae and broke up families and killed my mother.*

Her head shot up from the twisted nightmare as she lay in the catacomb next to a now empty room beyond the locked door. Where were the fae? Her joints and head pounded. Her body had a rough time moving. She sat up and groaned. Had everyone died? With an off par wig, she fixed it with ease, trying to stand, but her muscles failed and she sank back down to the ground.

Stomach roiling, she retched into the broken stone. While she finished losing her last meal, a vision of Enzo played in her head like a dream. He was fighting Aydevko with flames blasting from his hands. Did he have powers now? Her eyes shook as his embers ceased out and dark magic suffocated him.

Belyx curled her fists and stood on numb legs. She wouldn't lose him today. On her way out, a familiar voice like honey called. "Shall we think of a plan, flower?"

It couldn't be. It just couldn't. It was another trick.

Her mother stood in the distance, emulating grace in her stature. It was impossible. The imposter managed to mimic the well-pressed burgundy hair and intoxicating gleam correctly. Belyx blinked and looked back. Her mother was still there, smiling. Was this real? She even dressed how she remembered, in a green gown with a jeweled neckline. Something she would have designed.

"Who are you?" Belyx said in an accusatory tone. Her mother was dead.

The woman shook her head. "I am your mother. Have a seat, my flower. Oh, how you've grown."

Belyx couldn't believe it. She stood back, eyeing this woman who represented her mother, but it was one of Aydevko's tricks for sure. "My mother is dead."

Her mother tilted her head. "I am aware."

It was her. Belyx had the urge to reach out and touch her, but refrained. "Why are you here?"

She slumped her shoulders. "I tried to do what was best for this kingdom, but I fear even I couldn't stop the storm."

"What do you mean? The gangs?"

Her mother chuckled. "Goodness no. They were the product of grief and poor leadership. Bless your father."

A tinge of sadness slithered through her throat. "He is dead, too. His grief swallowed him up."

Her mother rubbed the rocky surface. "He was on his way there for years. I tried to tell him I couldn't be brought back, but he wouldn't listen. Stubborn, like someone else I know."

"Aren't you here now?" Belyx reached for her knife, but someone had taken it. If she wasn't her mother, she would need to fight it.

"His deal did work, but he trusted an evil entity and, as his reward for dying, they let me return momentarily. He rushed into the spell and was fooled. Grief is the most powerful dark magic."

Belyx gulped. "Figures. He would do the work and never get to see you. How long do you have?"

"Not much longer. No spell can alter death. Death is the greatest challenge, but also the greatest gift. I found peace in it, but it also made me thankful for the living. I put too much weight on my shoulders and it crushed me."

Her mother, the best queen ever, was telling her she took on too many responsibilities, but she made it look easy. All this time, they compared Belyx to her. It hurt, but it turned out her mother felt the same way. "The Order was supposed to protect everything and now it is crumbling. We failed."

"Dear flower." Her mother rubbed her wrists. "I am afraid the biggest illusion was that we needed to hide ourselves."

"We did it for our protection. The powers that be would have slaughtered us."

"My mother and grandmother did a great job of honing this order, but I realized in my last days, it wasn't needed."

"We do such great things! Of course it was!" Belyx's voice vibrated.

Her mother's face softened. "I'm not saying it wasn't important, but masks are like a seed, growing bigger and bigger into something completely different from what we planted. What was once a rose is now a sunflower. We have lost our identities."

Belyx clung to herself, remembering her wig and contacts were still on. "I feel secure as Doneque. She gets things done."

Her mother laughed, which surprised Belyx. "Flower. They are the same person."

Taken aback, Belyx turned away. "Well, I know, but as Doneque, I can save Aikradal differently on the streets."

"Belyx can do whatever Doneque can, and vice versa. You are letting yourself be held back by your alternate persona. This secrecy isn't protecting Aikradal anymore." Her voice was sharp, like a true ruler. Now Belyx longed for more time. "The continent is in more danger than we can ever imagine. It goes even beyond these gangs."

"What is it?"

"I can't say and I also can't say who killed me, but it sounds like you already know."

"Majeria." Her mother's face stayed neutral. "If we get out of this, I will make them pay."

"There is more to everything than what we think. Dying has taught me such." Her mother shivered. "I'm afraid I have to go."

"Wait! How can we beat Aydevko? He is unstoppable!"

"He was always filled with such hate. He could never accept the harmony between fae and humans. It was always us versus him." Tears welled in her eyes and she embraced Belyx. Touching was possible after all.

Although Belyx was young, the memories of her warm hugs came back to her in a flurry. The cold nights when Belyx had a nightmare. She was there. The sunny days that were stacked with laughter and sunshine, she was there. Her spirit woulds always linger and would continue in the good and bad moments.

Her mother pulled away. "Time is up, but there is something about the Tome you should know." Belyx's eyes widened, similar to her mother's. "In the Tome is a sort of reset spell. Get it, recite it, and it will banish him to hell."

"But, I'm not a witch."

"Like your father, you can read some spells, but you must refuse the temptations of other forces, like what your father failed at."

"Sounds easy enough." Her voice hitched. She knew it wouldn't be.

They hugged one last time, and in a flash, her mother was gone. Had this been a dream? Was she even her mother? Belyx didn't care. She had the drive now to fight back. Aydevko had an incomparable amount of power and would unleash havoc on the entire kingdom if she didn't stop him. With her fingers through her wig, she recalled those nights sneaking out, poisoning and killing for the Order. It was all her. Doneque was someone she created to work through her pain. Her mother's words echoed; Doneque wasn't needed to beat Aydevko. As Belyx, Princess of Aikradal, she would do anything for her people.

In one fluid motion, she ripped off the wig, tying her stringy auburn hair into a ponytail; and tore off her red contacts, letting her hazel eyes shine. She had no venoms or daggers, but it didn't matter; The greatest weapon was always in her possession...herself.

Princess Belyx would stop this threat. She prayed to The God for bravery as she would need it. Enzo couldn't fight this force alone.

After a quick stretch, Belyx charged up the stairs with one goal in mind, save her kingdom, even if it meant sacrificing herself. No murderous trespasser would ever hurt anyone else under her protection again. It was beyond personal now. For her father, for her grandmother, for the Order, for Enzo, and for the kingdom.

The blood of the Order painted her way to Aydevko. Nobles, maidens, servants, and too many members perished, along with the fae. Did they decide to work for Aydevko? Was Enzo in danger, or did he switch sides? A wave of nausea hit her as the thought of Enzo betraying her a second time manifested. That alone would kill her, but she would take out these fae with him if she had to.

Cook broke through the chaos of fae versus the Order and knocked them away, using her pure strength and size to her advantage. Why wasn't she killing the fae? "Princess!" Cook yelled as she kicked a fae about to launch a wind blast.

Belyx filled with dread as she removed a blade from a corpse of an Order member. Her face was too young to understand the place of death. She went to jab a fae killer in the back when Cook stepped in front of her and subdued him instead. Belyx screamed, "they will wake up and heal. We need to use lethal force!" Cook should have known.

Cook shook her head. "They are under a curse. They aren't acting in their own free will."

Belyx's breaths slowed. "How do you know?"

Cook arched a brow. "Your boyfriend told us."

Her cheeks flushed. "So Enzo isn't working with them?"

"No!" Cook shouted. "He was fighting them with us awhile ago, before going to find the shapeshifter." He was still on their side. Her heart lifted until it fell back to reality. They would be slaughtered by nightfall. "Sorry about Dara," Cook said.

She straightened. "She gave us a fighting chance, so let's honor her name and save this place. You good here?"

Cook peered over at more fae and Order members dueling like their lives depended on it. "We will be fine. Get to the shifter and end this."

Belyx squeezed Cook's calloused hand and hastened up the steps, weaving fae elemental attacks and helping the members. *Save your energy Belyx.* The real war had just begun.

Out of the painting spewed even more blood and pain. Now Aikradal soldiers dueled the fae and were losing. Her thoughts went to where Thomas and Freyja were and another to where Enzo was. No more of her loved ones would die today.

Belyx rolled to dodge a fire blast from a bald fae. They launched attack after attack, but Belyx moved in the shadows, just like Doneque did. Once she slunk close, she quelled the creature and slammed them to the ground.

Saying a silent apology, she headed for the sound of more screams and death, gasping at her previous peaceful home now in more ruins than the Berserkers left it. The portraits of her family were ripped to shreds. The tapestries were torn apart, and the statures were obliterated. Nothing remained of her palace. This had festered out of control. Her ears rang from the commotion, but Dara's words kept her going. That sacrifice provided time to defeat Aydevko, and she would not squander it. Things were replaceable, but lives weren't, no matter how much they tried.

By the main entrance outside, Aydevko's voice boomed. Belyx skidded to a halt and studied him. He had Enzo trapped in a dome thick as pitch, like in her vision. Two taller fae men surrounded him. His fathers most likely.

"This Fae has lost his sight." The energy around Aydevko twirled like a blizzard. "Our next step is to take this castle, then the kingdom, and then the continent. Move o—"

He stopped when Belyx walked out to him, her dagger hand shaking, but she held it down. She would not show fear here. His lips twisted into a smile. "Well, she survived my killing curse. How?"

Belyx returned the beam and looked to where Enzo lay, his soft body torn and still. "Witch curses don't work on me. You can thank the fae thief for that."

Aydevko twirled his fingers. "No matter. I don't need curses to kill you, anyway." He paused. "Where is Doneque? Surely Princess Belyx can't fight. Especially with these witnesses. What will your precious Order of pathetic females think?"

Air left her lungs, but she faced him head on. "Princess Belyx doesn't need Doneque anymore. She has enough strength to take you down and put an end to the turmoil you've started."

Aydevko spat. "You fool! It's almost comical how little you understand. Your own kind has tried to kill you many times and once they hear of this joke, they will eat you alive." He snorted. "An assassin princess. What's next? A pixie gladiator?"

Belyx raised her knife. "You once had purpose, Aydevko. As a merciful princess, I will give you the option to surrender." She knew he wouldn't accept, but if her last breath was near, she wanted the high road.

Aydevko cracked his neck, and the magic pooled around his center, giving his answer.

He growled as he launched a sinister blast right for Belyx.

The arc collided into the ground next to her, smoke rising from the impact. No weapon was required to face him, but a little help from ash pellets was appreciated.

Belyx rushed for the rose garden and Aydevko's frustrated sounds implied he lost her. He chuckled. "You can't hide, princess. Your heat signature is strong, but that will change soon." Belyx kept down, calling his bluff. "It is a shame for the roses," he said, launching a fire bolt, igniting flames around the garden. The sweltering air hit her face like a punch as she scanned every angle. Laughing like a madman, he had trapped her. The roses her grandmother worked hard to grow wilted in the pyres and it would be her hearth next if she stayed too long. She pressed the mechanism on the child statue and dove into the hideout, praying the embers wouldn't follow. If she could steal the Tome, that would end the destruction.

Belyx waited for the heat from the outside to reduce, keeping an ear to the trapdoor. "She is no more!" Aydevko's muffled cry said, followed with cheering. Little did he know. Smiling, Belyx went to her snakes. The new snake had grown twice its size since the last time. Its venom's effects were a mystery, but she needed to try something.

The snake's venom was hard to harvest due to the smallness of it, but she managed a partial vial full, stowing it in her bag, before enormous booms came from overhead.

Belyx ran back to the front and placed her hand on the switch to open the trapdoor. The thuds of his steps spread closer and closer. One more step and she would catch him. He stopped moving. "Where is she? Bodies can't burn that fast!"

Now.

She pressed the latch.

The door groaned, and his body fell in as he let out a gasp. She only had seconds. As he tumbled down the stairs, Belyx rushed by him and snatched the Tome from his talons, ignoring a slight sting on her arm. Belyx hit the latch to close the trapdoor. It wouldn't keep him there forever, but it would buy her time. Time was the greatest ally, now.

She leapt over the charred flower bushes and fended off the fae attacks, but members of the Order came from around the corner and fought them off. Belyx veered back to a temporarily safe place, and rifled through the Tome, looking for the spell her mother told her about. "Come on. Come on."

Like a noise from hell, the trapdoor exploded into smithereens and Aydevko rushed out, twin blades in hand as he bolted for the Order members. They tried to fight back, but their screams of death curdled the air. Belyx cursed as she put her book down and ran to them, refusing to let more people die.

"Looking for this." Belyx held up the Tome, not sure of her next plan.

Aydevko paused and tossed a maiden aside, her young body slamming into the ashes. "Hand it over and it will be a quick death for you and your whores!"

"Are you saying you can't defeat a little old princess without this piece of leather and paper?"

"Do not disrespect something you do not understand, you reckless child!" Aydevko's voice grew like thunder as he spun his blades around. Belyx didn't know if she had the skills to take him, but her grandmother always said those who act out of rage never swung a skilled sword. Why wasn't this Tome smaller?

As if it read her thoughts, it shrunk down to the size of her palm. Surprised, but happy, Belyx pocketed it in her pouch and readied her knife. It would be what she needed to take him down.

In a bang, he was upon her. They fought steel to steel. His swords were an extension of himself; a fierce storm, but Belyx shifted and weaved, refusing to fall like the last time. Aydevko kept a straight face, determined to take his revenge, but Belyx had her own revenge to settle. Every step he took, she would go opposite. Every slash of his blade, she would parry it. He grabbed for her pouch, but she sidestepped and cut his hand, drawing actual blood this time. His ambition blinded him.

Aydevko bounced back, but sucked the minor cut. "Nice. Too bad no venom laced it!"

Belyx smiled. "That's what you think." Aydevko's eyes widened. *Don't fail me now, unknown venom.*

Cursing in a language she had never heard before, Aydevko charged her. Belyx stepped back and blocked the strikes, but his aggression grew like a flame as he pushed her back. She hit the hard ground. How long would the effects take? Her strength depleted like the blood leaving her body as Aydevko came over her, a lurking shadow. He swiped at her, but she rolled with precision. Each slice struck closer and closer to meeting her face. Aydevko came down, but she twisted up and kicked his leg away, giving her time to stand.

"Foolish princess. If that old coot couldn't best me, what makes you think you could! You are only stalling your demise!" He rushed her with an array of attacks, and one strike slashed Belyx's arm. She barely dodged before the next slice nicked her cheek, taking her hair out of the tie. Trying to run, burgundy hair on her face, Aydevko snatched it and pulled her back, reaching for her pouch. "I preferred the blonde wig better, by the way," he sneered as his hands grasped around the Tome.

Seething against the pain, her roots exploded with pressure. He would rip her hair out if he kept pulling. Belyx's eyebrows shot up. *That's it!* Taking her knife, she swiped up and found herself free of his grasp.

Aydevko screamed as she faced him, a clump of reddish curls in his hand. Belyx would need a serious hair fix after this, assuming Freyja was still alive.

Aydevko continued his assault. Not much was in her tank, but she had to keep going, and had to keep fighting. The shifter came for the Tome, obsessed, and his weakness was visible. Belyx caught his arm and twisted, kneeing him in the stomach and pushing him away.

On his hands and knees, Aydevko laughed like a crone. "You fool! You fool!" He shook violently, like he would explode at any moment. "Enough fighting me! How about someone else!" A bright white glow came from his body and his form shortened; Belyx almost dropped her knife from what now stood in front of her, her mother.

"What? My flower? Something the matter?" Even his voice matched hers. *It isn't her. It isn't her.* Aydevko as her mother came for her, but Belyx kept back, unable to keep track of her confusion. Her mom's hair and eyes were perfect, down to an art. It was like a dream.

Aydevko twisted around and sent a back kick right into Belyx, and her knife went flying. He jumped on top of her and put his blade to her throat, the image of her mom staring back at her...was about to kill her. Reaching into her bag, he pulled out the Tome. "Grief is a funny thing," her mother's voice said. "It makes us deny reality and shrivel up like ants. You humans never had a chance."

Belyx closed her eyes. Why would her mother do this?

It is not your mother! Belyx, stop! Belyx!

In the heat of it, she grabbed his hand and bit it. Why hadn't the venom kicked in? Her experiment had failed. The face of her mother screamed in pain. Belyx head butted him, ignoring the fuzziness, and stood, attempting to twist the book out of his hands, but he had a grip of iron.

Glowing white, he changed back to his original form and shoulder checked Belyx, but she hung on, fingers burning. Blood trickled down her body as her joints cried for relief, but she would not give up. Aydevko gritted his teeth and released an evil sound piercing her eardrums. He tried to kick her, but she kept her hold, twisting and pulling like her life depended on it. She yanked back, and he did too and an audible tearing shook the area as they both flew in opposite directions; Belyx with a handful of pages and him with others.

They faced each other, panting like dogs. Aydevko opened his remaining shreds of the Tome and dark magic exploded from him.

Thirty-One

Enzo's head rumbled like a horde of rhinos. Like he had been close to jumping off a cliff and then someone yanked him back.

Embers danced in his hands, like an old friend. His powers pulsed at the surface, clawing to be let free. He only had seconds. His fathers ran to Enzo standing, ready to end their own son. Where was Aydevko? Had he made it to the kingdom?

Gritting his teeth, he marched forward only to be knocked down by his father, Thano.

The ground slammed against him and he tried to move when vines twisted around his body, squeezing his throat like a snake. As they approached him, he was forced to look up. His fathers were about to kill him. Why would the gods let this occur? This was a malevolent spell. The fae were immune to magic like this, but why were they affected?

His body thrashed. "Fathers. Please." Pleads were useless, as his parents were gone, only soulless walking figures. It was ironic he was finally reunited with them, and now they were going to kill him. Enzo kept his face in the dirt and almost laughed to himself. Why did he fight most of his life just for this to happen? The world was a cruel place, and he should have known it early on. His family was dead and soon, Belyx and the kingdom would be too.

He closed his eyes as his parents stood above him; the vines cutting off more of his blood flow. The air left his lungs like a gust of wind and he would join his brethren in the afterlife. Maybe Belyx would end up at the same place and they could be together. Belyx's face was what he thought about in his last moments. The way she judged everything, the way she made everyone's problems her own, no matter how small, and more importantly, how she never gave up, even for him. The true-fire was her. She burned brighter than anyone.

Suddenly, his body heated like a volcano. The vines grasping his life loosened, as if cowering away. Enzo opened his eyes and flames encircled him like it had a mind of its own. He sat up and his fathers backed away, unable to block out the heat. His flower tattoo covering his fae one burned away like paper, revealing the flame tattoos. His real power.

Clenching his fist, he declared an apology to his fathers, wherever they were, and launched a cyclone of pyres around them. They tried to fight against it, but were trapped. As his fathers panicked, Enzo pulled away. *I can't kill them. No matter what kind of spell they are in. They are my family.*

Screaming, he let his ability loosen, and the hot vortex lifted. His father's lay motionless. Was he too late?

He ran over and checked their eyes. The red was gone. They were knocked out, but this was different. They were cured.

My fire, Enzo thought, remembering when he freed Belyx from the Cabaret's curse. It had to work. The power to free the rest of them was in his grasp. Fire was dangerous, but it also acted like a reset to nature. Flames cleansed, and he would cleanse his tribe of this wretched spell.

Smiling, he advanced to fae after fae, absorbing them in flames until they passed out. They fought back, but Enzo was awake and full of fire. Every fae he faced was released of the curse, and he wouldn't quit till they were no longer slaves.

A familiar scream heightened his attention. *No way. She was dead.*

"You'll never get it! I won't let you take this kingdom!" It *was* her, around the corner. Belyx was alive. His happiness squelched when he realized who she was fighting.

Dismissing the fae trying to attack him, Enzo absorbed the air in his lungs and sprinted like he did as a child, heat climbing up his legs.

Aydevko stood over Belyx, a dark force looming around them. Belyx's life energy was visible as she screeched, clinging to something in her palm. He would not take away the girl he loved. She had sacrificed too much for him, and it was his turn to repay the favor.

Readying a fire blast like no other...years of stored energy ready to burst, Enzo launched it right at the witch.

Aydevko had the book and the page she needed. Her head vibrated as he recited a spell, but she couldn't hear over the ringing in her ears. With the intense focus of an eagle, she reached out. Aydevko was looking at the sky, assuming she was unconscious, but he messed with the wrong princess.

She had the leaflets in her grasp when a pluming flame plummeted into them.

A raging pain roared from her hands as she let go of the Tome. It mainly struck Aydevko, though. What dumb fae of his attacked their own master?

She turned and knew which dumb fae did, Enzo.

Aydevko flew like a ballista arrow and slammed into the side of the palace wall, dropping what was left of the Dark Tome.

Helping Belyx up, Enzo wrapped his arms around her. She grabbed his hands, but grunted. Her hands had been burned, and the pain clung to them like perfume as she struggled to make a fist. "You burned me." Belyx released Enzo, surprised at the first thing she said. Not to mention he had his long-lost powers back, which was a plus. But right now, she wished otherwise.

"Well, why did you put your hand in the way?" This reunion was going rather well...

Belyx blinked a couple times at his snarky remark. "We can discuss it later, but we have a shifter to take down."

Enzo grabbed her shoulders, his touch sent less lethal sparks through her body. "I can cleanse the fae with my powers. It was how I saved you from Scandeni. We can do this."

She was in shock. He had been the one to cleanse her before. She went to reply when Aydevko stirred. A huge fireball wasn't enough to take him out. "Hold him off. I'll get the book," Belyx commanded. "That can also end this."

Enzo nodded, flames swirling in his fists. Aydevko was charging for the other part of the book. He thrust his hands and sparks shot out, but Aydevko surrounded himself with his own magic and sent it gliding back.

Belyx chased the flying pages as Enzo and Aydevko dueled, embers and darkness spinning like stars in the sky. The palace grounds remaining were desecrated from battle. Whoever was alive in this fight wouldn't have long.

The Tome pieces spun in the breeze. Belyx gasped as a cursed fae ran for it too, hunger in his eyes. He launched a gust of wind, knocking Belyx to the ground. She went to stand, ignoring the pain in her hands, but he sent another gale smacking her into a nearby statue. Her head swirled and everything hurt. The wind fae had the sheets in his claws. If Aydevko retrieved the remnants, it would be over. Even Enzo's fire couldn't best him.

The fae retreated for Aydevko when an arrow stuck into his leg and he fell, followed with another arrow hitting the sheets from his hands. The fae growled when a blunted arrow knocked him in the head. Only one person shot with such skill.

Freyja came over, her signature bow/staff in hand, and helped Belyx up. "Figured you could use a hand." She looked at her burned hands. "Or two."

Belyx hugged her friend. "Thank you. I need time to look through those pages." A swirling blast of fire and wind slammed near them, demolishing a statue to pieces. "Cover me?"

Freyja grinned as she nocked an arrow. "With pleasure." Her face may have been tattered, but her battle spirit remained.

Belyx avoided the elements as she rifled through the pages. Fire and darkness exploded in the distance and Enzo had little time.

The right page wasn't there. It would be her luck Aydevko possessed the half she required. Relief swam through her veins when she came upon what she needed, but sank back as the page was ripped down the middle. The witch had the other parts. A burst of flame protruded toward Belyx when an arrow stopped it in the air.

"Go!" Freyja yelled as she and a couple others fought off the fae. They had no time left. The fae would make short work of them.

Belyx sprinted back to Aydevko, securing the sheet she needed and tossing the rest in the smokey air. Enzo tried to keep Aydevko back, but the witch had a lot of power. This distraction had to continue. Aydevko wrangled free of the flames and fired a dark bolt right into Enzo and he fell to the ground, but Belyx was in front of him.

Nothing would get through her this time. "Too late Princess! You failed! I have enough power to finish you and the rest of this land off!" Aydevko sneered as he raised a shimmering hand. Beams descended from the sky like lightning as he caught it, twisting it into a diabolical pulse of pure evil. He would not risk Belyx living again.

She stood tall, despite the nightmares radiating from his blast. It would take everything he had...and if she died; she would be remembered as the princess who never gave up. Her mother's face appeared. "I'll see you soon, mom."

Her mother shook her head as Aydevko's strength faded like a wilted rose. Aydevko cursed as he convulsed, his magic dimming in and out.

The venom. It must have taken effect. Aydevko screamed in agony as his magic flashed like torch lights.

"What are you waiting for?" Enzo said with a pained voice.

Belyx rushed to Aydevko. He fired a couple wild bolts, but Belyx dodged, giving him a rude gesture as she snatched the papers away. "Don't mess with venoms, creep." Aydevko slammed the ground, sending Belyx flying back, her head smacking into the brick.

Once she came to, Aydevko limped toward her, sword in hand. She exhaled through clenched teeth and clutched the parchment. *Doesn't he ever give up? He would not win today.* A searing fire bolt barreled into him as Enzo stepped in front of Belyx.

He didn't need to tell her to hurry as she pieced the pages together. Whatever the venom was only stalled him, as he still proved effective against Enzo's power. Her hands shook as she found the alignment and then, like a recital, read the words.

Cold darkness propelled around her and the world went black.

She reached in front, but nothing remained.

Then she descended into nothingness.

Her mind faded, as she couldn't even scream. What was happening? Would she ever hit the ground?

What felt like forever ended when a loud rumble thrust Belyx to her knees.

Standing in front of her was a figure from a nightmare. When they spoke, it switched between man and woman, child, and beast. It was nothing and everything.

Princess. You call upon dark magic. In a flash, her mother appeared before her as she saw earlier, but her face was expressionless. *I have the power to bring her back for real. Give up the Tome and you shall be together.*

Belyx went to retort, but no words came out. Then a twisting in her head crunched. *You cannot speak in my realm. I read your desires. I do not need an answer. I already know it. Losing a parent can be hard. Let me help you.*

No, Belyx thought. *I do not.* Her mother's body circled the area.

"Together, forever, flower," her mother said, but it wasn't her mother, or was it?

Belyx wanted her back with all her being. Everything would be fixed with her alive. She could do anything. Her emotions flared. *I want nothing more than to be reunited with my—*

"Stop!" A blinding beam of light broke through the surface as a figure resembling her grandmother pushed the evil force away.

You have broken the rules of the afterlife. You are damned to eternal suffering! the voice screeched.

Her grandmother, as majestic as ever, looked back at Belyx. Was what the energy said true? "It is worth it. I will not let the forces of evil taunt our world anymore."

The force laughed. *I will always be around. It was never your land. You will be sorry, eventually.*

Her grandmother exploded into a bright beam of energy and bolted to the entity, pushing it away. The walls fell around Belyx. She tried to scream, but nothing came out. What had her grandmother done?

In another blinding strobe, Belyx was back to her world, only it was quieter. Enzo lay on the ground, holding his side, now coated in crimson. The fae dropped like flies, and the guards and Order bent over in relief.

The curse had been lifted.

On the cobblestones away from Enzo, was Aydevko, panting, hand at his heart. His darkness wilted away like a dying weed. Belyx crept to him, afraid of his potential danger still, but he kept up his full toothed smile. "Humans. Always the humans thinking they are above everyone else." He coughed up a gel like fluid. "No matter what evil forces like myself are vanquished,humans will remain the true evil force. Remember in your reign, Queen Belyx."

It was the first time she had heard the title, and it left a weird taste in her mouth coming from him. His body began to dissolve, but he kept his eye contact with her. "Aikradal and this land will fall to each other. Good luck with the impossible, Queen." He said it again, and the claws worsened.

"What is that?"

He opened his mouth and dissipated into the wind like black dust, but not before getting out, "peace."

His words haunted her, but she paid him no mind. Wherever he went was where he belonged. Enzo was up now, and Belyx had a hard time containing herself. She tackled him to the ground, kissing him like the world was ending...which it almost did. Even though they were both in pain, losing each other was a sharper one.

After they pulled apart, Enzo gazed around. With a smirk, he said, "Well, it seems we have a lot of cleaning up to do, your highness."

Destruction, death, blood, and suffering were what she thought would remain of her kingdom, but then her allies circled her.

Freyja inclined her head, holding up an injured Cook, who still wore her injuries with pride. Other members of the Order and guards trudged up as well, but Captain Thomas was nowhere to be found. Was he still alive?

Onka was on her knees, holding her bloody side sobbing while Amenthya tended to her wounds and Belyx didn't even have to guess why. Beside her body was a motionless Inka, with other Order members crying. Still as a breath, Belyx let her tears fall. Inka fought with all she had and would be remembered. Would Onka recover though?

What remained was more than this devastation.

Belyx bowed back to her allies. It would take time, but healing, rebuilding, life, and happiness stood tall in the mess, proving they had a chance to be stronger.

They were Aikradal, the strongest kingdom.

Thirty-Two

"What is the damage report?" Belyx addressed her new council.

A week had passed since the attack and Belyx thanked The God she had prepared for a life of little sleep. The council room was not how it was before. The once roomy table was split down the middle and chairs were missing arms, but they had to make do with what they had. Rebuilding would take longer than she thought.

"Captain Thomas and Madame Jewella have turned in their resignations." Freyja sipped from her cracked cup, wearing battle armor with her hair tied in a frilled pony. It seemed fitting for Aikradal's new Captain of the Guard. Thomas's leaving hurt her the most. He had left the night prior to the attack, with no explanation, and no one could find him. The rumors of him claiming Aikradal was not fit to handle threats anymore haunted Belyx.

With a creak, Lady Lim readjusted herself, "trying" not to make a scene. Her face was in tatters and her hands shook. Her husband's betrayal and death plagued her to the core, but she helped house the children in the safe room when Aydevko and his fae minions attacked. Belyx took it in stride and appointed her to the Order as the new Master of Coin.

The Master of Trade left with some other workers too, indicating how Aikradal lost tradition. Of course, Maria, who also fought against the threat, was promoted to Master of Trade due to her uncanny knowledge of resources. At first they were offended they weren't invited sooner, but realized they would have to learn how to fight, which they stuck their noses up as "proper ladies didn't raise fists." Belyx had no idea what to do with them, but their admission to the council seemed like a start. Lim knew quite a bit of strategy being a wife to Kirk.

Her Aunt Hannah was another story. She tried to stop her father, and he slew her in his own bedroom. *To kill a sister*, Belyx thought. Her father was far gone by grief. That tempestuous road would never be crossed again.

"Well, Thomas was always a baby. Everything was his way or the highway. Good day, I say!" Lim fanned herself.

Lady Maria scoffed. "Right. That is why you fawned over him."

"Worthless sl—"

Belyx cleared her throat, and the ladies paused. "Sorry, Queen," Lim said. "I just love the sound of queen, don't you?"

With the silence, Lim sunk down, and Maria patted her shoulder.

Belyx was already nursing a severe headache. *Perhaps letting them in was a bad idea.* "How many members of the Order died? How many guards?" Her entire council needed to be aware of the Order, as there would be no more secrets. The council was in the Order anyway, besides Enzo of course. He was dressed in a clean and sharp uniform, making his eyes pop and his hair was neatly cropped. His injuries had healed, however. Leave it to a fae to recover quickly. Although their mental scars would be permanent.

"I can answer." Cook pulled out a parchment. "We lost about half of each. The crime in Aikradal has also increased. Although the gangs have been weirdly quiet."

Belyx hated sitting where her father did. In the past, she would look at him for advice, but their eyes were on her now. "Keep the patrols across the kingdom and a close watch at night. I don't want anymore surprises. The people need to know we will grow stronger from this." *Broken bones always grew back sturdier,* her grandmother would say. The death was still fresh in her mind as she repelled her tears. Her grandmother wouldn't want her squabbling. She would want her to take action.

"I couldn't agree more," Captain Freyja said. "But I believe it would be good for morale if the Queen addressed her people."

She gulped. Of course Freyja would say that. She was always in tune with people. "This would mean a coronation."

Enzo scoffed, ignoring Freyja's glare. "We don't have the security right now."

"It is the law." Belyx mouthed an apology to him after acknowledging Freyja. "The more laws and traditions we keep, the better. It will happen tomorrow and we will do the best we can for guards."

Freyja winked and scribbled in her frayed parchment.

"Our next order of business." Cook looked between Enzo and Belyx. "Who will be king alongside you?"

Belyx tried to stifle her blushing and ignored Enzo's gaze. Coughing, she replied, "I'm aware we need two rulers eventually, but because of the circumstances, I will be Queen on my own for awhile. It is a big decision to make." She couldn't deny her strong feelings for Enzo, but they still barely knew each other and needed time. "In the meantime, Enzo will remain head advisor and assist with the reintegration of the fae."

The council lowered their heads and Belyx prayed they would move on, but of course, Cook had to keep the wheel turning. "What about an heir? We need to think about the unlikely case of something happening to you." She paused. "Like your grandmother and father."

"The discussion of the heir will be had when the king is chosen." Belyx didn't know Cook had a political side. Where did she receive it from?

"When were we planning on having a service for—" She stilled and did a quick glance at Belyx. "Our previous king and queen regnant?" Freyja asked, taking notes.

"I think after the coronation, we can worry about such matters." In truth, Belyx had no time to grieve right now and if she stayed busy, she wouldn't have to. Honoring the rebuilding of the kingdom would honor them enough. Everyone kept silent, afraid to bring up anything else.

Belyx motioned to Enzo, and he added. "With the reintegration of the fae, we need to choose a thorough approach. A lot of the citizens have expressed fear of them despite the truth coming to light." Leave it to over a decade of negative propaganda to still meld the minds of the masses.

"Businesses in the Sehrlic Forest have requested compensation for having to move out." Freyja read from her notes with care. "They claim it is against their rights to move and change because quote, 'the savages have returned.'"

Enzo furrowed his brow. "We were taken! How can they—" he paused as Belyx shot him a stop talking stare.

"We will pay them for their trouble and that will hopefully be enough." Belyx shook her head. As much as she hated to appease such hate, it was the only way to prevent more civil war. A fifth gang was the last thing they needed.

Lim coughed. "Princess, I mean, Queen. Our funds are quite limited. Payin' them their requested amount would cripple us further."

Belyx scratched her head. "Ok, then we do what we can, but they need to leave. Those are homes." Lim opened her mouth, but stopped. Her first day as Master of Coin and she was already challenging her.

Although she had a point. "The people don't believe the fae were under a spell and actually wanted to take over. Multiple protests have sparked up around the kingdom. I will address it at the coronation. I will lay my life for them." She smiled at Enzo, who didn't return the sentiment. "I have appointed a couple fae to help with the rebuilding to make sure everything is done with sensitivity. Enzo's fathers, Gink and Thano Prekaro, will run these feats. I have asked and they will live in the palace as well. Their room is being made as we speak."

The council agreed, although Cook looked a tinge worried. Why couldn't she trust Belyx to do this?

Freyja flipped to her final page on the parchment, this had to end soon. Sitting through these as a princess was way easier, now as queen, and after such an attack, she wished she wasn't there. "Our last matter. How are we going to enlist more guards. Some left with the last captain." Belyx detected disdain as Freyja received the worst in this. She and Thomas had something passionate forming, but war broke up many things. "Our current low numbers are decreasing and the gangs will retaliate, but that is another issue."

A weight fell on Belyx's head as she struggled to keep a straight face. She pictured how her mother or grandmother would respond. "I will announce a recruiting station at the coronation. We will treat them right and remind them that they are strong for helping us." She paused, expecting push back on her next idea. "And I want all people, men and women."

The council gasped, but none retorted. Belyx stood, catching her wobbly self, and the pain in her charred hands returned. She would need another dab of salve to ease it again. It wasn't working like usual. Maybe the fae burns worked differently.

With a bow, Belyx turned to leave. "Thank you, council. We are adjourned for the evening. I will retire to my room and meet you for the coronation tomorrow. Be sure to get word out." Everyone agreed and Belyx brushed ahead, closing the door to her room and releasing her dinner into the toilet. After she was done, she almost screamed at Onka standing behind her, unsure what to say.

"Oh, Onka. I'm sorry."

Onka shook her head, turning to leave. Her hair was unkempt and her clothes were droopy. It had only been a week since she lost her sister, and Belyx was surprised she was awake now.

"Wait!" Belyx called her back, and she stopped. "How have you been?"

Onka took a couple of breaths and turned. Her eyes were puffy with white flecks at the corners from dried tears. She had her answer. "I'm fine, Queen. I just wanted this room to be clean for you."

Belyx wiped her mouth and went to embrace her maid when she tilted away. "Truly, Queen. I am fine."

"Onka. Take the week off. I understand what it is like—"

"Do you?" Onka yelled back, and her volume shocked Belyx. "We have been together since inside our mother's belly. We have never been apart! From birth, to the slavers, to here. She was a part of me. Now who am I?"

Belyx kept a distance from her, but gave a reassuring look, channeling her grandmother. Although less positive. "Onka, You fought bravely for us, and are more than just a twin. You were willing to lay down your life to stop Aydevko." Onka closed her hand around her stab wound.

Belyx's head flooded with sunshine at her next idea. "Since Freyja is Captain of the Guard now, I will need a new handmaiden and protector. I think someone with your talents would suffice."

Onka didn't smile, but stayed silent for a bit, tears welling in her eyes. "Queen. I don't know if I am up for the task. I am nothing like Freyja. Plus, I have the other Leaves to think of."

Belyx crossed her arms and smirked. "Are you disobeying an order from your queen?"

Onka smiled for a second and shook her head. "I would be honored."

She didn't pull away as Belyx grabbed her shoulder. "I, soon to be Queen Belyx, promote Onka to be my new handmaiden and protector as The God is my witness."

Onka bowed. "I won't let you down."

Belyx laughed. "I know, but as your first order, I order you to rest for a couple of days. Cook can run the Leaves and Freyja can handle double duty for awhile, even though I can be quite difficult."

"Never, your highness." Onka had a twist of humor in her voice, proving she would be well for now. "May I retire, my queen?"

Belyx pretended to think about it. "Yes." Onka tilted her head and left.

Before the door closed, a handsome fae snuck in, holding something behind his back.

"I hope this isn't an assassination attempt," Belyx said, trying to sneak a peek.

Enzo twisted his head. "Well, you caught me. If you consider sweets a silent killer?" He pulled out two fluffy scones, oozing berries and chocolate. "Cook didn't want these to go to waste, so?"

Belyx smacked his arm and took one, spit clinging to it like a happy memory in her mouth. "Sorry, I guess I was hungry."

Enzo shrugged and ate his, licking the crumbs off his hand like an animal. Belyx even swooned at these odd things. Love was strange.

"Intense council meeting tonight."

The tension grew in his voice. "It sure was."

The conversation turned awkward, and Enzo sat next to her on the bed, her face flushing. It had been a moment since the two of them connected. "How are the hands holding up?"

Belyx hid them, knowing he felt awful about it, but it had been worth it. "The healer says the pain should stop soon, but there will be scarring." A clever lie as she chewed the inside of her cheek. "Thank you for everything."

Enzo kept his head down. "For what? Putting this entire kingdom in jeopardy?"

Belyx grabbed his hand, ignoring the burning in her own. "Enzo. Your family was in danger. I would have done the same thing. You saved this kingdom. I could never have defeated Aydevko on my own." Even his name sent a searing acid down Belyx's throat. "You did what you had to. It will get better."

Enzo stared at her now, lips tightened. "How can you be sure? The people here are protesting. They hate my kind." His ear points started to grow back. Would he keep them? She hoped he would, as it was his authentic self.

"I know what it is like to hide and I don't want to anymore. The people will see your kind and learn they were victims in this mess. I know it will be hard at first, but the citizens need time."

Enzo wiggled his eyebrows. "Was that all you had trying to cheer me up? I rank it sub par." Belyx nudged him and came in close. Before she knew it, their lips were locked. The heat from his mouth radiated into hers, singeing her bad thoughts away.

Belyx pulled free. "Is the guest bedroom faring you well?"

As if catching her hint, Enzo replied, "Well, yes, but I find the bed too big. Do you have a smaller one?"

Gesturing to her own, she added, "I don't know if this one is smaller, but maybe sharing it would help?"

Enzo shook his head. "That gown of yours takes up an awful lot of room."

Belyx blushed and kissed him again, harder this time, and he returned the favor, sinking into her bed, becoming one.

Before things became too heated, Enzo cleared his throat. "You sure about the no king thing? I would rock a crown." He stuck his tongue between his teeth and Belyx's heart beat faster.

"One step at a time, advisor."

"Can I give you some advice? It's free this time."

Belyx rolled her eyes, rubbing his hard shoulders. "Yes?"

"Stop talking." He closed into her, and time slipped away like their clothing. In the heat of it, Belyx didn't even think about her coronation tomorrow.

After the turmoil, Belyx went to check on Amenthya. She had barely come out of her chambers since the incident. When she entered, a strong smell wafted across, but it wasn't like her usual salve. This had something stronger to it Belyx couldn't quite place.

"Queen," Amenthya said as she mixed her concoction. Her clothes were wrinkled and her hair was in shambles.

Belyx tiptoed forward, suddenly regretting her decision. "How have you been?"

Amenthya shrugged, not making eye contact. "It's been a lot with your father perishing and the fae returning." Her tone shifted at the mention of them as she handed Belyx more cream. She had almost forgotten the burning in her hand. Should she ask her why it's not working?

"It's peculiar they did nothing wrong." Belyx pocketed the medicine, sensing Amenthya may want to be left alone. How many Order members and soldiers died in this room?

"Sure." Amenthya kept mixing. Lots of people thought the fae were evil for long. It would take time to adjust.

"I hope this kingdom can move forward in peace. It's what it needs."

Amenthya stayed quiet. Everyone grieved in their own way and who was Belyx to judge? "I hope you plan to attend the coronation. I need all the supportive faces I can get."

Amenthya stopped what she was doing and stared into Belyx's eyes. They were reddened, most likely from sleepless nights and tears. "My Queen, Where I come from, the fae are said to be dangerous. I fear for a kingdom who allows them back in."

Who was this person? Amenthya's creed was to help everyone, and the fae must have been included. "They lived peacefully in the land for over 200 years when we settled. They were framed by a mad witch." Amenthya's face scrunched at the word. How did this slip by her? Her grandmother, who saved Amenthya, did.

Amenthya chuckled, which was rare. "Not before then. Don't you know what they did to the—" She stilled. "Never mind. You are right, my Queen. I look forward to your coronation."

Belyx wanted to press further, but a sick feeling crept inside her. "Take care and get some rest, Amenthya."

As soon as she saw it, her vision vibrated. *It couldn't be, it couldn't be.* Belyx halted and snuck back into the healing room, careful not to be heard. Amenthya stood, muttering a kind of incantation to herself and her concoction shimmered a bright citrine color. It was as if a light pulse radiated throughout her hut.

Holding her breath, Belyx retreated away, trying to ignore the melting in her insides. No wonder she was so perturbed about the fae and how her herbs worked so well. The burn on her hands couldn't be healed because witch magic didn't affect the fae! It was right under their noses.

Amenthya was a witch.

"This is how you have taken care of your hair?" Freyja pulled a tight knot on Belyx's scalp and she almost bit her tongue. After cutting it, she tried to even it as best she could, but clearly failed. "I will need to have a talk with Onka and make sure this never happens again." Even though Onka was Belyx's new handmaiden, Belyx wanted Onka to have more grieving time. Plus, she requested one last chance to work with Belyx, despite the other things she had to prepare for the coronation.

"Well, I certainly won't miss the aggression." Once Freyja stopped with the brush and switched to the styling, Belyx's head was numb.

Freyja smirked. "A queen can't look like slime on her coronation day. You have an entire kingdom to please."

Belyx fake frowned at her. "Oh, you mean the kingdom upset I am queen?" She heard of the outcries from the coronation invites. The people didn't want her.

Freyja huffed a breath and twisted her hair. "Only a little, but bringing the fae back are the main reasons. The people have been exposed to many falsehoods and the more hard-headed folks are skeptical, but you will impress them. How is the speech?"

Belyx gulped, and Freyja hmm'd. Even with a list of talking points, saying them had problems. She would most likely end up spewing a jumbled mess and then the gangs would take over. Sighing, she stayed silent as her new captain braided her hair. No brown-red strands remained when she was finished with it.

"What do you think, Prin — I mean Queen." Freyja spun her to a mirror and after the chaos Belyx faced, she looked beautiful again. The outside only hid the pain for so long, but Freyja had the skills to hide anything. If they appeared at a united front, the citizens would follow.

"I'm nervous, Freyja. What if I mess up?"

Freyja started applying her makeup, picking the bright tones Belyx cringed at, but didn't dare challenge her Captain of the Guard. "I think the only thing you should fear is not trying. And as much as I hate it sometimes, you never give up."

Belyx wanted to smile, but couldn't with the eye pencil close to her face. Freyja drew impressive black wing tips to complement the vibrant pinks and silvers of the blush. Her stomach tightened. It was almost time. "I couldn't have asked for a better protector, I mean Captain. Sorry about the candle business."

Freyja waved a brush hand. "I'll have plenty of time when I am older to mess around with such things. Right now I have to make sure Aikradal and the Order stay afloat."

Her morning meal threatened to leave her body. Like her grandmother, Belyx was supposed to keep the Order going, but Freyja knew Belyx would be stressed and she couldn't do it alone. The thought saddened her, as Dara should be here to run it while Belyx was queen. "Do you think we need the Order anymore?" Belyx asked, recalling her mother's words.

Freyja arched a brow. "I think it is up to you, but with the way this kingdom is now. I would say yes. Also, we need to keep your fashion line going. The Stems and Seedlings have adored helping." She winked. *Good, they could continue doing it.* Belyx would have even less time now to make sure the dress production was maintained and would pay whatever it took. Freyja had a point, though. They needed to clean up the kingdom, one secret at a time. Once the fae were acclimated, and gangs were eradicated, then the Order would be next. It had to be handled with delicate care, and maybe it never would.

Belyx gulped. "I hope it works out today." Freyja pulled out a silk gown with purple asymmetrical lines, plunging down to the hem. It had one shoulder with silver etched into the seams and the bodice was coated in a thin metal. Belyx's eyes widened as she felt it. It *was* actual armor. "It's divine."

"We figured the Queen of Aikradal needed something sharp and powerful. This is a new line we are trying and look," she opened an outside flap, revealing a holster for a daggers and venoms.

"This will serve my purposes." Belyx took no time to put it on. It fit in the right places and wasn't as heavy as she expected.

"It can also slit down the side for added movement. We don't want our queen defenseless." Belyx wrapped her arms around her friend and refused to let go. "Oh, another thing for now." Freyja pulled away and brought out her leather gloves. "Till it fades a little more. We don't need the people thinking the fae burned their new queen."

Belyx almost forgot about the scars, but most of the guards who witnessed the fae were no more, or swore to secrecy about the spell, to halt further hatred. Who knew how long the secret would stay hidden? She flinched as she slipped them on. "I guess the people shouldn't know about it."

"No. Probably not, especially because he is your advisor and—"

"I think just partner for now." She couldn't even fathom the idea of the king right now. "Any word on Thomas?" Treading with caution, she asked her friend.

Freyja's face stayed still. It wasn't often she expressed pain. "Still no word from him, but I fear the worst."

Belyx's stomach was in her throat. "Where is he?"

"Can't say for now, but the Leaves have seen him around Berserker areas."

"He wouldn't."

Freyja closed her eyes. "Whatever happens, we need to move on, queen."

Thomas needed a break. He had been through a lot. The Berserkers stood for everything he despised and he would be back, welcomed with open arms.

Belyx changed the subject, sensing her friends hurt. "Well, I think it is time." Freyja lead her out, but Belyx stopped and grabbed a parchment from her desk. "Almost forgot this." Noticing Freyja's confusion, she added. "You can wait and hear later." Her friend clutched her pained hand and they made their way to her coronation ceremony.

Thirty-Three

Almost the entire kingdom showed up for this. Suddenly, Belyx wanted to vomit, but the embarrassment would add poison to injury. Crowds from around the kingdom filled the front palace as she climbed the stairs to the top of the wall. Guards clad in dented armor acknowledged her, as well as members of the Order disguised as them. *Nice work, Freyja.*

Enzo and his parents waited as well. They were dressed in their fae brown and green tunics made from the forest. Maybe those would make a new fashion line. *Note for later.*

What surprised her was Enzo still had on his usual human clothes, a ruffled shirt and casual pants. Old habits died hard. Enzo winked, and she kept a straight face. *Advisors didn't wink at their queens!* She winked back.

The priest, ironically the one from the mausoleum where they stole a head, held the ceremonial crown. No ruler ever wore it, but it symbolized the approval of The God and paved the way for peaceful times. *Sure.*

Down below was a waving Lady Maria and Lim, both donned in their best dresses, of course. They were holding hands, giggling and most likely judging her new dress; while also keeping an eye on things, Belyx hoped. Their level of friendship would never be tested, despite their fighting. Belyx waved back, but her smile wavered as Amenthya lurked in the shadows, staring with no expression.

The witch realization had still creeped her out, but Amenthya was kind hearted. No matter where her abilities came from, she needed to monitor her from now on. If anything happened to the fae again, those responsible would feel the queen's wrath. She smiled back and Amenthya turned her head up with a half grin, but something in her eyes said, *I know you know.*

The people pointed up and shouted her name while others stood with their arms crossed. This would be a difficult sell indeed. Vendors lined the streets selling replica models of her with little tiaras to match. A few little girls put them on and Belyx grinned, waving back, trying not to pass out and fall off the wall.

Once Belyx stepped up front, the priest motioned for the trumpeters to play. Belyx tried to enjoy it, but kept an eye out for any assassination attempts, even though Freyja was on it.

After the musical number played the God March, the priest raised the crown. "In light of recent tragedy, we must name a new ruler." The crowd stirred a bit, but most listened. "King Terach ruled brilliantly for over twenty years and his untimely death has sprouted worry in our society." Belyx struggled to keep her head straight and not cry. No one could learn the truth of what he became. He was a competent king, consumed by guilt. *It won't be me.*

The priest continued. "Luckily, he had a named heir." *Luckily, indeed.* "By the power of The God and all their power and wisdom, I am pleased to announce Princess Belyx as our new Queen!" The people cheered surprisingly, and the priest waved Belyx to come forward. He held the crown up and everyone chanted the Ode to The God. Tears threatened to smudge her face, but she pushed them back. A ruler didn't show weakness.

He placed the crown on her head as he spoke the vows. "Do you, Queen Belyx Velena, plan to uphold the values of our kingdom and defend it from any threats." He stared at Enzo and his family for a second, which made her blood bubble. "And do you vow to rule for the people and uphold The God in every decision?"

Belyx tilted her head up and gazed upon the citizens, her people now. "I do."

The priest lifted his hands. "I declare Belyx the Queen of Aikradal!"

The crowd cheered and Belyx attempted a loose smile and approached the edge, fighting her shaking hands. The people quieted; she cleared her throat, readying her loudest voice. "Thank you, people of Aikradal. I know this last week has filled you with uncertainty and confusion, but I am here to address your worries. My father had a good rule, but he made one mistake." She debated going down this path, but it needed to be said. "He let his grief take over his judgment, and many suffered for it." Acknowledging Enzo and his fathers, she continued, "It made him act desperate and unlike himself. We know how losing Queen Abigail shook our kingdom." She was silent for a few beats to let the people mourn.

"It is dreadful timing to also lose the former queen, Dara. She fought a difficult fight, but her illness overwhelmed her. I vow to be strong for you. No matter the conflict, I am here and I am ready. I know you worry at my youth, but it only strengthens me. I am passionate and ready to take on the challenges. Our guards fought bravely against the dark forces and I would invite those of you who crave honor and glory to enlist. And I would like any adult who is able. Men, Women, and all others." Gasps echoed the streets. "I will not run from any conflict and I want to fight for you. My father's grief hurt many people, but especially the fae. They were wrongly imprisoned without a trial and, later, proven innocent. The fae will return to their home in the forest. They are a peaceful tribe who have harmed no one. Anyone who has a problem can bring it to me or my new fae advisors, Thano and Gink Prekaro." She motioned to them and they exchanged awkward glances. *Keep it going, Belyx.*

"I have another thing needing to be addressed, and if you are in the crowd, you better be listening. The gangs trying to steal this crown are fighting a failed battle. They can attempt their tricks and bribes, but they don't have the strength we possess. They are cowards trying to go against our God. Do not fear them. I have faced them head on and we can beat them." *More than they will ever know.* "We will reward anyone with information on their activities. Our streets will no longer be a place of fear, but one of love and success. I hope to one day see a great kingdom once again." Belyx took a breath and pulled out her parchment. "I wrote a poem to honor this kingdom. I hope you will find it inspiring." She stood tall and channeled her mother.

Our weapons make us strong.

Forged in the fury of our hearts.

But our forging is not all.

The fire making us is not coal.

It is the fire we carry

In our hearts.

We, the people of Aikradal.

Possess what no other kingdom has.

Love.

Love for each other.

Love for what we accomplish.

I pray one day we can have a world.

Where all people have a chance.

And we can put our weapons down.

When our best weapons.

Are our hearts.

She paused, taking in her powerful words. "As your queen today and until I take my last breath. I will fight for you always. Thank you."

The crowd erupted an applause greater than Belyx had ever imagined. Waving one more time, she took a bow, letting the excited crowds celebrate. She looked around to the allies who had supported and believed in her. She took a moment to reflect on who wasn't there, as they knew she had it in her to do well.

Taking in the sun, Belyx and the rest of her procession headed back into the palace. Enzo shot her the biggest smile, and she grabbed his hand, ready for what was to come. Belyx needed to back up her speech. For the first time in a while, Belyx felt hopeful again.

Belyx spent the rest of the day sifting through guard applications. More letters than ever had already been submitted and Freyja's gang tip line was swarming in scroll after scroll. The people of Aikradal truly wanted things to get better. She didn't doubt them, but they had losses too, and maybe this change would be for the best.

Belyx entered Enzo's fathers' new room, which used to be Kirk Sallo's room, but they added a bigger bed and one of them was redecorating.

"Apologies," the larger one with the short ponytail, Gink, said. "I just couldn't help myself. The room was so dull." His voice was light and airy, unlike someone who was trapped for over a decade.

Thano rolled his eyes at his partner while Belyx tried not to laugh. "Ignore him. He gets fixated on things easily. You should have seen his cafe when it opened up."

Gink strutted by him, an old dusty curtain in hand. "I detest that Than. And also how dare you say such things in front of our Queen."

Thano's eyes never returned down and Belyx waved a gloved hand. "Oh, please. Do whatever you want with the room. I am just thankful you agreed to be my advisors."

"How could we say no? What a gig, and this place ain't too shabby. Did you see the forest? I may be fae, but I am not a dog," Gink replied vivaciously.

"Look what we did." Thano sighed. "Give him a week and he will be bored again and start doing everyone's jobs."

"I don't do that! Well, I may have a few tips for the cook of yours, but save it for another time."

These were the beings who raised Enzo. No wonder he turned out the way he did. They were kind and rich in personality. Part of her wished she had the same bond with her parents, too.

Belyx smiled. "Well, I just wanted to check on things and make sure you were aware of the council meeting tomorrow. It is time to move the fae to the forest and fix their homes."

Thano rubbed the red scruff on his beard. His elongated nature tattoos glistened off his arms. It explained how he put up such a fight as Aydevko's mindless slave. "It will prove difficult, but you left the perfect faes in charge and if you ever need help with the clothing line, I have a knack for color." He spun to show his vibrant green and teal over-shirt, with brown fitted pants.

"Now, who is the dramatic one?" Gink arched a brow.

"I will let you to it then. If you run into Enzo, can you tell him I would like to see him?"

The faes eyed each other as if they were gossiping women at tea. "Of course," they said in unison and Belyx shook her head, going back to her room. It was getting late.

Once she closed the door, she pulled out her poetry and wrote a few things coming to mind, letting her tears flow. Despite her strong front, the sting of her grandmother and father's loss would take awhile to shake, but she knew they would be proud, and it made it easier to handle.

Belyx scrawled and sobbed until she had a filled collection of poems. Now, she had time to focus on using them to heal Aikradal. Art was a powerful motivator, and she refused to give up. The moonlight reflected from her balcony and she smiled at her closet, getting up.

Passed her opened doors, she was greeted by her "Doneque" outfit. Brushing her hands down the smooth, well-made surface as she put it on, along with the wig and contacts. "I need to keep her around a little longer," she whispered to herself.

Once Aikradal was back to normal, she would stop. She would. A queen couldn't be seen parading around the kingdom, anyway. The Thorns needed an earned break, and she would give them one. Belyx checked her vials and smiled at her refill, counting them again for good measure.

Opening the window, she said a prayer to The God for Them to take care of her family in the afterlife, and then she launched down the wall, into the heart of her kingdom.

Thirty-Four

One Month Later

"Very good, but we need to see a little more focus from a couple of you! Come on!" Belyx stared at her Captain of the Guard barking orders in the courtyard below her father's balcony. This was the third new batch of guards this week, and it was filled with people she never expected to join. The quiet masses wanted to fight back, too.

Belyx twisted the garland on the railing. She had finally finished redecorating (with the help of Gink, of course) and she still sensed her father's presence like a light never going out. At first, she didn't want to move bedrooms, but her ever-wise council suggested it would be helpful for morale. Enzo had his own room too, yet he barely slept in it.

The cold season was ending, but a chill breeze still spun through her kingdom like a force of energy. Aikradal's crime and gang activity had decreased. The Cabaret parties were dwindling, the fighting rings were down, the illegal trades were diminished, and no one whispered much anymore. Things had started to look up, but she wished her father and grandmother could witness it, as well as her mother.

There wasn't a second when Belyx didn't miss them. Each minor task reminded her of their faces, but for every thing she accomplished, she pictured their spirits congratulating her as if the pleasant feeling was them all along.

As usual, Belyx couldn't relish in her sad thoughts for long before her partner, Enzo, strode in like a hot delivery man, often with baked goods from Cook (and

Gink too). They learned to get along and Cook decided her old bones needed rest, which was fortunate for Gink. Today it was Baklava. The cinnamon and apple scent floated from it. Her stomach growled as she missed dinner again.

Some things never changed.

Enzo wore a fashioned suit with tailoring in all the right places and his hair was fixed, with his curls trimmed short. This adjustment to the palace life was treating him well. He handed her the slice and said nothing. They communicated in silence as well, and Belyx found Enzo to be more romantic than she imagined.

Beyond their days of work, Enzo took her out to picnics along the forest (with guards) and they would walk down the river where he played next to as a child and, to no surprise, he would read to her from his horrible romance stories. Although, she didn't hate the romances much anymore, understanding what the writers were talking about now. But she had to get past the atrocious way the women were written.

One act as queen was to have more woman writers!

The fae had moved back into the forest and were thriving. They started growing their crops again and trading with the vendors, which made the citizens more trusting. No fae joined the guards as they wanted to remain a pacifist culture. Belyx respected it; although disappointed to not have those powers fight for her, but if the time came, they would protect the kingdom. She visited every week to make sure everything stayed smooth, as the calm of the storm never lasted forever.

Amenthya appeared to adjust to their return as well, but she barely left her room now and hadn't spoken to Belyx much. Perhaps witches were misunderstood like the fae and needed help too. Belyx wouldn't know what to ask and minded her business with the problems at hand.

Enzo's fathers worked well reintegrating the fae and kept up her family's fashion line, as her grandmother would have wanted, per Belyx's approval. Not that her opinion mattered, as she had the design ascetic of a barkeep.

She sighed. Majeria had refused summons to discuss their accused wrong doings. The council agreed to fix things in Aikradal for now, and then move onto them. It killed Belyx every day. Her mother's death had many loose ends, but Aikradal needed help first, and then Majeria would be hers. Nothing would stop her, but the itch festered slowly.

"Coffee with your pastry?" As if on cue, Onka stepped in the doorway with a steaming pot. She had grown more confident in herself and developed a personality outside her sister. Although Belyx sensed her longing for her other half. Inka's dry comments would always be missed.

"Onka. You know we can get drinks too." Belyx laughed.

Onka set the pot down. "No way am I letting Freyja do better than me. I am with you for every beck and call." As she waited and shot eyes between her and Enzo, her face turned strawberry red. "But I can see I am no longer needed right now. I think I will check on the um, other things." She scurried out.

Enzo chuckled. "You sure know how to select them." He peered at the snake cage in the room and gulped. The new snake had grown into itself, with the spikes protruded even farther. Belyx had to use leather gloves to harvest the venom.

She moved him up to her room as it couldn't be in the Order; males weren't allowed in the hideout. It saddened her he wasn't female, but like Enzo, he still had his uses. Plus, Bruxo had made a colorful decor to her room. But his toxin was still unknown, as it didn't work on humans. *A venom only working on magical creatures. No wonder Enzo feared it. I wonder if that was what my grandmother tried using?*

"It is still creepy," Enzo said.

Belyx swatted him. "Shut up."

"Is that an order from the queen?" Enzo wiggled his eyebrows. Flirt.

"Always." She took him in and embraced him, tasting his lips of fresh pastry and cinnamon.

Belyx peered out again to a group of girls playing hide and seek in the new garden. The daughters of the nobles and guards were getting along swimmingly. One jutted her head up and waved to Belyx, and she graced them back when the other Seedlings joined in. Lady Lim stood with Maria, teaching them the art of etiquette, which wasn't as tortuous as it sounded. Ladies could play too, and the Order needed those skills more than ever.

Even though the Order numbers dropped, they had been recruiting across the kingdom. Belyx taught a class with Freyja a couple times a week and they continued stopping crimes around Aikradal, weeding out traitors, which had turned less and less. "They are lucky to have such a great role model," Enzo said with a cheeky grin.

"Some model I am. I kill in the night."

Enzo tensed his shoulders. Of course, this was a hard subject for him. After he found out she was still doing Thorn missions, he tried to confront her, but they refused to speak more of it. "You said you would stop going out when things were better. Well, they are. I can't fathom losing you." A tinge of guilt knocked on her spine. He had done a lot for her and here she was, taking out petty crimes, instead of letting the other members handle it.

"I need to make sure things are in order. I don't like it any more than you do, but I am the only one equipped to handle this kingdom."

"I'll tell the members of the Order you said that."

"They shouldn't have to risk their lives for my ideas. This is my kingdom and therefore, it is my responsibility." Belyx could at least say she was sleeping better, shockingly.

Enzo took Belyx's still burned hand, and sparks danced across her face. "Promise me. Promise me you end this persona and stick with only being my queen and incredible partner."

Belyx shook her head, but became lost in his pleading green eyes like an incubus. "Deal. Once the gangs are no more, I will put Doneque to rest. For good." Her mother would be saddened at her decision to keep herself and the Order a secret, but she needed to take things slow. Her mother would understand.

The sun began to fall like a petal in the warm season and the orange splashed across the sky like a canvas. Belyx and Enzo sat hand in hand, staring out at the stunning and resilient kingdom. Despite the conflict still brewing beneath the surface, the people of Aikradal were strong and resilient and they proved it in this last month. No matter what happened, they would stay determined.

Belyx kissed her partner's fiery hand and sauntered back inside. "You coming in?"

"In a second. These sunsets are my favorite," Enzo replied.

After closing the door, Belyx embraced this unfamiliar calm. She knew her mother, father, and grandmother's spirits were nearby, watching over her as usual.

"Thank you," she whispered as she lit the candles around the room. She stared at the flames an extra long time. They were like tiny heartbeats echoing in the darkness, always lighting the way. Despite her recent fear of fire, it faded like the footprints on the sand.

Before getting into bed, she spotted her partner enjoying his sunset like he did every evening. Thanks to him, Belyx had everything she needed.

Crawling into her covers, she smiled and curled up with a good book.

THANK YOU!

Thank you so much for reading A Flower Amidst the Flames. If you enjoyed the book, please consider leaving a short review on Amazon, Goodreads, and/or your retailer of choice. Reviews help us authors get noticed and you can help with my journey by doing so.

You can also follow me on social media to get a look into my life and interests, as well as more engaging content.
Instagram: @brettshafferauthor
Tiktok: @brettshafferauthor

Sign up for my newsletter to receive exclusive freebies, content, and more! As well as get an opportunity to join my ARC reader team for future books.
Sign up at my website: brettshafferauthor.com or click this link: https://brettsh afferauthor.com/newsletter/

ACKNOWLEDGEMENTS

Wow, that was a wild journey! Is anyone good at writing these? I think I will just start with a HUGE thanks to the readers and lovers of enchanting tales. Without your support, this book would not be possible. This story idea came to me when I was facing a rather difficult time in my life. Sometimes, when things seem hard, keep going...and always let your creativity shine.

I would like to give a shout out to my family and friends. Without your never ending support and listening to my book ramblings, I would never have made it here.

A big thanks to all the professors and teachers who supported my wild and convoluted stories about magical worlds and encouraged me that what I had to say mattered.

For anyone who read my book in the early, early stages of this story and gave me helpful tips on how to make it shine.

For my writing group. Those coffee shop sprints will always be treasured.

To my editors, K.M. Enright and Lisa Shaffer. Without your guidance, my story would still be this word salad in my brain.

To Megan B and Angie Alaya, for my incredible map and cover. You both brought my vision to life.

And lastly, thank you again for reading A Flower Amidst the Flames. I see a lot of myself in Belyx and I hope you did too. Always remember to stay true to yourself and never let anyone say you can't do something. I am so excited to continue this series with these wonderful characters in the fantastic world of Keyica.

About the Author

Brett Shaffer is an author and teacher, born and raised in Boise, Idaho. He has a BA in Elementary Education and Special Education. He is a writer of fantasy for teens and young adults. He currently lives in Boise with his partner, tuxedo cat, and bearded dragon. When he is not writing, you can find him reading the next best thing, playing tennis, and occasionally winning at Magic the Gathering. A Flower Amidst the Flames is his debut novel.

He invites you to visit his website at bretts hafferauthor.com or follow him on Instagram and Tiktok @brettshafferauthor

Sign up for his newsletter and be the first to know about bonus content and new projects!

www.ingramcontent.com/pod-product-compliance
Lightning Source LLC
Chambersburg PA
CBHW030133310726
48970CB00005B/1423